Ghost Moon

Also by Karen Robards
in Large Print:

Heartbreaker
Walking After Midnight
Nobody's Angel
Dark of the Moon
Desire in the Sun
Green Eyes
Morning Song

This Large Print Book carries the
Seal of Approval of N.A.V.H.

KAREN ROBARDS

Ghost Moon

G.K.Hall & Co. • Thorndike, Maine

Published in 2000 by arrangement with Delacorte Press, an imprint of The Bantam Dell Publishing Group, a division of Random House, Inc.

G.K. Hall Large Print Core Series.

The text of this Large Print edition is unabridged.
Other aspects of the book may vary from the original edition.

Set in 16 pt. Plantin by Anne Bradeen.

Printed in the United States on permanent paper.

Library of Congress Cataloging-in-Publication Data

Robards, Karen.
   Ghost moon / Karen Robards.
     p. cm.
   ISBN 0-7838-9110-5 (lg. print : hc : alk. paper) —
   ISBN 0-7838-9114-8 (lg. print : sc : alk. paper)
    1. Children of the rich — Fiction. 2. Mothers — Death —
Fiction. 3. Single mothers — Fiction. 4. Stepfamilies — Fiction.
5. Louisiana — Fiction. 6. Large type books. I. Title.
PS3568.O196 G46 2000b
  813′.54—dc21
                                            00-031961

This book is dedicated to my mother-in-law,
Frances Hagan Robards Sigler,
in honor of her seventy-fifth birthday.
It is also dedicated, as always,
to my husband, Doug,
and my sons,
Peter, Christopher, and Jack,
with love.

chapter 1

"Mom, I wet the bed." The small, shamed voice and the little hand that went with it tugged Louise Hardin out of a deep sleep. She opened one groggy eye to discover her daughter Melissa standing at her bedside in the darkened room. Behind her, the alarm clock glowed the time: one A.M.

"Mom." Missy's hand tugged once more at the long sleeve of Louise's pale green nylon nightgown.

"Oh, Missy, no! Not again." Louise's whisper was despairing as she rolled out of bed, careful not to disturb her husband, Brock, who slumbered peacefully beside her. Brock had to get up early, at quarter to seven, to be at the office by eight. As he said, the rest of them could sleep all day if they chose, but he had to earn a living. Besides, he hated the fact that

Missy sometimes still wet the bed. He was a pediatrician, he *knew* Missy should be over wetting the bed by now, and he tended to take her frequent accidents personally.

Consequently, Louise, Missy, and her ten-year-old sister, Heidi, conspired to conceal Missy's accidents whenever possible.

"I'm sorry, Mom," Missy offered in a tiny voice when they gained the relative safety of the hallway outside the bedroom. The blue shag carpet felt soft and warm beneath Louise's bare feet. Through the hall window, left uncurtained because it was small and high and on the second floor, Louise could see pinpricks of tiny stars and a wan sickle moon drifting against the black sky. "At least this time I dreamed I was on the potty. It seemed so real! And then I was all wet, and I woke up and I wasn't on the potty at all."

"All your dreams seem so real." If Louise's voice was just a tad dry, she couldn't help it. She was really, really tired, and this was getting to be almost a nightly occurrence. As a seven-year-old, Missy was getting her up at night almost as much as she had when she was a baby.

Light glowed around the partially closed door of the hall bathroom, illuminating the path to Missy's bedroom, which was at the far end of the hall, past Heidi's bedroom and a smaller guest bedroom. Louise had started leaving the light on at night because, in addition to wetting her bed, Missy had suddenly become afraid of the dark. She had nightmares about monsters hiding in her room and watching her as she slept. Sometimes she woke up screaming, and Louise would jump from bed like she had been shot and race down the hall to find her daughter huddled in the center of her bed, in a ball, with the covers pulled over her head, crying her eyes out and gasping something that made no sense. Inevitably, Louise ended up bringing Missy into bed with her and Brock, a practice of which he strongly disapproved. That, Brock informed her, was undoubtedly a large part of Missy's problem. Louise treated her like a baby, rewarding her misdeeds by giving her attention (which was what Brock said she wanted all along) when Missy should have been disciplined instead. Louise knew that Brock probably knew best — as he frequently pointed out, *he* was the expert — but she could not find it in her heart to punish her seven-year-old daughter for being afraid of the dark. Or for wetting the bed. Or, as Brock said, for nearly anything at all.

The ammonialike smell of urine struck Louise in the face as soon as she stepped inside Missy's room. She sighed. Missy's hand twitched in hers.

"I'm really sorry, Mom," Missy offered again.

Without a word, Louise let go of Missy's hand, closed the door, turned on the light, and crossed to the chest to extract a clean nightgown from a drawer. When she turned around, nightgown in hand, she was frowning. Maybe Brock was right, she thought. Maybe she should try being a little tougher on Missy. She was really becoming tired of getting up in the middle of almost every single night.

Accustomed to the ritual, Missy had already pulled her wet nightgown off and was in the act of dropping it on the floor. Lips thinning, Louise moved to her daughter's side and tugged the dry nightgown over Missy's head. As the gown fell into place, she reached around behind Missy's neck to free the long dark brown braid of her daughter's hair. When Missy glanced quickly up at her, her big hazel eyes questioning, Louise gave the braid a small tug.

"You can help me change the sheets," she said, with more sternness than was usual for her.

"Are you mad at me, Mom?" Missy asked humbly as the two of them worked together to strip the wet sheets from the bed. Louise's heart smote her. Missy was so very little, after all. And she was small for her age. She'd been born six weeks premature, and Louise had often thought that her early arrival might account for some of Missy's problems. Her body had just not yet matured as much as that of most seven-year-olds. Brock, of course, said that was nonsense.

Damn Brock.

"No, baby, I'm not mad at you." Her task made easier by the vinyl cover that saved the mattress from total ruin, Louise carefully tucked in the corners of the clean sheets that were kept, along with spare blankets, in a trunk at the foot of Missy's bed. She smoothed a pink wool blanket over the sheets and pulled back a corner. "Hop in."

"Don't tell Daddy," Missy said, obeying.

"I won't." It was a ritual, these words. Some part of Louise felt it was wrong to promise to keep something a secret from Missy's father, but the larger, practical part didn't want to listen to Brock's lectures if he discovered that Missy had wet the bed again. She didn't want Missy to have to listen to them, either. No matter whether Brock was the expert or not.

Louise tucked the clean, dry bedclothes around her daughter as Missy snuggled onto her side, a small smile curving her lips as her cheek burrowed deep into the pillow with its tiny white hearts on a deep pink background.

"Good night, baby." Louise brushed her lips across the warmth of her daughter's exposed cheek, and straightened.

"I love you, Mommy." Missy's voice was already sleepy, and her eyelashes were beginning to droop.

"I love you, too, Miss Mouse. Now go back to sleep." Louise gathered up the wet bedding and nightgown.

"Leave the bathroom light on."

"I will," Louise promised.

After opening the door and flicking off the light, Louise paused for a moment in the doorway to look back at her daughter with a faint, wry smile. So much for discipline, she thought. But Missy *was* only seven. . . . Lying there in her little white bed, which Louise had hand-painted herself with the colorful butterflies that were Missy's favorite creature, Missy looked no bigger than a minute. She would grow out of this bed-wetting phase one of these days, Louise consoled herself. It would be something to laugh about when she was grown. . . .

"See you in the morning," Louise whispered, turning away. She headed toward the basement, meaning to put the sheets in to wash and thus leave no trace of the night's misdeeds for Brock to discover.

What Louise didn't know was that, concealed in Missy's closet behind a double rack of neatly pressed outfits and a mountain of stuffed animals, a man listened and waited. He'd thought about running for it, when the child had gotten out of bed and gone for her mother. But he'd been afraid that he wouldn't get away in time, and indeed the little girl and the woman had returned within minutes. If he had left his hiding place, he would have been caught. During the few minutes the mother had been in the room, he'd sweated bullets as he listened to their exchange. All she had to do was open the closet door — but she didn't.

Now he and his little sweetie pie were alone again.

His heartbeat quickened as he waited, very patiently, for the mother to return to her room. When she did, he waited even longer, listening to the soft, light rhythm of the child's breathing.

Finally, he eased open the closet door.

The next morning, when Louise went to rouse Missy for her ten A.M. play date, her daughter was stretched out in bed as neatly as could be, lying on her back with the covers pulled up under her chin.

"Time to get up, sleepyhead," Louise said, laughing because Missy never slept late and, since she had, this might signal the beginning of a whole new phase that did *not* include bedwetting. Playfully she jerked the covers down.

In that moment she knew, and her laughter died, leaving her smile to deflate like a punctured balloon. Hoping against hope that she was mistaken, praying to all the gods that had ever existed in any universe that she was wrong, she grabbed her daughter by the arms.

Missy's body was cold. It was stiff, too. Rigor mortis had already set in.

The child was dead in her bed.

The next week, this banner headline appeared in the *New Orleans Times-Picayune*: "Prominent Baton Rouge Pediatrician Charged with Murdering Daughter, 7, for Wetting Bed."

The dateline was May 6, 1969.

chapter 2

Ghosts. They were everywhere on that steamy summer's night. Their white misty shapes hovered over the old graveyard that stood sentinel on the bluff beside the lake, played hide-and-seek behind the Spanish moss that dripped from the twisted branches of the bald cypresses, stretched heavenward above the inky surface of the water. They whispered together, their words falling like drops of water through the mist, almost drowned out by the other, more corporeal sounds of the night. *Run away. Go. Run away* was what they said. Whether the ghosts were real or the product of atmosphere and imagination, though, who knew? And what difference, really, did it make?

It was hot, still, although it was some ten minutes past one A.M. on August 19, 1999, which was a Friday night, or, rather, a Saturday morning. Hot with the thick, damp kind of heat that always lay like a blanket over Point Coupee Parish in August. The kind of heat that curled your hair or made it go limp, depending on what kind of hair you had. The kind of heat that made women "dewy" and men sweat, that exacerbated tempers and passions and bred clouds of mosquitoes and carpets of the slimy green floating plants known as duckweed.

LaAngelle Plantation heat. Courtesy of the swampy Louisiana low country to the south, the Atchafalaya River to the west, and the mighty Mississippi to the east. It came with its own feel, its own smell, its own taste.

She was come home at last, Olivia Morrison thought, inhaling the indefinable aroma of decay, swamp water, and vegetation run amok that she remembered from her earliest childhood. The knowledge both exhilarated and frightened her. Because the truth was that this was, and was not, her home.

"Are we almost there, Mom?" The tired little voice at her elbow was barely audible over the night sounds around them.

"Almost." Olivia glanced down at her eight-year-old daughter with mixed tenderness and concern. Sara looked dead on her feet, her sturdy little body drooping like a wilted flower. Her thick-lashed brown eyes were dark-shadowed and huge with fatigue. Her upturned face was pale. Tendrils of jaw-length coffee-brown hair, having been pushed back by an impatient hand once too often, curled and clung to the moist skin of her neck and forehead. The yellow and white gingham sundress that had been so pretty and crisp that morning in Houston was now as limp-looking as the child herself. Her dusty black ballerina flats — thriftily bought big to allow for growth — slipped off her heels with every step to slap against the spongy ground. The lace-trimmed white anklets she wore with them were grimy with dirt. They'd walked from the bus stop at New Roads, a distance of perhaps five miles, because nobody had answered the telephone at the Big House when Olivia called, and she didn't have the money for a taxi.

Not that she would have had much chance of rousting out Ponce Lennig and his beat-up Mercury anyway, Olivia thought, lifting strands of shoulder-length coffee-brown hair away from her own moist neck. LaAngelle's only taxi service had always been erratic at best, and Ponce had always turned off his phone promptly at six P.M. He didn't believe in working nights, he said.

Maybe Ponce didn't have the taxi service anymore. Maybe there was a new, modern taxi service — or none at all. Not that it mattered, since she was down to her last five dollars and change.

Ponce, if apprised of their circumstances, would have gladly given them a free ride out to the house, but Olivia would have had a hard time confessing to him or anyone else just how broke she was. Only to save Sara a five-mile hike could she have made herself do so. Once upon a time, as Olivia Chenier, spoiled and wild and the youngest of the golden Archer clan, she had been as glamorous and above their touch as a movie star to the people of the town.

Once upon a time. A long time ago. Now she was a dental office manager, barely scraping by from paycheck to paycheck. How the mighty are fallen.

No one but Aunt Callie knew she and Sara were coming, and Aunt Callie didn't know precisely when. Olivia couldn't blame any of the family for not being on hand when she called to fetch her and Sara home.

She hadn't seen them, any of them, for nine years.

With a twinge of anxiety, she wondered how they would react to her return. With something short of the proverbial killing of the fatted calf, she guessed. Her hand tightened around Sara's.

"I think I'm getting a blister on my heel," Sara complained. "I told you these shoes were too big."

Olivia focused on Sara again. "I have a Band-Aid in my purse."

"I hate Band-Aids."

"I know." It was all Olivia could do to suppress a sigh. Sara was not usually whiny, or grumpy, but she was rapidly becoming both. And who could blame her? The child had been traveling

17

since seven that morning, first by car and then by bus and then on foot. "Listen, baby, if we keep walking up this path, just a little bit farther, we'll come to some stepping stones, and when we reach the end of them we'll go up some steps to the top of a bluff, and you'll be able to see the house from there."

Sara's gaze swept their surroundings.

"It's spooky here." She shivered despite the heat.

"That's just because it's night." Olivia's words and tone were comforting, but she, too, glanced around, almost unwillingly. *Run away, Olivia. Run. Run away.* She could swear that's what she heard, murmured over and over again through the shifting pockets of steam, but she told herself that it was her imagination, nothing more. What with the insects out in full force, the water lapping at the shores of the lake, and all the other sounds of the night, the calling voices could be anything, and certainly did not belong to ghosts. It was just that the dirt path through the woods was so *dark*. They should have kept to the road until they reached the long driveway; taking the shortcut had been a mistake.

"Aren't you scared?" Sara asked, darting a glance up at her mother.

"No," Olivia said stoutly, as her daughter sidled closer against her side, but wasn't quite sure that she was telling the truth. Whether she was or wasn't, though, there was no turning back at this point. The road was farther behind them than the house was ahead. They had to keep on walking.

Overhead, a pale crescent moon slipped in and out of view behind a lacey overlay of lavender-tinged clouds, providing just enough silvered light to see by. Glittering stars peeked at them through the dense canopy of leaves. To their left, moonlight painted a shimmering white stripe across the polished surface of the lake, while a nodding ring of water hyacinths, black in this light, performed an eerie ballet close to shore. To their right, the darkness of the cypress grove grew impenetrable just a few feet beyond where they walked. All around them, leaves rustled, branches swayed, and twigs snapped as who-knew-what nocturnal creatures moved about. Insects whirred in never-ending chorus. The soprano piping of dozens of tree frogs was underscored by a bullfrog duet from the direction of the water. Not far ahead, where the ragged-edged lakeshore curved back toward itself, monuments to long-dead Archer family members tilted this way and that atop a kudzu-covered bluff. A long-ago patriarch's marble crypt gleamed faintly through the darkness. Surrounding it, the aged stone markers looked like ghosts themselves. Fingers of diaphanous white mist rose above all.

Spooky? Oh, yes. Although she would never admit as much to Sara.

"Is that the lake where your mom drowned?"

Trust her sensitive, imaginative child to hit

upon the one topic that Olivia really did not want to talk about just at that moment. The death of her mother had been the defining event of her childhood. It had changed her in a moment, like a catastrophic earthquake instantly reshapes the topography of the land. And yet, although the memory of the pain was sharp and strong even so many years later, she could conjure up no memory of how she had learned that her mother was dead, or of who had told her. No memories of her mother's funeral, or her stepfather, or the Archer family in mourning. It was as if her memory banks, where the events surrounding her mother's death were concerned, had been wiped clean. All she knew were the bare facts: Her mother had drowned at age twenty-eight in that lake.

The same lake from which voices now seemed to be calling to her.

"Yes." Olivia set her teeth against the sudden stab of loss remembered, and ignored the icy tingle of dread that snaked down her spine. She would not give in to the morbid fear of the lake that had been the bane of her growing-up years. She had always imagined that it was waiting to get her, to suck her down beneath its shiny surface as it had her mother. Her cousins, once realizing that she was afraid of the lake, had tormented her with it unmercifully, even going so far as to throw her in on one memorable occasion. Now, after so many years in hiatus that she had nearly forgotten about it, the fear threatened

chapter 3

"I think it's 'Twist and Shout,' " Olivia said incredulously after a moment, as some of the tension begin to seep from her fear-tightened muscles. It was impossible to remain sensitive to ghostly atmosphere with that sixties hit reverberating through the air, she thought with relief. After a couple of seconds, a reminiscent smile curved her lips. The family must be having a party. Of course, that was why no one had answered the phone when she had called from the bus station. The Archers did things like that. In the summer, particularly in August, they had huge outdoor barbecues/dances to which the whole town was invited, and came.

The Archers had always been bigger-than-life, more colorful and exciting than anyone else she had ever known. Since leaving them, Olivia realized, her life had turned as drably brown as an acre of parched land. Now, just as soon as she had set foot on Archer land again, peacock colors began seeping in.

How she had missed their brightness!

"It's a party. Come on, we're missing the fun." She tried to infuse a note of gaiety into her voice, and was heartened to see Sara smile in response. Hand in hand, they walked forward with renewed energy, buoyed by the infectious beat of the music that grew louder with every step.

"Wow!" Sara's reverent exclamation echoed Olivia's thought as they puffed their way up the last step cut into the twenty-foot-high limestone bluff. Standing side by side on level ground, they stopped by mutual, unspoken consent to absorb the scene before them.

Flaming six-foot-tall citronella torches formed a picturesque and, as Olivia remembered it, highly effective mosquito barrier around the perimeter of the five-acre lawn. Will-o'-the-wisps of mist danced with the guests. The grass itself seemed to stretch out endlessly, looking as soft and lush as a jade-colored velvet carpet in the uncertain light. The torches ended just a few yards in front of where Olivia and Sara stood, so Olivia had the sensation of being on the outside looking in at the festivities through a haze of pungent smoke. Beyond the torches, tiny white Christmas tree lights glittered everywhere. They were wrapped around the trunks and branches of the flowering dogwoods and redbuds that dotted the lawn so that each tree was entirely illuminated. They were strung through the neatly trimmed boxwood hedges that lined the stone path leading to the gazebo and, farther on, to the various outbuildings and the Big House. They adorned the ancient magnolias that stood near the house, ringed the rose garden with its center-piece bronze crane fountain, and dripped from the eaves of the gazebo and the Big House itself. In addition, the Big House, a twenty-four-room Greek Revival mansion of white-painted brick with a pedimented portico and more than two dozen soaring fluted pillars supporting twin galleries, was lit up like a jack-o'-lantern from within. Its long, rectangular windows glowed softly against the midnight-blue backdrop of the night. Although dozens of guests still mingled and danced on the lawn, it was obvious from the stream of headlights moving slowly down the long driveway toward the road that the party was beginning to break up.

Once upon a time, Olivia thought, on a night like this, at a party like this, she had worn a short red dress, and danced and laughed and eaten *boudin* and jambalaya until she thought she would pop, and fallen in love. . . .

The spicy scent of the rice and pork sausage that was *boudin* was in the air tonight, awakening her taste buds along with her memories.

If she could only go back and have it all to do over again, she would do things very differently, Olivia told herself.

A sharp slap on her left forearm brought her

startled gaze around and down.

"Mosquito," Sara said matter-of-factly.

"Oh." Olivia was thus recalled to the present, and realized in that instant that if she could live her life differently she would not, because living her life differently would mean that there would be no Sara, and Sara was worth far more than the sum of all the things that Olivia had given up to get her.

"Thanks." She smiled at the daughter who looked enough like her to be her own miniature, and twined her fingers more tightly with Sara's small ones. "Ready to go join the party?"

"Are you sure it's okay?"

Typically, when faced with a new situation, Sara's instinct was to hang back. Shy was not quite the right way to describe her, Olivia thought. Cautious was more like it, and reserved.

"I'm sure," Olivia said, with more confidence than she felt, and drew Sara with her through the ring of torches. The band stopped playing with a flourish as she and Sara walked along the stone path toward the gazebo. A glance around at the people they passed told Olivia that the tie-strapped sundresses she and Sara wore, even though they were cheap to begin with, slightly soiled from traveling, and limp from the heat, would attract no notice in this eclectic gathering. Guests were dressed in everything from party clothes to a Hawaiian shirt and shorts. Not that what they were wearing mattered a jot, Olivia told herself. They hadn't come to attend a party. That she should entertain so much as a niggle of unease about the suitability of her own watermelon-pink puckered cotton Kmart special surprised her. Apparently the style-conscious girl she had once been still lurked somewhere inside. For years now, she had been far more concerned about how much an article of clothing cost than about how fashionable it was. Their budget had not been able to stretch to include new clothes very often, and what little money she'd been able to scrape together for that kind of thing had been spent on Sara.

Sweet Sara, her baby and her rock, who deserved far more than her shortsighted mother had been able to give her.

Olivia breathed an inward sigh of relief as they drew one or two curious glances from the partygoers around them, but no real notice. She realized that she probably knew many of the guests, but from some combination of elapsed time and uncertain light and nervousness, she was not able to put a name to any of the faces she passed, and no one seemed to recognize her.

More guests were headed in the direction of the Big House now — there was a parking area immediately beyond it — and the traffic on the driveway streaming toward the road grew increasingly heavier. Looking away from the blinding stream of headlights toward the gazebo, Olivia was both pleased and frightened to recognize a familiar figure at last: her grandfather, or stepgrandfather, to be precise. Her feet faltered for a moment as she drank in the sight of him. Even at eighty-seven, as he must be now, he was still taller than the man he was talking to, although he was slightly stooped and thinner than she remembered and his age was obvious even at a distance.

She had been gone too long, Olivia thought, with a sharp pang in the region of her heart. Whether he had loved her or not, and Olivia was not sure that he ever had, she realized in that moment that she had always loved him. She was lucky that he was still here for her return.

Olivia was suddenly, fiercely glad to have this chance to put things right with him, with all of them. Despite everything, the Archers were the only real family she had ever known.

"There's my grandfather," she said softly to Sara, indicating with a nod of her head the old man who had cast a shadow as big as a mountain over her youth. Big John was what nearly everyone called him, including his grandchildren, not Papaw or Granddaddy but Big John. He'd once stood six feet five and weighed two hundred fifty pounds, which was how he'd earned the name. As head of the family, Big John Archer owned all this, the LaAngelle Plantation estate on which they now stood and the whole town of LaAngelle, practically, where Archer Boatworks was the main employer and the Archers had provided money for everything from a new fire truck to a library from time without end.

"Do you think he'll be glad to see us?" Sara's steps flagged, and her voice held the same doubtful note as before.

"Of course he will," Olivia said, a shade too heartily. She was not entirely certain herself about what kind of reception to expect from the old man, but it would never do for Sara to suspect that. Her daughter didn't need to be burdened with old family business that had nothing to do with her.

It didn't help her determined optimism to remember that Big John, like most of the rest of the Archers, had tended to be unforgiving at best.

"Mom, maybe we should come back tomorrow." Sara tugged urgently at Olivia's hand to slow her down.

"Pumpkin, don't be silly. This is my home. We're welcome here." Olivia's voice was firm, although she wasn't nearly as certain as she sounded.

"Then why haven't we ever come here before?" Sara sounded skeptical.

"Because — because . . . We're here now." Olivia answered the unanswerable with as much conviction as though her response made perfect sense. To her relief, Sara didn't question her further. Mother-speak had its uses.

They were nearing the gazebo, and the man Big John was talking to glanced toward them. Dressed in a tan sport coat with an open-necked dark polo shirt beneath and dark slacks, he was over six feet tall, which still made him several inches shorter than Big John. He had thinning gray hair, a square-jawed, big-nosed face, and a noticeable belly. His gaze drifted over them without much interest, and then returned in a classic double take to fix on Olivia's face. She recognized him then, although he was some thirty pounds heavier than she remembered, and much balder, too: Charles Vernon, Big John's son-in-law and the town physician. He would be around sixty now. Although he was, of course, no kin of hers whatsoever, she had always known him as Uncle Charlie.

His arrested expression attracted the notice of the two women in the group, and they looked at Olivia. She was still puzzling over their identities when Big John himself turned her way, seeming to peer at her through the darkness as if he, too, was curious to discover what had attracted his son-in-law's fascinated attention.

She and Sara were hand in hand, walking through pockets of guests and mist toward the gazebo, and Big John was no more than a dozen yards away, standing on the third from the bottom of the wooden steps. He was wearing a white linen sport coat and dark trousers, and his hair, which had been a thick crop of iron gray when she had seen him last, was as thinly white as the moon overhead. But his face, with its high forehead and long, hawkish nose, was un-changed as far as she could tell, except for, per-haps, the addition of a few more wrinkles. Olivia would have known him anywhere, and was sur-

prised that he did not immediately seem to recognize her.

Then she realized that she and Sara must be silhouetted against the blazing torchlight behind them. Although she could see him perfectly well, it was possible that her features were shadowed and he could not quite make them out.

And, too, he was now a very old man, with a very old man's vision. Allowances must be made for that.

She and Sara stepped into the circle of brighter light cast by the hundreds of twinkly white bulbs adorning the gazebo, and immediately their shadows were behind them, long and dark against the velvety grass. If darkness had been the problem, it should be no longer. She could feel the light on her face.

Still, Big John stared fixedly at her without making any attempt to greet her. Trying to ignore her growing discomfort — was she really so changed that he didn't recognize her, or was she really that unwelcome? — Olivia attempted a smile as she and Sara drew closer. Big John's lips parted slightly in response, and his eyes widened. He almost looked . . . horrified to see her, Olivia thought with dismay. Then he blinked rapidly, shook his head, took a deep breath, and stared again. One thin hand lifted toward her. But the gesture was not one of welcome. Rather, it was as if he would ward her off.

Olivia thought sickly that she should at least have had the sense to come alone so that Sara

31

would not be subjected to this.

"My God," Big John said in a hoarse voice. "Selena!"

Then Olivia knew, knew the cause of the horror on his face, of his failure to greet her. Instantly she opened her mouth to correct him, to ease his mind of the terrible misapprehension that apparently gripped him, but it was too late. He made a harsh sound. His hand curled into a claw and he clutched at his chest. Before anyone could react he pitched forward, tumbling down the steps to land face-first in the yielding cushion of carefully manicured grass.

chapter 4

Selena. He had thought she was her mother. Even as she let go of Sara's hand to rush forward, even as she flung herself to her knees at Big John's side, Olivia realized that. Of course, she knew that in appearance she was as much a mirror image of her mother as her own daughter was of her. All three had the same strong, square jaw, prominent cheekbones, straight nose, wide, full-lipped mouth, and large, thickly lashed brown eyes. They had the same tawny complexion, and the same coffee-brown hair with a tendency to curl in the low-country heat. Like her mother, Olivia was of no more than medium height, with a figure that could best be described as curvy rather than slender. The Chenier women were not classic beauties. At least, not in the Anglo sense. They were, rather, Cajun beauties, whose looks reflected their rich French-

Acadian heritage.

Selena had died at roughly Olivia's own age. Big John would remember her that way. Some trick of memory and/or lighting had made him think that he was seeing her mother again, twenty years after she had been laid in her grave.

"Big John! Big John!" Others were moving toward them, but instead of rushing they seemed to Olivia to be moving almost in slow motion. She was only vaguely aware of them as they began to cluster around. All her attention was concentrated on Big John.

Urgently, she grabbed his upper arm through the nubby linen of his sport coat, shaking it, only to find him unresponsive. He did not seem to be breathing. He was tieless, his collar open at the throat, and she placed her fingers against the warm skin at the side of his neck, feeling for a pulse.

Please, oh, please. Terror, sharp-tasting as bile, rose in her throat. Surely he wasn't going to die. Not now, not like this. Not on the very day that she was come home again.

If there was a pulse, she could not detect it.

"It's me. Olivia," she said pitifully, uncertain whether he could hear her but hoping that he could.

"Move!" Uncle Charlie dropped to his knees beside her, unceremoniously pushing her out of the way as he turned Big John onto his back and placed his own hand against the place where the pulse should be in his neck. Above them, one elderly woman began to scream, a nerve-shattering, high-pitched keening, while another ran toward the house, presumably to fetch help.

"Oh, please help him!" Rocking back on her heels, Olivia pressed both hands to her mouth, watching helplessly as Charlie repositioned Big John's head and jaw, and opened his mouth.

"Mom." Standing just behind her, Sara touched her shoulder, her voice hushed, scared. A glance back showed Olivia that Sara's face was as pale and frightened as her own surely must be.

For Sara's sake, Olivia fought to regain some measure of control.

"It's okay, pumpkin." Her voice was hoarse, but at least she could speak. She reached for the little hand on her shoulder, and clasped it. The warmth of Sara's fingers made her realize how icy hers had become.

"Mom, is he dead?"

"No. No, of course not." She prayed Big John was not, although she was terrified that her words were a lie. He lay unmoving, sprawled on his back now, his arms flung out to either side, his legs splayed. His skin was turning gray, visibly as she watched, the color leaching from his face, and the flesh of his cheeks and neck sagged in folds away from his bones.

Had she come home again only just in time to watch him die?

More and more people were crowding around.

The babble of their voices wove together so that Olivia could make sense of only a few disjointed phrases.

"What's happened?"

"Some kind of accident . . ."

"*Sacrebleu,* did anyone call an ambulance?"

"Help him, Jesus!"

"It's Big John. . . ."

Some of the newcomers hunkered down, so that in moments those crouched around Big John formed a protective circle, while what seemed like dozens more hovered above them. Shocked questions and exclamations overhead joined with the pounding of her own heart to create a relentless roaring in Olivia's ears; she felt dizzy, short of breath. Her vision was affected, so that Big John and the crowd around him became no more than a shifting blur of color. After a moment Olivia realized that that was because she was seeing them through the tears in her eyes. The full enormity of the tragedy she had precipitated made her numb. Grief closed her throat as Charlie blew into Big John's mouth, then straightened and with a grim face began performing the rhythmic chest compressions of CPR.

Hail Mary, full of grace . . . The prayers of her earliest childhood popped into Olivia's mind as they always did in times of stress, and she repeated them silently, grasping for comfort in the familiar litany. Behind her there was more comfort in the feel of Sara's solid little body pressed against her back. She could feel the knobbiness of Sara's knees like hard balls on either side of her spine. Sara's fingers squeezed her own, and Olivia clung to them as if to a lifeline.

Another man shouldered through the crowd to drop down on one knee on the opposite side of Big John's body from where she crouched. He had short, sandy hair, a powerful build, and was clad in a navy sport coat, a dark T-shirt, and khaki slacks.

"What in the name of God happened?" The question, addressed to Charlie, was low and rough.

"Heart attack, I think."

"*What?* What caused it? He was fine. . . ."

"*She* showed up," Charlie said briefly, his head jerking sideways to indicate Olivia. "He took one look at her and keeled over."

Across Big John's body, Olivia's stricken gaze met narrowed blue eyes that had once been as familiar to her as her own. Above them, straight ash-brown brows almost touched in a fierce frown. His eyes widened as he registered her identity. She supposed her eyes widened, too, as she recognized him.

Seth.

She must have said it aloud, because he replied with, "Olivia."

Just her name, no more, in a tone that was about as welcoming as stone.

"I think . . . Big John thought I was . . . my mother. He looked at me and said 'Selena' and —

37

and just collapsed," she said wretchedly. It was all she could do to force the words out around the lump in her throat. Tears filled her eyes, trickled down her cheeks. Surprised by the feel of their wetness against her skin, she wiped them away with her free hand.

"Jesus Christ, have you ever in your life done anything but cause trouble?" Seth's mouth twisted with anger. His gaze, hard with animosity, held hers.

Olivia felt as if he had slapped her. *Unfair!* she wanted to cry, but her tongue and lips would not form the word.

"I'm not getting anywhere with this." Charlie's voice was ragged. Despite his words, his hands were still rhythmically compressing Big John's chest.

Seth's gaze dropped away from hers as they both switched their attention to Big John. Charlie was pumping hard, his right hand crossed over his left on Big John's chest, his face red with effort. Seth's strong brown hand moved to grasp the old man's limp paper-white fingers.

"Big John, it's Seth," he said softly. "It's okay. You're going to be okay."

Seth was Big John's oldest grandson, his favorite, the one the old man, with unabashed pride, pointed out to all and sundry as his heir. If Big John could hear anything in this moment of extremis, Seth's would be the voice that would most comfort him.

Pray for us now and at the hour of our death. . . .

The words of the prayer ran through Olivia's mind in an endless loop. Behind her, Sara's knees still pressed into her back. Her daughter still clasped her hand. Drawing on these reminders for strength, Olivia once again dashed the tears from her cheeks.

"The ambulance is here!" a woman called with high-pitched excitement, both hands waving as she ran toward them from the direction of the driveway. Behind her, cars pulled to one side and people scattered as an ambulance came up the driveway, then pulled off the pavement to bump over the lawn toward them, its red lights flashing but its siren mercifully silent. When at last the vehicle stopped just a few feet away, emergency medical technicians leaped out and hurried toward the victim.

"Stand back, please! Stand back!"

Olivia stumbled to her feet, keeping Sara close to her, making room along with the rest of the crowd as the emergency personnel took over. With the sound of popping buttons, Big John's shirt was ripped open and the paddles of a portable defibrillator were applied to either side of his chest.

"One — two — three! *Clear!*"

With a sound like a watermelon hitting pavement, the defibrillator did its job, once, twice, lifting Big John's body off the grass only to allow it to flop back down like a landed fish. The smell of burning filled the air.

Olivia shuddered. Sara pressed close against

her side, her arms wrapping around her mother's waist. Olivia hugged her daughter close.

"We've got a pulse!" one of the EMTs cried. "Let's go!"

With a series of well-coordinated movements, the EMTs scooped Big John onto a stretcher, picked the stretcher up, ran the few steps to the open back door of the ambulance, and loaded him inside.

Seth and Charlie ran behind them, sport coats flapping in the breeze made by their haste. They were joined by a thin, sixtyish woman with short, carefully groomed auburn hair. She wore a blue floral dress, and her high heels kept sinking into the turf, giving her an odd, jerking gait as she ran. With a shock, Olivia recognized her as Belinda Vernon, Big John's daughter, Seth's aunt, and Charlie's wife.

All those years ago, Belinda Vernon had disliked her. *Swamp trash* was what Belinda had called her once, angry over the teenage Olivia's unrepentant attitude after Belinda took her to task for an outfit she was wearing. After that, Olivia had never again deigned to address her as Aunt Belinda, as she had been taught. The few times she'd had to call her something, she had said simply Belinda, in an insolent way that had only served to fuel the older woman's outrage.

In the face of the present emergency, though, past enmity merited no more than a flicker of remembrance. Olivia found herself instinctively running toward the ambulance, too, Sara's hand clutched in hers. She caught up with the others just as Charlie jumped in the back with Big John and the EMTs. Belinda clambered up next. Olivia grabbed at Seth's sleeve as he put a foot on the ambulance floor preparatory to heaving himself inside.

chapter 5

"Seth . . ." Instinctively Olivia wanted to go with them. In the face of this calamity, the years of separation vanished as though they had never been.

Seth glanced back at her, his face hard and unwelcoming.

"Stay here," he said shortly. Then he was inside the ambulance and the door closed in her face. Olivia recoiled inside. As clearly as if he had said the words, Seth's tone told her that she had no right to a place at Big John's side. No longer was she to be considered one of the family. How could she complain, though? She'd abdicated her place herself.

"Oh, my God, Olivia." A hand curled around her arm above her elbow as the ambulance jolted away. Olivia glanced up to discover another familiar face.

"Aunt Callie," she said in what was almost a

sob, as Seth's mother wrapped her in a warm embrace. Sara was still pressed close against her side and Olivia put one arm around her daughter's shoulders, holding her close, enfolding her in the hug. Callie had lost a great deal of weight, Olivia discovered, so that the once-sturdy woman felt almost fragile in her arms. Callie's hair was short now, framing her narrow face in spiky wisps, and the former brunette had gone completely gray. There were dark circles around her eyes, and her face was deeply lined. But the eyes, which were the same deep blue as Seth's, were unchanged.

In her invitation to Olivia to come home for a visit, she'd written that she was ill.

"I'm glad you came, Olivia. Thank you." Although she was clearly upset, Callie managed a shaky smile for Olivia as they separated. "Oh, my goodness, forgive me, but I've got to go to the hospital right away. Do you know what happened to Big John?"

"He had a heart attack, I think. At least, that's what Uncle Charlie said. He was standing on the gazebo steps and he just clutched his chest and keeled over. It was my fault. I'm almost sure — he thought I was my mother." Guilt and pain and shock had rendered Olivia almost numb. She *knew* what had happened, but at the moment she could not really feel it.

"Oh, my goodness," Callie said again helplessly. Her lips trembled. She took a deep breath, seemed to struggle to get hold of herself, and caught Olivia's hand, squeezing it. "Don't blame yourself, dear. Please. You and" — she glanced down at Sara, who was looking up at her with huge, frightened eyes from the protection of Olivia's skirt — "your daughter are very welcome. What happened surely wasn't your fault. Big John hasn't been well for some time, and he's been — a little unclear in his mind." She looked desperately around. "Oh, my, oh, my. I have to get to the hospital. Where is that car?"

"This is Sara." Olivia's arm was still around Sara's shoulders as she identified her daughter by name. It was clear from Callie's hesitation that she couldn't immediately call it to mind. Given the awful circumstances, though, that wasn't too surprising. Olivia herself felt as if her brain had ceased to function properly. Images of Big John as he had looked lying so still and gray on the grass filled her mind almost to the exclusion of all else.

"Please, let's head toward the house." With murmured acknowledgments and waves for other guests who came up to pat her consolingly or called out to her, Callie herded them forward with little shooing gestures. After a few moments and a few deep breaths, she managed a smile for Sara. "Hello, Sara. I'm your aunt Callie."

Sara said nothing, just nodded her head and peeped at Callie from Olivia's other side. With an arm still around her shoulders, Olivia hugged her a little closer. Sara would be overwhelmed by this crisis involving strangers and her mother's obvious emotion, and silence was the way she generally reacted. Not that Olivia blamed her: She was overwhelmed herself.

"Callie, how dreadful! Phillip just told me that Big John collapsed! Do you need a ride to the hospital?" A tall, slender blonde in perhaps her midthirties ran up to them, long-legged in high-heeled black pumps, and placed a hand on Callie's arm. She had rather sharp features that were carefully made-up, chic, chin-length blond hair, and wore a simple, sleeveless black linen sheath that looked like it had cost the earth. A stocky, dark-haired man in a red polo shirt, khaki shorts, and boat shoes with ankle-length socks followed a step behind her, looking agitated. Olivia recognized the man as Seth's cousin, Phillip Vernon. Actually, she had always thought of him as her cousin, too, although he wasn't. He and his brother Carl were the ones who had once thrown her in the lake, for which heinous deed Seth had obligingly beaten them up. Phillip would be about thirty-four now, Olivia calculated, some three years younger than Seth. He was quite a bit heavier than he had been the last time she had seen him, but Olivia would have recognized him anywhere.

"Oh, Mallory, yes, I do mean to go to the hospital, right away, but Ira's already fetching the car," Callie said, her voice quivering. "I am just about out of my mind —"

"Olivia!" Phillip interrupted, his eyes widening as they moved past Callie to fix on Olivia's face. "By all that's holy! What the hell are you doing here?"

"I asked her to come, Phillip," Callie intervened. "She and her daughter are my guests. And watch your language, if you please! Olivia, this is Mallory Hodges, Seth's fiancée. Mallory, this is Seth's cousin Olivia Morrison, and her daughter, Sara."

Seth's fiancée. As they all hurried toward the house, and Olivia and Mallory Hodges exchanged hasty greetings, Olivia turned the knowledge over in her mind. She had known that Seth had married and divorced, but she hadn't known he was planning to marry again.

But then, how should she? It was she, after all, who had cut the connection and chosen to stay away. For nine years.

"Did my father go with Big John in the ambulance?" Phillip asked as they neared the house.

"Both your parents did, and so did Seth," Callie replied, glancing around distractedly. "Olivia . . ."

They reached the Big House's wide front steps as Callie spoke, and began to ascend in a group to the first-floor veranda. The house was built in the fashion of southern Louisiana, with the first floor some ten feet above the lawn to combat groundwater. The cellar beneath was only partially underground, and had windows half the size of the upper-story windows looking out onto the mass of shrubbery that surrounded the house. The cellar walls were made of stone, as were the steps. The rest of the house was built of white-painted brick. Those used for the center section had been handmade and fired on the former sugar plantation by slaves before the Civil War.

A white Lincoln Town Car stopped by the walkway that led from the driveway to the house, and honked twice, causing Callie to break off in midsentence, stop climbing stairs, and glance toward it. Everyone else followed suit.

"Oh, thank goodness! I must go. Olivia —"

She was interrupted again.

"Do you mind if I ride with you? I feel I should be there for Seth, in case . . ." Mallory's voice trailed off delicately, but her meaning was clear: in case Big John died.

Hail Mary, full of grace . . .

"Oh, dear, oh, surely he won't need you that way! But of course you may come, Mallory. You're one of the family now. Olivia . . ." Callie cast a wild-eyed glance at Olivia. Olivia wondered if the icy shock she was experiencing was as visible as Callie's distress.

Before she could finish whatever it was she had been trying to say, Callie was cut off by a blond sprite in an ankle-length blue cotton nightgown who darted out the front door.

"Nana, what's happened? What's wrong?" The screen banged shut behind the child, the sound as loud as a gunshot. She was about Sara's age, and exquisitely pretty, Olivia saw, as she skidded to a stop at the top of the stairs, with hair

47

down to her waist, delicate bones, and huge cornflower-blue eyes.

"Oh, Chloe, what are you doing up? It's after midnight!" Callie said in a despairing voice.

"She ain't never been to bed, though I swear I tried." Martha Hendricks, the family's longtime housekeeper, followed on the little girl's heels. She was fiftyish, clad in a flowered cotton zip-front robe and pink terry-cloth slippers, a big-boned woman with a plain round face and an un-naturally black beehive of hair. She sounded ha-rassed. "She saw that there ambulance out of the window, and you know how Miss Curiosity is. Nothing would suit her but that she had to get out here and stick her nose in the middle of what was goin' on."

"Oh, dear," Callie said, her hands fluttering uncharacteristically. It was clear that she was torn between the waiting Lincoln and Chloe.

"Nana, what's wrong?" Chloe demanded again, resting a hand against a fluted pillar that soared two stories above her and looking down at Callie, who was a little more than halfway up the dozen steps.

"Honey . . ."

The waiting car honked impatiently. They all glanced toward it. At the same time, Martha saw and recognized Olivia, and her jaw dropped.

"Well, I never! Miss Olivia!"

"Hello, Martha." Olivia managed a smile. One hand curled tightly around the wrought-iron railing that ran up both sides of the steps. Her other hand clasped Sara's. The housekeeper had changed very little, she saw. Martha lived in town, coming into the Big House three days a week to do the heavy cleaning. On other days, she cut hair. Or at least, that was the way it had been when Olivia was a girl. "It's good to see you."

"You, too. Why . . ."

The car honked again.

Callie threw her hands up in the air and glanced distractedly from Chloe to the car. "Oh, goodness, I have to go. Big John's had a — spell, Chloe, and they've taken him to the hospital, and that's where I'm headed. It's nothing for you to worry about. Martha, you and Chloe take Olivia and her daughter in and get them settled for the night. Olivia, we'll talk tomorrow. At least . . ."

"Oh, my lord in heaven!" Martha said, one hand flying to press against her throat, her eyes round as saucers. "The ambulance — it weren't ever for Mr. Archer?"

"Nana, I want to go to the hospital with you!" Chloe was shrilly insistent.

"Honey, you can't. Hospitals don't allow children. Now, these are your cousins, come to visit, and I need you to stay here and help them feel welcome. I have got to go. Phillip, Mallory . . ."

Those two were already running down the steps. With another distracted flutter of her hands and an admonition to Chloe to be good, Callie followed them. Olivia, whose instinct was

49

to go, too, stayed where she was. Having relinquished her place in the family long ago, she was left to bite her lower lip, tighten her hold on Sara's hand, and carry on as best she could.

The front passenger door of the car swung open from the inside as the trio rushed toward it. Phillip snatched open the rear door, and he and Mallory jumped into the back. Callie, reaching the car last, clambered into the front seat. The car took off down the driveway while the doors were still closing. As there was a long line of traffic in the driveway in front of them, the driver honked his horn repeatedly. Other cars pulled over onto the grass to let the Lincoln pass.

Olivia stared after them, her stomach in a knot and her eyes burning with unshed tears. She should be speeding to the hospital, too.

"Well, we sure ain't doing ourselves or nobody else any good standin' out here. You better come on in, Miss Olivia." Martha's brisk words brought Olivia back to reality. Even if she were welcome at the hospital, even if Seth had not made it clear that she had no place at Big John's side, she could not go rushing off and leave Sara on her own among people who were strangers to her. For her daughter's sake, she had to stay where she was, had to present a calm, controlled exterior, had to deal with the situation as it existed.

Almost stealthily, Olivia brushed at her burning eyes with her free hand. Then she took a deep breath, looked up at Martha and Chloe, who stood on the veranda — as the downstairs gallery was properly called, some half dozen steps above them — and started to say something to Chloe.

But Chloe spoke first.

"If you're my cousins, how come I've never seen you before?" she demanded, scowling down at Olivia and Sara. "I know all my cousins, and none of them looks like you." She looked Sara over critically. "You're fat."

chapter 6

"Sara is not fat!" Olivia responded instantly, fixing Chloe with a look that should have shriveled her on the spot. She could feel Sara shrinking against her side, and tightened her own hand consolingly on Sara's smaller one. Sara's weight was a sensitive issue for the child. "Sara is the absolute perfect size for Sara."

"Miss Chloe!" Martha gasped at the same time, her shocked tone a reproof. "Say you're sorry right this minute!"

There was a moment of silence while the issue hung in the balance. Then, "I'm sorry," Chloe said sulkily.

"Are you Seth's daughter?" Olivia asked in a gentler tone, reminding herself that Chloe was just a child and had almost certainly not meant to be hurtful. She held tight to Sara's hand as they began to once again ascend the steps. She could sense Sara's reluctance to continue, but drew her daughter upward anyway. Sara's retiring nature was totally unsuited for this shattering homecoming.

"That's right," Chloe said, still sulky. "But you're not my cousins. You can't be. Phillip and Carl and Angela are my daddy's only cousins. And Melissa, and Amanda, and Courtney, and Jason, and Thomas, and Patrick are their children, and Nana says that makes them my cousins, too. But that's all. So who are you?" Her sweeping glance included Sara in what was unmistakably a condemnation.

"You're right, we're not precisely your cousins." Olivia held on to her patience with an effort. She reached the wide, plank-floored veranda with Sara's hand curled tightly in hers and Sara herself hovering close against her side. Everything about the veranda was just as she remembered it, from the weathered gray paint beneath her feet to the white wicker swing and rockers at its far end to the leafy ferns that hung in baskets from its eaves. Even the pair of stuffed ring-necked pheasants that Charlie, a skilled taxidermist, had hung by wires from the ceiling as a joke years ago were still there. "I guess you could call us courtesy cousins, though, if you wanted to."

"Why would I want to?" Chloe asked, looking Olivia and Sara up and down with narrowed eyes.

"To be polite?" Olivia suggested, in an even

53

gentler tone than before.

Martha put a silencing hand on Chloe's shoulder. Chloe made a face at Olivia, but said nothing more. Standing in the column of light that spilled through the open screen door as Chloe was, her hair looked almost platinum and, except for her sullen expression, she was as flawlessly lovely as a doll. Olivia wondered briefly if Seth's ex-wife was a blonde like her ex-husband and daughter, and as pretty as Chloe. Then Sara's hand twitched in hers. A glance down at her daughter's stricken face told Olivia that her silent child was totally intimidated by the other girl. She sighed inwardly — Sara's lack of confidence around other children was a source of never-ending concern to her — and gave Sara's hand another supportive squeeze.

"Miss Olivia grew up here, just the same as your daddy did," Martha said to Chloe in a scolding tone. "She's your cousin in all the ways that count, and this is her home, just the same as it's yours."

Olivia smiled gratefully at Martha, then looked at Chloe again. The child was scowling at her. Maybe she was just having a bad day, Olivia thought, trying to be charitable. She knew from experience that even the best-behaved child could occasionally turn into an adult-mortifying monster. Giving Chloe the benefit of the doubt, she tried to explain the situation in a way the girl would understand.

"Big John had four children, you know: Mi-

chael, James, David, and Belinda. Your grandfather was Michael, Big John's oldest son. My
stepfather was James, the second oldest. Your
father is the big cousin who looked out for me
when I was growing up. Your nana is my aunt
Callie, and Big John is my stepgrandpa, and
Phillip and Carl and Angela are the pesky
cousins who used to come over all the time to
bug me."

"So what you're saying is you're just a
stepcousin," Chloe said scornfully. They were
entering the house now with Martha, who kept a
hand on Chloe's shoulder, holding the screen
door open so that Olivia and Sara could precede
them inside.

"That's right," Olivia said with a flickering
smile, as the cooler air inside the house enveloped her. When she had left, there had been one
window air-conditioning unit downstairs and
two upstairs, and that was it. They had rattled all
the time, and had cooled the air a maximum of
maybe five degrees. This coolness felt different
— fresher and colder. Maybe Big John had finally sprung for central air. If he had, though, it
would surprise her. He had always been careful
with a dollar.

Chloe shrugged off Martha's hand to follow
them inside. "So if you grew up here, how come
I've never seen you before? Where've you been,
then?"

"Miss Olivia got married and moved away,"
Martha interjected before Olivia could reply,

shooting Chloe a warning look as she stepped into the hall and closed the door. "And that's about enough out of you, missy, or you'll make me tell your daddy that you were rude to guests."

To Olivia's surprise, the threat seemed to work. Chloe was silent. For a moment they stood rather awkwardly in the huge entry hall without speaking, bathed in the soft glow of the antique crystal chandelier that hung overhead. As far as Olivia could tell, nothing in the hall had changed so much as one iota from when she was a girl. Same well-polished hardwood floors with the same red-based Oriental runner leading toward the door at the far end of the hall that opened into the kitchen. Same cream-painted walls with the same quartet of mahogany pocket doors opening into living room and dining room and library and office. Same elaborate moldings accentuating the soaring fifteen-foot ceiling. Same oil paintings of dogs and horses, in the same places. Same wide, elegant staircase that rose with a graceful curve to the second floor. Even the smell was the same, a combination of faint mustiness from the never-ending damp, furniture polish, the rose-based potpourri that Aunt Callie used to combat the scent of everything else, and what Olivia had always thought of as just plain old. The house had always smelled old.

Taking it all in, Olivia felt, for an unsettling moment, as if she had been transported back in time. Nine years back, to be precise. On the surface, at least, nothing was different from the way it had been when she last saw it, on the night she had the quarrel to end all quarrels with Seth, and then had eloped with Newall.

"Martha, Carl Vernon's on the phone, wantin' to know what hospital they were taking old Mr. Archer to." A woman of about Olivia's own age, whom she did not recognize but who was clearly some kind of household help, from her black uniform dress and the white apron around her waist, entered through the swinging door that led to the kitchen. Her gaze touched on Olivia and Sara briefly, then returned to Martha. "*Did* something happen to old Mr. Archer?" she asked, agog.

Martha nodded, and gave Chloe a significant look as an obvious signal to the other woman to say no more. "Tell Mr. Carl that I don't know any more'n he does, and the rest of the family's done took off with the ambulance."

Eyes wide, the woman nodded acknowledgment and withdrew.

"Come on into the kitchen, why don't you?" Martha said to Olivia, then glanced at Sara and smiled. "I bet you're thirsty, hon. I've got some soda pop in the icebox. Or maybe you'd rather have a glass of milk?"

Sara pressed closer against Olivia's side, and shook her head no without replying.

"Doesn't she ever talk?" Chloe asked, frowning curiously at Sara.

"This is my daughter, Sara Morrison," Olivia said, addressing Chloe in a slightly stern tone without giving a direct reply to the question. Introductions, she felt, were in order, before Chloe's rudeness rendered Sara permanently mute. "Sara, this is Chloe Archer. Say hello."

"Hello," Sara produced, in a rough approximation of her normal voice, and actually raised her eyes to look at Chloe, although she continued to hang back, keeping Olivia's body partially between herself and the other girl.

"How old are you?" Chloe looked hard at Sara.

"Eight," Sara said, in response to a well-disguised maternal squeeze of the fingers.

"So'm I." Frowning, Chloe continued to look Sara up and down. Clearly unnerved, Sara dropped her gaze to the rug again.

Olivia sighed inwardly.

"Martha, I think we're just going to go on upstairs. It's late, and Sara needs to get to bed," Olivia said, earning a grateful finger squeeze from Sara.

"That's probably a good idea." Martha glanced at Chloe. "Miss Curiosity here needs to be headin' for her bed, too. She gets cranky when she stays up too late."

"I do not!" Chloe protested.

Martha sniffed eloquently. Then she looked at Olivia and rolled her eyes heavenward. Olivia understood the unspoken message: Chloe was definitely having a bad day.

"Let's see, I guess Sara can have your old bed-room for tonight, and you can have the room next door to it, that used to belong to Miss Belinda. They're all ready, and I just changed the sheets this mornin', in case anybody needed to stay all night after the party, if you know what I mean."

Olivia nodded. In case anybody got too drunk to make it home, was what Martha was really saying. "That sounds fine."

"Miss Chloe, you lead the way, why don't you."

Chloe obeyed, and they all headed upstairs. Family portraits, oils in elaborate gilt frames, marched one after the other up the wall of the stairwell all the way to the ceiling. There were many of them: Over the years, the Archers had tended to be a prolific lot. More examples of Charlie's handiwork were interspersed here and there among the portraits: a small, stuffed boar's head with graying tusks, a horned sheep, a three-point buck. The occasional landscape made an appearance, too, along with the odd memento, such as a framed fan. Beneath Olivia's fingers, the hand-carved cypress rail felt cool. Under-foot, the center of each uncarpeted step had a slight dip worn into the wood from generations of climbing feet. This, the main part of the Big House, was more than one hundred and fifty years old, and was as grand as any plantation house in any movie about the Old South. As a child, Olivia had always been a little awed by it, and she could see that Sara was, too.

"Oh, we don't want to forget about your suit-cases." Martha, who was following Chloe, paused midway up the stairs and spoke to Olivia over her shoulder.

"There's nothing to forget." Olivia grimaced ruefully. "We left our suitcases behind the counter at the bus depot."

"The bus depot! Don't you have a *car?*" Chloe piped up, turning at the top of the steps to give Olivia and Sara an astonished look.

"Lands, then, how'd you get . . ." Martha sounded perplexed. Then, with a scandalized gasp: "Never say you walked all the way from the bus dee-poe!"

Olivia nodded ruefully. "I tried to call some-body at the house to pick us up, but there was no answer here. And Ponce must have been at the party, because he didn't answer his telephone, ei-ther. If he even runs the taxi service anymore." If her statement was a trifle mendacious, then so be it. Coming home as the not-so-sure-of-her-welcome poor relation was hard enough without admitting to being dead broke as well.

"Ponce has done retired," Martha said. "His son — you remember Lamar? — well, he runs the business now. When he feels like it, that is."

There was condemnation in her voice. Olivia did indeed remember Lamar. Although he had attended the local public high school and she had gone to St. Theresa's, an expensive private school in Baton Rouge, their paths had crossed

60

with some frequency when they were teenagers. Two years older than Olivia, Lamar Lennig had been a good-looking, if sullen, boy who had seemed to spend most of his time finding trouble. He'd been a great admirer of hers, like most of the local boys.

She wouldn't have given him much more than the time of day back then, if Seth hadn't caught him hanging around once too often and ordered him to keep away from her. After that, she'd gone out with Lamar a few times, just to teach Seth that he couldn't run her life. Her open defiance had infuriated Seth. Looking back, Olivia had to admit that Seth had been right. Lamar had been a major-league loser. Just like Newall. Seth had warned her against him, too.

Olivia sighed. "I remember Lamar," she agreed.

"I bet you remember where your room is, too," Martha said with a smile. They were in the upstairs hall now. Olivia nodded, and turned left, toward the newer of the two wings that had been added to the main house decades after it had been built. The east wing, where her old room was, was built around 1930. The ceilings were lower than in the main house, only about ten feet high, and the crown moldings were not as elaborate. But they were spacious. Each of the four upstairs bedchambers boasted a fireplace and a little sitting area, and there were two bathrooms, although neither of them was en suite.

Her childhood bedroom was the second on the

right. Reaching it, Olivia opened the door and walked inside. It had been completely redecorated, of course. When she had inhabited it, the walls had been painted a bright, cheery yellow, ruffled chintz curtains had hung at the pair of long windows that opened out onto the upstairs gallery, and a matching chintz bedspread had covered the white-painted iron bed. The room had a more masculine feel now, sporting taupe wallpaper with a white windowpane check and simple white linen curtains and bedclothes. But the fireplace was still the same, with its small, elaborately carved mantel and creamy marble surround, and the windows, the moldings, and the narrow oak floors were unchanged, too.

Just walking into the bedroom that had been hers during her growing up years brought back emotions so powerful that Olivia was momentarily dizzy with them.

Her mother . . .

Staring at the bed, the same bed although the spread was different, Olivia was suddenly overcome by a long-forgotten memory of her mother bending over her, kissing her good night as she lay tucked up in bed in this room. The light floral scent of her mother's perfume, the warmth of her lips, the silken brush of her hair against Olivia's cheek as she straightened — all suddenly came back to her with such force that Olivia was shaken.

She almost felt as if she could actually see the scene taking place before her. At the same time, she was experiencing it as the little girl she had once been. That little girl had felt safe, sleepy, comforted by the warmth of her mother's presence.

She also had been dreading the moment when her mother would turn and go out of the room, because she was scared to death to be left alone in the dark.

chapter 7

"You can sleep in here, Sara, and your mama can have the room next door," Martha said. To Olivia, her voice sounded like it was coming from a distance. In reality, she was standing just inside the door, not four feet away, with Chloe beside her.

Olivia could feel the warmth of her daughter's fingers in hers, and the weight of her small body as she pressed close against her side. For Sara's sake, Olivia fought to overcome the sudden sense of disorientation that assailed her.

The vision, and the emotions that went with it, had seemed so real.

It was an old memory brought on by entering her childhood bedroom again, coupled probably with her upset over Big John, and nothing more, she told herself. The strength of the feelings that had accompanied it was disquieting, but that was likely because she had so few memories of her mother.

I'm here. She could almost hear the voice in her head. Which was ridiculous, of course. Making a great effort, she pulled herself together and focused on the present, and her daughter.

"If Sara doesn't mind sharing her bed with me, I think we'll both sleep in here, for tonight, at least," Olivia said, smiling at Martha. If her voice was a little thin and her smile a little forced, no one seemed to notice.

"I don't mind." Sara's free right hand was busy twisting a fold of Olivia's skirt, but she actually spoke without maternal prompting. From that, and the eagerness in her voice, Olivia knew how enormous her relief must be at not being left to sleep alone in these unfamiliar surroundings.

Martha nodded. "That's fine, then. Chloe's bedroom is next to Mr. Seth's, in the east wing. My room's across the hall from theirs, next to Miss Callie's. If you need anything, just come along and get me. I'm a real light sleeper."

Olivia's disorienting sense of having stepped back in time was fading. "We will."

"I'll scare you two up somethin' to sleep in, then, and we'll see about gettin' your things picked up from the bus dee-poe. Maybe, if I can get Lamar on the phone, he can run them out first thing in the morning."

"Thank you, Martha." Olivia glanced at Chloe, who was still staring at Sara. Sara, of course, instead of meeting that critical gaze head-on, was steadfastly regarding the patterned Oriental carpet. "Good night, Chloe."

"Good night," Chloe said with reasonable civility, and turned away as Martha grasped her hand. The two of them headed toward the opposite end of the house. When they were gone, Olivia looked down at Sara, who still stood pressed against her side, one hand in hers, one hand wrapped in her skirt, her gaze on the ground.

"You okay, pumpkin-eater?" she asked, dropping her daughter's hand to wrap her arms around her shoulders and give her a gentle hug.

Sara nodded, and hugged her back.

"I'm glad you're going to sleep with me tonight," she said, as Olivia released her.

"You better not hog all the covers." Olivia's reply was deliberately light.

That made Sara smile. "I won't. It's too hot."

She moved away from Olivia's side into the center of the room, and slowly revolved as she looked around.

"What do you think?" Olivia asked, smiling.

"This place is awesome," Sara said. "It's like a mansion."

Compared to their low-rent, two-bedroom apartment, Olivia guessed it was. "Told you."

"I thought you might be just making it up."

"*Me* lie to *you?* Never," Olivia said. Sara giggled. Olivia heard the sound with relief.

"See this bed?" Olivia continued, crossing to it

and throwing herself down on her back, arms spread wide.

Sara nodded.

"This is the bed I used to sleep in when I was a little girl. It had a yellow bedspread then with big cabbage roses on it, and lots of lace around the pillows. And there were *lots* of pillows."

"And you had a big doll with yellow hair and a pink dress named Victoria Elizabeth." Sara walked over to stand beside the bed, smiling down at her mother. She had heard the stories many times, and knew all the details almost as well as Olivia did.

"That's right."

"And you painted your hair yellow once, so you would look like the doll. And — and your aunt Callie tried and tried to wash it out, but it wouldn't come out, and you ended up having to get all your hair cut off." Sara's smile turned into a grin, and she flopped down on her stomach beside her mother. "I can't believe you would do something that stupid."

"It wasn't one of my better moments, I admit."

"And a nutria came down the chimney once, and when you woke up it was sitting on your pillow staring at you. You screamed so loud that you woke up everybody in the house, and they came running in, and the nutria was running all over the room and when Seth tried to shoo it out it bit him and he had to get rabies shots."

"Yup."

"It was all *true*," Sara said, enchanted. "There

really was a doll, and a nutria, and —"

A rap on the door caused Olivia to sit up, feeling slightly foolish about being caught in her abandoned posture on the bed. Beside her, Sara sat up, too, and scooted off the bed as though scared she had done something wrong. Martha stood in the open doorway, her gaze moving over them indulgently.

"I've brought both you girls nightgowns," she said, indicating with a gesture the articles of clothing draped over her right forearm. "And robes. And toothbrushes."

"Oh, Martha, you're wonderful." Olivia stood up and moved across the room to take the items from her. "Thanks."

Martha smiled first at her, then at Sara. "It's good to have you home, Miss Olivia. And you, too, Miss Sara."

Martha left, and Olivia closed the door. Turning back to her daughter, she found Sara standing beside the bed, wide-eyed.

"She called me *Miss Sara*."

"That's just the way things are done around here. Don't let it go to your head."

Sara wrinkled her nose. "I won't."

"Good. I'd hate to see your head get swelled up so much that it would just pop like a balloon. Your brains would go all over the walls and —"

"That's gross!"

"I know." Olivia chuckled at the expression on her child's face. She had been trying to cheer her up, and apparently she'd succeeded.

Moments later, nightclothes and toothbrushes in hand, Olivia and Sara went along to the bathroom across the hall to wash up and brush their teeth. It was too late for anything more, and to quiet her conscience Olivia told herself that missing her nightly bath wouldn't hurt Sara this once. After they were clean, and clad in borrowed nightgowns — Sara's was pink, but otherwise almost identical to the sleeveless blue one Chloe had worn, while the ownership of Olivia's knee-length green nylon number was murkier — they padded back to the bedroom, closed the door, turned out the light, and got into bed.

Olivia meant to wait until Sara went to sleep, then get up, go to the kitchen, and, if there was no news, call around until she found the hospital where Big John had been taken. She was certain that it would be in Baton Rouge, and that being the case there were only so many possibilities.

"Say your prayers," she instructed Sara, as she did every night. Lying close beside her daughter, with the tiny white lights that still twinkled outside penetrating the curtains so that, while the room was dark, it was not so dark that she could not see, Olivia listened to her daughter's murmured prayer.

"Now I lay me . . ."

She had said that same prayer, in that same room, as a child. In the gloom, it was easy to imagine that time had flown backward again, that *her* mother lay beside her listening to *her* prayer, and for a moment the illusion was so real that it sent a chill down her spine. Talk about déjà vu . . .

"Are you sad about that old man, Mom?" Sara asked, having apparently finished her prayers while Olivia had not been attending. Again Olivia forced herself back to the present.

"I'm worried about him," Olivia said. "I'm hoping he'll be all right."

"Should I say a God-bless for him, too?"

"That would be nice."

"God bless that old man," Sara said, and Olivia had to smile.

For a moment Sara was silent. Then she said, "That girl — Chloe — is really mean, isn't she? And she doesn't like us."

"She doesn't know us. Once she does, she'll love us, especially you. I mean, what's not to love?"

"Oh, Mom." Sara giggled sleepily.

"Hush, now." Olivia kissed her daughter's cheek as Sara snuggled close.

"Tell me a story about when you were growing up," Sara begged, as she did every night. Usually Olivia complied. But tonight, the memories were too close, too real. So real it was almost eerie . . . Anyway, she was tired and worried and knew that Sara had to be exhausted, too.

"It's too late, pumpkin. Go to sleep."

"But, Mom . . ."

"Go to sleep."

Olivia firmly quelled all of Sara's additional attempts to chat with firm repetitions of "Go to sleep."

Finally the sound of her daughter's breathing told Olivia that Sara had done just that.

Sliding carefully out of bed, she felt for the robe Martha had left her and pulled it on. Then, for no real reason except that it had always been her habit before she went to sleep in this room, she crossed to the long windows that were really more like French doors and made sure they were locked tight. Finally she turned on the small lamp by the bed so that if Sara awoke she wouldn't be in the dark, and left the room, quietly closing the bedroom door behind her. Then she headed downstairs. The anxiety over Big John that she had suppressed for Sara's sake surged into life, making her feel almost queasy.

She was terribly afraid that Big John would die. And if he did, it would be all her fault.

She should have stayed away.

chapter 8

There were two women in the kitchen when Olivia entered, both dressed in black uniforms with white aprons tied around their waists. Olivia knew neither of them, although one was the woman who had spoken to Martha in the hall earlier. Both had their backs to her, and both were busily engaged in wiping down the white laminate countertops with rectangular yellow sponges. Tupperware containers, some stacked atop each other, were lined up on one long counter. Their tightly closed lids could not quite contain the spicy smell of *boudin* and gumbo, and Olivia surmised that the help were taking leftovers home.

The kitchen itself was unchanged from Olivia's memory of it. Remodeled in the fifties with only an occasional change of appliances thereafter, it was huge, some forty feet long by twenty feet wide. At one time in the house's history, it had been three smallish rooms. Now it boasted oak-paneled walls that had been painted a soft cream, custom-built cherry cabinets that lined three walls to the ceiling, a massive Sub-Zero refrigerator, and a commercial-looking stainless-steel stove that was an obviously recent addition. A long, well-scrubbed and scarred oak trestle table in the center of the room provided seating for up to twelve. Above it hung a century-old wrought-iron chandelier that had been converted to electricity just before Olivia left home. The far wall was a bank of multipaned, floor-to-ceiling windows, which included two French doors that opened onto the lower of the two galleries that surrounded the house. At the moment, cream-colored drapes with a green ivy pattern were closed over the windows, keeping the darkness out. The kitchen itself was brightly lit by antique brass-and-copper lamps, original to the house, that had been converted from oil at some point, and the chandelier over the table, which was agleam.

As Olivia came through the swinging door that separated the kitchen from the hall, both women looked around.

"Hi," Olivia said uncertainly, realizing that, despite her overwhelming sense of having come home, in reality the kitchen help were more certain of their place in the house than she. "Has there been any news about Mr. Archer?"

Both women shook their heads.

"Not that we've heard," said the woman from the hall.

"You're Olivia Chenier, aren't you?" The one Olivia hadn't seen before looked her over appraisingly. If appearances were anything to judge by, she was the older of the two. She was around thirty, with obviously dyed dark red hair, blunt features, and a pear-shaped figure that the apron tied tightly around her waist only emphasized.

"Yes. Well, Olivia Morrison now," Olivia said, tightening the belt of the knee-length pink chenille bathrobe that Martha had provided. Her legs and feet were bare. While she was decently covered, and the only alternative garment she could have chosen was the limp sundress she had worn earlier, she felt hideously self-conscious under the other women's avid stares.

"I'm Amy McGee, Amy Fry, that was. You probably don't remember me, but I used to see you around a lot when you were growing up. I live in town. You ran off and married some rodeo rider, didn't you? Lord, when it happened that was all anybody talked about for months. Hot hot, is what we all said." The woman shook her hand suggestively.

"Amy!" the other woman protested. She was younger, slimmer, prettier, with mouse-brown hair pulled back into a ponytail at her nape. With an apologetic look at Olivia, she added, "I'm Amy's sister, Laura Fry. We own Sisters Catering. We did the cooking tonight, all except the desserts. They came from Patout's Bakery in town."

"The *boudin* smells wonderful, although I didn't get a chance to eat any." Glad to be rescued from a discussion of her past, Olivia walked across the cool, rough-textured brick pavers that tiled the kitchen floor. With her face scrubbed clean of any makeup and her hair brushed straight back and tucked behind her ears, she wondered how she stacked up to the Olivia they remembered. Not well, she guessed. "I just came down to use the phone. Is it still . . . ?"

She nodded toward the butler's pantry, which was basically a walk-in food closet with a sink and a telephone at the far end of the kitchen. When she had lived here, there had been two telephones in the whole huge house: one in the butler's pantry, for general use, and one in Big John's office, in the west wing. Big John had never liked telephones, and saw no need to have more than two of the noisy contraptions in his house. To his mind, two was pushing it. The restriction had played havoc with her social life, and as a teenager she had been impatient with Big John's autocratic decree. It had been hard to carry on a conversation with anyone, let alone boys, in the middle of the busy kitchen, where any chance passerby was free to listen in.

More than once she had driven into town to use the pay phone in the drugstore. Every time she had done it, the necessity made her mad.

"In there," Amy confirmed, jerking a thumb toward the butler's pantry. Her eyes were alive with speculation as she watched Olivia cross the room. Olivia guessed she would be the subject of a great deal of gossip in town the following day, and shrank a little inside. Where once she wouldn't have worried a jot about what anyone said of her, and indeed had enjoyed shocking everyone from her family to the local townsfolk, time and circumstances had changed her. Pride had well and truly presaged her fall, and she was stung by the knowledge that she would be the subject of probably unflattering gossip on the morrow.

"Amy, it's the middle of the night. What are you and Laura still doin' here?" Martha sounded scandalized as she came through the swinging door with far more assurance than Olivia had shown. Of course, Martha the housekeeper belonged now in a way that Olivia the not-quite-family-member did not. Martha looked as wide awake as ever, while she herself had passed beyond the point of exhaustion long since, and was sure it showed.

"We're just finishing up now," Amy said, gathering both sponges and tossing them into the top rack of the dishwasher. "We didn't want to leave the kitchen a mess." With a flourish she shut the door and turned on the machine.

"I hope Mr. Archer is okay." Laura was softer in manner than her sister. As she spoke, she picked up her purse, an inexpensive-looking tan

76

vinyl bag, from the counter, and slung it over her shoulder.

"So do I." Martha sighed. "I don't guess there's been any word?"

"Nobody's told us anything," Amy said.

"I was just going to start calling the hospitals in Baton Rouge." Olivia stuck her head out of the butler's pantry. The telephone receiver was already in her hand.

"Oh, Miss Olivia, are you up, too?" Martha's gaze found her, and she shook her head. "The day you've had, you should be sleepin' like the dead."

"I couldn't go to sleep without finding out how Big John is." Olivia's fingers tightened around the receiver. Once no one would have questioned her concern, or her right to it. It hurt to be treated like a guest, she discovered. Nine years away had changed nothing as far as her own feelings were concerned: To her, LaAngelle Plantation was still home, and the Archers family.

"No, prob'ly not," Martha conceded. "You go on and call, then. I'd try St. Elizabeth's first, if it was me. That's where Miss Belinda had her gallbladder out last year. Amy, did you two get your check?"

As Amy answered, Olivia ducked back into the butler's pantry and dialed Baton Rouge information.

At the same moment as the operator answered, the sound of one of the French doors opening caused Olivia to glance around.

"What number, please?" came the tinny inquiry over the wire.

"There's nothing we can do." Seth's voice, sounding the faintest bit testy, was clearly audible through the open door, although Olivia could not yet see him. Callie walked into the kitchen accompanied by a wave of humid air scented with honeysuckle, her face as pale as skim milk. She looked really old, far older than she had outside in the torch-lit darkness, and Olivia once again chided herself for staying away too long. She should have at least visited once or twice over the years — but then, how could she have done so without revealing how far down in the world she had fallen? If the family had learned what a struggle her daily life had become, she would have been humiliated beyond bearing.

On her last night at home, when she had screamed at Seth that she was going to marry Newall Morrison whether he liked it or not, he had warned her that if she did, the family would wash its collective hands of her. She would be on her own.

She hadn't listened, of course, to his threats or his warnings. She'd been so sure she knew everything about everything.

She'd been so young. Just thinking about how young she had been made her throat tighten and ache.

And dumb, too. Definitely dumb. Eloping

with a man she had known just four months was about as dumb as it got. Add to that the fact that she had run off three weeks before she was due to start her freshman year at Tulane, and dumb turned into downright stupid.

She knew better now, but of course now was too late.

In inviting her and Sara to visit LaAngelle Plantation, Callie had written that she was ill, without specifying the exact nature of the illness. Looking at her for the first time under a bright light, Olivia wondered just how serious that illness was. At the thought, she felt another icy pang of fear.

Had she found them again, this family that she had so foolishly spurned, only to begin losing them one by one? The thought chilled her.

Behind Callie came a man Olivia did not know. He was about Callie's age, just a few inches taller than she, bald except for the short white fringe circling his head just above his ears, paunchy, and dressed in a short-sleeved white shirt tucked into a pair of neatly pressed and belted brown slacks. His face was jowly and flushed from the heat, and beads of sweat glinted on his temples and forehead. His left hand, square and stubby-fingered, rested possessively on Callie's thin shoulder. He was followed into the kitchen by Seth's fiancée, Mallory, who was saying something over her shoulder as she entered. Despite the humidity, Mallory's blond hair was as smooth and sleek as if she had just stepped out of a beauty parlor, and her skin was perfectly matte. Her black linen sheath was unwrinkled, the big diamond on her ring finger and the smaller ones linked around her wrist sparkled, and even her crimson lipstick looked fresh. As the other woman walked by her without becoming aware of her presence, Olivia spared her an envious glance. Reed-slender, elegant, self-assured, and obviously affluent, Mallory was everything Olivia was not but wished she was. Only after Mallory appeared did Seth come into view, closing the back door behind him and locking it with a click.

chapter 9

What was it Seth had said to her? *Have you ever in your life done anything but cause trouble?*

A dial tone buzzed in Olivia's ear, telling her that her call had been cut off. Of course, she had never said so much as a word to the operator. Well, the information she had sought was obviously at hand now.

"Oh, Seth, we should have stayed," Callie said reproachfully to her son as the party walked across the kitchen. The bald man pulled out a chair. Callie sank into it as if her legs had suddenly given out, resting her arms on the table and leaning forward on them. The others sat, too, except for Seth, who stopped beside his mother to look down at her. He was frowning, and his hand closed tensely around the curved top rail of the Windsor chair.

"Mother, they only let one person at a time

Portville Free Library
Portville, N. Y.

into the Intensive Care Unit, and Belinda was there. She's his daughter, remember? And Charlie was in the unit, too, as his personal physician. Phillip was in the waiting room. Carl was on his way. There is nothing you or I or any of the rest of us can do for Big John tonight that they cannot."

"You would have stayed if I hadn't been there. You just came away to bring me home. I know you, Seth Archer." Straightening in her chair as if to deny the weakness she obviously felt, Callie tilted her head back to look up at him.

"Mother . . ." Seth's frown deepened. He, too, looked older in the bright kitchen light, Olivia saw. Time had etched fine lines around his eyes and deeper ones that ran from his nose to the corners of his mouth. His face was angular, with prominent cheekbones and a strong chin. His nose — the Archer nose — was long and straight with a faint bump on the high bridge. His lips were well-shaped but thin, and looked as if they scarcely ever smiled anymore. He was, as he had always been, deeply tanned, but there were glints of silver in the short blond hair above his ears, and his hairline was higher around the temples than it had once been. Tall, broad-shouldered, and lean, he exuded restless energy even at this late hour. There was an air about him of one born to command, as, indeed, he had been.

"You do need to rest, Callie, you know you do." This came from the bald man, who was seated beside Callie and who looked at her with undisguised concern.

"You stay out of this, Ira! I'm not an invalid yet." Callie glared at the speaker.

Seth made an impatient sound. "The fact remains that it would be stupid to stay there and exhaust yourself, when Big John is getting the best possible care and has absolutely no need of any of us. You need to take care of yourself now, Mother, not everybody else."

"Just what I keep telling her." Ira nodded in vigorous agreement, his gaze on Callie's face. She narrowed her eyes at him warningly.

"How's Mr. Archer?" This subdued question came from Martha, who stood near the counter with the caterers. In her flowered robe and slippers, she looked as at home in the kitchen as a loaf of bread.

"He's had a heart attack, Martha," Callie said, as though she could scarcely believe it herself. "They've got him in intensive care. I never even got to see him at the hospital. They let Seth in for a minute, then chased him out. Visitors aren't allowed, although they will let one person sit with him."

"Is it bad?" The words, instantly regretted, came out of Olivia's mouth before she could stop them. Mentally kicking herself, she stood just inside the butler's pantry, peeking like a guilty child around the doorjamb. As the eyes of everyone in the room focused on her, her greatest wish was to sink straight through the floor. Instead, she gathered her composure and stepped out into plain sight. Not for anything would she let them — Seth — see how intimidated she felt.

"Bad enough," Seth said shortly, his gaze raking her from head to toe. More than ever conscious of the deficiencies of her appearance, Olivia just managed not to flinch beneath that weighing look. She would be greatly changed from his memories of her, of course, and the knowledge was humiliating. Nine years ago she had been a headstrong teenager, convinced that the world was her oyster, sexy and flaunting it and head over heels in love with love. Now — what was she now? A twenty-six-year-old single mother, with five dollars and change in her purse and a lifetime's worth of hard lessons under her belt: the very antithesis of the girl she had been.

Callie looked at her, her face softening. "Oh, Olivia, come and sit down, honey. What a homecoming for you! But we're so glad to have you with us again!" Then, with a glance at the wide-eyed help, she added more severely, "Amy, you and Laura can go on home if you're finished. Martha, is there any coffee? I think we could all use a cup."

The caterers, routed from their positions as interested observers of this family drama, loaded up their arms with Tupperware dishes and headed for the door with murmured good-byes and plenty to prattle about the next day. Martha turned to the coffeemaker with a great show of getting busy. Olivia, meanwhile, reluctantly approached the table, all too conscious of her borrowed pink bathrobe, bare feet and legs, scrubbed face, and brushed straight hair pushed haphazardly behind her ears. Seth, Callie, Ira, and Mallory looked her over with very different expressions: Seth's was borderline hostile, Mallory's just barely interested, Ira's curious, and Callie's — dear Aunt Callie's! — was warmly affectionate. Olivia smiled at Callie alone, and sat down at the far end of the table.

"Is your little girl — Sara — asleep?" Callie asked kindly. "She's adorable."

"Thank you." Praising Sara was the way to Olivia's heart. "She's a sweetie. And yes, she's asleep."

"She's eight, isn't she?"

"Mmm-hmm."

"Like Chloe."

Seth ruthlessly interrupted this cozy exchange. "You and Olivia can visit tomorrow, Mother. It's late, and you need to go to bed."

"Were you always this bossy, son, or is it a recent development?" Callie asked with dry humor, flicking a glance up at him.

"Somebody's got to look out for you, since you won't look out for yourself." Right hand still closed over the top rail of Callie's chair, Seth shifted his frowning gaze to Olivia, who could have answered Callie's question about Seth's bossiness but refrained in the interests of keeping the peace. "Olivia will still be here in the morning — unless she intends to run off in the middle of the night again?"

This barb, and the look that accompanied it, brought Olivia's chin up. For a moment she was seventeen again and under attack, and her gaze clashed with Seth's. Then she remembered that she was all grown up now, for better or worse, and Seth had no power over her any longer. Her gaze dropped, and she smiled at Callie without deigning to answer Seth. Callie returned her smile with a gentle but humorously commiserating one of her own.

"Mallory, are you ready to go? I'll drive you home," Seth said abruptly, his attention moving to his fiancée.

"Anytime you're ready, darling." Mallory looked up at Seth in a melting way that told Olivia where he would most likely be spending the balance of the night.

"Don't you want coffee before you go, Mallory?" Callie asked. The welcome aroma was just beginning to fill the air.

"Not tonight, Mother," Seth answered for her, and pulled back Mallory's chair. Mallory made a comical face at Callie, and stood up. Clearly she was more than willing to put up with Seth's managing ways in return for his ring on her finger.

"I'm going, too. Seth's right, Callie: You need to go to bed." Ira pushed back his chair and got to his feet.

"If you two don't quit mollycoddling me . . ." Callie glanced from Ira to her son in exasperation. Then she looked at Olivia. "Olivia, by the way, this is Ira Hayes, our local sheriff. I don't

86

believe you've met him. He moved here about a year after you left home. Ira, this is our own Olivia, about whom I've told you, come back to us."

"Pleased to meet you, young lady," Ira said with a smile and a nod. Olivia realized now that the white shirt and brown pants he was wearing were part of a uniform. The only thing missing was his badge.

"I'm pleased to meet you, too." Olivia returned his smile. From the look of it, Callie had found a boyfriend, and Olivia was glad for her. She hadn't dated much while Olivia had been growing up. Her husband Michael had been killed in an accident at the Boatworks twenty-seven years before. She had married again, briefly, when Olivia was nine and Seth was in college, but that marriage had ended in divorce two years later. When it did, she had moved back to LaAngelle Plantation to make a home for Big John, whose wife was dying, and for Olivia, who had just lost her stepfather, Michael's brother James. Olivia had always been fond of Callie, and Callie had tried her best to do right by her niece-by-marriage, but at going on twelve, Olivia already had the bit between her teeth. It was too late for any kind of real mother-daughter bonding between them, and Callie had finally had to settle for being an affectionate if occasionally disapproving friend.

"Mallory . . ." Seth's hand curled around Mallory's arm above the elbow. As it did, his gaze just brushed Olivia's face. Its coldness was enough to wither her smile. As clearly as if he'd said the words aloud, his eyes told her that regardless of what his mother said, he, at least, did not welcome her return to the bosom of her family.

"I'm coming, I'm coming," Mallory said with a laugh, and then smiled at Callie and Olivia. "I'll see you tomorrow, Callie. It was nice meeting you, Olive."

"Olivia," Olivia and Seth corrected in practically the same breath. For an instant their gazes locked in surprise, and then Seth looked away.

"Go to bed, Mother," he said brusquely over his shoulder as he ushered Mallory toward the door. Ira dropped a quick kiss on Callie's cheek, and followed. They exited, and Olivia, Callie, and Martha were left alone in the kitchen.

Callie sighed, then flashed Olivia a quick smile that did nothing to conceal her exhaustion.

"Olivia, dear, we should have brought you home years ago," she said, as Martha set a cup of freshly brewed coffee before her. "I wanted to, but Big John and Seth said that you'd made your choice, and we had to let you live your own life. I let them overrule my better judgment. You haven't had it easy, though, have you? I can tell just by looking at you that you've had some hard times."

chapter 10

"Hard times are part of growing up," Olivia said lightly, unwilling to admit even to Callie how salutary were the lessons she had learned since leaving home. Martha set a steaming cup of coffee in front of her, and with a quick smile of thanks Olivia took a sip. The brew was faintly flavored with chicory and strong enough to melt the bowl off a spoon, just to Olivia's taste. If that didn't keep her awake, she thought, nothing would.

"But we hate for our children to suffer them." Callie's hands were folded around her own coffee cup as if relishing the warmth. She reached for the sugar bowl, added a spoonful, and then glanced up at Olivia. "And I have always considered you in some fashion my child, dear. Now more than ever."

"Aunt Callie . . ." Olivia began, then broke off

as Callie abruptly rested her head against the back of her chair and closed her eyes. Alarmed, Olivia leaned forward, reaching for Callie's hand and repeating on a more urgent note: "Aunt Callie?"

Martha came swiftly forward even as Callie's eyes opened and she focused with apparent difficulty on Olivia. Her eyes had a sunken look about them now, and her face seemed suddenly ashen. Her fingers felt cold to Olivia's touch.

"Aunt Callie, are you all right?"

"Can I fetch you something?" Martha asked quietly from beside Callie's chair.

"I'm all right," Callie said, straightening and lifting her head away from the back of the chair. Olivia was still concerned: Callie's face was even paler than before and her voice was weak. "I get to feeling bad sometimes now. I just need a second to catch my breath."

The three of them were quiet for a few moments as Callie took a series of deep breaths. Soon some of the color returned to her face.

"Martha, would you go get my pain pills, please? They're in my bathroom in the cabinet. I forgot to take the last one, what with everything, and I'm paying for it now."

Martha glanced from Callie to Olivia and nodded. "I won't be a minute." She left the room.

"When you wrote to me, you told me you were ill," Olivia said, still clasping Callie's hand, gripped by a terrible fear that was quickly crystallizing into a near certainty. "What kind of illness? What's wrong with you?"

Callie's gaze met hers. Her color was almost back to normal, and the blue-gray eyes, although still sunken-looking, were calm and steady. "I wish there was some easy way to say this, but there's not. I have cancer, dear. Non-Hodgkin's lymphoma. I was diagnosed two years ago. The doctors said it was slow growing, and recommended that I simply be monitored, so I didn't think it was anything to get too excited about. At the end of this past July, I went in for a routine checkup, and they told me that the disease had become aggressive. That's when I wrote to you to come home. I should have done it sooner, I know. All these years that you've stayed away, I've thought of you often, but I always thought that there would be plenty of time to get you back here and mend things between us all. Now time has started to seem a little precious to me, and I didn't want to wait any longer. I'm glad you came."

"Oh, Aunt Callie." Olivia's fingers tightened around the older woman's, and she felt breathless, as if she had just had the wind knocked out of her. "Are they treating you? What . . . ?" Olivia's voice trailed off.

"I started chemotherapy the first week in August," Callie said. She smiled a little. "The regimen is three weeks on, one week off, for six months. I actually felt fine until then, except for being tired. *Now* I feel like I have cancer. But it's

91

working, they tell me, so I can't complain."

For a moment Olivia stared at the older woman in appalled silence. Then she burst out with: "I'm so sorry! I'm sorry you're sick, and I'm sorry I stayed away so long. As soon as I saw LaAngelle Plantation — and Big John — and you — and, and everyone again, I realized how much I had missed you all. But . . . but . . ."

"But you were too proud to come scooting home with your tail between your legs. I know." Callie squeezed her fingers. "It's all right, Olivia. But it's time to put all that behind us. There's a good chance that I'll live a long time yet, the doctor says. I'm going to do everything I can to still be around for Chloe's wedding, and some great-grandchildren. But no more family rift! That nonsense has gone on long enough! I asked you to visit because I missed you and wanted to see you, of course, but also so that you could make up with Seth and Big John — and the rest of the family while I'm around to make sure it happens. I didn't even tell them you were coming, because they've been so ridiculous about the way you left. But whatever happens with Big John — and I pray to God that he'll be fine — we're all going to be a family again now. And I expect you to do your part to make that happen."

Olivia stared rather helplessly at Callie. "Seth said tonight that all I do is cause trouble, and I'm afraid in this case he may be right: I'm almost certain that I'm the reason Big John had the heart attack. I —"

"Nonsense." Callie shook her head at Olivia. "Big John has — wandered a bit in his mind from time to time the last few years, and his health hasn't been all that good. The man is eighty-seven, after all. I don't want you to blame yourself for what happened. It could have come at any time, for any reason. As for Seth — he's had a difficult few years of his own, you know. He's running the Boatworks completely now, and that's a lot of responsibility. And of course there's Chloe. Seth has sole custody of her. That bitch — pardon my French, dear, but there's no other word for Jennifer Rainey — that Seth married ran off to California five years ago. She took Chloe with her. Seth was — well, he was upset, to say the least. Last year Jennifer remarried and sent Chloe back to live with Seth. Just like that. She travels a lot with her new husband, she said, and having Chloe with them all the time made things awkward. She has seen Chloe once in the last year, two days before Christmas, when she and her husband just happened to be in New Orleans. I had to drive Chloe in to see her. Jennifer couldn't be bothered to come out here."

Callie paused, and Olivia had the impression that she was once again feeling poorly. Before Olivia could do more than squeeze her hand, Callie rallied and went on.

"Seth had a house in town, but when Chloe came to live with him he moved back in here so that I could help him raise her. I couldn't leave Big John on his own, you see. Chloe has had some — difficulty adjusting, which is only natural under the circumstances, I suppose. Now Seth's planning to get married again, which should give Chloe a little more stability. Except that, for right now, Chloe doesn't seem to care for Mallory." Callie sighed. "Life is never simple, is it?"

"Never," Olivia murmured with a crooked smile. Callie's revelations about Chloe prompted her to feel a rush of compassion toward the child. She knew what it was like to feel unwanted. As the child of her mother's first marriage, left behind with her stepfather and his family when her mother died, she had never quite felt like she belonged in the Archers' privileged world. She had always felt that this larger-than-life clan had somehow just gotten stuck with her, and was having to make the best of a bad bargain. "Chloe's a beautiful little girl. Seth must be very proud of her."

"She looks like her mother, poor little mite," Callie said with some acidity. "If only she doesn't take after her in personality, we'll be all right."

"Have Seth and Mallory set a date yet?" Olivia asked.

"November sixth. Only ten weeks away. Mallory's planning this big blowout, even though she and Seth have both been married before. She wants Chloe to be her bridesmaid." Callie's despairing tone told Olivia how likely she thought that was to occur. "She keeps inviting Chloe to go shopping for dresses with her."

The swinging door from the hall opened with a soft sound, and Martha came in, holding a small brown vial.

"I've got your pills here," she said, coming toward the table.

"Thank you, Martha." Callie took the vial gratefully and opened it, shaking two small pink tablets into the palm of her hand. Meanwhile, Martha removed a glass from the cabinet, filled it with water, and brought it back to Callie. Olivia saw that Callie's hand was slightly unsteady as she raised first the pills and then the glass to her mouth. Swallowing and setting the glass back down, she grimaced and closed her eyes. After a moment she opened them again, and looked at Olivia very directly.

"How long can you stay, Olivia?"

"I could only get a week off from work," Olivia said. "Even if I called and asked for more time — they might give me a few days unpaid leave — Sara starts back to school in eleven days. We have to be home before that. But if you want me, I'll come back to visit just as often as I can, I promise."

"If I want you —" Callie shook her head at Olivia. "Honey, of course I do. We all do. With all the twists and turns and barriers and potholes we've encountered along the road, we're family. One thing I've learned since getting sick is that family is all that matters." She took another drink of water, then grimaced. Olivia watched Callie's changing expression with concern, but this time Callie seemed to recover swiftly. With only a slight hesitation, Callie continued: "But we can talk more tomorrow."

She took a deep breath, then let it out slowly and looked up at Martha. "I think I better take Seth's advice and go to bed now. I'm so tired I can hardly sit upright, all of a sudden."

"It don't surprise me none," Martha said with a sniff, reaching for Callie's chair as if she would pull it back for her. "What with everything that's happened today, anybody'd be plumb wore out. And you bein' sick like you are, well, that's just too much. Like Mr. Seth says, you need to let everybody else worry about everybody else, and you just take care of yourself for a change."

"Martha's been staying with us since I've been ill, helping to look after things. She won't even go to bed until I do. I don't know what I'd do without her," Callie said to Olivia, with a tired smile for Martha.

"Kill yourself with exhaustion, most like," Martha muttered, giving the chair a tug.

"I'm going to bed, too." Olivia stood, watching with increasing worry as Callie slowly and carefully got to her feet. Martha's proffered help was rejected, and Callie led the way out of the kitchen, her movements determined but slow. At the top of the stairs, the three paused. Callie looked at Olivia, and smiled at her rather mistily.

"Oh, honey, I *am* glad you're home," Callie

said, enfolding Olivia in a warm embrace. Returning the hug, Olivia once again became aware of how fragile her aunt's body had become, and it frightened her.

"I'm glad I'm home, too," Olivia murmured. Her heart swelled with love and pity and regret as she let Callie go. She'd been wrong to stay away so long, she thought with sorrow. Wrong to let pride and stubbornness keep her away from her family. But until tonight, she'd been too young to realize how truly fleeting life was.

The lesson was being taught her with a vengeance.

They parted, with Callie and Martha heading one way and Olivia going the other. Even after she was curled up next to Sara, Olivia couldn't get out of her mind the way Callie had felt as she'd hugged her: Her body had felt like it was wasting away. She was scarcely more than a bag of bones.

And Big John had suffered a heart attack. No matter what anyone said, the guilt of causing it would stay with her forever.

Please, God, don't let him die, Olivia prayed. And keep Aunt Callie safe, too.

She needed time to make amends. To both of them. To all of them, this family that she had once been so eager to leave behind.

The fear of imminent loss, as sharp and sour-tasting as bile, rose in Olivia's throat and settled like a stone in her heart. Tears welled in her eyes, and trickled down her cheeks to wet her pillow.

For a long time she lay there in the bed that had been hers as a child, weeping silently so as not to disturb her own beloved child snuggled next to her, until finally exhaustion claimed her and she fell asleep.

chapter 11

Jeanerette, Louisiana — April 14, 1971

It was the middle of the night, and something was outside her bedroom window. Becca Eppel heard the faint crunch of footsteps in the pea gravel her mother used for mulch around the shrubbery, followed by rustling in the shrubbery itself, and then a thumping sound as whatever it was hit repeatedly against the glass. She was too afraid to look. It might be a werewolf, which was the monster she feared most of all, trying to get in. Or a vampire — her big brother, Daniel, thought vampires were scarier than werewolves — or even Frankenstein, although they both agreed that Frankenstein wasn't as scary as the other two because he was easier to outrun. Whatever it was, she didn't want to know about it. She huddled on her side, her knees drawn up to her chest and her back to the window, hoping that whatever it was would go away.

But the thumping continued.

Becca wished she could go to her mother. But her mother was in the hospital having another baby. Number five, like they really needed more kids in the family. Daniel was nine, she was eight, David was six, Mark was three, and then this baby, a girl who didn't have a name yet. She'd been born that morning. Dad had taken them all to the hospital so they could see her through the glass window. She and Daniel and David had all looked at each other and rolled their eyes when Dad said, "Isn't your sister beautiful?" because that skinny little bald-headed baby was about the ugliest thing any of them had ever seen. But they hadn't let Dad see. He might get mad. Dad was like that. He got mad at the stupidest things.

That baby girl was going to have to share her room, because they were the only two girls. She and her mom had already rearranged everything to make room for the crib, and a little chest with a pad on top for changing the baby's diapers.

Becca didn't want to share her room with a loud, smelly baby. She knew how babies were from Mark. Basically, all they did was poop, puke, and cry.

Thump. Thump.

Becca shivered. Mrs. Granger from across the street was sleeping in her parents' bed. She was staying with them while her mom was in the hospital, because her mom needed her dad with her. Which was okay, except Mrs. Granger was about a hundred and smelled like cabbage and hardly ever smiled.

No matter how scared she got, Becca couldn't go to her.

But maybe she could go to Daniel. He would tease her for being a baby, but that was better than being ripped to shreds by a werewolf.

Thump, thump.

Becca couldn't stand it any longer. She eased the bedclothes away from her face. If she was going to make a run for the room the boys shared, she wanted to take a good look around first. Maybe something was already in her room, but hadn't noticed her yet. Maybe it would see her only if she moved.

Their house was a three-bedroom brick ranch house, and her window looked out into the backyard. Mrs. Granger hadn't pulled the shade down like Mom always did at night, and moonlight poured right in through the window. Her bedroom wasn't really that dark at all, Becca discovered, peeking. The moon made an awful lot of light.

She could see the thing at the window.

Becca's eyes widened, and for a moment she forgot to breathe. It wasn't her imagination at all. Although it was just a black shape with the moonlight pouring in around it, she could definitely make out two pointy ears.

Sylvia. Her cat. In all the confusion of her family going to see her mom at the hospital earlier, Sylvia must have slipped out the door. Now she was sitting on the windowsill, asking to be let in.

Even as she watched. Sylvia butted her head against the glass.

Thump.

Smiling with relief, Becca got out of bed and crossed to the window. Her bare feet padded silently over the hardwood floor. She was wearing only a T-shirt and panties because of the heat, and her long light brown hair was twisted up on top of her head in a bun, but she was *roasting*. If her mom had been home, they would have gotten out the fans, hot as it was, but Mrs. Granger had opened up all the windows instead, saying the night air would be cool enough. Well, Becca couldn't sleep with only a screen between her and whatever monsters lurked in the night, so she had shut her window and paid the price in sweat.

Now she unlocked the window and raised it, then lifted the screen, too, just enough for Sylvia to swarm in along with a breath of relatively cool air. The breeze felt so good on her overheated skin that Becca stood there for a minute, wishing she was brave enough to just leave the window open and go back to bed. After all, the windows were open everywhere else in the house. But she was not. Just because Sylvia wasn't a werewolf didn't mean there wasn't a werewolf out there.

There was a full moon tonight.

Sighing, Becca closed and locked the window again, then bent to pick up her cat. Sylvia was weaving around her legs.

"What a smart girl." Becca stroked the animal, who began to purr and butted her chin with a cold nose, and turned to head back to bed.

She wouldn't be afraid with Sylvia to sleep with her, she thought.

She was still smiling faintly when something grabbed her from behind and yanked her back against a warm, strong, adult-size body. Hard arms, bare and hairy with gloves on the hands, wrapped around her. A werewolf? No . . .

Sylvia leaped for safety. Becca tried to scream. As her mouth opened, a sick-smelling rag was clamped down over her face, suffocating her.

Becca never even managed to make a sound.

It had been a long time. Almost two years. Carrying the little girl's limp body to his van, he quivered with anticipation. He didn't know how he had managed to hold out for so long. The need to do this had been building up inside him, spiraling tighter and tighter until he could hardly stand it. He'd fought it, he really had. But when he'd seen this little girl, and followed her home, and realized that he *could* do it, that it would be easy, his control had snapped. He just couldn't resist, couldn't hold out anymore. And it wouldn't be like the last time. The last time had been messy, with newspaper headlines and a circus of a trial that had resulted in the girl's father being convicted of murder — well, he had learned from his mistakes. He should never have taken Missy back to her bed. With this girl he'd do better.

Nobody — except him — would ever see her again.

chapter 12

Even after she finally drifted off, Olivia slept fitfully. For a moment or two after she awoke, hazy remnants of the night's dreams floated through her mind. Her mother had appeared in one, sitting in the small wooden rocking chair in the corner of the bedroom softly singing a lullaby to the little girl, Olivia, in the bed. The smell of her perfume — White Shoulders, Olivia remembered with sudden clarity — had been the most magical thing in the world. But another dream had been terrifying. Olivia wasn't quite clear on what had happened in it, although she had a vague impression that it involved the lake and a voice calling to her from its depths. *Run away. Run away.* Except for the voice, the details were lost in the mists of sleep. Not that she wanted to remember anyway. Her morbid fear of the lake was not something she wanted to dwell on, waking or sleeping.

Olivia rolled onto her back, determinedly banishing the last cobwebs of sleep from her mind. They were dreams, nothing more, and she was glad to let them go. She glanced at her daughter. Sara lay sprawled on her stomach, deeply asleep, her arms outflung and one bare brown foot thrust out from beneath the covers. Olivia smiled. Even as a baby, she had never been able to keep Sara's feet covered at night.

Beyond Sara, a few slivers of pale, early-morning sunlight filtered through the crack in the curtains. Olivia thought almost longingly of turning onto her side and going back to sleep. But she knew as well as she knew her own name that she would sleep no more that morning. Therefore, she crept from bed without waking Sara and was in the kitchen at ten minutes before seven, according to the big clock that had hung above the stove for as long as she could remember. Wide awake but fighting the incipient pangs of a headache, she turned on the coffeemaker and looked over at the chalkboard next to the telephone for any messages.

There were none, which Olivia supposed was good news.

A knock sounded at the door. The curtains were still drawn over the wall of windows, leaving the kitchen gloomy and concealing the identity of the visitor. Who on earth would come over so early? Still clad in the chenille robe and gown that Martha had loaned her, Olivia considered ignoring the brisk taps. Then it occurred to her that perhaps some family member had been locked out. Or maybe it was news of Big John. If he died, would they call, or would they send someone like a friend or a priest to break the news?

That thought made Olivia's heartbeat quicken with dread. Pushing her hair back from her face with one hand, she hurried to the door, then hesitated with a hand on the knob. Instead of opening it, she parted the curtains slightly so that she could check the identity of the visitor first.

There, on the wide veranda, bathed in bright shafts of morning sunlight, stood Lamar Lennig, her cheap black suitcase and Sara's cheap red one at his feet. He was gazing off toward the lake, which gave her a moment to study him. An inch or so less than six feet tall, he was broad-shouldered and muscular-looking in jeans and a white T-shirt. His black hair was long enough so that it curled into small, flat ringlets at the nape of his neck, and his features, just as she recalled them, were bluntly good-looking. He had matured physically from the teenager she remembered, although she would have recognized him anywhere. Relief made her feel suddenly limp: No one in the family would ever dream of using Lamar as a bearer of bad tidings.

He must have felt her eyes on him, because he glanced at her then, just as she was considering letting the curtain drop back into place again.

She was not exactly dressed to receive visitors, she thought, especially not a visitor like Lamar Lennig. As a teenager, he'd been the local hunk, and the girls had made collective fools of themselves over him. As the hot-to-trot daughter of the town's preeminent family, she had caught his eye early on. Not that she had minded. Not then. Then she had considered Lamar Lennig exciting. Though he'd never formally been her boyfriend, they'd gone out a few times on the sly and messed around a little. All right, more than a little. Too much, in fact.

Now she found herself embarrassed to see him. Total amnesia on his part seemed too much to hope for.

That he recognized her even through glass and the narrow gap in the curtains was not in doubt. A broad smile spread slowly across his face, and his eyes lit up with pleased surprise.

Seeing no help for it, Olivia parted the curtains and opened the door.

"Hello, Lamar," she said without enthusiasm.

"Well, as I live and breathe, Olivia Chenier," he said. His gaze ran over her. Knowing herself to be looking less than her best, Olivia's expression soured as he glanced up to meet her eyes. "Still lookin' babe-alicious as ever, I see."

For Olivia, his audaciousness had once been part of his charm. What she had liked best about him, though, besides his handsome looks, was the aura of the forbidden that had clung to him. Years ago, when she'd snuck out to be with him, she had felt that she was being very, very bad.

And, to the teenager she had been, that had been good.

"Thanks for bringing the suitcases," she said, stepping onto the wooden planks of the veranda and reaching down to pick them up. Even so early in the morning, it was hot out, although the humidity level was not as bad as it would be later. The distinctive sweet smell of LaAngelle Plantation, composed of magnolia and honeysuckle and roses and a hundred other plants and flowers, hit her nostrils, and she breathed it in deeply. In the yard below, a pair of drab brown peahens and a gloriously colored peacock scratched in the thick green carpet of grass for sustenance. The birds would delight Sara, who loved all animals, Olivia thought. She could hardly wait to show them, and everything else about her old home, to her daughter. Sara was going to love it here.

"No problem." Lamar's gaze ran over Olivia again as his hands beat hers to the handles and he hoisted the bags in the teeth of her attempt to pick them up. "Nobody told me these belonged to you. I would have been here earlier if I'd known. Like the middle of last night."

A wide grin still split his face as he brushed past her to carry the bags inside. The grin spoke of remembered intimacy and a continued assumption of familiarity. Olivia didn't like what it implied, but there was nothing wrong with her memory, either, and she realized that she had well and truly earned the expression on his face.

Lamar glanced back at her over his shoulder. "Where do you want me to put these?"

"Right there is fine," Olivia said, following him back into the kitchen and pointedly leaving the door open behind her. Lamar set the suitcases down on the brick pavers near the table and turned to face her, thrusting his hands into the front pockets of his jeans.

"You here for a visit?"

Crossing her arms over her chest, Olivia nodded without speaking. She meant to do nothing to encourage him. Bad boys didn't do it for her any longer. She had grown up and wised up.

"Been a long time, hasn't it?"

"Yep."

"Planning to stay for a while?"

"A week, probably."

"If you want to go out . . ."

"I doubt I'll have time," Olivia said pleasantly. "My daughter's with me, and —"

"Got a daughter, do you? Left hubby at home?"

"I'm divorced."

That nugget of news seemed to amuse him. Cocking his head to one side and rocking back on his heels — Olivia wasn't surprised to observe he wore cowboy boots — Lamar grinned at her again. "Everybody in town knew that rodeo rider you dumped me for was a bad bet. Except you, I guess."

"I guess. And, anyway, I didn't dump you. We were never —"

"Hello, Lamar." The unexpected greeting made both of them glance around. Seth had entered the kitchen through the open French door, where he had paused for an instant, squinting as his eyes adjusted to the difference in the light. Taller, leaner, and less obviously handsome than Lamar, he was also, on this occasion, unshaven, bleary-eyed, and frowning. He still wore the navy sport coat, T-shirt, and khakis he'd had on the night before. Obviously he had spent the night out, and Olivia's thoughts immediately flew to Mallory.

"Mornin', Seth." The grin with which Lamar had teased her vanished from his face as if by magic. He stood straighter, his hands no longer in his pockets, his attitude respectful, as Seth continued across the kitchen. Although most of the younger generation of townsfolk did not address the Archers by honorifics such as *Mister* Seth and *Miss* Olivia like the older ones did, the inbred deference was there in Lamar's demeanor. "I just came by to drop off some suitcases."

Having reached the counter and stopped, Seth looked pointedly at the bags sitting on the floor at Lamar's feet. Then he reached into his back pocket and withdrew his wallet. "How much do we owe you?"

Olivia hadn't considered that they owed Lamar money for fetching the bags. Of course, payment was in order: He hadn't done it for free. Remembering the scant state of her own funds, she was suddenly glad that Seth had appeared.

"Ten dollars should about catch it."

Seth opened his wallet and extracted a bill, which he held out to Lamar. "Thanks," he said. It was obvious dismissal.

"Anytime." Lamar accepted the money and his fate with good grace. He turned to leave, casting a humorous glance and a crooked smile at Olivia where Seth couldn't see. "Good to see you, Olivia."

"You, too, Lamar."

With a wave for both her and Seth, Lamar exited, closing the door behind him. Seth looked at her then, his eyebrows lifting questioningly.

"Entertaining already?" he asked, heading toward the coffeemaker. The rich, heady aroma of freshly brewed coffee filled the air. Just the smell of it went a long way toward banishing Olivia's headache.

"Not at all. I just happened to be in the kitchen making coffee when Lamar dropped off the suitcases." She fought hard to keep her voice from sounding defensive.

"I'm sure you'll be glad to get your clothes." As he opened the cabinet where the cups were kept, his gaze ran dispassionately over her pink bathrobe and bare feet.

Although there was nothing pointed about either his words or tone, Olivia had warred with Seth often enough in the past to know when he was verbally jabbing at her.

She gritted her teeth, but decided to take the high road. "Yes, I will," she agreed sweetly.

Pouring coffee into a cup, he leaned one hip against the counter to drink it and looked at her consideringly over the cup's rim.

"If you're interested, it looks like Big John's going to pull through. They said he's stable this morning."

That got to her, as it was undoubtedly meant to do. Still standing beside the table, with one hand resting on its scarred surface, she met his gaze with sparks in her eyes. "What do you mean, *if* I'm interested? Of course I'm interested. I know it was my fault that he collapsed, but I couldn't help it! How was I to know he would react to seeing me that way? And he's my grand-father — at least, I always thought of him as my grandfather — just like he's yours."

Seth made a derisive sound and swallowed some more coffee. "If you hadn't stayed away for nine years, having you pop up like that might not have been such a shock to him. To everyone."

Olivia's hands clenched by her sides at the un-fairness of that. "Aunt Callie invited Sara and me to come for a visit. She knew we were coming. Ask her. If you and Big John weren't so gall-darned bullheaded, she probably would have told you we were coming in advance, in-stead of planning to spring it on you when it was too late for you to object. Anyway, for years now you — you all — have known where I live. You could have come to see me anytime. Nobody did. All I got was an occasional card from Aunt Callie." Certainly she had expected them — Seth, to be specific — to come after her when she'd run off with Newall. Blissfully in love with her new husband, she had been relieved at first when no one had. Only after Sara was born and her marriage went bad and she was left to pick up the pieces of her life did she realize how much their just letting her go had hurt.

But then, what had she expected, really? She had never truly been an Archer, after all. Not by blood, and with this bunch blood was all that mattered. You were either kin, or you weren't.

"You were married. There wasn't much point." Seth took another swallow of coffee. "What God hath joined, let no man put asunder."

Olivia discovered that she hated him just as much as she always had.

"Oh, shut up," she said, glaring at him. Grabbing a suitcase with each hand, she stalked from the kitchen.

It infuriated her to realize that he was smiling a little as the door swung shut behind her.

By the time she was halfway up the stairs, Olivia could have kicked herself. She had responded to Seth exactly as she would have when she was a teenager and he was the older, wiser pseudocousin who thought he had the right to tell her what to do. In fact, she had said those same words to him so many times over the years that that was probably why they had risen so automatically to her lips.

The next time he baited her, she vowed, she would ignore him. If he hadn't matured in nine years, she had.

Sara was still sleeping when Olivia entered the bedroom, and she realized that it was still very early. Sara slept like the dead most of the time, so Olivia did not fear waking her as she unpacked clothes for the two of them to wear that day. Stowing the suitcases under the bed — she would unpack later — and leaving Sara's outfit for the day on the foot of the bed, she left the bedroom for the bathroom. She took a shower, washed her hair and blew it dry, put on makeup, and pulled on a pair of cut-off jeans, a lime-green T-shirt, and Keds before returning to check on Sara again. A glance at the alarm clock by the bed told her that it was eight fifteen. Sara still slept.

Stymied, Olivia headed back downstairs. Faint sounds from the kitchen told her that someone was there — perhaps Seth still, or maybe Martha. She certainly didn't want to encounter Seth again so soon, and didn't feel much like talking to anyone else, either. Trying to ignore the fact that her head still ached, and temper had cheated her out of her much-needed morning coffee, she went out the front door into the enveloping warmth of the day. Just in time to keep it from banging shut behind her, she caught the screen door and eased it closed. No need to alert whoever was in the kitchen to her presence.

For a moment Olivia stood beneath the shelter of the veranda, looking past the fluted columns and hanging ferns at the sun-drenched grounds. Not so much as a blade of grass seemed to have changed in nine years. Once a vast sugar plantation that had been reduced over time to forty acres of scrub woods and swamp and five acres of lawn, LaAngelle Plantation stretched out around her as far as the eye could see on three sides. On the fourth, past the bluff, she could see part of the lake, glimmering silver in the morning light. Deliberately she made herself look at it. It was no more or less than a body of water, with nothing inherently sinister or evil about it. Certainly no voices called to her from it. Any ghosts from the night before were either the product of her imagination, or had been burned away by the rising sun.

Crossing the veranda, Olivia headed down the wide stone steps, running a hand lightly over the hard surface of the wrought-iron rail. She stopped for a moment on the flagstone path that led to the driveway, glancing around, uncertain of where she wished to go. Birds chattered and called. Insects droned. In the distance she could just faintly hear the sound of some sort of farm machinery, like a tractor. The pair of giant magnolias that were the centerpiece of the lawn were as magnificent as she remembered them, with white waxy blossoms the size of dinner plates bursting through glossy green foliage. The sweet olive and jasmine near the gazebo were in bloom, as was the rose garden. Tendrils of pale yellow honeysuckle vine twined with the deeper yellow forsythia bushes that formed a hedge around the property. Closer at hand, crimson amaryllis was massed in glorious profusion in front of the neatly clipped thicket of dark green boxwoods that circled the house. The air was redolent with the scent of flowers; just breathing in was a pleasure.

Although the grounds were beautiful, the reminders of last night's party were not, and they were everywhere. The Christmas lights were turned off, but they still hung from the eaves of the house and gazebo and clung to the bushes and trees. Festive the night before, this morning they made the property look unkempt, like a just-wakened woman who had gone to bed without washing off her makeup. At the far end of the lawn, a quartet of workmen labored. Two of them, toting black plastic garbage bags, were engaged in picking up trash, while the other two wielded rakes. Plastic cups and forks, napkins, the remnants of balloons, and other odds and ends littered the ground near Olivia's feet, and she assumed it was as bad everywhere.

As she looked around, a peacock strolled into view from around the side of the house.

Leaving the path, Olivia walked across the grass toward the bird, watching with a smile as it lowered its head and grabbed something in its beak. As the object disappeared down a feathered throat to the accompaniment of enthusiastic head bobs, Olivia realized to her dismay that the peacock had just swallowed a cigarette butt with as much avidity as if it had been a bit of leftover cracker. With no obvious ill effects, the bird then continued on his dignified way. Behind him came the two peahens Olivia had seen earlier, still pecking busily at the grass, and a second peacock, strutting with his head up and his tail fully extended.

All iridescent greens and blues, he was a beautiful sight on a beautiful morning.

LaAngelle Plantation was just the same as it had always been, Olivia thought, as she rounded the side of the house and headed toward the backyard: a place that belonged more to the past than to the present. But on this morning, with the perfume of flowers in the air and her rebellious teenage years a wry memory, that seemed like a good thing rather than a bad one.

A movement of some sort on the very edge of her peripheral vision drew her attention, and Olivia glanced toward the house. A huge white Persian cat was walking delicately along the rail of the upper gallery, its tail waving plumelike through the air. One false step would send it plunging about twenty feet to the ground, but it kept on its way as serenely as if it walked on solid earth. Only at the last minute did Olivia see its goal: Chloe, still wearing her blue nightgown, her blond hair in two ponytails caught up by elastic bands at either ear, leaning over the railing at the far end of the upstairs gallery, something cupped in her hands. As Olivia watched, the child let go.

The object plummeted downward, glittering brilliantly in the sun as it fell, and landed in the sweet bush below with no more than a faint disturbance to the leaves.

Chloe straightened and saw Olivia at the same moment that Olivia glanced up at her again. Olivia was too surprised to call to the child, or even to wave, and Chloe did not speak, either. Shooting Olivia a baleful glance, Chloe snatched up the cat that had by now almost reached her, disappeared into the shadowy depths of the gallery and from there, presumably, into the house.

Curiosity piqued, Olivia moved to the sweet bush and peered in and beneath it. The delicate vanillalike aroma that gave the bush its name wafted around her. Its fragile white flowers and umbrella-shaped foliage concealed an inner hollow that, Olivia remembered from her own childhood, was an ideal hideaway. Stooping, pushing aside the fragrant canopy, and keeping a wary eye out for the bees and wasps that liked to drink from the blossoms, she ducked beneath the leaves and looked around. Almost instantly she spotted it: a bracelet. It dangled from a branch just a few inches off the ground.

That was what Chloe had dropped from the gallery. Olivia's earlier perception of an object that glittered like fire in the sun resolved itself into this sparkling piece of jewelry. Disentangling the bracelet carefully, Olivia ducked out into the sunlight again, prize in hand. Straightening, she looked at it as it lay across her palm.

It was a watch, not a bracelet. A delicate woman's watch, with a braceletlike band made of linked diamonds, and a face encrusted with them. The numerals were indicated by tiny rubies. Olivia turned it over in her hand, wondering where Chloe had found something so obviously expensive, and why on earth she had chosen to drop it into a bush.

Made of platinum or white gold, the casing of the watch face felt cool and smooth beneath Olivia's fingers as she smoothed them over its hexagon shape.

There was engraving on the back in delicate script. Olivia had to hold the watch closer to her eyes and tilt it into the sun so that she could read what was written there: *Mallory Hodges.*

chapter 13

Frowning, Olivia tucked the watch into the front pocket of her cutoffs and continued on her way, pondering what to do. Obviously the watch had to be returned to its owner, but her every instinct shrank from describing the circumstances that had led her to discover it. Whether Chloe was difficult or not — and from every indication that was the only word to describe her — the child was just a child, after all, and was having a rough time.

Perhaps she could simply say that she had found it on the lawn?

Olivia walked along the pea-gravel path that led to the *garçonnière,* the small, two-story frame lodge at the edge of the property that had once housed the single, young adult males of the family, and, more recently, was used as a guest house. She paused at the perennial garden, stepping through the trellised archway that served as a garden gate, and spent a moment admiring the beauty within. The white bells of the yucca that had been trained to grow over the arch and around the fence served as a perfect frame for the profusion of colorful flowers that bloomed with abandon around the garden's centerpiece, a five-foot-tall marble angel that looked as if it had been lifted, at some time in the distant past, from one of New Orleans' raised cemeteries, or cities of the dead.

Butterflies floated over the garden, looking like fluttering blossoms themselves, and a pair of glossy-winged blackbirds perched on the edge of the fence, watching a third peck at the rich black earth below.

Sara's going to love all this, Olivia thought again, and then turned back toward the house to see if her daughter was awake yet. Sara did not usually sleep past eight o'clock, even on weekends, but yesterday had been physically and emotionally exhausting for both of them.

At the back of the house, the driveway widened into a paved area that could, in a pinch, provide parking for as many as twenty cars. It also served as a basketball and shuffleboard court. Seth was walking across the pavement toward the stone carriage house that had been converted into a four-car garage at its far end. He had changed into loose khaki slacks and a dark green polo shirt, and was busy talking into a cell phone that he held pressed to his ear.

They saw each other at the same time. Olivia paused, loathe to encounter him again so soon, but he didn't so much as check his stride, even as his gaze slid over her. Neither acknowledged the other by so much as a wave.

If it had not been for the diamond watch in her pocket, Olivia would have given him a wide berth. As it was, she thought crossly, she might as well go on and hand the thing over and get done with it. As Chloe's father and Mallory's fiancée, Seth was the person to whom it should be given.

She started walking toward the carriage house just as he closed the phone and slid it into a pocket. Reaching down to grasp the handle of one of the four separate garage doors, he paid no attention to her approach.

"Seth, wait a minute!" she called, when the heavy metal door had rattled to its apex and he headed into the shadowy depths of the garage.

He stopped just inside the garage and turned to look at her as she came past the edge of the building toward him.

"What?" The question was faintly impatient. His hand rested lightly on the trunk of his car, a dark-colored Jaguar.

Olivia moved out of the bright sunlight into the relative darkness near where he stood, and blinked. Until she felt the skin around her eyes relax, she had not realized how she had been squinting. Even so early in the morning, the Louisiana sun was blinding.

"I — I need to give you something." Not

122

having expected to see him so soon, she had not really thought out what she was going to say. Consequently, she stumbled over her words a little.

"What?" The impatience was more pronounced as he met her gaze. As her eyes adjusted to the gloom, she saw that he had shaved. His eyes were still bloodshot, though, and he looked tired and irritable.

"This." Olivia reached into her pocket and drew forth the watch, which she held out to him. It sparkled even in the dim light.

"Mallory's watch." His tone changed to one of surprise. He took it from her and looked down at it as it lay across his fingers, then glanced up at her sharply. "Where did you get this?"

Here was the tricky part. "I found it outside." Which had the merit of being the literal, if not the whole, truth.

His eyes narrowed at her. "It was on top of the bureau in my bedroom not more than an hour ago. Mallory left it in the car last night."

"So what are you implying?" Olivia bristled at the accusation she thought she discerned in the words. The sound of running footsteps distracted her, and both she and Seth looked around to try to identify the source.

"Daddy, wait!" Twin ponytails flying, wearing short white shorts and a navy-and-white striped T-shirt and carrying a tennis racket, Chloe darted across the pavement into the garage, where she came to an abrupt stop, her gaze swinging from her father to Olivia and back. After that single hard glance, she ignored Olivia to address Seth. "Where are you going? You promised to take me over to Katie's so we could play tennis this morning!"

The impatience in Seth's face lessened only slightly as he looked at his daughter. "Chloe, I can't. I —"

"Where did you get that?" Chloe interrupted, her voice suddenly shrill as she spied the watch that lay across Seth's hand. Her gaze, narrowed with suspicion, shot immediately to Olivia. "Did you give it to him? What did you tell him? Did you make up some big lie about me?"

Olivia's eyes widened. "No, of course not. I —"

"Watch your manners, young lady!" Seth's voice was low and furious.

"Whatever she told you, it's not true!" Gripping the tennis racket in both hands and holding it in front of her body like a shield, Chloe looked appealingly at her father. With her wide blue eyes and the long blond ponytails streaming over her shoulders, she was the picture of childish innocence. "Are you going to believe her or me?"

"Chloe . . ." Before Seth could continue, Chloe's lower lip trembled.

"You're going to believe her, aren't you? You always believe everything everyone else says about me! I hate you!" she choked out. Bursting into noisy tears, she ran from the garage, still clutching the tennis racket and shooting Olivia a venomous glance as she bolted past.

For a moment afterward there was silence as the two adults gazed after the departing child. Then Seth looked at Olivia.

"I apologize for my daughter," he said heavily. His face was flushed dark with anger or embarrassment, or some combination of the two, and his eyes were hard. "She'll apologize for herself later."

"It's all right." Olivia felt a spurt of sympathy for both Seth and Chloe. Obviously theirs was not an easy relationship. "My theory is you haven't really put in your time as a parent unless your child embarrasses you thoroughly at least once a month."

Seth's gaze moved over her face. His lips compressed into a thin line as he closed his fist around the watch in his hand. "My ex-wife spoiled Chloe rotten. Then she married again, and apparently her new husband didn't want a stepdaughter as part of the deal. So she sent Chloe back to me, as if the child were no more than a pet she'd grown tired of. It hurt Chloe badly."

"Your mother told me."

"I figured she would." Seth's expression changed, grew wry. "Now, suppose you tell me what Chloe obviously thinks you've already told me. Where did you really find the watch?"

Olivia stood silent for a moment, chewing on her lower lip, thinking the matter over. "I'd rather not say," she said finally. "I think you should ask Chloe."

"Livvy . . ." He broke off at the stubborn expression on her face, and shook his head impatiently, shoving the watch into his pocket. "I don't have time for this right now. I have to be at the hospital at nine thirty to talk to Big John's doctors. I'll deal with Chloe — and you" — he shot her a dark look — "later."

He opened the car door and slid behind the wheel, slamming the door behind him. Seconds later the engine turned over with a purr and a burst of exhaust. Olivia moved out of the way, into the sunlight and toward the edge of the pavement. The Jaguar backed out of its bay, maneuvered around so that it was facing the driveway, rolled forward a dozen feet, and then came to a sudden stop. It was, Olivia saw as it wheeled into the light, gunmetal gray with a cream interior. The engine died, the car door opened, and Seth got out, looking grim.

"Damn it to hell and back." He slammed the door with considerable force. His gaze met Olivia's. "Did you see where she went?"

"Toward the front yard," Olivia offered.

Seth swore again, pinned Olivia with an evil look, and headed toward the front yard. Watching him go, Olivia had to smile. Having Seth stomp off in a temper brought back memories. Years ago, she had been the object of his wrath more often than she cared to remember.

He had called her Livvy, as he used to when she was a child. That he could use the nickname

126

gave her hope that perhaps he was ready to forgive and forget. It would be nice to be on friendly terms with Seth again. As a little girl, she had thought her big stepcousin hung the moon. Even when she was older, for all she had butted heads with him at every turn, somewhere underneath it all she had still admired, respected, and, yes, loved him.

Now they were both adults, divorced, with daughters the same age. For the first time in their lives, they were on more or less equal footing. Except, of course, that Seth was rich, successful, and sure of his place in the world. While she . . .

Another car pulled into the parking area next to the Jag. This was a white Mazda Miata, a sporty two-seater convertible with the hood down. Mallory, sunglasses in place and a white silk scarf tied around her blond head, was driving. Olivia spared an envious glance for the car. She possessed an ancient Mercury Cougar with more than one hundred thousand miles on the odometer and bad tires. It had not been up to the trip from Houston, which was how she and Sara had ended up on the bus. But if she'd had her druthers, she would have chosen a car just like Mallory's.

"Hi!" Mallory waved and got out of the car, removing her sunglasses and pulling off her scarf at the same time.

"Hi," Olivia answered with a smile.

Mallory walked toward her. She was wearing a

cute little tennis outfit with a tiny pleated skirt that left her long, tanned legs bare. Olivia felt a pang of envy for the outfit, too.

"Have you seen Seth, or Chloe? I'm supposed to take Chloe to a friend's house to play tennis. Seth said he had to be in Baton Rouge at nine thirty." She glanced at her wrist, then shook her head. "Drat, I keep forgetting I'm not wearing my watch. Anyway, have you seen either of them?"

Lightning fast, Olivia processed a whole jumble of conflicting thoughts and emotions. Her first instinct was to protect Seth and Chloe from intrusion from an outsider at this delicate moment. She had to remind herself that this woman was going to be Seth's wife and Chloe's stepmother, and thus was not an outsider after all. "I think they're in the front yard."

Mallory frowned. "Why on earth . . . ?" Then she brightened. "Here they come."

Olivia looked around to discover that Seth and Chloe were indeed approaching around the side of the house. Seth had his hand on Chloe's shoulder. He was grim-faced, while Chloe, still clutching her tennis racket, looked sullen.

Watching them, Mallory sighed, then, summoning a smile, waved cheerily.

Seth waved back. Chloe didn't. If anything, she just looked more sullen.

"Honestly, that child," Mallory muttered under her breath, then shot a quick look at Olivia to see if she'd been overheard. Her gaze on Seth

128

and Chloe, Olivia pretended to be deaf.

Seth marched Chloe right up to Olivia. A paternal squeeze of the child's shoulder prompted a barely audible "I'm sorry," and a lightning glance brimful of dislike.

"That's all right," Olivia said gently, wincing inside at Seth's handling of the situation. Forcing an apology out of an obviously reluctant child would only serve to make her more rebellious, in Olivia's opinion.

Mallory's eyebrows lifted in delicate inquiry as she looked from Chloe to Olivia, then shot a quick glance at Seth. His expression was forbidding. Mallory, having the good sense not to comment on the exchange, instead addressed Chloe a shade too heartily: "Your dad asked me to take you over to Katie's. I called her mother, and we decided that we're going to play tennis, too. Maybe we can work in a doubles match, you know, kind of a mother-daughter thing. Wouldn't that be fun?"

Chloe scowled, and Olivia held her breath, waiting for what, on the strength of her brief acquaintance with Chloe, she was already sure would be an ear-shattering outburst. But something — Seth's warning hand on her shoulder, probably — kept it from coming.

"Yeah, fun," Chloe said.

The sarcasm was unmistakable, and all the adults present chose to ignore it. Olivia could see their point: Sarcasm beat a tantrum hands down.

"Well, let's go, then." Mallory smiled at Chloe,

a mere stretching of her lips that didn't reach her eyes, then smiled at Seth more genuinely. "Don't worry about us."

"I won't." His expression relaxed a little as he exchanged glances with Mallory. He squeezed Chloe's shoulder once more before releasing it. "Behave." His tone was a warning.

Chloe climbed into the passenger seat of the Miata, and Mallory and Seth walked around to the driver's side. Seth opened the door for Mallory, who rested a hand on his shoulder and kissed him lightly on the mouth before settling into her seat.

"Bye, darling," she said, smiling up at him as Seth closed her door. Olivia's glance slid almost involuntarily to Chloe. The child's scowl had turned ferocious.

Once again, Olivia held her breath waiting for the outburst that did not come. Mallory put the key in the ignition, then looked up at Seth, who was stepping away from the car.

"Oh, darling, would you mind fetching my watch for me before we go? I'm absolutely lost without it."

Seth flicked a glance at Chloe, who was staring stonily through the windshield and appeared not to have heard the question.

"I just happened to have it on me." Seth reached into his pocket and withdrew the watch, which he handed to Mallory.

"Thanks." Mallory fastened the watch around her wrist. "I was so relieved when you called last night to say you found it. I should never have taken it off in the car."

Seth's expression changed subtly. "No," he agreed with a glimmering smile, and the way he said it made Olivia wonder what else Mallory had taken off in the car.

"Can we *go,* please?" Chloe's tone was hostile, and Seth's smile disappeared. Mallory glanced at Chloe, her lips tightening.

"Behave," Seth said again to his daughter, and stepped away from the car.

With a wave from Mallory, the Miata revved to life and headed down the driveway.

Seth looked after them for a moment. When the Miata was out of sight he glanced at Olivia.

"I've got to go," he said. "I'll see you later."

Then he, too, got into his car and drove off.

chapter 14

The Jaguar ate up the miles between LaAngelle and Baton Rouge with no trouble at all. Which was only to be expected for a car with a monthly lease payment of almost seven hundred dollars, Seth reflected. Attracting wealthy buyers was the name of the game for someone like himself who built yachts for a living, and an image of success was necessary to attract wealthy buyers. But still, the money that he paid out for the car was money he didn't have to spare.

Only no one knew that, except himself and Big John and maybe a couple of loan officers down at the bank. And, if he had his way, no one else was going to find out. Unless Big John died. Then the cat would be out of the bag, because the estate would be probated and everyone would know that Archer Boatworks had teetered on the verge of bankruptcy for a long time.

He didn't expect Big John to die. His grandfather was a tough old coot. Too mean to die, his grandmother would have said if she were alive. Seth half smiled at the thought. Big John had been the opposite of warm and nurturing, but Seth loved the old curmudgeon nonetheless. From the time he was ten, when his father had died, Seth had looked to Big John as the closest thing to a father in his life. Big John, grouchy and acerbic as he was, had always come through for him.

Now it was his turn to come through for the old man.

A couple more years of hard work, paired with a little good luck, and he could turn the company situation around. Archer Boatworks would be soundly in the black again. The big commercial orders for barges that Big John had not wanted him to accept — they were *yacht* builders, the old man argued — were making the difference. There was money out there for barges. The money for fine luxury yachts seemed to have dried up.

Big John was counting on him to save the company. Seth meant to do his best. If the old man had listened to him earlier, things would never have gotten this bad. But no, Seth was always the "boy" who had a lot to learn in the old man's eyes. And the old man was as stubborn as a mule in a corncrib. There had been no persuading him that things had to be done differently if Archer Boatworks was going to survive.

The family, the house, the town and its people were all dependent on the Boatworks. If it went down, they went with it. His relatives lost a large chunk of their income. The estate, LaAngelle Plantation, which had been in the family for generations, would be taken by the bank because he'd had to use it as collateral for a loan to finance the building of the barges. One-fifth of the town worked for him directly, and the other four-fifths of the population owned or worked for businesses, like grocery stores and dress shops, that were dependent on the existence of the Boatworks for their survival. By his calculations, that was almost three thousand people whose lives and livelihoods he held in his hands. That huge burden of responsibility accounted for the eighty-hour weeks he put in, and his increasing inability to sleep nights.

Jennifer hadn't been able to take it. When they'd met, at a Mardi Gras party thrown by a multimillionaire whose one-hundred-twenty-foot yacht had been built by the Boatworks, she had thought he was a rich man, too, and a gentleman of comparative leisure. That was a large part of why she had married him, he figured out later. The truth had come as a shock to her, and she had hightailed it out of Dodge as soon as she found a better prospect.

He didn't miss her. Not now, not for years. Hell, he was glad she was gone. She'd been a high-maintenance luxury item that he didn't need and couldn't afford.

But it humiliated him to remember that when she had left him — for another, richer man — and taken their daughter with her, he'd broken down and cried like a baby, then drank like a fish for weeks.

It had been Big John who pulled him out of the abyss into which he was sinking. Big John who poured his Wild Turkey down the sink and slapped him upside the head and told him to shape up or get the hell out of the company.

When he had jumped to his feet, furious at being hit and ready to pound the hell out of the old man, it was Big John who had stood his ground with his fists raised, cursing a blue streak and daring him to bring it on.

Thank God he had retained enough decency to turn around and walk away. Later, when he was sober, he was shamed by the thought of how near he had been to coming to blows with his then eighty-two-year-old grandfather.

He'd taken a good, hard look at the bad-tempered drunk he'd become, and realized that Jennifer wasn't worth it. From that moment on, he'd been as sober as a preacher.

Sometimes, though, when the burdens of work and family felt as if they might suffocate him, he caught himself thinking longingly about just chucking it all, climbing into his leased vehicle, and taking off into the sunset. No more responsibility. No more pressure. He could start a new life somewhere else, build up his own business without other people's needs and mistakes weighing him down.

He could be free.

But the price for that freedom was too high, and he knew it. It meant letting go of his heritage. It meant letting people he loved — people who loved him — down.

He couldn't do it. He didn't even really want to do it. Not often. Only sometimes.

Like today.

His daughter was a brat. His mother had cancer. His grandfather was in intensive care. His business was struggling to survive. His personal litany of woe was so long it was almost comical.

Only he didn't feel the least bit like laughing.

Deliberately he thought of Mallory. With her, he'd gotten lucky. She was beautiful, educated, with her own solvent business. She loved him. She was great in the sack. She was going to make him a fantastic wife.

Except he wasn't one hundred percent certain that he was in love with her. And Chloe hated her. And Mallory wasn't any too fond of Chloe, either, although she tried to hide it. Hell, he couldn't even blame Mallory. Chloe was his own daughter, and he felt like throttling her about half the time.

But he and Chloe were a package deal, for better or worse, and if he didn't love Mallory then he certainly should, because she was absolutely what he needed in a wife and Chloe needed in a mother. Unlike Jennifer, Mallory was a mature adult. Mallory was stable. Mallory loved the town of LaAngelle, and the plantation and his family (Chloe excepted, for the moment). Mallory understood about his work. Mallory was capable and successful and a heck of an organizer.

Maybe that wasn't entirely a good thing, though. Maybe that was why, over the last several weeks as preparations for the wedding had moved into full swing, he had sometimes felt like a small corporation caught in the grip of a larger one bent on a takeover. Maybe Mallory should knock off trying to organize him. Maybe he wasn't quite ready to marry again after all.

Who knew why he felt the way he did? All he knew was that right now, his relationship with Mallory was starting to feel like just one more problem.

Olivia was home. Seth had been shying away from coming to terms with that. He hadn't really thought much about her in a long time — years. But all he had to do was see her again, and everything came rushing back.

She and her mother had come to live at LaAngelle Plantation when Livvy was a year old. Almost immediately she had started toddling about after him, and he, twelve years old and an only child just as she was, had been enchanted by the big-eyed, chubby little girl. All through her childhood, he had played the part of big brother, ordering her around and bopping her on the head when he felt she deserved it, but letting her tag after him and protecting her from everybody else. Then he left for college and grad school and his first and only job away from the family business. By the time he'd come home again at Big John's request she had been fifteen and running wild. His mother, who was sweet and kind and the most loving woman on earth, was no kind of disciplinarian. And Big John, who certainly was, showed no inclination to exert his authority over a troublesome teenager who was, as he frequently pointed out, no blood kin.

Since nobody else seemed willing or able to do the job, Seth had done his best to take Livvy in hand. But trying to control the teenage sexpot she had become was like trying to hold back the tide, he'd discovered: It couldn't be done. God help him, that last year when she was seventeen and he was a grown man of twenty-eight, sometimes he'd found himself sexually attracted to her, too.

And why not? She'd been mouthwatering in the tight jeans and skimpy tops she'd worn almost as a uniform. Chubby no longer, she had become voluptuous instead, with full, lush breasts and a round ass and a slim, taut, tanned waist she had pretty much kept bared. Her hair had been longer then, almost down to her waist, dark and silky-straight. With her big brown eyes and pouting lips, she'd looked like one of the girls in the Hawaiian Tropic commercials.

He would have had to be a eunuch not to notice.

To his credit, he hadn't done anything about it. Not then. Not ever. In a way, it had been a relief when she'd run away.

Now she was back, thinner, paler, more subdued, having obviously learned some hard lessons about life over the intervening years, with her own daughter in tow.

A sexpot no longer.

But to his dismay, he'd had only to take a good look at her in the kitchen last night, bathrobe, bare feet, and all, to discover that he still found her sexy as hell.

Add another problem to the list.

Pulling into the parking lot of St. Elizabeth's Hospital, Seth sighed. He could deal with only one crisis at a time, and right now he had to focus on making sure Big John got the medical treatment he needed to get well.

Charlie was waiting for him, leaning against his own leased vehicle, a '99 Lexus. Which, presumably, his uncle-by-marriage really could afford. As Big John's personal physician, Charlie would have the latest on the old man's condition, but the only reason for Charlie to be in the parking lot waiting for him was to tell him, Seth, something that he wasn't ready to tell the others who would be gathered inside.

Great. Seth parked and got out, locking the door with the careless push of a button on his key ring, his muscles already tightening in anticipation of what he would hear.

Charlie didn't disappoint him. Rumpled and

tired-looking from the all-night vigil they had shared, he straightened away from his car and walked over to clap a hand on Seth's shoulder.

The two men's eyes met. "I'm sorry," Charlie said, "but I've got some bad news."

Was there any other kind? Seth thought.

Not lately. Not for him.

chapter 15

This time, Sara was awake when Olivia went up to check on her. She was standing on the edge of the mattress, fully dressed except for her white tennis shoes, which were on the floor. Facing the head of the bed, she was looking back over her shoulder at her rear view, which was reflected in the small, gilt-framed oval mirror over the chest on the opposite wall. Trying to decide if she was fat? Olivia guessed the reason for Sara's tortured posture almost instantly. As a child, she'd done the same thing herself, more times than she cared to remember.

When Olivia entered, Sara immediately altered her position, shooting a guilty glance toward her mother and jumping to the floor.

"What were you doing?" Olivia asked casually, as Sara made a production of sitting down on the edge of the bed and putting on her shoes.

Sara shrugged without looking up. The chin-length wings of her dark brown bob had swung forward, effectively hiding her expression.

Olivia accepted that nonanswer without comment. She didn't want to make Sara's perfectly fine weight an issue, or push Sara into confiding uncertainties that she might not be ready to share. Instead, as Sara tied her shoes, Olivia crossed to the windows and drew back the curtains, letting bright sunlight pour into the room. Immediately the taupes and creams of the new decor lost their gloom and even took on a certain brightness. The old wooden floor glowed where the sun touched it, and dust motes danced cheerily above the tumbled bed.

"It's a beautiful day," Olivia observed, looking back at her daughter. Having finished with her shoes, Sara stood up, turned around, and automatically reached for the rumpled covers that were listing toward the floor on her side of the bed. It was a rule in their Houston apartment that beds were made before they left their bedrooms each morning.

"Where have you been?" Sara asked as Olivia moved to the other side of the bed to help.

"I went for a walk." Olivia tugged her portion of the bedclothes into place and smoothed them as Sara did the same. "Did you have a good sleep?"

"Yeah." Sara tossed her mother a pillow. Mother and daughter placed their pillows against the headboard at approximately the same time in approximately identical positions on their respective sides of the bed, exchanged congratulatory glances at the symmetry thus achieved, and the bed-making was complete. "What are we going to do today?"

"I don't know." Olivia smiled at her daughter. "I thought we'd start by washing your face and brushing your teeth and brushing your hair and —"

"Oh, Mom, I meant what are we going to do today that's fun?" Sara asked impatiently. "This is our *vacation*."

"We could explore," Olivia suggested, coming around the foot of the bed to put an arm around her daughter's shoulders and give her a hug. Sara had never had much in the way of vacations; at least, nothing fancy, although Olivia had tried her best to make the one week she could take off from work every summer special. Last year, as always, finances had dictated that they stay close to home, but they had taken day trips to the beach at Galveston and to a local amusement park and gone to movies and the mall. "I've already seen all kinds of interesting things this morning."

"Like what?" Sara hugged her back, both arms around Olivia's waist, and looked up at her mother. Olivia dropped a light kiss on her forehead. She loved this child so much that sometimes the emotion felt like a physical ache inside her.

"A big Persian cat." Sara loved cats, although

143

she'd never been allowed to have one. Their apartment complex did not allow pets. "Some peacocks."

"Peacocks!" Sara's eyes widened. "Really?"

"Mmm-hmm." Olivia nodded as she smoothed Sara's hair away from her face. "But first things first. To the bathroom with you, miss."

By the time Sara was clean and brushed and they were heading downstairs, it was almost ten o'clock. Sara went ahead of her, bouncing from one step to the next, looking cute as a bug in a sleeveless, pink-and-white striped blouse and pink denim shorts, with twin pink barrettes holding her hair behind her ears.

"Breakfast," Olivia decreed, as Sara reached the bottom, and pointed toward the kitchen. Sara obediently turned in the indicated direction, and Olivia followed a step or two behind. Muffled voices from the kitchen made Sara hesitate just outside the swinging door.

"Can we go look for the peacocks now instead of having breakfast?" she whispered to Olivia, whose hand was already flat against the door. "I'm not very hungry."

"Well, I am," Olivia said firmly, and pushed the door open. When Sara still hung back, she put a hand between her daughter's shoulder blades and ushered her into the kitchen. Callie and Martha were sitting at the table. Callie had a glass of orange juice, a cup of coffee, and a plate of scrambled eggs and toast in front of her. Except for the coffee, the meal appeared untouched. Martha was sipping at a cup of coffee. Her plate was empty. Both looked around as Olivia and Sara entered.

"Good morning!" Callie greeted them with a smile. She wore khaki slacks and a white silky-looking camp shirt. Rosy blush and lipstick made her appear well-rested and deceptively healthy. "Did you two sleep well?"

"I did," Olivia answered, while Sara, her fingers entwining tightly with Olivia's, merely nodded.

"What can I fix you ladies for breakfast?" Martha got to her feet. In plaid Bermuda shorts, a forest-green T-shirt, and wedge-heeled sandals, with her black hair teased high and an abundance of red lipstick on her mouth, she looked both out of place and out of date. But her smile was warm and her eyes were friendly. Olivia was reminded that, even when she was at her teenage worst, Martha, at least, had never appeared to judge her.

"Sit back down, Martha. I'll get it," Olivia said, waving Martha back into her seat at the same time as she discreetly detached herself from Sara's hand and pointed her toward the table. "Sara only ever eats toast, and I'll have coffee."

"It won't take more'n two shakes to fix scrambled eggs, or I can make pancakes if you'd rather, or there are some muffins in the freezer. . . ." Stopped halfway out of her chair, Martha

145

frowned at Olivia.

"No, thanks." Heading for the toaster, Olivia shook her head with a smile, and proceeded to locate what she needed to make toast.

"My goodness, you look like your mother," Callie said, smiling at Sara, who was hesitantly approaching the table. "Come on and sit down." She pulled out the chair beside her own, patted the seat, then glanced at Olivia, who was putting slices of bread in the toaster. "Seeing the two of you together sure takes me back. It seems like only yesterday that you were that age, Olivia, and Selena was fixing toast for you."

"My mother fixed me toast for breakfast?" Olivia questioned lightly, pleased to see that Sara took the seat beside Callie without further urging. Having ignored Olivia's request that she sit down, Martha rummaged in the refrigerator for orange juice and milk, and poured out two glasses of each.

Callie laughed. "That's all you would eat: grape jelly on toast with the crusts trimmed off, cut into triangles. Only your mother could fix it to suit you. You never would eat anybody else's."

"I only like Mom's toast," Sara said shyly, interested as she always was in stories of her mother's childhood. "And I like grape jelly on it, too."

The toast popped up just then, so Olivia missed out on Callie's reply. Spreading butter and jelly, she searched her mind for a memory of her mother doing the same for her, but drew a blank. There were so many holes in her memory where her mother was concerned. For the first time, it occurred to Olivia that perhaps something was not quite right about that.

"What are you two going to do today?" Callie asked, as Olivia carried the toast — crustless, spread with grape jelly and cut into triangles — to the table. Striving to purge another disquieting stab of déjà vu from her mind, Olivia smiled and sat down beside her daughter.

"Explore."

"There's a new pool in town. The Marguerite T. Archer Memorial Swimming Pool. Big John funded most of it, and it was finished two years ago. You and Sara might like to go swimming there, Olivia. Chloe and her friends spend a lot of time hanging out at the pool."

Her smile turning a little tight-lipped, Olivia shook her head as she took a revivifying sip of coffee. "That's a wonderful way for Big John to honor his wife, isn't it?"

"My mom can't swim," Sara offered, biting a corner off her toast. Sara always ate two slices of toast cut into eight triangles, corners first, then the centers. "She made me take lessons, though. But I'm not very good."

Callie sent Olivia a swift glance of concern. "Oh, honey, forgive me, I forgot. Sometimes I think this medicine they've got me on fogs up my brain."

"It's all right." Olivia managed another, more genuine smile. Her fear of the lake had expanded

147

and generalized over the years to include all water, something of which she never liked to be reminded. It was ridiculous, and limiting, especially when Sara wanted to go swimming, but it was something she had found impossible to overcome. At least she had not infected Sara with the same fear. And she had managed to pay for and grimly taken her daughter to lessons until Sara could swim the width of a swimming pool on her own.

Callie and Martha exchanged glances as Martha sat back down after pouring herself another cup of coffee, and the subject was quickly dropped.

"Do you like to play tennis?" Callie asked Sara. "Chloe and her friends have been playing tennis a lot this summer. She's over at a friend's house playing right now, as a matter of fact, but she should be back before lunch."

"I've never played," Sara said, consuming another bite of toast. "I think I'd like it, though."

"Sara likes animals," Olivia put in, sipping the orange juice Martha had set before her. "We're going to go outside and check out the peacocks. And maybe see if we can find that big Persian cat I saw this morning."

"That's Ginger." Callie smiled. "Named for Ginger Spice, actually. Chloe was a big fan of the Spice Girls when we got the kitten for her two years ago. But I think that craze has kind of died out now. Like the Beanie Baby thing. This time next year, it'll be gone."

"Oh, does Chloe collect Beanie Babies?" Sara asked excitedly. "I love Beanie Babies."

"So does Chloe." Callie smiled at Sara, while Olivia smiled at both of them. Sara loved Beanie Babies with a devotion she showed few playthings. For the last few birthdays and Christmases, a Beanie Baby was tops on her list, and she saved her money diligently between holidays to buy new ones. Olivia knew that if at any time she wanted to give her daughter a special treat, she could do no better than to bring home one of the little beanbag animals.

"Miss Chloe has a whole bookcase-full up in her room," Martha put in. "I'd say she has just about every one ever sold in a toy store."

"Does she have Nip the cat?" Sara was so intrigued that she forgot to eat. A toast triangle hung ignored from her hand. "Or any of the bears? Like the Princess bear?"

Obviously Sara found this possibility dazzling.

Martha shook her head, and Callie laughed. "Honey, you'll have to ask Chloe. She probably does, her daddy's bought her enough of them. But I don't know any of their names, and I don't think Martha does, either."

Martha shook her head again. "They all look alike to me."

"Finish eating, Sara," Olivia interposed quietly. It would be wonderful if, by talking Beanie Babies, Sara and Chloe could connect. On the other hand, she had seen enough of Chloe in action to be just slightly skeptical.

The telephone rang.

"I'll get it." With a quick glance at Callie, Martha pushed her chair back. Getting to her feet, she moved quickly toward the butler's pantry. The phone had just started to ring for a third time when Martha picked up the receiver.

"LaAngelle Plantation," she said, then listened. After a minute she covered the voice piece with her hand and looked at Callie. "It's Mr. Seth calling from the hospital. He wants to talk to you."

A worried frown creased Callie's brow at the news. Standing up, she crossed to the butler's pantry and took the phone Martha held out to her. The conversation was brief, but Olivia could tell it contained bad news, not so much from what Callie said, which wasn't much, but from her reaction. Her face went gray beneath the carefully applied blush, and she sagged against the doorjamb.

Hanging up, Callie stood motionless for a moment, then turned back to find the eyes of everyone in the kitchen fixed on her.

"Big John's had a stroke," she said heavily. "He was recovering from the heart attack well, but now he's had a stroke. Seth says it's serious. But he says I should stay home, and not come to the hospital, because Big John doesn't know anybody, and there's nothing any of us can do."

"Oh, no." Olivia's hand flew to cover her mouth, then dropped. Her stomach lurched, and she felt suddenly queasy. "Oh, no."

"Mr. Seth's right," Martha said firmly to Callie. "It won't help Mr. Archer if you go making yourself sicker."

"He wants me to call David again and tell him he needs to come home." Callie's voice sounded hollow. "Right now."

"Oh, no," Olivia said again. David was Big John's second youngest child and sole surviving son. He lived in San Diego, where he owned and ran a restaurant called Barney's. Olivia had always liked him, and he had been kind to her whenever they met. But that was infrequently, because Big John and his third son were like oil and water. Whenever either one of them could possibly avoid it, they did not mix.

If Seth was asking his mother to summon David *right now,* then Big John must be on the brink of death.

chapter 16

No matter what Martha or Olivia said to dissuade her, Callie insisted on going to the hospital. Olivia was elected to drive her despite Callie's protests that she was perfectly capable of going alone. Martha and Olivia agreed that Callie's health was too uncertain for her to safely drive herself. Martha needed to stay at the house because chances were that Mallory would drop Chloe off before Callie returned, and the consensus of those who knew her well was that Chloe would behave better with someone acquainted with her quirks. Sara would stay with Martha. Olivia wasn't perfectly happy with this arrangement — she didn't like leaving Sara in a strange environment, with someone who was to all intents and purposes a stranger to her, and the prospect of Chloe returning home anytime soon did not help — but she felt a strong need to be at Big John's bedside herself in this moment of crisis. Or, if not exactly at his bedside, at least in the waiting room outside, if that was as close as she could get.

Never mind that some members of the family might not want her there.

In her heart, Big John was *her* family, whether or not she was his.

She left Sara in the kitchen with Martha. The two of them were happily contemplating making peach ice cream with the old-fashioned ice cream maker that had been in the family for decades. Having had no idea that making ice cream at home was even possible, Sara, an equal opportunity devotee of Baskin-Robbins and Dairy Queen and every other ice cream parlor to come down the path, was wide-eyed with wonder as Martha wrapped an apron around her waist and started setting out the supplies they would need.

"I'll be back as soon as I can." Olivia dropped a quick kiss on Sara's cheek on her way out the back door.

"I'll be okay," Sara said. "Don't worry about me, Mom."

It struck Olivia how very adult she sounded, almost as if she were the parent reassuring the child. Not for the first time, Olivia reflected on how very different Sara's childhood was from her own. With no extended family, limited financial resources, and more worries than an eight-year-old should be aware of, Sara had been forced to grow up fast. Maybe too fast.

Or maybe not. Maybe being a little more mature than her mother would stand her in good stead. Maybe, at least, it would keep her from repeating some of Olivia's own mistakes. Olivia fervently hoped so.

"Sara seems like the sweetest little girl," Callie remarked in the car on the way to the hospital. They were traveling south on Highway 415 in Callie's navy-blue Lincoln Town Car, one of the older models that was as big as a boat, with Olivia behind the wheel. On the east side of the raised, two-lane road was the brackish water of a freshwater swamp, where cattails, alligator grass, and marsh elders grew higher than the levee that held back the Mississippi River. On the west, enterprising farmers had taken advantage of the swampy conditions to grow rice and raise crawfish. Flooded fields stretched as far as the eye could see. "Is she always that good?"

"Sara is a sweetheart," Olivia said with conviction. The putrid smell of rotting vegetation that was as much a part of the swamps as mud was starting to creep inside the car, so she cranked up the air-conditioning a notch, hoping to defeat the increasing heat and the smell at the same time. Outside, from a cloudless blue sky, the sun beat down relentlessly, raising heat shimmers on the pavement in front of the car and pouring through the windows, making the navy leather upholstery burningly hot in places. Olivia shifted uncomfortably as her bare legs stuck to the seat. "I don't know what I'd do without her."

"It's obvious you've done a good job mothering her." Callie sighed. "I just wish Chloe had been as lucky. Seth has tried his best, and so have I, but . . ." Her voice trailed off. "Well, I don't guess Jennifer was any great shakes as a mother anyway, so she's no real loss."

"I can't take too much credit for Sara. She has been as good as gold from the time she was born. Even as a tiny baby, she only cried when she needed something. As a toddler she never went through the terrible twos, never threw tantrums. I have never had a complaint about her behavior from a teacher or a baby-sitter or anyone. I think being good just must be in her nature."

"She doesn't take after you much, then, does she?" Callie sent her a sudden, teasing smile that reminded Olivia of Seth. "I can remember you throwing some ungodly tantrums when you were a little bitty girl. I used to think Selena was a saint for dealing with you so patiently. She never spanked you, you know. Not even when Big John told her she should."

"Big John told her to spank me?" Olivia took her eyes off the road to glance in surprise at Callie. It was hard to imagine Big John paying any attention whatsoever to child-rearing matters. It was even harder for her to formulate an image of how she and her mother must have been together. All she had was the mental equivalent of a few hazy snapshots of the two of them, although over the last twenty-four hours, since coming home to LaAngelle Plantation, she felt

155

more connected to her mother than she ever remembered feeling in her life. It was almost as if, in this place where Selena had lived and died, some essence of her remained and was reaching out to her daughter.

"I think it was after you threw a plate of spaghetti at the table in the midst of a temper fit. We had guests at the time, and noodles and sauce flew all over them. Big John yelled at you and at your mother for not disciplining you better, but she looked him in the eye and said she would raise her own child, thank you very much, and then picked you up, screams and all, and walked away. I admired her for that. Standing up to Big John took real courage in those days. But Selena was never meek. She was quiet, and careful to be respectful of her elders, but if you pushed her she had quite a temper. And God help anybody who did something she didn't like to you."

Olivia was silent for a moment, feeling a sudden tightness in her throat as shadows of memories danced along the edge of her consciousness. None was specific. What stood out suddenly was an overwhelming sense of feeling loved. My mother loved me, she thought, and as she acknowledged that the constriction in her throat increased. She swallowed, took a deep breath, and swallowed again. Finally she managed to say in a near-normal voice, "You know, I don't really remember much about my mother."

Callie glanced at her. "I'm not surprised. You were only six years old when she . . . died."

156

That brief hesitation did not escape Olivia's notice. Had Callie been about to say something else? There were so many questions Olivia wanted to ask, but this was not the time, or the place. Her emotions were already running too high.

If she talked any more about her mother, she feared she would cry. Which, under the circumstances, Callie didn't need to have to deal with.

"Tell me about the plans for Seth and Mallory's wedding," Olivia said a little too brightly, changing the subject. "Is it going to be held at St. Luke's?"

St. Luke's was the Episcopal church in LaAngelle. Founded in 1837, it was almost as old as the town. The Archers had been mainstays of the congregation for generations.

Callie shook her head, smiling. "Mallory's expecting about five hundred guests, so that lets St. Luke's out. It's too small. The ceremony's going to be at St. Bartholomew's in Baton Rouge, and the reception will be held at the Baton Rouge Country Club. Mallory's having a ball planning everything, but I think Seth would prefer something a shade less elaborate. He hasn't said anything, but I know him. He's starting to get nervous."

"Is he?" Olivia smiled, too, at the idea of Seth's suffering from prewedding jitters.

"This is hard on Seth, you know." Callie's tone turned suddenly serious. "My cancer, I mean. He's a fixer. Anything that's wrong, any problem

157

that anybody has, he tries to fix it. But he can't fix this."

Olivia didn't know what to say. Fortunately, the turnoff into Baton Rouge loomed just ahead, and the topic was lost as she concentrated on getting over the long, crowded bridge that spanned the Mississippi River and into the city.

The Intensive Care Unit was on the fourth floor of St. Elizabeth's Hospital. By the time she stepped off the elevator, Olivia was already starting to shiver from the air-conditioning. Before coming, she had changed her shorts for a more appropriate knee-length denim wrap skirt. With it she wore a white T-shirt and brown strappy sandals. Even without panty hose — it was too hot for extraneous pieces of clothing — the outfit had felt almost too warm for the smothering heat outside. Inside, it was barely adequate. She found herself envying Callie, who'd had the foresight to bring a very pretty white cardigan, and had put it on over her slacks and blouse within minutes of entering the hospital.

"I hope we're not walking into more bad news," Callie murmured, curling a hand around Olivia's elbow as they walked past the busy nurses' station toward the Intensive Care Unit. Callie's fingers were cold, and felt almost skeletal as they pressed into Olivia's skin. She was reminded once again that Callie was gravely ill, and covered the older woman's hand protectively with her own.

"Seth only called an hour ago." Olivia glanced

sideways as a green-coated orderly pushed a hospital bed past them. The rubber wheels squeaked over the slick gray-speckled terrazzo floor. Motionless on the bed lay an emaciated woman with disordered tufts of sparse white hair. Her eyes were closed and her face was turned away. An IV bag dangled from a metal pole attached to the bed. Its contents dripped down a clear tube into the woman's arm.

Callie took one look and averted her gaze. Olivia could feel her aunt's shudder.

Of fear? Olivia was quite certain that Callie was imagining herself sharing the woman's fate.

"Oh, Callie, you shouldn't have come!" Dressed in a celery-green summer pantsuit, her short auburn hair meticulously sprayed into place but her face pale and tired, Belinda Vernon was coming down the hall toward them. Both hands were outstretched toward Callie. Behind her, a sign marked WAITING ROOM hung above an open door to the left. Phillip Vernon walked out that door, glanced after his mother, spotted Callie and Olivia, and headed toward them, too. At the very end of the hall was the Intensive Care Unit.

Wide double doors of blond wood and metal were closed, and bore a sign warning NO ADMITTANCE: AUTHORIZED PERSONNEL ONLY.

"You know I had to," Callie said, embracing Belinda. "How is he?"

"Not good." There was pain in Belinda's

voice. "They're doing everything they can for him, but Charlie says all we can do now is pray."

"Hello, Olivia," Phillip said in a subdued tone, coming up to stand beside his mother. He was wearing a short-sleeved blue dress shirt tucked into khaki slacks. His dark brown hair was neatly combed, and he was freshly shaved. Obviously both he and his mother had managed to shower and change since the events of the previous night, and Olivia assumed they had gotten a few hours of sleep, too.

Olivia echoed Phillip's greeting as Callie and Belinda broke apart. Belinda's gaze then alighted on Olivia, and she nodded without speaking. Civil but not friendly, Olivia thought. Well, she could live with that.

"Mom, it's your turn." Telephone receiver in hand, Carl poked his head out of the waiting room door, glancing down the hall toward his mother. He disappeared back inside for a moment, then emerged into the hall *sans* telephone. Like Phillip, his elder by three years, Carl wore khaki pants and a short-sleeved dress shirt, though his was white. Also like Phillip, he was stocky and blue-eyed with dark brown hair. As a youth he had been mischievous, prone to teasing and pranks, and it was he who had thrown her into the lake. Despite that, Olivia had always liked him, and he greeted her now with a quick hug and a smile.

"We can only go in one at a time," Belinda explained to Callie as the whole group began to move in the direction of the Intensive Care Unit. "It doesn't really matter. Daddy doesn't seem to know anybody anyway."

"I'm sure some part of him senses you're here and is comforted," Callie said. One of the double doors to the Intensive Care Unit swung outward, and Seth walked into the hall, talking to someone over his shoulder all the while. He paused for a moment, finishing his conversation, then glanced their way. Frowning, he moved toward them, and the door swung shut behind him.

"How is he?" Belinda asked as he joined him.

Seth shook his head at her. "No change." His glance slid past her to touch on his mother and Olivia, and his lips tightened. "Mother, you shouldn't have come."

"I told her that," Belinda said.

"I wanted to," Callie answered with quiet dignity. "Big John is my father-in-law, and he is as dear to me as my own father was. Of course I came."

"You have to think of yourself, Mother." Seth sounded grim. He glanced at Belinda. "I know it's your turn to sit with him for a while, but would you mind letting her go in now, for just a minute, so that she can go back home? With the chemotherapy, her immune system is weakened, and she particularly needs to stay out of hospitals, which, for some reason I can't begin to fathom, tend to harbor a whole spectrum of really nasty germs."

161

"Who told you that my immune system is weakened?" Callie demanded challengingly, sounding surprised and a little defensive.

"I've been talking to your doctors."

"They have no business telling you anything without my permission!"

"Maybe they think you need a keeper, Mother."

Mother and son exchanged measuring looks.

"You go ahead in, Callie," Belinda said, drawing their attention. "Seth is right. You should head back home just as quick as you can."

"Seth is too bossy," Callie muttered under her breath, more to herself than anyone else, but allowed Seth to take her arm and escort her to the door of the Intensive Care Unit. He pulled it open, said something briefly to someone inside, and then, as Callie disappeared within, stepped back out into the corridor.

"You weren't planning on seeing my father, I hope?" Belinda asked Olivia as Seth came toward them. "Since the sight of you is what made him collapse in the first place, I just can't permit it. I'm sure you understand."

Olivia nodded unhappily. She did understand, however unpleasant she might find Belinda's edict. After all, if the sight of her *had* brought on Big John's heart attack, her presence at his bedside was the last thing he needed until he was perfectly cognizant of who she was — and wasn't. Anyway, if he didn't know anyone, it didn't matter, did it? She had just hoped to get a chance to mend fences with him while she still could.

"That's a little harsh, don't you think?" Carl protested, giving his mother a reproving look.

"It's all right, Carl. I really only came to drive Aunt Callie," Olivia said.

Joining them, Seth lifted his eyebrows inquiringly as he caught the tail end of the conversation.

"You can't blame Olivia for the old man's heart attack," Phillip added, talking to his mother.

"No, you can't," Seth said, surprising Olivia, who was sure he did blame her for it. He fixed his aunt with a steady gaze. "You know as well as I do that Big John could have had a heart attack at any time, for any reason. Or no reason. What happened wasn't Olivia's fault."

Olivia sent Seth a small smile of thanks, which he acknowledged with a glance and a wry twist of his lips.

"You always did take her part," Belinda said bitterly, and turned on her heel, walking into the waiting room with her head held high.

"She's upset," Phillip said excusingly to Olivia.

"You wanna go down to the cafeteria, get a cup of coffee while you wait for Aunt Callie to be ready to go?" Carl asked, smiling at her.

Olivia hesitated, then nodded. "That'd be great." She certainly didn't want to stay in the waiting room with the others in the face of

Belinda's hostility.

"I'll bring Mother down when she's ready to go," Seth said. "And — when I feel it's appropriate to do so — I'll tell Big John you were here."

"Thank you." Olivia smiled at him briefly, then turned away with Carl.

As Olivia and Carl walked toward the elevator bank, Seth went into the waiting room with Phillip. Olivia could hear the murmur of their voices joined with Belinda's. She guessed, without really knowing for certain, that they were talking about her.

That was because the single word she overheard clearly before moving out of earshot was uttered by Belinda, in a tone of high-pitched contempt. It was *trash*.

chapter 17

The big white cat sat on the porch rail, looking at her. Sara glanced up from her book, and there she — or he — was. The Persian was really fluffy, with big blue eyes. For a moment Sara returned the stare. Then with a flick of its tail the cat jumped down to the floor, heading toward the blue earthenware bowl that held the melted remnants of her peach ice cream. Sara had finished eating it about an hour ago, set the bowl down on the porch floor beside the swing, and forgotten about it while she curled up with a book she had found. It was *Misty of Chincoteague*, a horse book, and it was really good.

If she could have anything she wanted in the whole world, Sara reflected, what she would wish for first would be a horse of her own.

The second thing she would wish for would be a cat. Or maybe she would wish for the cat first.

It was hard to say.

No, the very first thing she would wish for was that her mom would have lots of money, enough money so that she wouldn't ever have to worry again. Then her mom could buy her the horse, and the cat. That would be best of all.

The cat — the real cat — was licking up the melted ice cream, its little pink tongue moving busily in and out of the pale orange goo. Setting the book print-side down on the blue-upholstered cushion, Sara slipped off the swing and dropped to her knees on the wooden planks beside it.

"Hello, kitty," she said. When the cat did no more than flick her a look and continue to lap at the ice cream, she reached out to pet it. Its fur was silky-soft and thick, and as she ran her hand along its back the cat began to purr.

"What a nice kitty," Sara said in tones of praise, stroking it, and its purr grew louder. The cat glanced at her, and she saw that a drop of melted orange-colored ice cream dangled from its whiskers. Sara began to smile. Her vacation so far had been more tiring and scary than fun, but the presence of the cat made it a lot better.

"What are you doing to Ginger?" The accusing voice was so unexpected that Sara jumped. Her shoulder hit the swing's metal frame. The swing bounced away, then into her shoulder again, and it hurt. Wincing, she scooted forward out of the reach of the swing, rubbing her shoulder and looking around at

Chloe, who had materialized out of one of the long window-door things that opened onto the big upstairs porch.

"What are you doing to Ginger?" Chloe demanded again, as the cat abandoned the now-empty bowl and began to walk in stately fashion toward her.

"Nothing. I was just petting her."

"She's *my* cat." Chloe took a step forward and snatched Ginger up, cradling the cat tightly in her arms. Ginger suffered this with good grace, merely running her tongue over her whiskers to get at the last drops of ice cream and fixing Sara with an unblinking gaze. For a moment two pairs of eerily similar blue eyes stared hard at Sara.

"She's beautiful," Sara said with sincerity, looking at Ginger. "I wish I had a cat."

"Why don't you get one, then?"

"We can't have one in the apartment where we live. Pets aren't allowed."

"You live in an *apartment?*"

"Yeah."

"Just you and your mom?"

"Yeah."

"Where?"

"In Houston."

"You're really poor, aren't you?"

Sara shrugged. She'd never considered the matter in quite that light, but . . . "I guess."

"I could tell from your clothes."

"What's wrong with them?" Sara looked down at herself questioningly. Her pink shorts and striped blouse looked fine to her.

"They're cheap."

"How do you know?"

Chloe made a face. "I can tell." Her gaze slid past Sara and lit on something behind her.

"Hey, that's my book!"

"I didn't know it was yours." Sara glanced at the book. "It's really good."

"You shouldn't have touched it without my permission!"

"I'm sorry," Sara said humbly.

Chloe frowned. The cat stirred in her arms, and her hold on it shifted as she lifted it higher and rubbed her cheek against its fur. "Do you like horses?"

"I love horses." Sara's reply was fervent.

"I'm going to get one for Christmas. My dad promised."

"You are so lucky."

Chloe looked her up and down. "Do you have any Beanie Babies?"

Sara nodded. "I have almost thirty."

Chloe snorted. "Is that all?" she asked scornfully. "I have all of them. Well, nearly all, except for some of the very rarest ones like Trap the mouse. But my dad says he'll get them for me when he can find them."

"Do you have the Princess Bear?" Sara asked, awed. "That's the one I want most right now."

"I have *two*. My dad bought me one, and my nana bought me one. Want to see them?"

Sara nodded with open eagerness.

"Come on, then."

Sara stood up, and followed Chloe along the porch. Chloe disappeared through one of the open window-door things. Sara didn't like having that kind of window in the bedroom where she slept, it made the room too spooky, like anyone could come in anytime they wanted, even when she was asleep. But everybody else, even her mom, didn't seem to mind, and she didn't like to be a baby and act scared.

Following Chloe through the opening, Sara found herself in Chloe's bedroom. It was decorated in shades of blue and yellow, with fluttery blue gingham curtains draping the open windows, and a matching bedspread that cascaded to the floor in layers of ruffles on the four-poster. Chloe was standing in the doorway of a smaller, adjoining room as Sara entered. Stopping beside her, Sara saw that the room was lined with shelves, and the shelves were stuffed with toys. More toys than in a toy store, Sara thought, eyes widening.

"See?" Chloe pointed to a painted cabinet that took up all of one corner. The cabinet was fitted with shelves, and the shelves were filled with Beanie Babies.

Sara stared for a moment, then glanced at Chloe.

"You are so lucky," she said again, meaning it.

Chloe smiled. "Want to play Beanies?"

chapter 18

The following morning, Sunday, the family went to church. Although she and Sara had been less than regular churchgoers in Houston — the lure of a Sunday morning to sleep in was often just too great to resist — Olivia remembered the Sundays of her growing-up years with fondness. Every week, without fail, the Archers attended church en masse. The only excuse was sickness — and sickness did not include staying up too late on the Saturday night before. As a child, Olivia had enjoyed the togetherness of the church community, with its Friday fish fry and its summertime bring-a-dish suppers. As a teen, she had hated being dragged to services. But at LaAngelle Plantation, the rule was every member of the family attended church. No excuses.

Remembering, Olivia had packed accordingly.

Her own dress was an inexpensive (Kmart again) knee-length white cotton pique, with short sleeves and a self-belt, which she wore with nude panty hose and white high heels. Sara's dress was costlier (it had been on end-of-season clearance in a pricey Children's World catalogue). It was a three-tiered pale pink cotton knit strewn with deep pink flowers. Cut very loose, in floater style, it had short sleeves and reached just past her knees. With white lace-trimmed socks, her black ballet flats, and a deep pink headband to keep her hair out of her face, Sara looked darling. Chloe, who was seated next to Sara in the back of the Jaguar, wore an obviously expensive pale blue dress with short puffed sleeves, a white Peter Pan collar, and a sheer organza overlay. Her blond hair was tied with blue ribbons at the crown, and allowed to cascade down her back. Looking at the two girls together, Olivia was thankful that she had splurged on Sara's dress: Her daughter would have no reason to be ashamed of what she was wearing.

On this steamy Sunday morning in August, St. Luke's bell pealed in a beautifully melodic call to worship. The sound could be heard from the edge of town, and it immediately transported Olivia back to her childhood. The ringing of that bell had marked Sundays in LaAngelle for as long as Olivia could remember.

There were three other churches in LaAngelle: Our Lady of Sorrows Catholic Church, which was the largest; LaAngelle Baptist, which was

171

larger than St. Luke's; and a Pentecostal church that was so tiny Olivia wasn't even sure it had a name.

"I hate church," Chloe muttered resentfully as the Jaguar nosed toward St. Luke's. Earlier, she had tried — and failed — to get out of attending by using the argument that nobody went to church anymore. Olivia, who had tried that one herself as a child, could have told her that she was wasting her breath.

"No, you don't." Callie's response was tranquil. She was in the front passenger seat beside Seth, who drove. Olivia sat with the two girls in back.

"Oh, yes, I do." Chloe's expression was mutinous. She was scowling with her lower lip thrust out, and she had her arms crossed over her chest. Glancing at her, Sara chewed her lip nervously. Olivia didn't blame her. Chloe looked like she could explode at any minute.

"That's enough, young lady," Seth said, in a voice that brooked no defiance. Chloe's scowl grew even more fierce, but she said nothing more.

The Catholic Church predominated in most of the southern parishes of Louisiana. In the northern parishes, Protestants were the dominant religious group. In this area, which was right on the borderline between Acadia and the upstate parishes, Catholics and Protestants mixed in roughly equal numbers. The Anglo aristocrats, such as the Archers, attended St.

172

Luke's. The congregation of LaAngelle Baptist were basically the town's typical rural southerners, who worked for a living at the Boatworks and at other area businesses. A few had their own hardscrabble farms. Some drove a few miles north or south to work in the gas or lumber industries. Those of French Creole descent, although there were few who could claim such ancestry in LaAngelle, attended Our Lady of Sorrows. So did the Cajuns, who made up the bulk of Our Lady of Sorrows parishioners. Descended from the Acadians of Nova Scotia who were forcibly relocated to southern Louisiana in the eighteenth century, the Cajuns were historically looked down upon by the other groups. In years past, "Cajun" was a pejorative term, and Olivia had been raised with a vague sense of shame about her Cajun origins. The family had openly felt that James Archer had married beneath him when he wed the Cajun widow Selena Chenier.

They passed Our Lady of Sorrows, which was housed in a white clapboard building at the end of West Main Street. The antebellum courthouse with its graceful green lawn was situated directly opposite, in what had once been the center of town. Olivia had always found it amusing that the main artery through their small town was called West Main Street, because there was no East Main Street. It had existed once, but all its buildings and the roadway itself had been washed away in the hundred-year flood of 1927, and no one had bothered to rebuild it. West Main Street now ended abruptly at Chitimacha Street, which ran perpendicular to it. The T-shaped intersection where the streets met was where Our Lady of Sorrows and the courthouse stood. St. Luke's was on the other end of town, on Cocodrie Street, more gracefully situated atop a small rise amidst a stand of live oaks.

Besides the churches, LaAngelle was home to an eclectic mixture of houses and businesses that were thrown randomly together as if the town fathers had never heard of zoning (which, at the time most of the houses were built and the businesses were established, they probably hadn't). The newer, bigger houses were mostly located on several-acre lots on Melancon Pike, on the far west side of town. The house where Seth had lived with his wife and Chloe was there, as were Phillip's house and Charlie and Belinda's. The houses in town tended to be smaller and older, and their city-size lots were jumbled in among the local business establishments. These businesses included Mike Lawson's Grocery and Gas Station, Patout's Bakery (the Patout family had been making mouthwatering desserts for generations), Mary-Jeanne's House of Style, the LaAngelle Inn and Restaurant, Like-New Consignments, Broussard's Pharmacy, and Curly's Hardware, among others. LaAngelle Elementary was at the northern end of Chitimacha Street. It was a long, one-story building with a red-tiled roof that educated local children from kindergarten to grade eight. After that, they moved over to the LaAngelle High School, a newer, two-story brick building that stood next door for grades nine through twelve. Olivia had never attended either school, although she had many friends who had. The Archers, for generations past, had attended private school in Baton Rouge. Olivia assumed Chloe did as well.

"See? I told you nobody would be here." This came from Chloe, as the Jaguar pulled into the parking lot of the gray stone church. There were, indeed, only about ten other cars in a lot that could easily have held fifty. To judge by the vehicles dotting the parking lots of the other churches they had passed, none of the houses of worship were enjoying capacity crowds that morning. Which was not surprising: Sundays in August were traditionally a somnolent time. Come September's marginally cooler weather, and increasing steadily as the year wore down toward Christmas, the churches would begin to fill up.

"*We're* here," Callie said with gentle emphasis.

Chloe made a rude sound that indicated quite clearly that she would rather not be. Olivia's gaze automatically flew to Seth. As she was seated directly behind him, she had to gauge his reaction through the rearview mirror. Engaged in parking the car, he seemed not to have heard. Callie, who had to have heard, ignored Chloe.

As Seth turned the engine off, a man emerged from the white Lincoln Town Car in the adjacent parking space. Olivia recognized Ira Hayes. Dressed in a navy sport coat that did a great deal to hide his paunch, red tie, pale blue shirt, and white slacks, he looked much more attractive than when Olivia had first met him in the kitchen two nights before. He opened Callie's door for her, and stood waiting. Looking way too thin in a butter linen dress that had obviously been purchased when she was heavier, Callie got out to stand beside him. Her smile of greeting was so warm that Olivia realized her aunt must be fonder of this man than she had guessed.

Olivia released her seat belt as Chloe scrambled out the door with Sara right behind her. Olivia's own door swung open from the outside. She glanced up to find Seth holding the door for her, an inscrutable expression on his face as he looked down at her. He appeared very distinguished in a light gray summer suit with a white dress shirt and a navy tie that brought out the blue of his eyes. With the sun glinting down on his blond hair, and a slow smile stretching his mouth, he was — handsome. The realization rattled Olivia. She had never before had such a thought about Seth.

"Are you planning to get out?" he inquired politely, reaching in a hand to assist her to alight. Olivia realized that she had been sitting there staring up at him for several seconds. Flustered, she dropped her gaze away from his face. Grasping his hand, she scooted out. His hand was warm and strong, and far larger than hers.

Clasping it made her suddenly very aware of him as a man. It occurred to her that she could be — might be — *was* — attracted to *Seth,* a mind-boggling thought. Not daring to glance at him again lest he should somehow be able to read the stunned realization in her eyes, she dropped his hand with all possible speed. Apparently un-aware that anything untoward had occurred, he shut the door. As she walked across the parking lot, she was conscious of him behind her. He was close enough so that their shadows touched on the pavement. His shadow was tall and broad-shouldered. It engulfed her petite one.

His hand came up to cup her bare elbow, in a gesture as automatic as it was polite. Olivia had to repress an urge to pull her arm away. Seth had touched her before, casually and in anger and to help her in or out or up or down, countless ways and countless times over the years, and it had never affected her one bit. What was wrong with her, she asked herself, that out of the blue she was reacting to him this way?

"Olivia! My stars, young lady, it's good to have you back with us! I had heard you had mar-ried and had a child, of course." Father Randolph took her hand and pumped it vigor-ously, a broad smile splitting his face. Seth's hand dropped to his side, and Olivia was con-scious of a strong sensation of relief as she smiled back at Father Randolph. She had al-ways liked the priest. Not much taller than she was, he was a rotund man with a ruddy face, pale blue eyes behind silver-rimmed spectacles, and a full head of white hair. He wore his black priest's robes with dignity. "Was that your little girl who just ran by with Chloe? Of course it was! She looks just like you."

"Yes, that was Sara," Olivia confirmed with a smile.

"We're glad to have you both in church this morning," Father Randolph said. Then he turned to Seth, and the men shook hands. "I stopped by to see your grandfather at the hospital yesterday. We're all praying for him."

"I appreciate it, and he would, too, if he knew."

Father Randolph's voice lowered. "Your mother is handling the chemotherapy okay?"

"As well as can be expected."

"We're praying for her as well. You all know you can call me at any time if you need anything. In any case, I expect I'll see you at the hospital next week."

"I'll be there. Take care, Father."

"You too, Seth."

Another woman came up to the priest, and Olivia started to move on. Seth followed her, only to pause as the woman called after him.

"Seth! Where's Mallory?"

Olivia instinctively turned to look as Seth stopped. The woman appeared to be about forty, with short, feathery blond hair, crow's feet around blue eyes, and a comfortably plump figure in a navy summer suit. Although her hand was still being shaken by Father Randolph, her gaze was moving with open curiosity over Olivia.

"She's showing houses in Baton Rouge today," Seth replied courteously.

"That real estate business of hers certainly keeps her busy!" The woman withdrew her hand from Father Randolph's with a distracted smile for the priest and another pointed look at Olivia. At that juncture, Father Randolph's attention was claimed by another new arrival, a man in a navy business suit.

"Yes, it does," Seth agreed. Glancing around, his caught Olivia's gaze and he smiled. For a moment something almost wicked danced in his eyes, and Olivia thought for the second time, *Why, he's handsome.* Then he reached out a hand to catch hers and draw her forward. "Olivia, this is Sharon Bishop. She's the new principal of the high school. She and her husband — that's her husband, Tom, talking to Father Randolph — bought Jett Paley's old house. Sharon, this is Olivia Morrison."

The women exchanged polite greetings, and then Seth excused himself and Olivia, and followed Olivia on into the church. With her hand once more free, Olivia could concentrate on something besides her sudden, stunningly unexpected response to Seth, and she became aware of the other woman's covert looks following them. She knew what Sharon Bishop was thinking. To tell the truth, it was not too far from what was in her own mind at the moment — but in fact it was totally untrue. She and Seth —

there was nothing to it at all. There never had been.

"You should have told her I was your cousin," she whispered scoldingly over her shoulder at him.

"She'll figure it out," he said in her ear, and then it was time to take their places for the service.

St. Luke's was a beautiful church, designed to hold no more than a hundred, with high ceilings supported by dark carved beams, walls of rough white plaster, and rows of gleaming mahogany pews divided by a center aisle. The choir loft was to the left of the pulpit. Only three women and one man in maroon and gold robes were seated there today. To the right of the pulpit, in pride of place, was an intricate church organ, donated by Big John years before. Of the twenty or so worshipers in the chapel, Olivia estimated that she knew at least fourteen. That was how little things had changed in LaAngelle, even after nine years.

The church service included a special prayer for Big John and another for Callie. Except for that, it was the traditional Episcopal service, and Olivia found it comforting. Although she had grown up reciting the prayers of her mother's Catholic faith in times of need, and indeed had been baptized as a Catholic at birth, she had been raised Episcopalian. The Archers had seen to that.

Olivia sat between Sara and Seth. On Seth's

other side was Chloe, and next to Chloe was Callie. Ira sat beside Callie, and the two shared a hymnal. Although Sara and Chloe had originally been sitting together, Seth had shifted his daughter to his other side after the two girls succumbed to a muffled fit of giggles over a dropped hymnal. Olivia silently agreed with him that, for decorum's sake, it might be wiser to separate the children. But sitting so close to Seth did nothing for her peace of mind. With six of them in one pew, it was a bit crowded, and her arm brushed Seth's sleeve whenever she moved. Although she shared a hymnal with Sara, while he shared with Chloe, she was conscious of his height when they stood up to sing, and of the pleasingly deep timber of his voice. When he turned sideways to deposit Chloe in her new seat, she found herself admiring the breadth of his shoulders, and the strength that allowed him to pick up his daughter as though she weighed nothing at all. Seated beside him, she became more aware with every breath she drew of the warm male scent of him, with its overnotes of shaving cream and soap. A glance down acquainted her with the long muscles of his thighs, and the flatness of his abdomen beneath his tailored slacks. As the service wore on she grew so aware of him that it was embarrassing. I'm getting turned on by *Seth,* she thought. The realization disturbed her so much that she slid infinitesimally closer to Sara, and forced herself to think about something else.

Sara. She would think about Sara. To her mingled surprise and relief, she had returned from the hospital the day before to find Sara and Chloe playing Beanie Babies on the upstairs gallery. Bonded by a common interest, the girls had apparently made friends. Her offer to take both girls exploring had been rejected, and they had played together with relative amity for the rest of the day. Still, Sara was wary of Chloe's temper, and, Olivia thought, perhaps a little too eager to please her new friend.

Seth knelt, along with everyone else in the church. Realizing that she had completely lost track of the service, Olivia followed suit, sliding to her knees on the padded prayer bench and piously closing her eyes. As she murmured the words to the prayer that she knew by heart, Seth was close beside her, his body brushing hers every time one of them moved. After a few moments, no matter how hard she tried to concentrate on church and faith and prayer, Seth and Seth alone filled her mind.

Maybe being back in LaAngelle was awakening the old Olivia, she thought. Maybe that was why she was suddenly so attracted to Seth. As a teenager, she had liked men, liked their attention, liked their bodies. She had enjoyed sex, which was really why she had imagined herself to be so in love with Newall: They'd been great together in bed. At first. But then she'd gotten pregnant and Sara had been born and sex had become the last thing on her mind. After Newall had left her, her mind had been occupied with feeding and clothing and caring for her child, and her body had been routinely exhausted.

It shocked Olivia to realize that she hadn't had sex in six years.

No wonder Seth suddenly looked good to her, Olivia thought with relief. Back in the familiar environs of LaAngelle, she was simply reverting to her old self. And the Olivia that she had once been would have died at the idea that she might go six years without sleeping with a man.

Sara had taken over her existence, and for those six years taking care of her daughter had been paramount. But her life in Houston, while not affluent, was at least stable now. Sara was growing up, and she was still young, Olivia reminded herself. When she got back to Houston, there was no reason why she couldn't start a relationship with someone if she chose. She'd gone out with several of Dr. Green's dentist colleagues over the years, and with the brother of a patient and her upstairs neighbor. She'd been asked out by and had turned down a lot more, including her divorce lawyer. The point was, if and when she decided she wanted a man in her life again there would be plenty of men to choose from. There was nothing wrong with her renewed interest in sex, she told herself. She just needed to redirect her lust to a more suitable candidate.

Anyone but Seth.

chapter 19

On Sunday night, when the gray Jaguar pulled into the parking area behind the house, its lights cutting bright swathes through the darkness, Olivia and the two girls were out in the yard. It was about ten o'clock, not long after nightfall, which, given the heat of a LaAngelle summer, meant that it was the best time of day to be outdoors. Overhead, a pale three-quarter moon just skimmed the treetops. Although it was as dark as the inside of a cave under the trees and along the hedge, translucent moonlight bathed the rest of the yard. The marble angel in the center of the perennial garden looked almost alive in the unearthly light. The scent of honeysuckle lay heavy in the humid air. Insects and amphibians joined together in their usual nightly chorus. Occasionally one of the peacocks perched in the trees near the lake would scream, making Olivia jump.

It always took her a second or two to remember that birds made that nerve-shattering sound.

Slathered with bug repellent and armed with mason jars, Sara and Chloe were darting about chasing lightning bugs, which they dropped into the jars to make one-night-only "lanterns" for their bedrooms. Olivia had loved catching lightning bugs as a child on this same lawn. The limitations of their Houston apartment meant that Sara had never had the opportunity to flit about outside at night in pursuit of the glowing insects. To Olivia's surprise, upon proposing this activity she discovered that Chloe had never chased and caught lightning bugs, either.

Fifteen minutes into their game, Chloe and Sara were running and giggling and in general having a wonderful time, their darting progress marked by the blinking illumination of the "lanterns" they carried about with them. Taking care to keep within their general vicinity as they swooped about, Olivia laughingly served as referee, cheerleader, and bug spotter. Callie and Martha sat in rocking chairs on the rear veranda, watching the action as they talked.

The arrival of the Jaguar coincided with an unearthly shriek from Chloe. Stopped in her tracks by the sheer, paralyzing intensity of that scream, Olivia ran to the child's rescue as soon as she recovered the use of her limbs. Her progress marked by her bobbing lantern, Sara flew toward Chloe from another part of the yard. After playing together all afternoon yesterday and today, the two girls were now friends.

"Chloe! What on earth . . . ?" Olivia gasped out as mother and daughter converged on the still-screaming girl.

"It's on my arm! It's on my arm!" Clearly panic-stricken, Chloe hopped about, her bare right arm extended out from her body with as much stiff horror as if a snake were coiled around her wrist.

"What is?" Olivia's mystified glance at Chloe's arm found nothing out of the ordinary.

"A bug! Get it off me! Get it *off* me!" Chloe was on the verge of hysteria.

"It's okay. Hold still, now, and let me see."

Placing a hand on her shoulder to hold the dancing child still, Olivia grasped Chloe's extended wrist and took a second, more thorough look at her arm. She then perceived that the shrieks had been precipitated by the escape of one of Chloe's bugs from her jar, which she still clutched tightly in her hand. Instead of flying off to safety like a sensible bug, it had chosen to go crawling up her arm, where it now fanned its wings in the vicinity of her elbow.

A relieved smile curved Olivia's lips. She resolved the crisis by the simple expedient of recapturing the bug with a gentle swipe of her hand. She then let go of Chloe's wrist. Chloe let out a shuddering sigh, and her arm dropped to her side.

"My God, what is it?" Seth came pounding to the rescue just a few seconds too late.

186

"It was on me!" Chloe's voice quivered piteously — but she hung on to her jar, leaving Olivia to surmise that the trauma hadn't been all that severe. Instead of flinging herself on her parent, as Sara would have done in like circumstances, Chloe only looked at Seth with huge eyes and a trembling lower lip. He didn't make any move to hug or physically comfort his child, Olivia noticed. It flitted through her mind that Chloe might have caused such a commotion just to get her newly arrived father's attention.

"*What* was on you?" Seth's gaze darted from his daughter to Olivia and back. Unable to verify her suspicion, Olivia pushed it to the back of her mind to contemplate later.

"A lightning bug," Olivia said, the merest hint of dryness in her voice as she opened her palm for just a second so that he could see the evidence in her hand. The bug spread its wings and flashed its light, but before it could escape she closed her fist around it again. "Chloe, if you'll give me your jar, I'll put this one in for you."

"That scared me to *death*," Chloe said with conviction, eagerly handing over the jar.

"Me too," Sara said, as Olivia unscrewed the lid and carefully scraped the bug off her palm so that it could join its fellows in the jar. "I thought something had you. A monster or something."

"In our yard?" Chloe's voice was scornful. Recovering with amazing quickness from her fright, she gave Sara a disdainful look. "What kind of monster could there be in our yard?"

"A yard monster?" Sara suggested.

"You mean like a giant frog?" Chloe asked, intrigued by the idea but still scornful.

"More like a giant lightning bug," Sara said. "Maybe the king of all lightning bugs, who's come down from the sky on this beautiful night to rescue the lightning bugs we've caught and wreak dreadful vengeance on us for catching them."

"Do lightning bugs even have kings?" Chloe asked doubtfully.

Sara nodded. "Sure they do, just like bees have queens. And this particular lightning bug king probably has fangs," Sara added with a delicious shudder, getting into the spirit of the story. "We've enraged the vampire lightning bug king, and he's come down to drink our blood," she finished dramatically, and giggled. "*That's* what I thought had you."

"You're making that up!" Chloe stared wide-eyed at Sara, who giggled. Suddenly Chloe giggled, too, and then both girls were laughing and scrunching up their shoulders and looking around with pleasurable fear for the imaginary creature.

"Here." Having screwed the lid back on, Olivia passed the jar back to Chloe. Chloe's quick passage from terrified victim to giggling coconspirator strengthened her suspicion that some of her terror, at least, had been put on for her father's benefit. "Next time a lightning bug lands on you, remember it won't hurt you and just brush it off. You scared me to death, screaming like that."

"I guess that makes it unanimous, then," Seth said under his breath, as the girls scampered off to resume their game with this new variation. "From the amount of noise she was making, I thought she was being murdered at the very least."

"Yes, well, your daughter obviously likes lightning bugs better in a jar than on her arm." Olivia glanced up at him. He was wearing khakis and a dark-colored polo shirt that contrasted nicely with his moon-silvered hair, and his eyes gleamed faintly as he watched the girls play. The attraction she had felt for him earlier had not faded, Olivia discovered, as she caught herself measuring her height against his — at six feet two, he was exactly a foot taller than she was — and admiring the breadth of his shoulders and the narrowness of his hips.

Dismayed, she switched her gaze to the girls, and switched her focus to them as well. They had played Beanie Babies for a while that afternoon, and then Olivia helped them build a fort on the upstairs gallery, where they held a tea party. After supper, they had watched a tape of *Beauty and the Beast* on the television in the den. Chloe had really been very good all day, and Olivia was beginning to feel almost fond of the child.

"*Your* daughter obviously has quite an imagination." From his tone, Olivia wasn't sure that it was exactly a compliment.

Olivia made a face at him. "Yes, she does, thank you very much. And we just finished reading *Bunnicula*, which accounts for the vampire lightning bug king, I think."

"*Bunnicula?*" He obviously had no idea what she was talking about. Olivia wasn't surprised. She had already figured out that he actually knew very little about his daughter.

"It's a children's book about a vampire bunny. I bet Chloe would love it, if she hasn't already read it."

He shook his head. "I have no idea. You'll have to ask her. Or check with Mother. She buys Chloe's books."

Olivia said nothing, although telling him that *he* should know more about his daughter than anyone else hovered on the tip of her tongue.

"Any problems this afternoon?" Seth asked after a moment, glancing down at her, the question carefully casual. It was obvious that he was referring to problems with Chloe's behavior, and Olivia found herself wondering again about the state of their relationship. Clearly he loved Chloe. She just as clearly loved him. But something was obviously not right between them.

"Chloe's been wonderful all day," Olivia replied, not pretending to misunderstand. Seth smiled wryly.

"I'm glad to hear it" was all he said.

"How's Big John?" Olivia changed the subject. Seth had been gone since just after church, and she assumed he'd been at the hospital for at least part of that time.

Seth was once again watching the girls, a slight frown on his face. He slapped absently at his bare forearm — Olivia suspected a mosquito — then glanced at her again. "No change to speak of. He's still unconscious, still on a respirator. Charlie says every day he hangs on his chances improve, though." His gaze slid the length of her body, which was clad in cutoffs, a red tank top, and her Keds, and lingered for a moment before returning to her face. "You're going to get eaten alive out here, dressed like that."

Olivia shook her head, smiling a little. "Sara and Chloe and I are wearing so much insect repellent that we're slimy with it. Don't forget that I know what these mosquitoes are like: I lived here as a little girl."

"I don't forget, believe me," Seth said, his gaze running over her body once more. Olivia was suddenly conscious that the raggedy fringe of her cutoffs ended at midthigh, and her tank top, besides being skimpy, clung. For a second she thought that Seth was looking at her breasts, and her breathing suspended. Then, before she could be sure, he turned abruptly away, heading toward the parking area. "I've brought David home with me. And Keith. They flew into Baton Rouge this morning and took a taxi to the hospital. They'll be spending the night here. Come and say hello."

He spoke over his shoulder.

"I'm glad David came." Keeping one eye on

the girls, Olivia trailed him to the parking area, where the single yellowish bug light on the far side of the garage revealed Callie just stepping back from an embrace with a tall, well-built man in a pale sport coat and dark slacks. Immediately Callie turned to another man, shorter, stockier, but dressed similarly to and standing beside the first, and hugged him.

"Big John's his father," Seth said with a shrug that implied *no matter what*, then advanced on the group. "I told you Olivia was home." Seth spoke to the newcomers as he and Olivia reached them.

The taller of the two men turned to Olivia, smiling. In height and build he resembled Seth, but his face was square rather than angular and his blunter features reminded Olivia of Big John. He was about sixty years old, and had the wrinkles and incipient jowls to prove it. His hair was still dark and thick — Olivia wondered if it was dyed — and he sported a neatly trimmed black mustache. This was Seth's uncle David, whom she had met perhaps half a dozen times in her life.

Olivia returned his smile.

"Well, hello, Olivia!" David greeted her jovially. "The last time I saw you, you were — what? Twelve years old? At Mother's funeral, I believe it was."

Murmuring assent, Olivia submitted to a quick embrace, and they exchanged air kisses in the general vicinity of each other's cheeks. Then

192

David gestured at his companion. "You remember Keith Sayres, of course?"

Certainly Olivia remembered Keith Sayres, although she had met him only twice before. The last time had been when David brought his live-in companion to his mother's funeral. The resulting explosion had been unforgettable. Big John had nearly gone off into an apoplexy at the idea that his gay son would so publicly flaunt his homosexuality, and Belinda, taking her father's part, had ranted on and on for days about how reprehensible it was of David to bring his "friend" to such a solemn family occasion. "For he only did it to get back at Daddy, you know," Olivia had overheard her tell Callie at the time. "He hates Daddy, just like Daddy hates him."

Oh, yes, Olivia remembered Keith Sayres.

"How are you?" she said cordially to Keith, and they did the hug and air kiss thing.

"Worried about David because of his dad, but otherwise fine," Keith replied, stepping back from the embrace and smiling down at her. "It's a shame that it takes things like this to get families together, isn't it?"

"It certainly is," Callie answered, and then at Callie's urging they all went inside. Left to gather up the children, Olivia finally managed to get them inside. Everyone was sitting around the kitchen table when the three of them entered, Sara and Chloe with well-filled lightning bug lanterns in hand. Declining offers of coffee and cake or a sandwich, Olivia turned Chloe and her precious lantern over to Martha, and took Sara upstairs for bath and bed. Sara's lids were drooping and she was yawning by the time she was in bed, but she still begged for a bedtime story. Olivia settled down on the bed beside her, listened to her prayers, and then told her about a fairy house of mud and rocks she had once made in the front yard. Later that night, she had risen from her bed, looked out her bedroom window, seen lightning bugs disappearing inside the house she had made, and decided they were fairies. She had crept from her room and . . .

Sara was asleep.

Smiling, Olivia got up, tucked the covers more closely around Sara's shoulders, and, instead of joining the others downstairs, headed for the bathroom for her own bath. The bathroom overlooked the back of the house, and while she was in the tub she thought she heard one or more cars pull up. Finishing her bath, she brushed her teeth, smoothed moisturizing lotion onto her face, and freed her hair from the high ponytail she had worn in the tub. Running a brush through the tangled strands, she peeped out the window and saw that, actually, three cars were parked in the parking area. One was Mallory's Miata, and she thought the white Lincoln must belong to Ira Hayes, but she wasn't sure about the ownership of the other. The mystery was solved as she headed back toward her bedroom and encountered Carl walking toward her from the direction of the stairs.

"What are you doing here?" she asked, surprised. She was wearing her own robe, a knee-length zip-front of floral cotton, over a sleeveless pink nylon nightgown, but with Carl looking at her like he was she suddenly felt less than adequately dressed. She had not expected to encounter anyone, much less Carl, in the hallway that led to her bedroom. With Big John in the hospital, she and Sara were the only ones sleeping in this wing of the house.

"I came up to see if I could talk you into coming down again," Carl said easily. "Everybody's here, and we're havin' a big ole family party downstairs. When Seth said you'd gone to bed, I just thought I'd come along and fetch you back down."

He grinned engagingly. Six feet tall, stocky but not fat, with dark brown hair, his father's hazel eyes, and a warm personality, Carl was an attractive man. As that thought occurred to her, Olivia's eyes brightened, and she looked him over almost hopefully. But attractive man or not, her mind refused to see him as anything other than her occasional childhood playmate and ultimate pesky cousin. It was probably just as well, she thought resignedly. Getting excited about Carl posed just about the same problems as did getting excited about Seth, with the addition of Carl's witch of a mother's reaction thrown in. Just imagining how Belinda would be likely to respond to any hanky-panky between Carl and herself made Olivia smile. It would *almost* be worth it.

Carl's face lit up at her smile. Seeing that, Olivia shook her head at him.

"I'm not dressed, and I'm tired. I think I'll go on to bed. But thanks for thinking of me, though."

"You sure?" Carl sounded disappointed.

Olivia nodded. After a couple more attempts to persuade her, Carl gave up and headed back toward the stairs. Olivia checked on Sara, then went to bed.

As she drifted off to sleep in the room next to Sara's, a memory of the way Seth had looked at her in the backyard tonight swam through Olivia's head. Just remembering the way his eyes had run over her body made her breathing quicken. If he were to touch her . . . She shivered at the thought. That woke her up, and, awake, she was horrified at the direction her subconscious had taken. She absolutely, positively refused to have sexual fantasies about Seth.

In the end, unable to fall back asleep without uncomfortable images of Seth filling her mind, Olivia resorted as she sometimes did to counting her blessings: God thank you for Sara; God thank you for my health; God thank you for the roof over my head and the food in my stomach and my warm bed; God thank you for Sara. . . .

With a small smile curling her lips, she finally drifted off to sleep, only to be awakened what could have been anything from minutes to hours later by a piercing scream.

chapter 20

Sara! Olivia came awake instantly, knowing without knowing how she knew it that the scream had come from her daughter. Throwing the covers aside, leaping from her bed, she ran for Sara's room, thankful that she knew the way so well that she could get there blindfolded, because their section of the house was now so dark that it was *like* being blindfolded as her bare feet stumbled over the transitions between the resilient wool surfaces of the Oriental carpets in her room, the hall, and Sara's room, and the buffer zone of the slickly smooth hardwood floor in between.

"Sara! *Sara!*" Flinging open the door to her daughter's chamber, Olivia saw in a glance that the bedside light she had left on was out. She saw, too, that the curtains over one window were slightly parted, allowing a shaft of moonlight into the room. By its light she could see Sara sitting bolt upright in bed, the bedclothes puddled around her waist.

As was her habit, she had checked the window locks before leaving Sara to sleep. Had she not pulled the curtains completely closed again, allowing that shaft of moonlight to enter? She didn't remember seeing moonlight when she'd taken a last look back at Sara after turning off the light — but maybe the moon just hadn't risen sufficiently then.

"Sara!" Olivia flipped on the light switch by the door. The room was flooded with warm yellow light from the fixture overhead. A quick, comprehensive glance saw no sign of injury to Sara. Olivia was relieved, so relieved, to discover her daughter apparently unharmed that for an instant she sagged against the doorjamb. Her heart was pounding wildly, her breathing came in sharp gasps, and her big toe ached where she had stubbed it on something. None of it mattered: Sara was safe. Although what she imagined could have possibly happened to Sara in this secure environment, she couldn't have said.

"Mommy!" Voice shaking, Sara stretched out her arms toward her as if she were a very little girl again. As Olivia hurried to her daughter's side she saw that Sara's face was as white as the sheet upon which she sat, and her dark eyes were huge with shock. "Oh, Mommy!"

Sara scrambled for the side of the bed even as Olivia reached the edge. They wrapped their arms about each other, and Olivia sat down on the mattress. The clock on the nightstand read 4:28 A.M. Sara's pink Barbie nightgown was damp with sweat.

"There was something — it was standing at the foot of my bed!" Sara was nearly incoherent as she pressed her face into the curve between Olivia's neck and shoulder. Olivia tightened her hold as an unexpected chill raced down her spine. Something — at the foot of Sara's bed — at the foot of *her* old bed, in her old room . . . ?

"Something was standing at the foot of your bed?" Olivia tried hard to ignore the disorienting sense of having played out this scene before. But she couldn't resist glancing at the rocker in the corner, the rocker where memory had resurrected her mother, and where, she realized with some deep instinct that was surer even than conscious memory, her mother used to sit while she slept. *Why* had her mother sat with her as she slept? Hazy memories teased the outer reaches of Olivia's mind, but she could not quite seem to access them. They were there and yet . . .

"It was big — it had this big, bald head — it was *looking* at me . . ."

"What was, baby?" Olivia let go of her own thoughts to concentrate on comforting her daughter.

"The thing at the foot of the bed. It — it was wearing something dark, like a cloak, or — or something, and when it saw me looking at it — it — it smiled — and — and it had fangs!" Sara shuddered at the memory.

"Fangs?" Olivia questioned, holding Sara close. Strangely enough, the mention of fangs was reassuring. Whatever fuzzy remnants of her own childhood terrors might be lurking at the edges of her consciousness, she was almost certain they did not include fangs.

"I think it was the vampire lightning bug king!" Sara disclosed with a sob, and shuddered in her mother's arms.

Olivia took a deep breath. Her own sense of horror was fading. The vampire lightning bug king? It rang no bells with her psyche. Suddenly she remembered. "From your game?"

Sara nodded, her face hidden, her arms tight around Olivia's neck.

"Sara." Olivia kissed Sara's averted cheek. "Baby, I think you just had a bad dream."

Sara shook her head. "It was real. I woke up and it was standing there. The room was dark — you promised you'd leave a night-light on, Mom! — but it was standing in the light from the window. I could see it! I could see it looking at me, and I could see its fangs when it smiled, and then when I screamed it turned and went toward the window and — and disappeared!"

"It was a nightmare, baby." The relief she felt as her certainty grew that her child's scream had been due to a nightmare and nothing more was palpable. Olivia squeezed Sara tightly and smoothed her hair back from her face. When Sara looked up at her Olivia gave her a reassuring smile.

"Let me check the light," Olivia said, easing Sara's arms from around her neck. "I *did* leave it on. Something must have happened."

The small bedside lamp was of white china with an inexpensive white pleated shade. Leaning sideways, Olivia reached under the shade for the switch and pressed it. Nothing happened. Disentangling herself from Sara, she stood up and looked behind the night table at the cord. The lamp was plugged in. Finally she grasped the bulb, checked to see that it was tight in its socket, then unplugged the cord and unscrewed the bulb, all under Sara's unblinking gaze.

Finally she raised the bulb to her ear and shook it. The ensuing rattle confirmed what she had suspected.

"The bulb's burned out." Olivia was cheerfully matter-of-fact by this time. The sick dread that had threatened to overtake her when she'd considered the possibility that something — some*one* — actually *had* been in her daughter's room had faded. She put the bulb down and moved toward the parted curtains. "Let me check the window."

Pulling the curtains farther apart, she visually checked the latch. It was an old-fashioned brass hook-and-eye latch, and it was firmly locked, just as it had been earlier when she had checked it. Olivia touched it to make sure.

It felt secure, and she didn't see how anyone could have gone out the window and then locked it from the gallery. If anyone had gone out the door when Sara had screamed, Olivia might not have seen them because of the darkness of the hall. But she would have heard them, felt them, known they were there. It had taken her only seconds to reach her own bedroom door. There had been no time for an intruder to get away.

"The window's locked," she said. To make doubly certain, she checked the latch on the other window again, too. It, too, was locked.

"It was just a bad dream?" Sara quavered uncertainly. Some of the color had returned to her cheeks but she was still a far cry from her normal buoyant self.

"That's what it was." Olivia nodded as she twitched the curtains back into place. She moved over to the white-painted chest between the windows and extracted one of Sara's nightgowns from a drawer. "Here, baby, change your nightgown. Yours is damp."

"I sweated." Sara caught the nightgown Olivia tossed to her, pulled the one she was wearing over her head, and donned the fresh one. It, too, was a pink Barbie nightie — Olivia had gotten a half dozen on sale for $3.99 each at Kmart — identical to the one it replaced. Sara threw the damp nightgown to her mother, who placed it in the mesh bag she kept for dirty clothes.

"Mommy — can I sleep with you for the rest of the night? I'm still scared."

Since reaching the advanced age of eight in April, Sara only ever called her Mommy when she was in trouble of one sort or another. *Mom* was the cool, preferred term.

"Sure thing, pumpkin." Olivia would have suggested it if Sara had not. As a single parent, she worked hard at not being overprotective, or overpossessive, and not babying Sara too much. Consequently, her child had had her own room and her own bed from infancy, and even when Sara was at the stage when she persisted in getting out of her bed and climbing in with her mother every night, Olivia had patiently, night after night, waited until the child had fallen asleep beside her, and then gotten up to carry her back to her own bed. Not because she didn't want Sara with her — she did — but because she felt it was better for Sara. But on special occasions, such as when Sara was sick or upset or they just needed each other more than usual, she let Sara sleep with her. Those were the nights when Olivia slept best of all, because she knew then, with absolute certainty, that Sara was safe.

It had never before occurred to her to wonder why she didn't entirely feel that Sara was safe when she was in her own bed.

There was something about a child's being alone in bed. . . .

"Mom?"

Olivia realized that she had been standing beside the bed staring blankly into space for several seconds. Her daughter was looking at her with the beginnings of concern.

Olivia blinked. "I was just wondering whether

we ought to sleep in your bed, or mine."

"Yours," Sara said positively, and Olivia didn't disagree. She nodded and held out a hand to Sara, who scooted off the bed. They exited the room together, leaving the door open and the light on behind them. Certain as she was that there was nothing to be afraid of, Olivia still didn't want to turn out the only source of illumination in the whole pitch-black upstairs.

"Bathroom?" she asked, looking down at her daughter.

Sara nodded. They headed to the bathroom, then to Olivia's room. For no reason except that she just felt she wanted to, Olivia turned the lock on her bedroom door once they were inside, without letting Sara see. They got into bed, cuddling together in the middle of the mattress with the bedside lamp burning brightly, while Olivia told a very funny (and mostly invented) recollection from her childhood. Sara giggled herself breathless before finally falling asleep.

Then Olivia switched off the lamp, wrapped an arm around Sara, and tried to get back to sleep herself. But the niggling thought remained:

Had something — or someone — been in Sara's room?

Like the vampire lightning bug king? On that absurd note, Olivia dismissed the suspicion as ridiculous. Sara had had a bad dream. Nothing more.

God thank you for Sara. . . .

Just before she dozed off Olivia thought she heard a floorboard creak in the hall. Her eyes popped open, and she was instantly alert. But strain though she might, she heard nothing more. Old houses always had creaks . . . didn't they?

She lay awake for a long time, listening. Finally, with her arm curved protectively around her daughter, Olivia at last fell into an uneasy sleep.

A long time after they were gone, after listening to them go to the bathroom, then enter the room next door and settle down for the night, he took one last peek to make sure the coast was clear and slid out from under the bed.

That had been a close call. He was rusty. It had been a long time. Too long.

Good thing mommies never thought to look in closets or under beds.

That thought made him smile. He felt good. Surprisingly good, really. Alive, and sharp, and ready for more.

His plan might have been foiled tonight, but his appetite had been whetted.

He would be seeing little Miss Sara again.

Very soon.

chapter 21

Grand Isle, Louisiana — July 17, 1974

"Daddy, could you stay in just till I go to sleep, please? If I'm already asleep when you go out I won't be scared." Maggie Monroe's voice was softly pleading. Dressed in purple baby doll pajamas with little pink flowers all over them, her legs as skinny as a crane's below the ruffled panties she wore, and her hair as yellow and frizzy as a dandelion's, she was standing in the doorway of their rented vacation cottage two blocks from the beach. Her father, Vince, was already halfway across the shabby screened porch. He was going out, he'd said, and she should go on to bed. Ordinarily she would never dream of arguing with him. She was half afraid of him at the best of times. But she was more afraid of being left by herself in this tumbledown shack after dark.

"Gawd-damn, Maggie, you're nine years old.

Plenty old enough to stay by yourself whilst I go out for a while." Her dad was irritated, but not yet mad, and he actually paused to look back over his shoulder at her.

Prodded by the shadows that were creeping over the scruffy patch of grass in front of the cottage and her dread of being left alone as twilight deepened into full dark, Maggie swallowed and tried again.

"Please, Daddy? It won't take me long to go to sleep, I promise. I'm real sleepy already."

"If I'da known you was gonna need a babysitter, I wouldn't've taken you on no vacation." He scowled at her, and Maggie shrank inside herself. He was starting to get mad, she could tell. "You go on to bed now, and I'll be back directly, you hear?"

With that he pushed on out the screen door, which banged shut behind him. Maggie stood watching forlornly as he climbed into his bright blue Chevy Impala and roared off. Knowing her daddy like she did, Maggie figured he probably wouldn't be home before dawn, and when he did get home he'd be drunk and mean with it.

Oh, why had her mama made such a stink about his never spending time with her anymore? That's what had brought this whole blamed thing on. Her mama had screamed it at her daddy in front of the judge at their divorce, and her daddy had called later on the telephone and told her mama he was taking Maggie somewhere special over summer vacation, to a house on the beach that he had rented just for the two of them so they could spend some time together, so she could just quit bitching about his never doing anything nice for his daughter. He did, too. She just liked to bitch.

Mama had tried to take it back then, to say that Maggie couldn't go, but it was too late. The judge had ordered it. So Maggie had to go.

When he had come yesterday morning to pick her up, her mama and daddy had gotten into one of their screaming fights right in the yard in front of the neighbors. It had ended with her mama yelling thank God she'd finally had the sense to divorce him and kick him the hell out of her life. Her daddy had looked around at all the nearby houses with their windows open and people listening behind them, said "Bitch," under his breath, and gotten in his car. Then her mama had looked at Maggie, given her a kiss on the cheek, and told her to take real good care of herself because her daddy never would. Then Maggie had had to get in the car, and her daddy had driven them away.

To this shack, where he'd left her alone last night as well. Look, he'd said, it was his vacation, too, and he didn't want to hear her whining about it.

Now the yard was getting darker, gloomy almost. Maggie shivered and went back inside the cottage and carefully shut and locked the door. If she got into bed now, before it got too dark, she might be able to fall asleep before it was full night and then she wouldn't have to see it and know she was alone in it.

Maggie scurried to the bedroom — there was only one bedroom, so her daddy slept on the fold-out couch — and jumped into bed, huddling down and pulling the covers up over her head. Then she realized that it would be dark soon and she hadn't turned on any lights. So she hopped out of bed and ran from room to room, flicking on switches until the three-room cottage blazed with wattage. Finally she got back into bed, pulled the covers over her head, curled into a little ball, and prayed to go to sleep.

The bed smelled musty, and sort of like somebody had peed on it a long time ago. What with the bad smell, and the heat, and the air conditioner in the kitchen not working right, she pretty soon started to feel sick to her stomach. But she would have to get up and go into the bathroom if she was going to throw up, and she was too scared to do that, so she just lay where she was and started imagining, started thinking about herself as a beautiful princess named Allyson who lived in an enchanted castle on a faraway isle and had a unicorn named Dazzle for her best friend.

It was her favorite fantasy when she was scared or lonesome, and pretty soon, as Princess Allyson, she was riding Dazzle through the clouds, and that was how she fell asleep.

Maggie didn't know what time it was when she woke up, but she knew it was a long time later because her dad was home. He'd opened the bedroom door and turned out the light, and now he was coming across the floor to check on her.

"Daddy?" Blinking, she pulled the covers away from her face, glad to be able to breathe in air that didn't smell so bad at last. Her dad was right by the bed, looking down at her. Scooting her butt around on the mattress, she started to sit up — and then her dad swooped down on her, jamming a wet cloth that smelled sort of like gasoline over her nose and mouth while his other hand pressed hard against the back of her head so she couldn't get away. She gagged and tried to fight him off, and as she did she looked up and saw that it wasn't her daddy doing it to her at all, but a stranger.

Stark terror released a rush of adrenaline that gave her the strength to kick and flail.

It wasn't enough. In less than a minute Maggie's eyes rolled back in her head and she went limp.

Stealing little girls out of their bedrooms was the best, the ultimate thrill. They had usually just had a bath, and they smelled sweet and clean. He liked that. Plus, inside their own houses they thought they were safe, their parents thought they were safe, and he got off on imagining how horrified the mommies were in the morning when they got up to discover their babies missing. The last one, he had seen her face on a milk carton a couple of weeks ago. HAVE YOU SEEN THIS CHILD? the caption read.

That had made him chuckle. Oh, yes, he'd seen her, all right. But he didn't think he'd be calling the 800 number anytime soon.

This one looked like she might be a fighter. If so, he was going to enjoy her even more. Of course, once she woke up and saw where she was and what he meant to do with her the fight would go out of her pretty damn fast. Still, it was going to be fun to watch her face while she figured it out. He might keep this one awhile, in the place he had rigged up. Keep her until he couldn't stand it anymore, until he just couldn't hold out another minute.

But it would be fun to fight the urge for as long as he could.

Fun for him, that is. He chuckled as he drove along the interstate toward his destination. His toy was locked in a dog cage in the back of the van. From the sounds she was making, she was already starting to regain consciousness.

"Mama . . ." she moaned.

Sweetheart, he thought, you won't ever see your mama again.

He smiled with an anticipation that was almost orgasmic. Then he had a thought that caused the smile to ripen into a full-throated chuckle. The white panel van he was driving was perfectly plain so as not to attract undue attention.

In the interests of truth in advertising, maybe he should hire somebody to paint a smiley face on it with the legend MONSTERS R US.

Would that bring the kiddies running, or what?

chapter 22

What was left of the week passed swiftly for Olivia.

Lamar Lennig called twice, once to invite her to a movie in Baton Rouge and the second time to ask her to lunch or dinner or anything else she cared to do, as long as she did it with him. Olivia turned him down both times. An old friend of hers from St. Theresa's, LeeAnn Hobart, now James, who was living in LaAngelle as the wife of the pharmacist, of all things, called, then came by at Olivia's invitation to reminisce over past, wilder times. From that visit, Olivia gleaned that the news of her return to LaAngelle Plantation was the talk of the town.

The rest of the time she spent with Sara, and getting reacquainted with her family. One or more of them — usually more — dropped by for dinner nearly every night, so, except for the occasional personality clash, evenings were generally merry affairs.

Callie's chemotherapy regimen called for three weeks on, one week off, for six months. Since this was an off week, Callie stayed pretty much close to home, trying to gain back what strength she could before, in her word, they started dripping poison into her veins again. Seth, on the other hand, was hardly ever home. Olivia assumed he was dividing his time between the Boatworks and the hospital, but she didn't know for sure. David and Keith were around, having settled into the *garçonnière* for what David described as an "indefinite period." What that actually meant, Keith said candidly when David wasn't present, was until Big John either died or was pronounced out of danger. Since David no longer participated in the day-to-day running of his restaurant, a lengthy absence would do it no harm.

Chloe was away from the house a lot, too, involved with her own activities from early morning to late afternoon. She had swim practice and tennis practice and piano lessons and play dates, all prearranged. At Callie's insistence, Sara was invited to join in the play dates — Callie was sure Sara would love Chloe's friends! — but Sara privately begged her mother not to make her go. She always preferred not to meet strangers unless she had to. Olivia saw no reason to force her daughter into trying to make friends with the local little girls, given the fact that their presence at LaAngelle Plantation was to be so brief, so Sara stayed home.

In the evenings Sara and Chloe played together — usually Beanie Babies or a video game on the TV set in Chloe's room. The rain that had been intermittent since Monday precluded any more lightning bug hunts, which in Olivia's opinion was just as well. Sara was back to comfortably sleeping alone in Olivia's old room, and Olivia wasn't anxious for a repeat of the vampire lightning bug king episode. It had been too unnerving for both of them.

Even if it was just a bad dream.

Chloe had the occasional unpleasant outburst, but since Sara seemed ready to do most anything Chloe asked, the girls got along fairly well.

Olivia and Sara spent the days together very happily, exploring outside when the weather permitted, reading when it rained, going into town for an ice cream and to view Olivia's girlhood haunts in Callie's Lincoln, which they borrowed, and basically just hanging out.

During most of the year, Olivia felt guilty because, as a single working mother, the amount of time she had to spend with Sara was limited. Even when they were together after Olivia got off from work and picked Sara up at the neighbor's where Sara stayed after school, there was supper to be made and homework to be done and baths to be taken and clothes and lunches to be prepared for the next day — in other words, a whole litany of chores. What Olivia craved most in the world, always, was time. Unpressured time to just be with her daughter. So being free to wander and read and talk with Sara was the vacation she needed.

The plan was that she and Sara would return to Houston on Friday. Olivia had bought round-trip tickets on Greyhound that required them to leave New Roads at six A.M. They would arrive back in Houston late that night, pick up her car, which they had left in the bus station's parking lot, and drive home to their apartment. That would give them the weekend to recover from their trip and do the necessary shopping and planning for Sara's opening day at school the following Wednesday. Olivia had to be at work at eight A.M. Monday morning.

Thus would life get back to normal. With one exception. Now that the connection with her family had been reestablished, and especially given Callie's and Big John's illnesses, Olivia meant to come visit again as often as she could. LaAngelle Plantation was no longer a dream of faraway places and better times with which to beguile a little girl to sleep. It was, once again, simply home.

On Wednesday afternoon, Olivia and Sara came running back to the house through a sudden shower. The day had been so hot that even the raindrops felt warm as they struck Olivia's skin. The lawn seemed to steam. The air smelled of damp earth and honeysuckle. They'd been hunting for dropped peacock feathers because Sara was utterly enchanted by them, and, having already found four, she was bent on starting a collection. As they sprinted, laughing, hands clasped, heads ducked against the rain, up the front steps to the protection of the veranda, Callie and Keith called to them. Callie, in navy slacks and a short-sleeved print blouse, and Keith, in white slacks and a black T-shirt, were seated in the two white wicker rocking chairs near the swing that was the twin of the one on the upper gallery. Fifteen feet above them, the two ring-necked pheasants that Charlie had stuffed and hung from the ceiling twenty-five years before still winged their way skyward. On the floor between them, there was a big brown cardboard box.

"Come join us, you two," Callie invited, beckoning.

Uncomfortably damp and feeling slightly grubby in a rain-splattered yellow T-shirt and another pair of the cutoffs that she wore almost constantly when not at work (recycled from her worn-out jeans, they were the most economical of shorts), Olivia almost declined. But there was so little time left, and she had not said nearly everything she wanted to Callie. She therefore smiled assent and headed toward the others. Tugging on her mother's hand, Sara resisted. Olivia looked down at her questioningly.

"Can I go watch cartoons instead?" she whispered. A big satellite dish behind the *garçonnière* brought a dazzling array of programs into the house, including three channels of nonstop cartoons. Since they were not even able to afford basic cable in Houston, Sara was in TV lovers' heaven. Sometimes she would watch in Chloe's room with Chloe, or, if Chloe was not home, on the big set in the den.

"Sure, baby." Olivia let go of Sara's hand, and with a quick, grateful smile for her mother Sara scampered into the house.

"Looking at pictures?" Olivia approached Callie and Keith. It was fairly obvious, from the snapshots they were exclaiming over and passing back and forth, that they were, indeed, doing just that. With David spending a lot of time at the hospital, and Keith, like Olivia, decidedly persona non grata there, Keith had a lot of time on his hands. He had been spending most of it with Callie, with whom he got on like a house on fire. She even referred to him, in and out of his presence and only a little jokingly, as her new favorite sister-in-law. He seemed to take that as a compliment, and even returned the favor.

"Oh, Olivia, I kept these for you," Callie said, looking up as Olivia reached her chair. She gestured at the box at her feet. "I thought you'd want to have them someday."

Glancing down, Olivia saw that her aunt was holding out a snapshot for her to view. The picture showed a pretty dark-haired woman smiling as she crouched behind a cherubic little girl in a ruffle-bottomed playsuit. The little girl was clutching a yellow-haired doll that was nearly as big as she was.

The doll was Victoria Elizabeth.

Olivia realized that she was looking at a photograph of herself with her mother.

chapter 23

For a moment it was as if she had inadvertently stepped onto a carousel and was being spun back through time. Olivia felt light-headed, nauseated almost. The photograph in Callie's hand blurred until she couldn't make out the images, and then it seemed as if she were looking *out* from the picture, as if she had become the round-faced little girl and was looking out at her adult self.

She could almost smell the scent of her mother's White Shoulders perfume.

"You look just like Selena," Callie said with satisfaction, her attention on the print in her hand rather than her niece. "I don't think there's a hair's worth of difference between you. And Sara is going to look just like the both of you when she's grown."

"Amazing resemblance," Keith agreed, looking up at Olivia and then back down at the picture in his hand.

Olivia did not want to take the picture. She did not want to see, to remember. Her instinct was to back away, to refuse to look, to do whatever she had to do to keep from touching the photo that Callie was holding out to her. But that was silly — worse than silly. It would be a repudiation of her mother, and of herself, and by extension of Sara.

"It *is* amazing," Olivia agreed in a hollow voice, and accepted the snapshot from Callie. It was a Polaroid, taken with an instant camera, and the colors were starting to fade a bit. The paper edges felt as stiff and slick as plastic between her fingers. Unable to bring herself to look directly at the mother and daughter who'd been caught laughing into the camera with no knowledge of what the future would bring, she turned the picture over.

On the back, on the white bottom border of the photograph, a line was written in black ink. The small, precise letters were heavily slanted to the right. *Livvy and me,* it said, followed by a date: June 13, 1976.

It was her mother's handwriting. Olivia knew it as well as she knew her own name.

There was a sudden roaring in her ears, and for a moment Olivia thought she might faint. Grasping one of the pair of spindles at the top of Callie's rocker, she held on, grimly determined not to be such a fool.

What on earth was wrong with her? Hadn't she

always yearned for mementos of her mother? One of her greatest regrets had always been that she had taken nothing but a suitcase full of clothes with her when she had eloped with Newall. She had left everything behind, all her possessions, from the stuffed animals on her bed to her high school ring. They hadn't seemed important at the time — being with Newall had been the important thing.

Dear God, how stupid she had been!

But there had never been mementos of her mother in any case, not even when LaAngelle Plantation had been her home. Everything, from photographs of Selena to her clothes, had disappeared almost immediately after she had died.

Put away so the healing could begin. Olivia remembered hearing that explanation from someone at the time, although she couldn't remember who had said it, or the context. Perhaps she had asked a question. She didn't know.

Had she, Selena's daughter, the laughing, chubby little girl being hugged by her obviously loving mother in the picture, had she healed? Until returning to LaAngelle Plantation, Olivia would have said yes with no hesitation at all.

Now she knew that she would have been wrong. The wound had healed over, maybe, but it hadn't healed.

Maybe she needed to look at the pictures, to talk about her mother, to feel the reality of her life and death, for the true healing to begin.

"Are you okay, Olivia?" Keith asked, looking at

her with gentle concern.

"I'm fine. I just didn't know that pictures like this still existed. I thought they'd all been thrown away, or something." Olivia took a deep breath, and turned the snapshot over, forcing herself to look at it objectively. The resemblance *was* uncanny, she thought. She could almost be looking at a picture of herself with Sara as a three-year-old.

"Oh, honey, do you think I would have let anybody throw things like these pictures away?" Callie asked reproachfully. "They're yours. They've been in the attic all these years. And your things are up there, too: everything of yours, everything that was in your room the night you left us. It's all in boxes. I packed it away myself."

"You did?" Olivia looked up from the picture then to smile a little shakily at her aunt. "I can't believe you did, after I — well, after I left the way I did. But thank you. And thank you for saving these pictures of my mother." She glanced down at the snapshot in her hand, then back at Callie. "I think I — needed to see them."

"Olivia, why don't you sit down here and go through these with Callie?" Keith stood up, vacating his rocking chair. When Olivia started to protest, he waved his hand at her dismissively. "Do you think I'm going to let *Martha*, fine woman though she certainly is, prepare our meal? When I am a culinary *artiste?*"

He said it jokingly, but Olivia got the sense

222

that he meant what he said. She remembered that he had trained as a chef, and had gotten to know David when the two men, one a waiter and one a cook, had worked together at a New Orleans restaurant some thirty years before. Waving her into his chair, Keith disappeared inside. Olivia was left to do something she was not sure she wanted to do: sink down in his abandoned rocker, and pore over a box of old photographs, with their accompanying memories of her mother.

She wasn't ready to remember. Not when just looking at a picture of her mother and herself together made her feel physically ill.

And yet, as if compelled to do so, she was already reaching down into the box and picking out a silver-framed, five-by-seven portrait from the jumble of photos. A wedding picture: her mother in a form-fitting ivory suit, a bouquet of pink orchids and freesias in one white-gloved hand. Beside her stood James Archer, tall and fair-haired and handsome in his dark blue suit, an orchid in his lapel, beaming broadly into the camera. At their feet was plopped a baby in a ruffly pink dress, sitting on her diapered bottom with white booties on her feet and a wreath of tiny pink flowers in her dark, feathery hair.

She was that baby.

Olivia remembered with a flash of blinding clarity that this picture had once sat in pride of place on the nightstand beside her mother's bed, and felt dizzy again.

"Did you know that Selena was working at the Boatworks when James met her?" Callie asked conversationally.

Unable to speak, Olivia shook her head. The picture felt increasingly heavy in her hand. She laid it faceup across her lap and rested her head back against the uneven weave of the chair. She remembered — she remembered that bedroom. It was the room across the hall from her bedroom, her old bedroom, that is, the room Sara was sleeping in now. Her mother had slept across the hall with her husband, and she, Olivia, would run in there most mornings and jump into bed between them. Her mother would hug her, and her stepfather would laugh. . . .

The walls had been painted pink. Pink was her own favorite color. And Sara's. It must have been her mother's, too, for her to paint a room she shared with her husband in such a feminine hue.

"She was. She was from Bayou Grand Caillou, you know."

Callie was frowning at her. Olivia's face was turned toward her, and she could see her aunt perfectly well, but — it was almost as if she were looking at her through glass. Olivia continued to rest back in the chair, her hands, limp in her lap, just touching the edges of the picture. She felt strange, immobile, as if even the smallest movement would require too much effort, and she guessed her face must have paled.

"Do you want to hear the whole story, Olivia? Or would you rather not?"

Making a great effort, Olivia moved, glancing down at the photograph in her lap. Her mother looked so young in that picture, younger by several years than she was herself. She knew so little about her. . . .

Livvy and me. The words written on the back of that snapshot swam through her mind. They sounded so homey, so cozy.

Life with her mother had been cozy. They had shared laughter, and warmth, and love.

Olivia's heart ached suddenly. Although specific memories were lost to her, the emotions that went with them were coming through loud and clear.

"Of course I want to hear," Olivia said. To her own ears her voice sounded hoarse. But she needed to know. It was suddenly very important to her that she know everything that there was to know.

Callie nodded, her expression sympathetic. "I never knew your natural father, but Selena always said he was part Houma, and that he had worked as a shrimper until he was killed in some kind of boat accident a couple of months before you were born. Your mother was left with nothing, no money, no house, no job, no family she could turn to. She came to LaAngelle because a friend of hers worked as an upholsterer at the Boatworks. The girl asked Big John to give her friend Selena Chenier a job, and he did. My husband, Michael, had been dead for several years by that time, and it had fallen to James, as the next brother in line, to take over as general manager of the Boatworks. But Big John was still very much hands-on then, and it was he who hired Selena. In any case, James was instantly smitten. He didn't care that she was pregnant with another man's baby, he didn't care that his mother — forgive me, dear! — considered her unsuitable marriage material for an Archer, he didn't care that he was so much older. He was head over heels. After the baby — you! — were born, he kept going round to the little house on Cocodrie Street where Selena and you lived with an older woman who rented out rooms, bringing her things for the baby — you! — and trying to get her to go out with him. Finally she did, and they got married three months later." Callie shook her head. "I thought his mother — Marguerite — was going to have a stroke. Well, you know how she was. So proud! I have to tell you that Marguerite and Belinda were not very nice to your mother then, or, to tell the truth, later. I've always thought Belinda was jealous of Selena. She was so young and pretty, you know! So — fiery. I think that's what James loved best about her. She had an unquenchable spirit. They were very happy after they married. She doted on you, and James treated you like his own child. When she died, he was inconsolable." Callie broke off and glanced at Olivia rather guiltily, as if she thought she might have said too much. After a moment she went on, in a different, almost apologetic tone. "He changed so much after she died, you know. I don't know if you remember him like he was before, but afterward — well, he just withdrew. I always thought he wanted to die, too, so he could be with Selena again. And, a few years later, he did."

Callie paused, biting her lip. Her gaze met Olivia's. "Olivia — I always felt bad that I didn't do more for you after Selena died. But Marguerite was alive then — your grandmother! — and I just couldn't stand up to her. Well, you know how she was! She wanted to raise you up as her idea of a lady, and she talked James into going along with whatever she wanted. James was her son, you know, and after Selena died he never again strayed across the boundaries she set for him. They were too strict with you, and . . . and not very loving, I guess. After Selena — well, you were the sun and the moon and the stars to your mother. It must have been very hard for you to adjust. Thinking back on it now, well, I feel bad that I didn't try harder to help you, that's all."

"Please don't feel bad." Olivia reached for her aunt's hand. Callie's skin felt dry and thin, almost like crepe paper. "You were always so kind to me, even when I didn't deserve it. I know you did the best you could."

"I should have done more. I wish now I had." Callie smiled wryly, her hand gripping Olivia's. "That's one of the things about having cancer, you know. It makes you think back over your life, think about what you did, and what you didn't do. The things you didn't do hurt the worst, I think. I should have married again, I should have had more children. And I should have done better by you."

"Aunt Callie . . ." At the regret in the older woman's voice, Olivia's hand tightened around hers. "Sometimes I think things work out the way they're supposed to no matter what we do. If I hadn't been so rebellious, I wouldn't have run off with Newall. And if I hadn't run off with Newall, I wouldn't have Sara. And Sara is the best thing that ever happened to me in my life. I don't regret her, or anything that brought her to me, not for one instant."

"I'm glad to hear you say that, dear. It makes me feel better." Callie smiled a little tremulously. Her eyes were bright with unshed tears.

A white Mazda Miata, its convertible top up, burst past the shrouding trees and hedges at the base of the lawn, and sped up the driveway with a swoosh of tires. As it passed them to disappear behind the house, Callie blinked, sniffed, released Olivia's hand, and stood up, suddenly brisk. "Well, there's certainly nothing to be gained by making ourselves maudlin, is there? Here's Mallory, with Chloe. I think I'll just go in and see how the shopping expedition went. You come on in when you're ready."

"I will." Olivia stayed in her rocker, watching as Callie went inside. She had wondered, since finding out about Callie's illness, how much of her cheerful let's-get-on-with-it attitude was assumed. Now that she had been given a glimpse into the well of fear and pain and regret concealed beneath Callie's prosaic manner, she could only respect her aunt more. Callie was coping with cancer the way she had coped with every other blow she had suffered in life, by simply keeping on keeping on. In Olivia's opinion, that was courage.

The rain had stopped, although thunderheads still loomed like great purple mountains in the sky. The sound of water dripping from the eaves was soothing. Insects hummed, birds called. Silvery puddles lay amidst puffs of steam on the lawn. The peacocks emerged from the shrubbery near the bluff to pick their way across the grass, no doubt greedy for the worms the rain always forced from the ground in droves. Olivia watched the birds idly, her fingers once again resting on the glass-fronted picture in her lap. The gentle creak of the rocking chair as she moved back and forth brought with it a feeling of peace.

In a moment, she would turn her attention to the contents of the box at her side. For now, for just this instant, she was content simply to be.

"I hate you, I hate you, I hate you!" The shriek was followed by the sound of shattering glass. Olivia jumped, and looked around in alarm as the screen door burst open and Chloe barged through it. As the door banged shut again Chloe was already all the way across the porch, still screaming "I hate you" at the top of her lungs and running as if the seat of her cute white shorts were on fire.

Before Olivia could move, or do or say anything to try to stop the child, Chloe flew down the steps and across the lawn along the path that led down to the lake, fleet-footed as a gazelle, her long blond hair streaming behind her.

chapter 24

"Chloe Archer, you come back here this instant!" Mallory pushed through the screen door, for once less than perfectly groomed. One side of her chic blond bob was soaked flat and dripped water onto the shoulder of her lavender linen coatdress, which was itself liberally splashed with water. Her face was flushed scarlet and her eyes flashed fire.

"Chloe Archer!" As the door banged shut behind her, Mallory raced to the edge of the porch to scream after the fleeing child. But if Chloe heard she pretended not to, disappearing over the bluff as she darted down the steps cut into its side.

For a moment Mallory stood there, fists clenched at her sides, glaring impotently after Chloe. Then she pivoted on her beige high heels, and seemed to become aware of Olivia's presence for the first time.

"That child is the worst brat I have ever seen in my life," Mallory said through her teeth, meeting Olivia's gaze.

The screen door opened again, and Callie came out onto the veranda. Mallory's incensed gaze swung to her.

"Oh, Mallory, I am so sorry!" Callie said, tsk-tsking busily as she walked up to her furious future daughter-in-law. "Oh, dear, Chloe shouldn't have done it, but . . ."

"But nothing!" Mallory was still talking through her teeth. "She shouldn't have done it, period! She threw a vase of flowers at me simply because I showed her a picture in a magazine of a bridesmaid's dress I thought would look nice on her! If I hadn't ducked she would have hit me with it! That child needs professional help!"

"Oh, Mallory, no, she's just a little girl going through a bad time. . . ."

Mallory closed her eyes for a moment as Callie's hands fluttered ineffectually around her wet hair and dress. She seemed to take a deep breath, and opened her eyes again.

"I realize that," Mallory said, and her voice was calmer. "Believe me, I'm trying to make allowances, Callie. I'm trying to be her friend. I've rearranged my entire schedule these last few weeks so that we can do things together. I've taken her to play tennis. I've taken her swimming. I've taken her to piano lessons. I just this afternoon canceled a showing of a half-million-dollar property in Baton Rouge so I could take her school shopping. I'm certainly trying, Callie."

"I know know you are, dear." Callie sent an appalled, eye-rolling look over Mallory's shoulder to Olivia, and tsked-tsked some more. "Let's get you dried off, and then we'll see what we can come up with. Stepparenting is so difficult. . . ."

Callie's eyes met Olivia's again, this time with a silent plea for help. Olivia understood that she was being asked to go check on Chloe, and nodded. Callie looked relieved, and ushered a still-fuming Mallory into the house.

Olivia carefully put the picture in her lap back into the box with the others, and headed down the stairs. Her movements were reluctant. Chloe wasn't her child, and she *was* difficult. How Callie thought *she* was going to be able to do anything with Chloe when the child's own father, grandmother, and stepmother-to-be couldn't, she didn't know.

On the other hand, there was no one else available to go after Chloe at that precise moment, and she did have an eight-year-old daughter of her own, which surely had taught her something about young girls. Not that Sara was anything like Chloe. Sara had never had a bratty episode in her life.

But Olivia had. All at once Olivia remembered the fits she had thrown at her grandmother, at Callie, even at Seth. Sara never threw tantrums, but Olivia had.

233

Why? Olivia reached the top of the bluff at the point where she and Sara had first emerged from the woods below, stared unseeing at the silvery lake with its picturesque ring of purple water hyacinths, and made a fundamental discovery.

For all her characterization of Chloe as "difficult" — and that, in her opinion, was being polite — she had been much the same at Chloe's age, and even older.

Because she had felt unloved. That truth hit her like a blow, making Olivia feel slightly sick to her stomach, but there it was. After her mother had died, Olivia had never again felt loved.

Chloe was acting out because she felt unloved.

The stone steps cut into the side of the bluff were wet, and that meant they were slick, as Olivia knew from experience. She was careful going down them, and careful, too, as she picked her way through mud and puddles along the path that led to the lake. She remembered the line *Snakes! Why did it have to be snakes?* from one of the Indiana Jones movies, and smiled wryly. Of all the places for Chloe to run, why did it have to be to the lake?

Because life was like that. No matter how hard you tried to get away, no matter how many corners you turned, you were constantly coming face-to-face with yourself.

She could hear Chloe's gusty sobs before she got there. She'd had an idea where Chloe was, of course. Every child who grew up on this property knew about the overhang. Not quite a cave, it was more of a depression in the face of the cliff. At about five feet deep and maybe six feet wide, it had a craggy, curving roof of rock that soared some twelve feet overhead. What made the spot irresistible were the vines. Tangled tendrils of bright green kudzu stretched over the opening like a curtain, hiding the hollow within.

Anyone who didn't know the overhang was there would never have seen it.

With her goal in sight, Olivia paused and considered. Approaching Chloe, either with sympathy or a lecture, was destined to meet with failure. Chloe was clearly in a mood to wreak havoc on all comers.

Olivia, therefore, wouldn't approach.

Working quickly, listening to sobs all the while, she gathered a small pile of sticks and rocks, then squatted just off the path opposite the overhang and began arranging her trove into a structure.

She also started to sing.

Olivia was *not* a singer. She knew it, had known it since she had tried out for St. Theresa's annual musical in seventh grade and been laughed out of the auditorium. But then, this particular application didn't require that she be able to carry a tune. It just required her to attract the attention of one very unhappy little girl without it being obvious that that was what she was trying to do.

"Jimmy crack corn . . ." she began softly. She had worked her way from that song through a half dozen others and was on a lusty chorus of

"Zip-a-dee-doo-dah" when a hand smacked against her shoulder. Rather harder than a polite can-I-have-your-attention-please tap, but still within the outer realms of acceptability.

Olivia stopped singing, and glanced over her shoulder in feigned surprise.

"Oh, hi, Chloe," she said, just as if she did not notice the child's swollen eyes, tear-wet cheeks, and still-trembling lower lip, and had no idea what had gone on in the house earlier.

"What are you *doing?*" The question was petulant, hostile even, but curious. Chloe's gaze was focused on the small, four-walled rock and mud structure that Olivia had constructed beside the path.

"Putting on the roof," Olivia replied, and began to lay on twigs, working sideways and placing them so that their tips crossed over the larger one she had positioned lengthwise over what would be the peak of the roof.

"What is it?"

Olivia scooped up a good-size glob of mud and patted it down on top of the twigs. Her hands were already caked with mud, and from the feel of it she had at least one streak across her cheek, but it was all for a good cause, she thought, risking another glance back at Chloe. The child was still sniffling, but she looked intrigued.

"A fairy house."

"A *fairy* house?" There was a wealth of scorn in the question.

"Mmm-hmmm. When I was a little girl I used

to build them all the time. After it rains is the best time. Mud makes the house easier to build, and there seem to be more fairies out when it's damp."

"There's no such thing as fairies." This time, if Chloe's scorn had had weight, Olivia would have been crushed beneath it.

Olivia shrugged. "How do you know?"

"I *know*, that's all. Everybody knows."

Olivia shrugged again, her hands still busy patting mud down over the roof.

"When I was eight, like you, I used to feel bad sometimes, and when I felt bad I would build a fairy house, and then I would lie in my bed — I always built the fairy house where I could see it from my bed — and watch for the fairies to come. They always came."

"Fairies?" The single word brimmed with skepticism.

"Well," Olivia temporized, "*something* came, with little lights. I could see little lights flying all around my house, and going in and out the windows."

"Lightning bugs!" Chloe pronounced scathingly.

"Maybe," Olivia agreed, finishing the roof and wiping her hands as well as she could on the damp leaves beside the path. "But I liked to pretend they were fairies."

"It's stupid to pretend."

Olivia shook her head, and stood up, surveying her handiwork with pride. A neat little stone, twig, and mud house stood beside the path. It was about a foot tall. "Pretending is wonderful, Chloe. If you can pretend, you can do anything, or be anything, or have anything. I used to pretend I could fly. I would lie on my back on the grass behind the house and look up at the clouds and pretend I could fly up there where they were. . . ." Suddenly Olivia hesitated, shaken, as she realized that she really was unearthing a memory; her voice softened. "So I could visit my mother in heaven."

How she had wished that pretend game would come true!

"How old were you when your mother died?" Chloe was looking up at her, her tears and anger momentarily forgotten. She seemed genuinely interested.

"Six," Olivia answered, trying to ignore the sudden disorienting feeling of seeing things through the eyes of the child she had once been. It was important right now to concentrate on Chloe and nothing else.

"I was six when my mom got married again," Chloe said, and all of a sudden her lower lip started to tremble. "That's how I got to be *here*. She didn't want me after that."

Tears swam in Chloe's eyes. Responding instinctively, Olivia wrapped her arms around the child, hugging her close. Bad move. Chloe jerked free, glaring at her.

"Pretending's stupid!" she said, her face contorting. Before Olivia realized what she meant to do, she lifted a foot and stomped through the roof of the fairy house. Then she turned and ran back up the path.

At least, Olivia thought, ruefully surveying the ruins of her creation, Chloe was headed in the direction of the house.

It was only when she looked up again that Olivia realized she was alone in the one place on earth she least wished to be: not twenty feet from the edge of the lake where her mother had drowned. Her throat tightened even as she told herself that it was absurd to feel afraid.

Run away. Its origins were unclear, but the whisper was not, and Olivia blinked as she absorbed what she was hearing. *Run. Run away.*

Olivia stared wide-eyed at the lake for a solid minute before she realized the truth. Of course the words were in her mind. Yes, she had heard the voices before, when she and Sara had walked through the woods on her first night back. But there was no ghostly presence calling out to her from the smooth surface of the water. There were no specters talking to her from the trees, or the clouds, or the earth.

Her fear was speaking, and when Olivia realized that she made up her mind: It was time to silence that fear once and for all.

Standing stock-still, she forced herself to take a long look at the lake. It was a big lake, covering perhaps twenty acres, and deep. As the sun moved farther down in the western sky, the surface of the water turned almost purple, rather than the silver it had been earlier. The water hyacinths formed an outer ring around the tattered shoreline, their bobbing heads a deeper purple than the water, their foliage the same deep green as the duckweed that grew between them, giving the appearance that the flowers grew on solid ground. The twisted shapes of live oaks and bald cypresses looked like living sculptures when viewed from across the expanse of water. Their branches, like the branches of the sylvan canopy above her head, were adorned with Spanish moss that draped and hung from bent limbs like ratty silver-green feather boas.

Run. Run away. A breeze had come up, bearing with it the slightly fetid smell that Olivia had always associated with the lake. Involuntarily she shivered, suddenly cold. With the best will in the world, she could not help being afraid. The lake . . . It had always been the stuff of her most terrible nightmares.

She would not run away from it anymore. Earlier today she had come face-to-face with the memory of her mother, and the experience had been healing. Now she would face her fear of the lake.

Run away, Olivia! Run away! The voices seemed stronger, more urgent, their warning underlined by creaking branches and rustling leaves and swells of water slapping at the shoreline. The towering purple thunderheads that had brought the afternoon's showers had gentled into an early evening sky of pink-tinged clouds against a background of pale amethyst. Dipping low on the distant horizon, the sun was the color and shape of a scoop of orange sherbet.

Taking a deep breath, ignoring the voices, Olivia took one step off the path, then another. Then she was walking determinedly toward the lake, weaving among trees, dodging cypress knees, wading through tangled undergrowth. She meant to stand on the shore, right at the very edge where the water could lap at the toes of her Keds, face her fear, and, by facing it, conquer it. She refused any longer to feel a shiver of dread every time the lake came within her view.

Olivia! The voice from the lake was shouting at her now, warning her to stay back, afraid of her assault on its sovereignty. Olivia reached the edge of the trees, set foot on the sliver of rocky, muddy beach, and took the final step needed to bring her to the edge of the water.

To her surprise, she immediately sank up to her ankles in ooze. As the brackish water rose, lapping at her calves instead of her toes, she looked down in dismay.

Without warning a hand caught her arm from behind, yanking her violently backward.

chapter 25

Olivia screamed, flailed, stumbled, and would have fallen bottom-first into the muck if someone had not caught her under the arms in the nick of time.

"What the *hell* do you think you're doing?" It was Seth, she discovered, bending her head back to look at him from the ignoble position in which she found herself. He was scowling, his thick, straight brows nearly meeting over his nose as his eyes collided with hers. He looked, and sounded, equal parts angry, amazed, and alarmed.

"What am *I* doing?" Olivia felt the panic that had exploded into life when she was grabbed from behind dissipate as quickly as it had come. "What are *you* doing, grabbing me like that? You scared the life out of me!"

It was hard to project the true degree of her indignation, she discovered, when her bottom was approximately six inches above the muck and his hands under her arms were all that kept her out of it.

"Didn't you hear me calling you? I yelled, but you kept going like you were in some kind of trance. You walked straight into the damned lake, just like you were trying to . . . What the hell were you trying to do?"

His face was flushed beneath its usual sun-bronze, and he seemed to be short of breath, as if he'd been running. He was handsome from any angle, Olivia discovered, still looking up at him from a position that made her practically supine. Though he frowned ferociously at her with his mouth set hard and his blue eyes snapping, her body responded with an instant quickening. She couldn't believe her reaction to him under the circumstances, which were laughable, and after all her self-talk explaining away what she had lately felt when in his presence, and she wouldn't allow it. This was *Seth,* for God's sake. She simply would not think of him that way.

"I said, what the hell were you trying to do?" His tone was so fierce that her eyes widened. It occurred to Olivia that she had frightened him, and that, in turn, was what had made him angry.

"I was just trying to get over being afraid of the lake," Olivia confessed in a milder tone than any she had used with him so far. "What did you think I was trying to do, drown myself?"

She'd meant that last question to be hu-morous, but from the uneasy flicker in his eyes she divined the truth.

"You *did* think that, didn't you?" She hooted, grinning, and for a minute she thought he was going to drop her into the goo. His mouth tightened, his eyes darkened, and then she was being thrust back into an upright position, his hands leaving her just as soon as he saw that she could stand alone.

"Next time you plan to go wading, take somebody with you. It's stupid as hell to go walking into the lake alone." He looked down, and his expression became one of angry disgust. "You always were more trouble than anybody I ever knew."

She followed the direction of his gaze. Like herself, she discovered, he was some eight inches deep in slimy mud and water. Unlike herself, he was dressed for work in a navy suit, white shirt, red tie, and, Olivia presumed, expensive dress shoes just now hidden from sight because they were sunk deep into the ooze.

"Oh, dear," she said, her eyes meeting his, and then, because she just couldn't help it, she grinned. "I appreciate you coming in after me. I really do."

"Next time I'll let you drown yourself." His tone was so sour that Olivia had to laugh. He looked at her, his expression grim, and then the beginnings of a smile began to tug at the corners of his mouth. "Olivia, you are a pain in the ass."

"Why, thank you, sir."

Moving carefully as the ooze bubbled and sank

around him, Seth turned, lifted a dripping, slime-covered foot from the mud to the accompaniment of a sound like a vacuum seal being broken and the smell of rotten eggs, and set it down again halfway to shore. He repeated the operation with his other foot. Another step saw his right foot planted on the firmer ground of the muddy strip of beach. With his left foot, he was not as fortunate. Lifting it free of the goo one last time he swore, and Olivia saw as his foot came into view that it was minus its shoe.

"Oh, dear," she said again, knowing the response was inadequate but unable to come up with anything less inflammatory on the spur of the moment. As his gaze met hers for a pregnant instant, she began to giggle helplessly. He stared at her without saying anything at all, his expression thunderous. Then, swearing every inch of the way, he waded back in, bent, thrust an arm into the muck, and felt around for his shoe. Olivia, meanwhile, squelched toward shore. *Her* shoes stayed on her feet. Clambering onto solid ground, ooze coating her bare legs to midcalf, she turned to observe his efforts. A mosquito landed on her thigh just below the fringe of her cutoffs, and she slapped at it absently. Her gaze was on Seth. She watched as he straightened, shoe in hand, moving with an easy, athletic grace despite the impediment of being mired in over-the-ankle mud. He really had a great body. . . . Not that it interested her at all, she reminded herself firmly. She was watching him only be-

245

cause she was amused.

Mud covered the arm of his suit coat to the elbow, water poured from his recovered shoe, and a swarm of bugs — gnats or mosquitoes, she couldn't be sure which — enveloped his head. As he turned for shore, swatting at the insects with his free hand and swearing under his breath, she saw that he looked extremely put out, to say the least.

She grinned at him.

"I came down here looking for Chloe," he said, fixing her with a look that dared her to laugh again as he took two long, squelching strides onto solid ground. "Have you seen her?"

Olivia nodded cautiously, uncertain of how much he knew of his daughter's transgression. Probably quite a bit, if he had come down to the lake in search of her. "I talked to her for a few minutes, but then she ran — I *think* she ran back to the house."

Seth made a disgusted noise, dropped his shoe on the ground, and worked his foot back into it. The shoe was muddy, slimy, stinky, and soaking wet, but no more so than both his pant legs from the knee down and his right arm from the elbow. "Apparently she threw a vase full of flowers at Mallory."

"I know."

The look he sent her did not bode well for Chloe. "I don't know whether to tan her backside until she can't sit down or take her to see a psychiatrist. Mallory votes for the psychiatrist."

Against the bronze of his skin, his teeth flashed white suddenly in a quick, humorless grin. "At least, that's what she says. Given the choice, though, I think she'd really go for the spanking."

"Oh, Seth, you wouldn't."

"Wouldn't I?" He sounded grim.

They turned toward the path, and as they made their way through the undergrowth Seth automatically reached out to cup Olivia's elbow for support. As his hand was still slimy wet, Olivia jumped, startled, and looked down at it wide-eyed.

"Oh, sorry," he said, withdrawing the offending hand. A touch of real humor lit his eyes. "We've got a full house for supper tonight, by the way. Mallory, her *mother*, David and Keith, Charlie and Belinda, Phillip and Connie — Connie's Phillip's wife, I don't think you've met her yet — and their kids, and Carl. Oh, yes, and Ira, I'm sure. No doubt I'm leaving someone out."

"Good God," Olivia said, appalled.

"My feelings exactly. So of course I'm thrilled out of my mind to get home and find that my daughter has disgraced the pair of us again. The fact that I'm now going to have to face my future mother-in-law and explain how I ended up looking like the Creature from the Black Lagoon just adds an extra element of interest to what has been an already very interesting day."

They were almost to the path, and once again

Seth reached automatically to support Olivia as they stepped out of the tangle of vegetation onto the well-trodden trail. This time, Olivia glanced down before he touched her. At her glance he remembered, grimaced apologetically, and withdrew his muddy hand. Olivia started walking with Seth behind her.

"Why so many?" she asked over her shoulder, noting the ruined fairy house with a sideways glance as they passed it but not saying anything to draw his attention to it. He was already angry enough at Chloe as it was.

"Charlie wanted to have a family meeting to discuss possible treatment options for Big John. And Mallory's mother apparently went school shopping with Chloe and Mallory. Mallory needed her for moral support, she said, in dealing with my spoiled, capricious, totally undisciplined child. Of course, Mallory was kind of mad when she said all that. I'm pretty sure she only meant about two-thirds of it."

"Seth." Olivia turned abruptly to face him, one hand coming up to flatten against his shirtfront, stopping him in his tracks. He looked down at the dirt-streaked hand splayed out over his red silk tie, and then up into her eyes. His expression changed in that instant, becoming impossible to read. The anger seemed to have disappeared, but she couldn't be sure what had replaced it. His eyes were narrowed and almost hard as Olivia looked up at him earnestly. "Does Chloe remind you of anyone?"

One corner of his mouth lifted. "Linda Blair in *The Exorcist?*"

"Seth!"

He laughed. "All right, then, maybe that's a little bit of a stretch. Who did you have in mind?"

"Me."

His eyes widened. "Good God, I'd almost rather have Linda Blair."

"Seth, I'm serious!"

"So am I."

"Fine." Olivia turned on her heel and marched away from him. "If you're too damned pig-headed to listen . . ."

"Livvy. *Livvy.*" He caught up with her, both hands closing around her upper arms, stopping her. The mud on his right hand was nearly dry, and anyway she didn't care anymore if his hand was muddy, because she was suddenly too darned mad. He never would listen; he never had! He always thought he knew better than everybody else. . . .

"Olivia." He turned her around to face him, his hands still on her arms, a smile lurking around his mouth and in his eyes. "Wait. Tell me. Why does Chloe remind you of yourself?"

"Because she thinks nobody loves her," Olivia said brutally, glaring up at him. She'd meant to be more tactful, but her newly resurfaced, long-simmering sense of injustice chased the tact right out of her.

He didn't like that, she could see. For a moment his hands tightened almost painfully on her arms, and his eyes widened. Then his mouth twisted in a silent message of repudiation.

"Bullshit," he said.

That made her madder. "Think so?"

"Yeah, I think so. What do you mean, she thinks nobody loves her? I love her, and Mother loves her, and . . ."

"How does she know that? I've been here a week, Seth, and all I've seen you do is go off to work and go off to the hospital and go off here and go off there without so much as a thought for your daughter, and when you do finally see her you're either fighting with her or telling her to behave. Do you think that feels like love to her? Aunt Callie's good to her, but she's desperately ill and can't focus on Chloe like the child needs to be focused on. Martha's fond of her, but she's hired help. Mallory — well, I won't even get into Mallory. And her mother — Chloe's mother broke her heart by sending her home to you. The child feels *abandoned*, Seth. She needs your time and your attention, not punishment."

"Bullshit!"

"It is not bullshit! It's the truth, only you're too damned stupid to see it!"

They were standing practically nose-to-nose by this time, her hands clutching the lapels of his jacket for balance, his hands curled around her upper arms. In her flat shoes, the top of her head reached no higher than his chin, so she had thrown her head back to meet his glare head-on. She could feel the strength in his hands, the hard menace of his body, the anger that emanated from him in waves, and she wasn't backing down an inch.

She never had.

"You don't know what the hell you're talking about!" he said through his teeth.

"You just won't listen! You never would listen! You always know everything, and everybody else is wrong, and —"

"Was I wrong about Newall Morrison? Huh? Was I? If you'd listened to me, instead of being so goddamned eager to climb into bed with that lowlife —"

"Shut up! You just shut up, Seth Archer!" Olivia yelled. Maddened, she jerked an arm free and slapped him full across the face. His head jerked to one side. The sound of the blow reverberated in the air. Her palm stung. Horrified at herself the instant after she did it, Olivia could only stare at him as the imprint of her hand on his cheek reddened and his eyes bore furiously into hers.

It was an uncanny replay of the quarrel they'd had just before she'd eloped with Newall. She had slapped Seth then, too.

"Go to hell," she whispered, shaken, and pulled the arm he still held free. He let her go; she was under no illusions that he couldn't have held her there if he'd wanted to. Head high, she turned and stalked away from him, up the path, heading for the house. She would go straight upstairs, and with any luck no one would even see her.

The best-laid plans of mice and men . . . The entire company was assembled on the front veranda, enjoying predinner drinks and watching the sunset, when Olivia emerged at the top of the bluff. As the hum of voices and laughter alerted her to their presence, she hesitated. Her first impulse was to skulk along the hedge until she reached the back door. But they would see her — *someone* was bound to see her; there wasn't enough shrubbery between herself and the house to provide any real concealment — and then she would look like an utter fool.

So Olivia walked up to the house along the path as nonchalantly as though she hadn't just had a terrible fight with Seth, as though she hadn't gotten mired in mud and heard voices calling to her and tried to calm an angry eight-year-old and in general been through what amounted to an emotional wringer. She even managed to fix a pleasant expression on her face as she reached the steps.

chapter 26

Archers and their guests were spread out all along the veranda, some seated, some perched on the rail, some standing. All had one thing in common, however: They watched Olivia with interest as she came up the steps and onto the porch.

Muddy, sweaty, and angry, dressed in grubby denim cutoffs and a dirt-smeared yellow T-shirt that probably clung more than it should have, with a mosquito bite on her thigh and drying mud caked midway up her calves, Olivia was definitely not prepared to be the cynosure of all eyes.

There was no help for it, however.

"Olivia! Just in time for supper!" Keith, perched on the rail nearby, greeted her first with a jovial tip of the half-filled glass he held. Leaning against the rail beside him, David eyed her thoughtfully and tipped his own glass toward her in greeting. Beyond them, Charlie and Ira were seated in chairs carried out from the house. They broke off their conversation to glance at Olivia. Charlie waved. Ira smiled.

Out on the lawn, four wiry, fair-haired children in shorts and T-shirts whooped gleefully as they burst out from behind the house, taking turns kicking a soccer ball across the grass. A glance back told Olivia that their ages ranged from about two to six. These had to be Phillip's children, she thought. Funny to think of him as married with four little ones.

"Pipe down, guys!" Phillip cupped a hand around his mouth to yell after his children, with no discernible effect on the volume level. "Can't you quiet them down a little?" he asked a plump woman of approximately thirty with a light brown boy cut and a sweet smile. Olivia assumed the woman was Phillip's wife, Connie, whom she had not yet met. With Phillip standing over her, Connie was sitting in the rocking chair next to Callie, who was at that moment getting to her feet, her eyes on Olivia.

"Oh, let them play," Connie replied comfortably, smiling at Olivia. Olivia smiled back. Phillip's reply to this was lost as Olivia's attention shifted to Callie, who was moving toward her with obvious purpose.

"Chloe came back about fifteen minutes ago. I sent her to her room," Callie whispered as she reached her. "I think Sara's up there with her.

Oh, dear, was Seth very mad?"

Olivia answered this with a nod.

"Can I get you a drink, Olivia?" Smiling, Carl came toward her from his place beside his brother. Olivia shook her head, smiling back. Carl was clearly interested in her as something other than a cousin. It was a pity, all things considered, but she was not interested back, and the sooner he realized that the more comfortable things would be for both of them. At the moment, especially, all she wanted was to go upstairs.

"Why, you're covered with mud! You ought to go in the back way." Shouldering through the screen door bearing a tray piled high with crackers and grapes and chunks of yellow cheese, Belinda stopped to look Olivia over with disapproval.

"She's fine, Belinda," Callie reproved, her voice low so that the others wouldn't overhear.

"I really need to go in and take a shower . . ." Olivia began, edging forward in hopes that Belinda would move away from the door.

"Oh, look, Mama, there's Seth! I told you he wouldn't be long!" Mallory had been sitting on the swing beside an older, look-alike blond woman whom Olivia guessed was her mother. She jumped up, moving to the rail and waving, presumably at Seth. Grasping the edge of the screen that Belinda still held ajar, Olivia refused to look around to make sure. She could only hope that the mark on his cheek had faded by this time. What the present company would make of that she didn't even want to guess.

"Why, he's covered with mud, too!" Belinda said loudly, the placement of her body in the doorway preventing Olivia from edging past her. Her gaze, sharp with malice, swung back to Olivia. "Whatever have you two been doing together?"

All eyes turned toward Olivia. Mallory's and her mother's went round as they weighed the evidence on Olivia's legs. Carl, who had almost reached the bottleneck at the door, looked at her mud-covered calves and frowned.

"Making mud pies," Olivia said, smiling sweetly at the gathered company. Then, to Belinda, she said with just the barest hint of bite, "I really *do* need to take a shower. If you'll just let me by . . ."

There was nothing else Belinda could do but step aside. Let Seth explain, Olivia thought, and made her escape.

He must have come up with something reasonable, because later, when she was fresh out of the bath and headed toward her bedroom, Olivia heard him laughing as though he hadn't a care in the world. The sound floated to her ears from the dining room, where the company had gathered for dinner.

Not for anything — not even chicken in sauce piquante, which, from the smell, was what they were having — was Olivia going back downstairs. When Martha came in search of her, she pleaded a headache. Kind Martha brought her up a plate. Sara put in an appearance around tenish, having had supper with Chloe in her room. After Sara's bath, and the obligatory bedtime story, Olivia finally went to her room and crawled into bed. She was asleep as soon as her head hit the pillow.

Of course, given the way her day had gone, she dreamed about the lake. She could hear the voices calling to her — *Run. Run away!* — as she stood on the shore, just as she had that afternoon. But in her dream she was able to identify the source of the voice: It belonged to her mother, a tiny, barely glimpsed figure desperately flailing in the center of the turbulent water. As Olivia watched in horror, her mother called out a warning one more time and then disappeared from view. Olivia knew, without knowing how she knew, that Selena had been pulled beneath the surface by some unseen force.

At that point Olivia woke up in a cold sweat. For several minutes she lay without moving, heart pounding, as she convinced herself that she was safe in bed. The dream had seemed so *real* — but then, it was based on reality, she told herself. She had been standing beside the lake that day, she had imagined voices, and she had been looking at a long-forgotten picture of her mother.

Was it any wonder that all those elements had combined into a truly terrifying nightmare? The wonder would be if they hadn't.

Although the logic of that was irrefutable, the residual fear was stubborn. It lingered long after she knew it was ridiculous, and thus it was quite some time before Olivia fell back to sleep.

By morning, Olivia had recovered from the dream, and was pretty much over her anger at Seth as well. In fact, what she felt most strongly when thinking back over their quarrel was shame at her own behavior. She'd fought with him just like she had as a teenager. Hadn't she grown up one bit?

She and Sara were leaving for home the next morning, Olivia reflected, as she and her child spent the afternoon in a last, largely fruitless search for peacock feathers. She needed to smooth things over with Seth before she left. But he was gone all day, frustrating her good intentions. Since Chloe was confined to her room, with no TV and no playmates allowed, it was clear that he hadn't taken to heart what she'd told him about his daughter feeling unloved and needing his attention.

Why should she care whether or not they parted on an angry note? Olivia asked herself. There was certainly nothing new about that.

But she cared nonetheless.

It was almost eleven o'clock and Sara was already asleep next door when a soft knock sounded at one of the pair of French windows in Olivia's room. At the sound, a little frisson of unease stirred inside her. She tensed, her hands stilling on the blouse she was folding, tempted not to answer the knock. She didn't like knowing that anybody could get to her room just by walking along the gallery. It made her nervous.

But that was silly. Who would be knocking at her window but family? Moving to the window, pulling the curtain aside, Olivia was rewarded for her fortitude by seeing Seth. Any vestige of fear vanished, to be replaced by a small spurt of pleasure that he had cared enough to make up their quarrel before she left.

"Come outside. I want to talk to you," he said softly when she pushed open the window.

With only a single glance behind her for the half-filled suitcases that lay open on the bed, she did as he asked. She could always finish packing later. Seth said nothing after she stepped through the long French window into the soft warmth of the night. He closed the window behind her without a word, then stood for a moment with his back to it looking at her with such a pensive air that she was immediately alarmed.

Maybe he had not come to apologize, but to bring her bad news.

"What's the matter?" Olivia asked, tensing. She had known Seth a long time, basically all her life in fact, and she could tell that he had something besides making up their quarrel on his mind.

His face relaxed into a wry smile. "You see me, and you immediately assume something's the matter? What am I, the official bearer of bad tidings?"

"Something like that."

"Come and sit down, Olivia. I want to talk to you."

She followed him to the pair of rockers and the swing at the far end of the gallery, and when he stopped in front of one chair and indicated with a gesture that she should sit, she did so. Instead of sitting in the other one, he leaned a hip against the rail.

By the soft glow seeping from behind the curtained windows, she could see that he had changed from his muddy suit to rumpled khakis and a white T-shirt. A healthy growth of five o'clock shadow darkened his cheeks and chin, and his short hair was mussed, as if someone (Mallory?) had been running her fingers through it. Olivia realized that she didn't much like that idea. Then she realized that she didn't like not liking it. Feeling jealous of Mallory was, to all intents and purposes, the same as feeling attracted to Seth.

She just wasn't going to go there.

Anyway, she thought he looked tired.

Well, of course he was. It was late, and she was tired herself.

"Been busy packing?" He took a sip of the gold-colored drink he held in one hand. The muted light from the window shone through the glass, throwing a golden rectangle onto the white-painted rail on which he leaned.

"Yes." Olivia felt herself begin to relax, beguiled by the beauty of the night. She breathed in the sweet scents of honeysuckle and magnolia, listened to the chorus of insects, and admired the magnificent vista just beyond the colonnade of a thousand twinkly white stars strewn over a navy-blue sky. Seth was in her line of vision, a comforting presence against the glittery backdrop. If she was honest, she would have to admit that having him there relaxed her, too. Her gaze moved over him despite her best efforts to keep her eyes focused anywhere else. It touched on his short fair hair, brightened to platinum by the moon; on the smooth plane of his forehead, his high cheekbones and straight nose, and the slight smile playing around the corners of his mouth; on the firm lines of his jaw, the breadth of his shoulders and the solid length of his body, all outlined by the night. Colorless in this light, his eyes gleamed at her, and as she met their gaze she felt the now familiar flutter of attraction he roused in her stir anew.

And she realized to her dismay that she was helpless to do anything about it.

This time, when leaving LaAngelle Plantation, the thing she was going to miss most of all was Seth.

His eyes narrowed as he watched her. He knew her so well, Olivia was afraid that he might somehow be able to read her thoughts. She hurried into speech, reaching for something, anything, to distract him.

"I'm sorry I slapped you," she said abruptly, leaning back in the chair and transferring her gaze to the stars that winked and blinked behind him. "I apologize."

"That's a first, coming from you," he said with a laugh, moving to sink down in the other rocking chair. The rocking chair creaked under his weight. His hands — one cradling the glass, both bronzed and strong-looking — rested on the chair arms, and his legs — long and muscular, ending in sockless feet thrust into boat shoes — stretched out in front of him. Olivia registered those details, and the length and breadth of his body sprawled in the delicate, lacey chair, with a single glance, and determinedly returned her attention to the stars.

"You're not going to apologize, are you?" she asked, nettled. Focusing on his shortcomings — such as his really world-class ability to make her angry — might keep her from focusing on how aware of him she was.

"What makes you think that?" The question was lazy, teasing almost.

She glanced sideways at him, smiling a little. "I know you, Seth Archer."

"I know you, too, Olivia Chenier —" The tenor of his voice changed, hardening just enough to be noticeable, as he added, "Morrison."

His opinion of her married name was apparent from his tone. Olivia sighed.

"All right, let's get this over with. You were right and I was wrong, okay?"

"About what?"

"You know about what. About Newall. I was a fool to run off and marry him like I did. I know it. You don't have to keep rubbing my nose in it."

Seth was silent. Still doggedly watching the heavens, Olivia could feel the weight of his gaze on her.

"If you thought I was rubbing your nose in it, then I do apologize. I didn't mean to. We all make mistakes, God knows." After another long moment of silence in which she could feel his gaze on her face, he asked quietly, "Was it bad, Livvy? Being married to him?"

Absurdly, the gentleness in his tone made Olivia want to cry.

"Pretty bad," she said in as light a tone as she could muster. "Try to picture never-ending groupies, no money for anything that wasn't something he wanted or needed, and constant travel from one cheap motel to another while he followed the rodeo circuit. By the time he left me for another starry-eyed teenager, I had certainly learned my lesson about eloping with strange men, believe me."

"Want to talk about it?" Seth's tone was still very gentle.

Careful not to look at him, Olivia shook her head. "Nope. It's water under the bridge."

"It's not where you've been, it's where you're going that counts?" he suggested with a smile in his voice. That was one of Big John's favorite axioms, known to everyone who knew him well, and Seth's use of it coaxed a smile from Olivia.

"Exactly," she said, and risked a glance at him. He was still looking at her, but she couldn't read his expression in the darkness. Absurdly, she felt this sudden urge to be comforted by him. If, at that moment, she could do anything she wanted in the whole world, she thought, she would crawl into his lap and have him wrap his arms around her and . . .

"I want you to stay here," Seth said abruptly. "*We* want you to stay here. That's what I wanted to talk to you about."

chapter 27

"What?" This time Olivia looked directly at him, wide-eyed with surprise.

"I'm offering you a job at the Boatworks, and a home for you and Sara here at LaAngelle Plantation for as long as you care to stay."

Olivia was stunned. She had never considered such a possibility.

"Well?" Seth prompted, when she didn't say anything.

"Are you serious?"

"Of course I'm serious."

Olivia wet her lips. A thousand tangled thoughts and emotions swirled through her head. To stay here, to live here — to step back into the life she had spurned so many years ago and bring Sara with her — she didn't know if it was a very good idea, or a very bad one.

"Oh, Seth, I don't know what to say. Our

home's in Houston now, Sara's and mine. Sara starts back to school in just a few days, and I have a job that I like, and —"

"Olivia," Seth interrupted. "I know your job doesn't pay very well. I know you live in a small apartment in a not very affluent section of Houston. I know life's a struggle for you and Sara there. I can offer you a better job, one that pays more, has a future. For right now I need an office manager, somebody to keep track of appointments, stay on top of the books, answer the phone, do some typing or whatever else is needed. Ilsa Bartlett, who has the job now, is going on maternity leave in two months. She needs help now, and I'll need a trained replacement for her then. I'd like to hire you for that position now, at a better salary than you're getting in Houston — you can tell me what that is; I trust you." There was a touch of humor in his voice as he said that. "And then, later, when Ilsa comes back and you know more about the business, I'll move you into a sales position, which involves a good salary plus commission. I don't know why I never thought of it before, but given our clientele a pretty woman could probably do very well." He held up a hand when Olivia would have said something. "Hear me out. The hours would be adjusted so that you could be home when Sara's home. You could drive her — and Chloe if you would — to school in the morning, come to work, and then leave in time to pick them up and be with them all afternoon. Yes, I'm including

266

Chloe in that, at least until Mallory and I get married. Then we'll see. You seem to like her, Chloe seems to like you, she behaves relatively well with you, and I think you — and Sara — could do her a lot of good. Plus Mother starts chemotherapy again next week, and she's going to be fighting this thing for another five months. She needs you here. She wants you here. Big John's in bad shape. He may or may not pull through. You want to be here if he's not going to make it. Between him, and Mother, and work, I don't have much time for Chloe right now. You were right about that. *I* need you here. I'd want you to live here, at the house, until things settle down a little. Actually, since Chloe and I are moving back into my house in town after Mallory and I get married, I'll want you to stay here with Mother until she's back on her feet. But then I'd see that you got a house, in town, a nice house of your own for you and Sara. All yours, all paid for." He was watching her. "How does that sound?"

"Seth . . ." Olivia took a deep breath. "Oh, Seth, it sounds fine, but I have to think. I never thought about staying. I — where would Sara go to school? Where does Chloe go to school?"

Seth smiled faintly. "Right here in town. LaAngelle Elementary. After seeing the results of Grandmother's sending you to St. Theresa's, I thought I might do better to keep Chloe closer to home."

Olivia was surprised by that. An Archer, in the

local public school? It was unprecedented. Her feelings must have shown on her face, because Seth laughed. "Hey, I may learn slow, but I learn."

Olivia was still trying to sort things out in her mind. "Belinda hates me. She'll have a fit."

"Hate is a strong word," Seth observed mildly, without denying it. "And I run the Boatworks. She doesn't."

"I know — but — gosh, Seth, you're asking me to take a big step."

Seth took a sip of his drink. He looked away from her, out at the night. "Is there a boyfriend? Somebody you don't want to leave?"

Olivia shook her head, a rueful smile just touching her lips. "Believe it or not, there hasn't been anybody important since Newall. Like you said, I may learn slow, but I learn."

Seth took another sip of his drink, rested it back on the flat arm of his chair, and looked at her again. "So what's the problem?"

"Well . . ." Olivia hesitated. There were so many objections they almost tangled her tongue as she tried to give voice to them. "I have an apartment. With a lease. I have a job. They depend on me. I have friends. Sara has friends. She's all settled in her school. I have furniture. My car is at the bus station in Houston, for goodness sake. I can't just stay here."

"Sure you can. If you want to."

He looked at her. She looked at him.

"Well?" he said.

"I have to talk to Sara," she said slowly. "I can't make a decision like this without talking to Sara."

"So talk to Sara." Their eyes met again. "Livvy," he said. "We need you. You need us. Stay."

She wanted to, she realized suddenly. Oh, she wanted to. To come home again — wasn't that what she had dreamed about since the grim truth about her marriage had started to sink in? And to bring Sara back with her, under the conditions Seth had described — it sounded almost too good to be true.

There had to be a catch somewhere.

She wouldn't have to leave Seth. At that thought, a warm glow began pulsing in the region of her heart. Try though she might, no stern thoughts she could summon up would make it go away.

"Our bus leaves tomorrow morning at six A.M. The tickets are in my purse. Can — can I call you from Houston and let you know what we decide?"

"You're not going to ride in a goddamned Greyhound bus all the way back to Houston. What did it take you, something like twelve hours to get here?" Seth stood up abruptly, walked to the rail, set his glass down on it, and turned to face her. He sounded almost angry. "If you want to go back tomorrow, I'll take you. Or, if you'd rather, you can take one of the cars and drive yourself. But forget the bus."

Olivia looked at him for a moment without saying anything. Then she said mildly, "The bus isn't really all that bad, Seth."

"To hell with the bus. This is not about the bus." He moved toward her, stopped short, and stood frowning down at her. His hands balled into fists at his sides.

Olivia looked up at him, met his gaze, and quite suddenly ceased to breathe. He was close. So close that if she stood up, she would be in his arms.

How she wanted to stand up!

"Forget the bus," he said again, his tone almost rough. "Sleep in, talk to Sara, and let me know. If you still want to go to Houston tomorrow, I'll take you. Okay?"

Clinging to the arms of the chair as though, if she just held on tight enough, she could prevent herself from doing what she suddenly wanted to do more than anything else in her life, Olivia nodded. "Okay."

For a moment their gazes remained locked together. Then Seth pivoted, walked to the rail, leaned both hands against it, and stared out at the night. Olivia looked at the hard, long line of his back and hips and legs, and felt her mouth go dry. But she stayed in her chair.

Her bond with him spanned a lifetime. He was the big cousin she had always looked up to, bossy and maddening as he could be. She could not spoil their relationship by introducing a sexual element to it. She would not. He was too important to her. Besides, he was going to marry Mallory.

"We'll talk tomorrow," Seth said over his shoulder. "Go to bed, Olivia."

If she wasn't going to make a fool of herself and a mess of her relationship with Seth, she had better take some of the best advice she had ever heard in her life.

Olivia let go of the arms of her chair and stood up.

"Good night," she said softly to his back. He murmured something in reply, but he didn't look at her, continuing to stare out into the night.

It was an effort to pull her eyes away from him, but Olivia did it. Then she very purposefully walked away, along the gallery to her room, and through the French window to safety. She locked it tight, then stood with her back against it for a very long time.

chapter 28

In the end, it was a family party, which was probably a good thing, Seth reflected. It was around nine thirty on Saturday morning, and they had been in the air for over an hour. He was at the controls of a company-leased, twin-engine Beechcraft — aircraft were expensive to operate, but necessary for a business like the Boatworks, where there were wealthy clients to impress and court all over the country — his mind almost solely occupied with trying not to imagine what it would be like to take Olivia to bed. She sat beside him in the copilot's seat, wearing a pair of snug white shorts that hugged her butt and left the tanned length of her legs bare, and a tomato-red T-shirt that clung with loving attention to the curves of her breasts. Her hair, which he had always thought of as being the color of dark chocolate, was pulled back into a ponytail at the nape of her neck. Nothing provocative there — except that it left the tawny curve of her neck and the smooth line of her jaw more exposed to his view. She was laughing, her lips parted to reveal even white teeth, her beautiful eyes alight with merriment.

He wanted her so much that he ached with it, so much that if the intensity of his wanting didn't wane by the time they landed in Houston he was going to embarrass himself by not being able to stand up, and there was absolutely nothing he could do about it. Nothing he planned to do about it.

He was getting married in a little more than two months. To Mallory, who should by rights be starring instead of Olivia in the X-rated pictures that he could not seem to banish from his mind.

Olivia was family, and now his employee as well. His policy toward her was going to continue to be, as it had always been, strictly hands-off.

Even if it killed him, which right at the moment he could easily imagine it might do.

Fortunately, strapped into the seats directly behind him and Olivia were the two best chaperons he could have wished for: Chloe and Sara, both yakking away nonstop to each other and Olivia.

Olivia had insisted on bringing Sara, saying the little girl needed a chance to gather up her personal belongings and say good-bye to her old home. Then she had suggested bringing Chloe as well, and somehow the whole thing had turned into a family outing, which Seth had not, at the outset, intended. But for all his initial misgivings, it was working out surprisingly well. The girls seemed to get along with each other and with Olivia, and Chloe, excited about being included, was on her best behavior.

Sara had never flown before. Seth was both amused and touched by her wide-eyed awe over everything, from the instrument gauges to the view out the window. Smug with previous experience, Chloe explained everything to Sara, not with one hundred percent accuracy, perhaps, but so earnestly that Seth had to smile.

Listening to Chloe's chatter about Beanie Babies and Pokémon and a show called *Sailor Moon*, Seth reflected that he knew very little about his daughter's inner life. He loved her, made sure she had everything she needed, and tried to provide her with some sort of discipline and structure, but he realized to his shame that he had never really had a conversation with her. Oh, he asked her about school sometimes, and about which friend she wanted to take on which outing and that type of thing, but other than that, if they talked, it was usually him telling her to do something or scolding her. Since Jennifer had sent Chloe back to him, he had basically left the raising of her to his mother. After all, he defended himself from the stab of guilt that suddenly assailed him, what did he know about bringing up a little girl?

The girls were chattering away again about some musical group he had never heard of, but Olivia seemed to know just what they were talking about.

Mallory would have been as at sea as he was.

Of course, Livvy had an eight-year-old daughter of her own, and Mallory did not. The comparison between the two women in such an area was unfair, and he knew it.

But he couldn't get it out of his mind.

A wall of heat radiating down from the sky and up from the pavement greeted them when they descended from the plane at the airport in Houston. Texas heat differed from Louisiana heat in that it was dry and baking, while Louisiana heat was moist and suffocating. All things considered, he'd take Louisiana heat any day, Seth reflected. With every step he took, he felt as if he were walking on the top of a stove, and Chloe's pale-skinned face was flushed pink within minutes. His own khaki pants and white polo shirt felt like the warmest of dark wool suits.

They took a taxi from the airport to the Greyhound bus terminal to pick up Olivia's car. The terminal itself was a low, flat building beneath a blue sign adorned with a greyhound dog. A line of big silver-and-blue buses was parked next to it, about a third of them emitting copious amounts of pollution to add to the haze that lay over the city. The rest of the parking lot was about half filled with cars of various descriptions. Olivia headed straight toward the worst of the bunch, a ten-year-old dinged and pitted faded blue Cougar. When he saw it, Seth was aghast. The thing was a junker, with more than 123,000 miles on the odometer and bald tires, worth maybe a thousand dollars at best. The idea that Olivia and Sara had been driving around a big city like Houston in a vehicle that was a breakdown waiting to happen appalled him. If the car had given up the ghost in the wrong place, the result could have been disastrous. Something of his revulsion must have shown on his face, because Olivia grinned at him as he looked her car over.

"Now you see why we took the bus," she said in a near whisper so the children wouldn't hear.

"You sure wouldn't have made it in this thing," he agreed grimly, just as Chloe piped up, making no effort to keep her voice down.

"This is your *car?*" she asked Sara with obvious horror.

Trust my tactful daughter, Seth thought, shooting a glance at Olivia's face. She, in turn, looked swiftly at Sara. Good mother that she was, her concern was all for her child, and it showed in her expression.

"Yeah." Sara's voice was low, and her whole demeanor was suddenly so downcast that Seth realized the child was embarrassed. She looked so much like Olivia had as a little girl that from the beginning it had been easy for him to like her, although from what he could tell her per-

276

sonality was far different from her mother's. Sara struck him as shy, quiet, and vulnerable, and he didn't want her to feel bad about something as unimportant as a banged-up old car.

"I used to have a car just like this when I was a college student," he lied cheerfully, walking around the hood of the car. "The great thing about it was that I never had to worry if somebody dented it, or if it would get stolen at night while I slept. If you live in a city like this, you have to worry about those kinds of things, you know."

"You mean if we brought the Jaguar here, somebody would steal it?" Chloe asked, round-eyed.

"They might," Seth answered, grasping the driver's door handle and feeling a spurt of surprise when it didn't immediately fall off in his hand. Sara looked much more cheerful suddenly, and Olivia smiled at him, a slow and charming smile that thanked him without words for saving face for her daughter.

For the sake of that smile, Seth would have told ten times as many lies.

"I'll drive," Olivia said, moving to stand beside him as he opened the door. She slipped past him, sliding into the driver's seat before he could protest. "*I* know where we're going. You don't."

He let her drive. Having taught her to drive himself, he had no very great opinion of her skill behind the wheel, but, after a stop to pick up some boxes, she managed to get them safely to their destination. Her apartment was in a working-class section of town, and when he saw the building — it was seven stories high, brick, with tenement-style windows, on a block with five other identical buildings — he was reminded of the car. The apartment building was a junker, too.

The apartment itself was better. A quick glance told him that it was small, although all he could see from the door was the tiny, galley-style kitchen, a part of the hall, and the living room–dining room combination, which the door opened directly into. The carpet was faded tan, and obviously cheap. The walls were basic white. But what he could see of it was immaculately clean, and it looked like a home, with comfortable if inexpensive furniture and dozens of thriving green plants.

Sara's face lit up as she walked inside. As plainly as if she had spoken, Seth could read the word *home* on her face, and he wondered suddenly if Olivia had had to talk her into the move to LaAngelle Plantation. Olivia must have seen the same thing, because she leaned over to whisper something in her ear. Sara looked up at Olivia, and nodded solemnly.

"Olivia! Is that you?" A woman burst through the apartment door, which Seth, the last person to enter, had not yet closed. The first thing he noticed was her red hair, obviously dyed, which was done up in some sort of kooky knot on top of her head that left the ends sticking up like feathers. Her gauzy purple pants and top caught his eye next. Only then, when she had brushed by him as though he wasn't there, did he realize that she was tall, attractive, and from the looks of her maybe just a little older than Olivia.

"Sue!" Olivia turned, smiling, and the two women hugged. "Thanks for watering the plants. They look great."

"Hi, Sue," Sara said, already on the way out of the living room with Chloe following close behind her. Both of them were dragging large, empty boxes.

"Hi yourself, pipsqueak," Sue called after Sara, as the children disappeared down the hall. Then she focused again on Olivia.

"Tell me you were just kidding on the phone last night!" she demanded, stepping back from Olivia but keeping her hands on her shoulders while she looked with tragicomic intensity into her face. "You're not serious about moving to some little backwater in Louisiana, are you?"

One corner of Seth's mouth turned down wryly as he closed the door. Although he supposed, from the perspective of Houston, a little backwater in Louisiana was exactly what LaAngelle was.

"It's where I'm from," Olivia said excusingly, as her friend released her. "Sara and I are moving back to my old home."

"*Today?* Don't you know moving takes weeks — *months?* These things have to be planned!"

"Sue, I explained the whole thing over the

phone. We're just picking up clothes and a few personal items today. Movers are coming next week to get everything else."

"But you're *leaving* today! What am I going to do for a best friend?" Sue almost wailed. "I'll miss you!"

"I'll miss you, too," Olivia said promptly. "But we can talk on the phone. And you can come visit."

Seth felt a stirring of alarm at the idea — this woman didn't look like anyone ever seen before in LaAngelle. Before he could take the thought any further, Olivia was introducing him.

"Oh, my, I didn't realize you had a new boyfriend," Sue said, eyeing Seth up and down. "So *that's* why . . . But what's Mark going to say?"

"Seth's my cousin," Olivia said firmly, although she knew as well as he did that he technically was not. "And Mark and I have dated exactly twice. We're really just friends. He doesn't have anything to say about this at all."

Mark — he'd known there had to be a man, Seth thought. With Olivia, there had always been men.

"If you say so, girlfriend. But I don't imagine he would agree with that. Does he know about this?"

"I called him when I called you, and Anna, and Marybeth, and Dr. Green. . . ."

"What did Dr. Green say about your quitting your job?" Sue was instantly diverted.

"He was very nice about it. He said he understood that I needed to get Sara settled before school started. He wished me well."

"Mom, can we take my Beanie Babies with us today?" Sara emerged from the back part of the apartment to ask.

Olivia glanced at Seth. "Is there room? She has quite a few."

"Sure." Seth spoke to Sara. "Bring anything you like. Except the furniture. I don't think there's room for your bed on the plane."

Sara giggled. "Okay," she said, and left the room again.

"Plane?" Sue was mouthing at Olivia as Seth looked back at them. "*His* plane?"

Olivia nodded.

"Oh, my. And he's sexy, too."

"He's getting married in two months."

"To *you?*"

"No, nincompoop. He's my *cousin*, remember?"

Olivia was looking at him by this time, and from her expression she realized that he was perfectly well aware of what they were saying. Her cheeks pinkened. Seth watched with interest. He had rarely seen Olivia blush. She didn't have the complexion, or the temperament, for it.

"What do you want me to do?" he asked, pushing away from the door. Sue was eyeing him with a calculating gleam in her eyes that he had seen dozens of times before. He'd just as soon take himself out of her orbit.

Olivia put him to work clearing out kitchen

cabinets, while she and her friend carried most of the plants down the hall to Sue's apartment. Olivia was giving them to her, all except for a cactus garden that belonged to Sarah and a huge fern of which she was particularly fond. Seth guessed that, like the Beanie Babies, it was destined to go back on the plane with them.

Seth finished emptying the cabinets, and headed down the hall toward Chloe's bedroom. Just before he reached the open door, he got a glimpse of the little girls, who were sitting on the floor, apparently putting the contents of Sara's small white chest into a box. He stopped just outside the room as he overheard part of their conversation.

"Who's that?" Chloe asked, holding a small, gold-framed picture that Sara had just removed from a drawer.

"My dad." Sara reached out and took the picture, handling it carefully.

"I thought you didn't have a dad."

"Yeah, I do. It's just — he and my mom are divorced, and I don't see him much anymore. He lives in Oklahoma now, and he's got a new wife." There was a wealth of sadness in her voice.

"My mom's like that, only she lives in California. After they get married again, they don't want you anymore." Chloe was so matter-of-fact that Seth winced. Was that really what those children thought?

He retreated back to the kitchen so quietly that the girls never heard him, leaned against the counter, and took a deep breath. Guilt stabbed him again. He'd been seeing Mallory when Chloe came to live with him. Soon afterward, they'd gotten pretty hot and heavy. Chloe's misbehavior had worsened as his involvement with Mallory had increased, he realized as he thought about it. Once they got engaged, she'd become unbearable. Seth wondered that he hadn't made the connection before.

Chloe was afraid that once he and Mallory were married he wouldn't want her anymore.

Olivia had seen it. She had told him Chloe felt unloved.

Seth felt like the biggest prick alive. It was suddenly as clear as a pane of glass to him that he had been neglecting his daughter.

The problem was, he didn't know quite what to do to make things right. Something more was required of him, he thought, than just sitting Chloe down and telling her flat out that she was his daughter and he would always want her, whether he was married to Mallory or not.

He was still pondering the question on the flight back to Baton Rouge. In contrast to the nonstop chatter that had marked the flight to Houston, it was quiet in the plane for the return trip. Lulled by the drone of the engines, Chloe and Sara were both asleep in their seats, he saw with a glance around. Chloe's head lolled sideways onto her shoulder while Sara's rested back against the gray leather seat. Behind the girls, the enormous fern he had known Olivia would want

283

to bring took pride of place. Next to it was a box filled with Sara's Beanie Babies, with which the girls had played until they had fallen asleep. The rest of the gear was, thankfully, in the hold.

"Is Sara okay with moving?" he asked Olivia softly, after checking again to make sure the girls really were asleep.

Olivia looked sideways at him. "She's excited, I think, but a little scared, too. It's hard for a child her age to change schools and friends and everything."

"Did you have much work persuading her?"

It was growing dark outside. The horizon was limned with vivid pinks and oranges and silvers, but up where they were the sky was nearly purple, and a handful of stars had popped out. Just enough light remained to enable him to see her clearly without turning on the inside lights.

Olivia had one leg drawn up under her, one hand on the armrest and the other in her lap, and her head rested back against the seat. She looked tired, faintly rumpled — and so beautiful that he couldn't believe the woman he was looking at was the girl he had known for so many years.

"I didn't really have to persuade her. It was the possibility of a cat that did it, I think," she said, not very clearly. Or maybe he had missed something. He'd been so busy looking at her that it was entirely possible.

"A cat?" His question was wary. If, by chance, what she'd said made sense, he didn't want her to know he didn't know it.

"Sara wants a cat more than anything in the world. We can't have one in our apartment. I told her she could have one at LaAngelle Plantation. You don't mind, do you?"

"Livvy, you don't have to ask me if Sara can have a cat at LaAngelle Plantation. It's your home. Sara — and you — can have anything you like."

Olivia smiled at him. "Sara will be thrilled."

"I overheard them talking today, Sara and Chloe," Seth said abruptly. "From something Chloe said — you were right. I think she does feel unloved. The problem is, I don't know what to do about it."

For a moment she looked at him without saying anything. "Are you asking me for advice?" There was a note to her voice that told him their quarrel had not been entirely forgotten.

"I guess I am."

"My goodness, this is a first."

"A watershed moment in our relationship, hmmm?" Seth said dryly. "Okay, Livvy, quit gloating. What do you think I should do?"

"Spend time with her. Do fun things with her. Don't just drop her off to play tennis, play tennis with her. Get involved in her school activities. That kind of thing." A sudden smile, quickly suppressed, made the corners of her mouth quiver. "Play Barbies with her."

Knowing when he was being teased, Seth shot her a quelling look. "I'm serious."

Olivia laughed. "All right, so I was kidding

285

about playing Barbies. The key is for you to spend time with her in a way you both enjoy, I think. Let her know you like being with her. Hug her. Tell her you love her. And Seth . . ." She hesitated.

"Hmmm?" He glanced at her questioningly.

She looked at him without speaking for a moment. He got the impression that she was hesitant to say whatever was on the tip of her tongue.

"Go on," he said.

"Maybe you and Chloe and Mallory should spend time doing things together, too. Fun things. So Chloe can get used to the idea of the three of you as a family."

"Good idea," he said. And he knew it was. But he had trouble picturing himself, Chloe, and Mallory doing anything together that would not end with a tantrum from Chloe and a diatribe from Mallory. Suddenly he realized that he was having trouble picturing the three of them as a family, too.

And that gave him something else to think about all the way home.

chapter 29

Donaldson, Louisiana — October 19, 1976

I hate school. According to the chimes of the big grandfather clock downstairs, it was just after two A.M. Unable to sleep, Kathleen Christofferson lay sprawled on her stomach in the too-soft double bed in her grandmother's guest bedroom, her head with its hated flaming-red mop hidden under a pillow, her hands closed into fists around folds of fresh-smelling white sheets. *I hate school, I hate school, I hate school.*

Little and skinny for ten years old, cursed with waist-length hair and freckles that all the kids teased made her look just like Pippi Longstocking, she had been, that day, the butt of jokes from the entire fifth grade.

Carrottop! Carrottop! Call the bunny rabbits!

It would help if her mom would let her get a pixie cut like a lot of the other girls so her hair wouldn't be so noticeable, but her mom wouldn't hear of it. *Your hair's beautiful,* she said. *You'll be thankful for it one day.*

Yeah, right, Kathleen thought with an inward snort. Like maybe if I were to get lost in a fog and needed somebody to find me, I might be thankful for it.

Everybody stared at her hair. This afternoon, some creepy guy followed her all the way to her grandmother's house after school. Her hair was what had attracted his attention, she knew. Without her hair, and her freckles, she wouldn't stand out at all. She would be perfectly ordinary, and that was what she wanted.

Be proud of being different. That was her mother again. Her mom was full of little snippets of advice like that. Of course, her dad had had red hair. That was why her mother and grandmother both liked her hair so much: It reminded them of him.

He'd been a helicopter pilot who had died in Vietnam a month before she was born.

Her mom was a librarian. The school librarian. It was her mom who had suggested that Ellen Maddox, the most stuck-up girl in her class, read *Pippi Longstocking* at the beginning of the year, as a matter of fact. Ellen had showed the book around, with the picture of skinny, freckle-faced, red-pigtailed Pippi on the front, and that was when everybody had started calling her names.

Just ignore them and they'll stop. That's what her mother said. But ignoring them didn't work.

Kathleen had tried that, had tried it today in fact, by burying her nose in a book and pretending she was deaf. But they'd just kept on and on and on until she couldn't take it anymore. To her eternal shame, she had finally burst into tears and run away to hide in the girls' bathroom.

She wasn't going back to school on Monday. She didn't know how she was going to get out of it, but she wasn't going back to school. She was absolutely determined about that.

Her mom was at a librarian convention in New Orleans this weekend, which was why she was staying with her grandma. Grandma was her father's mother, and she was really old, like ninety or something. Kathleen loved her, though. She wished she'd known her father, Grandma's son. Grandma said that she looked like him, even without the hair.

There was a picture of him in a brass frame beside her bed. Even with the red hair, he'd been handsome. Kathleen kind of thought she looked like him, too. Anyway, she hoped she did.

All her life it had been just her and her mom, living alone in their own little house, and Grandma, living alone in this big one two blocks away. When Kathleen had asked why they didn't just all live together, her mom had said she and Grandma got on each other's nerves.

Unexpectedly, the third step from the top of the stairs creaked, jerking Kathleen from her reflections. It was the one that always creaked, whenever she went up or down the stairs. She would know the sound anywhere. Coming out of nowhere in the middle of the night, the sound was enough to make the hairs rise up on the back of her neck. For some reason, or no reason really except she just *was,* Kathleen was suddenly very, very scared.

Grandma was asleep in her bedroom at the end of the hall. *She* couldn't be coming up the stairs.

It was pitch-black with her head under the pillow. Kathleen couldn't see a thing. After that one creak, she didn't hear anything, either. Not another sound. But she was positive, absolutely positive, that someone was in her room, which was the one closest to the top of the stairs.

She lay still, hardly daring to breathe. But to her horror she realized that she could *hear* breathing — in and out, in and out, not very loud but really, truly there.

Someone *was* in the room with her.

Suddenly the pillow was plucked right off of her head.

"Peekaboo," a man's voice said.

Kathleen's eyes popped open. Her mouth popped open. Starting up, she got just a glimpse of a weird-looking head and huge shoulders bending over her. Then, before she could scream, before she could run, a cold, wet, sick-smelling rag was clamped over her nose and mouth.

Kathleen was so surprised that she gasped,

drawing in lungsful of the sweetish fumes. She gagged, coughing, and that was the last thing she knew.

He'd spotted this one coming out of a school. Her hair was beautiful — deep, flaming red. The sun had caught it, making it glow like it was lit from within. He'd never taken a redheaded one before, and he just couldn't resist. He'd been trying to be so good, too, really he had. He'd thought a lot about his little fetish since the last one — Maggie — and he'd decided that he wouldn't do it again. He'd even prayed to God in church to be delivered of his affliction. But prayers or no prayers, the urge had come on him with increasing strength in recent months, like there was a spring inside him that just kept getting wound tighter and tighter. He knew that if it got too tight the spring was going to break — and that's just what it had done today.

The monster in him was once again on the loose.

Like Charlie Brown in *Peanuts*, he was a sucker for a little redheaded girl.

The thought made him smile. He was still smiling as he stuffed the little redheaded girl in a canvas laundry bag, and, swinging the bag with her in it over his shoulder, carried her right out the front door of her own house.

chapter 30

The next month was so busy that Olivia barely had time to catch her breath. She settled into her job at the Boatworks, Sara and Chloe started school — they were in the same class, and Olivia didn't know if that was a good thing or a bad one — and Callie endured another cycle of chemotherapy. Big John remained hospitalized. Olivia was finally permitted to see him — Seth drove her in one day a week during lunch — but since he had not regained consciousness it wasn't the catharsis she had hoped for. The frail old man in the hospital bed with tubes sprouting from every part of his body bore almost no resemblance to the grandfather she remembered. Each time, she held his hand, murmured a few words, and then it was time for her and Seth to go.

As it became apparent that Big John was going to be in the hospital on a long-term basis, David and Keith had begun dividing the week between their home and LaAngelle Plantation. Weekends, which were the busiest time in the restaurant business, were spent in California. Monday through Thursday mornings they spent in LaAngelle, or, more properly, at the hospital. David and Belinda divided up the days, so that one or the other of them was pretty much always at the hospital. The rest of the family took turns as their schedules and responsibilities permitted. Even Keith went to the hospital, although he stayed away from Big John's bedside. But, as he said, he wanted to be nearby for David.

Seth obviously felt that he should be at the hospital more, but his first responsibility was to run the Boatworks. As Olivia, with her access to the books, had quickly learned, the business that had provided the family with its comfortable lifestyle for so long had started to deteriorate badly over the last decade or so. With Seth's insistence on taking commercial work, which many in the family still thought was beneath them, the company was slowly climbing back to financially sound footing, but every business transaction mattered. Seth oversaw every detail of the operation, from sales to production schedules to quality control. Without him, Olivia realized, Archer Boatworks would have gone the way of many longtime family businesses: sold to outsiders, or bankrupt.

Archer Boatworks had been in the business of turning out gentlemen's yachts for almost a hundred years, and the office systems seemed to be almost that old. Ilsa Bartlett, whom Olivia would be temporarily replacing, was a tall, thin (except for her midsection, which bulged ominously as she entered her eighth month of pregnancy) thirty-year-old of moderate attractiveness but a great deal of humor. She handled all the routine business of the office, and, as she candidly told Olivia, the job was a killer. Papers dating back to the company's inception were stored in a room in the main building that Ilsa referred to as the catacombs. It contained dozens of file cabinets squeezed into every available inch of space. In those file cabinets were what seemed like every scrap of paper ever generated by the business. In between answering the phone, keeping track of Mr. Archer's (Seth's) appointments, boat specifications, delivery dates and status, ordering and inventorying supplies, taking visitors on tours, and performing general secretarial tasks, Olivia was expected to transfer data from those long-stored documents onto the company's newly acquired computer system. It was a daunting task, complicated by the fact that no one, including Ilsa, seemed to be able to keep the computers up and running on a consistent basis. From her first hour on the job, Olivia perceived that she was going to be earning every penny of her generous salary. That relieved her mind of one worry: that Seth had offered her a "gimme" position either out of the kindness of his heart or just to get her to move back to LaAngelle.

Carl and Phillip both worked for the Boatworks, Phillip as assistant general manager and Carl as sales manager. As Seth's right-hand man, Phillip was always around, but Carl also seemed to have frequent business that brought him to the central office. Olivia never questioned the legitimacy of his visits until Ilsa remarked, dryly, that she had seen more of Carl since Olivia started work there than she had in the previous three years of her employment.

The Boatworks itself was located five miles to the west of town. It was a sprawling complex, consisting of a yacht storage facility, a repair shop, a retail sales center complete with four huge showrooms, a central office, the yacht design and building complex, and another construction facility devoted to barges. A twelve-foot-tall chain-link fence topped with razor wire surrounded the operation, making it look, to the uninitiated, rather like a prison. Approached from town, visitors were greeted by two large rectangular slabs of polished granite marking the entrance, both bearing the legend ARCHER BOATWORKS. A paved driveway then led across the flat, grassy lawn to the sales center, a two-story brick and glass building half as wide as a city block. Behind the sales center, directly atop the great earthen barrier of the levee that held back the mighty Mississippi, were two dozen warehouse-style buildings lined up one after the other that housed the rest of the operation. The location of these buildings on top of the levee was necessary because of the requirements of launching the completed or repaired vessels. When a yacht, or, increasingly, a barge, was ready, a crane would position it at the apex of a ramp composed of huge metal rollers that formed a path from the top of the levee to the river. With gravity to propel it and heavy-duty steel cables directing its slide, the vessel would be released and simply roll down the ramp into the water. The resulting splash made a giant wave capable of swamping anything in its path. Whenever a launch was planned, the Coast Guard was notified to stop traffic on the river for the required amount of time. It was a system that had worked beautifully, with some minor variations, for nearly a century.

As general manager, Seth put in long hours. He arrived at the Boatworks before seven most mornings, and basically worked until there was no work left to be done that day. Since their trip to Houston, he'd made an effort to get home no later than seven so he could spend a little time with Chloe before she went to bed. Some nights, when problems arose or there were prospective customers to be wined and dined, or he had a date with Mallory, he wasn't able to make his self-imposed deadline, but he was obviously trying to focus more on Chloe.

At Olivia's suggestion, he went with Chloe to her classroom on the first day of school — Olivia was surprised to learn that he had never done that before — and attended a midday library awards program a week later to watch Chloe (along with nearly all of her classmates except Sara, the newcomer) receive a medal for reading a certain number of books over the summer. Seeing Sara's downcast face after the program, Seth, all on his own, hit on the perfect way to both cheer her up and make her feel included: That evening, when he came home, he was carrying two small, exquisitely wrapped presents, one for Sara and one for Chloe. When the girls opened them, searching frantically through layers of tissue paper when it appeared that there was nothing inside, what they each found was his business card. Olivia watched, as perplexed as her daughter as Sara stared blankly at the card she held in her hand. Then Olivia saw, scrawled in Seth's handwriting on the back, the words *Look in my car.*

"Turn it over," she suggested softly. When they did, both girls squealed with excitement and tore out the back door and down the steps to where Seth had left his car parked on the pavement, instead of garaging it as he usually did.

Olivia, Seth, Martha, and Callie followed the children only as far as the veranda. From that vantage point, they watched as Sara and Chloe, chattering animatedly, peered through the windows, squealed again, and jerked open the right rear door. Seconds later, both girls emerged, clutching something close to their chests.

"Mom, come look!" Sara called, her voice

tremulous with awe.

Olivia went down the steps with the other adults behind her to find that Sara cuddled a tiny, fluffy smoke-gray Persian kitten. It had a pink ribbon tied around its neck with Sara's name on it. Chloe was holding an identical kitten, with her name on it.

"Oh, Sara!" Olivia exclaimed, giving her daughter a hug.

"A kitten's what I wanted more than anything else in the whole world," Sara said, the words solemn as if she couldn't believe her good fortune. She looked up at Seth, who had come up behind Olivia, shyly. "Thank you, Seth."

"You're welcome, Sara," Seth said, and Sara smiled at him, her eyes luminous with joy. He put a hand on her head, and then Chloe thrust her kitten under his nose and he exclaimed over it, too.

Later, when Olivia had a chance, she thanked him for his kindness.

"You notice I got two," he said, settled on the couch in front of the TV, his arms crossed over his chest as he watched the girls playing with their kittens on the floor of the den. "Absolutely identical, so they wouldn't have anything to fight over. You think I did good, huh?"

"You did good," Olivia confirmed. She was sitting on the couch, too, at the opposite end. Their gazes met, and she smiled at him, a warm and affectionate smile. He looked at her for a moment, smiled rather wryly in turn, and after a few moments got up and left the room.

Although Seth was still not quite comfortable with the more hands-on aspects of parenthood, like tucking his daughter in at night or giving her the occasional hug, he was making great progress, Olivia felt, by simply trying. Chloe responded to his increased attention by being — at least, for the most part — better behaved.

Time remained the problem. There was simply not enough of it for all Seth had to do, Olivia realized. Besides work, and Chloe, and Big John, there was Callie. Chemotherapy rendered her weak and ill, and she needed him, too, although she would have pooh-poohed the notion. But Seth was her only child, and they were devoted to each other. He spent as much time with her as he could, taking off from work a couple of mornings a week to sit with her while the cancer-killing chemicals dripped into her veins, and being there with her in the evenings after Chloe went to bed. In addition to everything else, the plans for his wedding were proceeding apace, and Mallory stopped by the Boatworks nearly every day to get his opinion on, or approval of, something concerning the ceremony or reception. With so many competing demands on his time, Olivia sometimes wondered how he could function at all, much less as efficiently as he always did.

By the end of September, Olivia's routine was firmly established. She rose at six thirty, got herself and the girls up, dressed, and fed, had Sara and Chloe at school by eight, herself at work by eight fifteen, worked until two forty-five, then picked up the girls at three. After that, she had her afternoons free for Sara — and Chloe. She supervised homework, arranged play dates, chauffeured the girls to soccer games, attended PTA meetings, and volunteered to assist with the Brownie troop, among countless other mommy-type activities. For the first time since Sara's birth, she had plenty of time to spend with her daughter. Except for her ever-present concern for Callie and Big John, and the bad dreams that increasingly plagued her, she was more content than she had been in years.

The dreams did not come every night. Olivia almost thought it would be easier if they did, because then she would expect them. As it was, there seemed to be no rhyme or reason to it: Some nights the dreams came, and some nights they did not.

In them, it was always night, she was always standing on the shore of the lake, and her mother, in some kind of flimsy white top with wide lace straps, was always in the water. Her mother cried out to her: *Run, Olivia! Run away! Go! Run away!* Then Selena would disappear beneath the surface of the water, pulled down by something Olivia could not see.

But what made the dreams especially terrible was that each time some new detail emerged: In one she saw that her mother's eyes were huge with terror, and her screaming mouth was bare of lipstick; in another she caught the ripples of something swimming in the water behind Selena as her frightened face turned toward shore; in a third she was a helpless observer as Selena sank, only to have one hand break the surface, fingers stretching frantically toward the sky, before it, too, was gone.

One thing never changed: Each time it happened, Olivia awoke terrified. She would lie in her bed, bathed in sweat, her eyes wide in the darkness as she reminded herself, over and over, that it was only a dream.

Or was it? She had never had dreams like this before returning to LaAngelle Plantation. Now they were so persistent, and so disturbing, that she was beginning to wonder if they were more than just products of her subconscious.

More than once, when the dream jarred her from sleep, she could almost swear that she caught a whiff, the merest whiff, of White Shoulders perfume.

It was her imagination, of course. Just like the dreams were almost certainly a manifestation of her fear of the lake. And she was afraid of the lake because her mother had drowned in it. When she thought it through rationally — which meant, in the daylight hours — the whole thing was perfectly logical.

Still, she made up her mind to ask Callie, or Seth, or someone, to tell her, in detail, about the night her mother died.

Just the thought gave Olivia cold chills. So she

put it off, enduring the dreams, telling herself that knowing the details would make no difference. Besides, everyone was so busy. Surely, sooner or later, the dreams would just go away.

The big event in LaAngelle at the end of September was the Fall Festival. Held on a Friday night on the combined grounds of both the elementary and high schools, it was a combination carnival, picnic supper, and dance, designed to raise money for PTA projects. Seth, as general manager of the Boatworks and one of LaAngelle's leading citizens, had been asked to serve a turn in the dunking booth. He was unenthusiastic but knew his duty, and left home around six thirty wearing swimming trunks and a T-shirt and taking dry clothes with him to change into later when his stint as target ended. Mallory and Chloe went with him in the Jaguar. Olivia had agreed to help out at the Cook's Corner booth, where homemade baked goods were for sale. She and every other elementary school mother had contributed cookies, cakes, brownies, and fancy breads in massive quantities so the booth wouldn't run out during the four-hour course of the event. Olivia had been assigned the first shift, from seven to eight, which would leave plenty of time for her to enjoy the other activities when she was finished. It was just getting dark when she and Sara drove into town with Callie and Ira and a trunk full of late-arriving baked goods in Ira's big Lincoln. Dressed in a black short-sleeved sweater and a short white denim skirt, lugging an armful of miscellaneous goodies loaded into brown paper bags — Ira and Sara were similarly laden down — Olivia reached her booth just as the first customer arrived. Setting out the best of what she had brought with her on the U-shaped trio of tables that was the sales area, she got down to work. She was glad to see that her shift partner was LeeAnn James, who had a kindergartner in the school. Looking adorable in jeans and a pink sweater set, Sara went off with her teacher, Jane Foushee, and a trio of third-grade girls who had agreed to take the early shift with their grade's fund-raising project, a cakewalk.

"Gosh, we're going to sell out in an hour," LeeAnn said after fifteen minutes of brisk business had depleted their stock by about a quarter. It was the first chance they'd had to talk since Olivia had sat down.

"Oh, no, everybody rushes over here first to get the really good stuff, like Mrs. Ramey's caramel cake and Louise Albright's chocolate chunk cookies. Once they're gone, the other things usually last awhile." It was amazing how fast she had gotten back into the swing of life in LaAngelle, Olivia reflected, answering LeeAnn with knowledge gleaned from years of attending the Fall Festival. Except for Sara, it would be easy to imagine that her nine years away had never been.

"I keep forgetting you grew up here," LeeAnn said with a laugh. "Since we went to high school together, I can't seem to get it out of my head that you're from Baton Rouge like me."

"Olivia, do you have any of Lurleen Sprewell's brownies left? My boys like 'em something fierce, but I'm late getting here tonight."

Olivia looked up at the speaker, Augusta Blair, with a smile. She was a contemporary as well as a friend of Callie's, and Olivia had known her, as she had the greater portion of the town, for most of her life. The boys she referred to were her three sons, grown now and all employed in various capacities at the Boatworks.

"Let me look." A glance around the table and then at the inventory underneath revealed two red paper plates piled with brownies, covered with plastic wrap and tied with Lurleen Sprewell's signature big red bows. Olivia produced them. "Sure do."

Mrs. Blair paid with a pleased smile, and carried her purchases away. The next customer in line was Father Randolph. He wanted a chocolate cake, but wasn't particular as to the cook. Knowing that, of the ones left, Ellen Gibbs's was probably the best, Olivia sold it to him. After that, she was so busy that she barely had time to exchange more than a word or two with her customers, almost all of whom she knew. When the second shift arrived, she surrendered her seat to them with relief.

"What are you going to do now?" LeeAnn asked, as they emerged together from the back of the booth. Olivia flexed her neck, which was stiff from looking up at customers for an hour, took a deep breath of the warm night air, and smiled.

"Check on Sara. She's helping out with the cakewalk."

"I'm going to go find Tom" — her husband — "and Michael." Michael was LeeAnn's five-year-old son. "See you later."

Olivia echoed her farewell, then headed toward the elementary school where the cakewalk was taking place in one of the classrooms. Light shone through every one of the two-story building's uncurtained windows, and Olivia could see people milling around inside. Besides the third grade's cakewalk, each grade had its own fundraiser. Olivia knew that inside the school were a doll-walk, a dart throw, a silent auction, a coin toss, and a pet beauty contest, and there were many other activities as well. A constant stream of people moved in and out of the main entrance.

Weaving through shifting throngs of townspeople, glancing at the booths on either side, Olivia exchanged greetings left and right but paused only once, to join the crowd at the dunking booth. Seth was seated on the platform, yelling good-natured insults at the beefy young man who was getting ready to hurl a baseball at the flat metal disc, which, if struck properly, would drop him into the tank of water above which he perched. He was already wet, his hair plastered to his skull, his plain white T-shirt clinging to his chest. Olivia watched, a smile lurking about her mouth. If she was not mistaken, the man throwing the baseball was a Boatworks' employee. The informality between employer and employee, the kind of banter that Seth was exchanging with him, was what made the Fall Festival fun. Seth spied her, grinned, waved — and promptly went down with a gigantic splash as the baseball struck the disc with a bang. Laughing, Olivia watched as he surfaced, slicking his hair back with both hands and shaking the water from his face.

"Lucky shot!" he yelled after the thrower, who was retreating with a wide grin and the prize of a stuffed animal. Another hopeful had already taken the winner's place, baseball in hand. Seth hoisted himself back into position on the platform. Water streamed from his body. Olivia's gaze moved over him as he yelled insults at the newcomer, noting how the wet T-shirt clung, revealing the broad strength of his shoulders and the solid muscles of his chest. His trunks were black and shiny-wet. Below them, he had an athlete's knees and calves, tanned and faintly fuzzed with hair. Long, narrow bare feet dangled above the pool. Her heartbeat quickened. There was, simply, nothing she could do about that. But she could move herself out of the way of temptation. A month of working for Seth, of having easy access to him every day, had taught her the wisdom of that. When he came near, she went elsewhere. It made life much less complicated.

chapter 31

Accordingly, Olivia turned her back on the dunking booth and walked on toward the elementary school. Sure enough, in moments her pulse had returned to normal. Her attraction to Seth was pure folly, and if she resisted it resolutely enough it would, sooner or later, go away.

She really needed to start seeing someone, she told herself. Olivia made a face, thinking about the candidates. Lamar Lennig still called her twice a week to ask her out, and Carl had also made it clear that he admired her. There were other possibilities, too: some of the Boatworks' employees who were available and interested, according to Ilsa, and a brother-in-law of LeeAnn's, with whom LeeAnn wanted to fix her up.

"Olivia, would you drop this off by Linda Ryder at the beanbag toss? Jamie needs to go potty." The speaker was Hailey Fragione, a pretty brunette of about her own age who had grown up in LaAngelle. Hailey, having gone to the local high school, had not been a friend of hers while they were growing up. In fact, they'd barely known each other. But now, hanging on with one hand to a Ziploc bag filled with change and a struggling-to-escape toddler with the other, she turned to Olivia as she would have to any other young mother of her acquaintance.

Olivia realized that her return to LaAngelle was no longer the nine-days wonder it had been at first, for which she was thankful. She was once again simply a citizen of the town.

"Sure," she said, accepting the bag, which was surprisingly heavy. Hailey thanked her with a smile thrown over her shoulder as she was dragged off by her child. The beanbag toss was about a dozen booths farther along. She would drop it off, then go check on Sara.

The theme of this year's Fall Festival was FrancoFete, in accordance with the statewide celebration to honor the three hundredth anniversary of France's establishment of a colony in the Louisiana Territory. The colors of the French flag were everywhere, from the bunting adorning the booths to the balloons tied to the trees, and the fleur-de-lis abounded, too. White Christmas lights were strung between the booths, lighting the area and dividing the soccer field to the side of the elementary school, where most of the outdoor booths were located, into a

308

series of impromptu walkways.

The picnic tables that had been set up under a huge white tent on the blacktop front parking lot of the elementary school were filling up with people who had ordered box suppers from the school cafeteria. A band playing zydeco music serenaded the diners. In the distance, strains of contemporary rock from the dance in the high school gymnasium could be heard. This close to the dining tent, though, the zydeco all but drowned the other out.

"Olivia! All by yourself?" The voice, and the hard male arm that slid around her waist, belonged to Lamar Lennig. She glanced at him, surprised, instinctively resisting his hold, and he grinned down at her as he held on tight. "Hello, beautiful!"

"Actually, I'm with the family." Olivia succeeded in twisting free. He rocked back on his heels — she saw that he was wearing the cowboy boots again, with tight jeans and a plaid shirt with the sleeves rolled up and tails tucked in — and stuck his thumbs in his belt loops. His black hair waved around his face and his dark eyes twinkled at her. He was undoubtedly handsome, what a lot of women would term a hunk, and he stirred not the tiniest bit of response in her.

"Family, huh?" Lamar looked around at the crowd milling past, raising his eyebrows in an exaggerated expression of skepticism. "You must have gotten lost, then."

"I've been working in the Cook's Corner. My

shift just ended, and I'm on my way to fetch Sara."

"Let me buy you dinner first." He reached out, touched her mouth with a hard forefinger, and smiled at her. "For old times' sake."

Old times with him were just what she wanted to forget.

"No, thanks, Lamar." She stepped back, smiled, shook her head, and started to walk away.

"Hey, wait a minute." Catching her arm, Lamar pulled her back around to face him. He was frowning, and his dark eyes were intent on her face. "I don't mind a chick playing hard to get, but this is getting stupid. What do I have to do to get you to go out with me, get down on my knees and beg?"

"Nope." Without making a big production out of it, Olivia tried to pull her arm free. When he wouldn't release her, she sighed. The only thing to do was very gently set him straight. "Let me go, Lamar. You can't talk me into going out with you, not now, not ever. It wouldn't be good for either of us."

"What do you mean by that?" His eyes narrowed at her, and his hand tightened on her arm.

"I mean I've changed. I'm not the girl you used to know. I'm a mother now, a straight arrow, a homebody. I'd bore you to tears in an hour."

"Baby, the way you look, you could never bore me." He moved closer, gripping her other arm as well. His gaze ran suggestively up and down her body before fastening on her mouth. As a seventeen-year-old, she would no doubt have found such an open display of desire sexy. As a twenty-six-year-old, she was just plain annoyed by it.

Olivia glanced around. Although literally dozens of people she knew were nearby, she didn't know them well enough to be able to use her eyes to signal her wish for a tactful rescue. The music prevented them from overhearing what was being said, even if anyone was paying attention, which no one seemed to be. She was in no real danger in the midst of such a crowd, of course, and almost certainly in no real danger from Lamar in any case. She had only to tell him to let her go convincingly enough, and he would. Wouldn't he? She hoped so. If he forced her to make a scene, the ensuing gossip would linger for weeks.

"Let me go, Lamar." The words were a quiet order.

"If you let me buy you supper."

"Thanks, but no." It was a definite refusal, as she tried again — subtly, so as not to attract too much notice — to free herself from his hold.

"Tomorrow night, then." He was no longer smiling, and his eyes had grown hard.

"Thanks, but no."

"Next Friday? Or Saturday?"

"I don't think so. But thanks."

"In other words, get lost?"

Olivia was losing her patience. "Something like that, yeah." She succeeded in pulling her arms free. The flesh above her elbows where his fingers had dug in stung a little, and she guessed she would have marks there later.

"Think you're too good for me now, Olivia?"

This was definitely starting to get ugly. Olivia shrugged, and turned away without replying. Lamar stepped in front of her, blocking her path.

"Baby, I've *had* you, remember? And if I was the daughter of the town slut turned suicide, I wouldn't think I was so all-fired high and mighty."

Ordinarily, the reminder that she'd been fool enough to sleep with him would have stung. But she was too stunned by what had come after. She gaped at him soundlessly, her lips parting, her eyes growing huge.

"Get the hell away from her, Lamar." The voice, with its dangerous, quiet threat, and the hands that came down on her shoulders, belonged to Seth. The solid strength of his hands tethered her, held her still, kept her upright. She drew strength from them, from the knowledge that Seth was behind her, even as she felt the color leach from her face and the world beyond the three of them blur.

Lamar looked over her head, his expression belligerent. Olivia knew he was looking at Seth, felt the silent clash of wills, saw the sudden flicker in Lamar's eyes as he gave way. His mouth tightened, his gaze fell, and then without another word he turned on his heel and walked away.

Olivia was left standing there, staring after

him, feeling as if she had been kicked in the stomach.

"Seth . . ." she said piteously.

"Livvy." Seth turned her around to face him. A glance must have sufficed to reveal the shock she had suffered, because his jaw tightened along with his hands.

"Lamar said . . . he said . . ."

"I heard what he said." His voice was grim. He looked quickly around, at the crowd of friends and neighbors brushing by on either side without casting more than an occasional casual glance toward the drama being played out in their midst.

"Seth . . ." She wanted to ask if it was true, but she couldn't get the words out. Her mouth felt as if it were full of cotton. Her chest was so tight she could hardly breathe.

"We can't talk here." With another glance around, he let go of her shoulders and caught one of her hands instead, his fingers entwining with hers. "Come with me."

He started walking and she went with him, still mindlessly clutching the plastic bag full of change. He responded to the greetings that came his way with a smile and a wave, but never slowed his pace. Olivia, on the other hand, could neither smile nor wave. She felt like a zombie, sleep-walking through the night.

He led her away from the festival, away from the music and lights and people, around the far side of the school to a gray metal door that led into the gym. The gym was deserted. Lit by fluorescent fixtures high overhead, it was a cavernous space with a highly polished wood floor and metal bleachers folded back against three of the white-painted concrete block walls. She followed him across the basketball court to an alcove at its far end. The entrance to the locker rooms, girls' and boys', were on either side of the alcove. Seth pushed open the door marked boys, and pulled her in with him.

Like the gym, the locker room was deserted. Olivia barely registered the banged-up gray lockers that lined the walls, the gray-and-white-and-scarlet tiled floors, the showers and toilet facilities in another room off to the left. Even the smell — of damp, dirty socks and disinfectant — didn't reach her. Olivia would have gone anywhere Seth took her. That he had chosen to take her into a boys' locker room was immaterial.

"Give me a minute to get dressed, okay?" Only then did Olivia notice that he was still wearing the soaked T-shirt and shorts, with shower thongs on his bare feet. With the part of her mind that remained capable of noticing such things, she thought, *he must be freezing* — and indeed, she could just see the tiny puckered nubs of his nipples pressing against his wet shirt. The air-conditioned building was much cooler than the warm night outside, and she thought she felt goose bumps springing up along her arms. Looking up her arm from where his hand was joined with hers, she saw that it was so.

"Sit down." Seth pulled her to one of the long, closely spaced wooden benches with which the room was furnished and gently pushed her down on it. Setting the Ziploc bag on the bench beside her, Olivia obediently sat, leaning forward, bare knees together, hands clasped on top of them. Giving her a frowning glance, he moved a few paces away and opened one of the long, narrow lockers. His clothes — khaki pants, navy polo shirt, underwear, socks and shoes — were inside.

"Seth."

Bunching his clothes in one hand and holding his shoes in another, he turned to look at her.

"Is it true?" Her voice was thin, high. Her eyes met his with silent entreaty. *Please let it be a lie.* But she knew already that it wasn't.

"Livvy . . ." He didn't have to say anything more. She'd known him too long. The answer was written all over his face, as it had been ever since Lamar had said the thing. Still, she had hoped against hope. Her eyes widened as if from a blow, and her mouth went suddenly dry. She licked her lips, trying to moisten them. Her chest felt as if it was being crushed by lead weights.

"Jesus Christ, Livvy, it was twenty years ago." Seth dropped his shoes on the floor with a clatter, his clothes on the bench nearest him, then yanked his wet T-shirt over his head, dropped it on the floor and replaced it with the dry polo shirt. Olivia was so upset that she barely registered the brief sight of him dressed only in trunks. She retained only a blurred impression of a wide, strong-looking chest with impressive muscles, and a wedge of brown hair. Then Seth stepped over the bench on which the rest of his clothes lay, and stood for a moment in front of her. Her head was bent, but she felt him looking down at her, sensed his concern.

"He said — my mother was a *suicide?*" Hard as it was to move, she tilted her face up to ask the question, knowing she could read more in his expression than he would tell her. He met her gaze, his eyes narrowed, his mouth tight. She knew that he hated her pain, and his helplessness in the face of it.

"Livvy." He sank down on the bench directly opposite her, so close that their knees almost touched, and leaned forward to take both her hands in his. She met his gaze, reading anger and sorrow for her in his blue eyes.

"Seth, please tell me. I need to know."

"You don't need to know. You never needed to know." His voice was rough. His eyes were dark with the reflection of her distress.

"Seth . . ." The rest of her plea trailed away unspoken. He knew her well enough. He could read it in her eyes.

"Okay. Okay." He glanced away from her, wet his lips, and looked back. "Your mother apparently just walked into the lake one night. She'd gone to bed earlier. Uncle James had been away for a couple of days, traveling on business. He got home a little after midnight, went up to see his wife, discovered she was missing, and started looking for her, first in the house and then outside. There were a lot of people in the house that night, and everybody eventually spread out to search the grounds. Big John found Selena floating in the lake. Charlie tried to revive her — he'd been at the house with Belinda — but it was too late. Her death was later ruled a suicide."

Olivia closed her eyes and held on tightly to his hands, which were the only warm things in a suddenly icy world. After a moment she opened her eyes and looked at him. That bare-bones account was undoubtedly designed to save her pain, but it left too much out.

"But why?" she asked. "Why did they think it was suicide? Couldn't it have been an — an accident?"

His eyes as she met them reflected her misery. "She was still wearing her nightgown when she was found. There was no reason for her to be anywhere near the lake at that hour of the night. And — and they said she'd been depressed in the weeks before it happened."

"Who said?"

"Charlie. He was treating her for depression. Apparently she was taking some kind of medication."

"But why would she be depressed? What was wrong?"

"Livvy, can't you let this alone?" He sounded, and looked, wretched at the idea of having to tell her whatever more there was. And there was more. She could tell by looking at him.

"Seth, please."

His clasp on her hands tightened, as though he would impart some of his strength to her.

chapter 32

"I was only a teenage kid at the time, okay? I may not have everything one hundred percent right." Seth sucked in a breath, then let it out slowly, his eyes never leaving her face. "They said she killed herself because she'd been having an affair, and Uncle James had found out and was threatening to divorce her. They said that's why he came home unexpectedly that night, because he was hoping to catch her with whoever the man was."

Olivia cringed. Jumbled memories of her life with her mother and stepfather spun through her consciousness. Although she could not slow them down enough to concentrate on any one, she thought — the impression she had was that they were happy together. All three of them were happy together.

"Who was it? The man." Her voice sounded strange, like it did not belong to her.

"I don't know. Hell, I don't even know if there was a man. That's just how the story was told to me."

"Oh, God." That explained it, then. Explained Lamar's remarks, and Callie's odd hesitation when talking about Selena's death, and even Seth's concern when he saw her, as he thought, walking into the lake. Her gaze met his. "That's why — you came after me when you saw me at the lake that day. You thought I might be going to kill myself, didn't you? Like mother, like daughter, hmmm?"

His mouth thinned in an apologetic grimace. "I didn't really think that. It was just an — instinctive reaction."

"I should have been told. I should have known this a long time ago."

"Why?" His hands tightened on hers. Their knees touched. His eyes were intent as they met her gaze. "It's over and done with. In the past. Nothing you, or I, or anyone else can do can change anything about it. And it has nothing to do with you. Nothing to do with your life, or the person you are. Nothing at all, you hear?"

He sounded so fierce that she managed a wavery smile for him. "I hear."

"Good." He took a deep breath. "You okay?"

She nodded.

"You sure?"

"I'm sure." In truth, she was anything but okay, but if she told the truth about how she was feeling she would scare him to death.

"Okay. I'm going to put the rest of my clothes on now, and then I'm going to take you home." He let go of her hands and stood up. "Okay?"

It was an effort to collect her thoughts. Lifting her gaze to meet his was one of the hardest things she had ever done. "Sara. I can't go home without Sara."

"We'll get Sara. Or you can let her stay and have fun, and Mother or Mallory can bring her home."

Unable to say more, Olivia nodded.

Seth looked down at her for an instant longer, his expression troubled. Then he grabbed his clothes from the bench and headed into the anteroom that held the showers and toilets.

Left alone, Olivia slowly bent almost double, wrapping her arms around her legs and resting her head on her knees. Nausea assailed her, and her head throbbed and spun. Visions of her mother — or was it herself? — walking into the night-dark lake evolved from the first blurred images of what almost seemed like an out-of-focus movie into an experience that was suddenly, startlingly real.

She was wearing a nightgown, an ankle-length, flimsy white nylon nightgown with wide lace straps, and no shoes. The night was hot and muggy, and there were mosquitoes. Moonlight reflected off the shiny surface of the lake, lighting a path for her to follow. As she stepped into the water and it rose around her, it felt warm and brackish, just as it had the other day when she

321

had stepped in it. The smell was the same, too, the slightly fetid smell of stagnant water and rotting vegetation: the smell of the lake. Her bare feet sank deep into the mud; it squished between her toes, swallowed her ankles. Water rose higher and higher, swirling about her as she waded out, wetting her nightgown to the knees, the waist. . . .

Suddenly she was no longer a participant, but an observer. From the vantage point of the lakeshore, she watched her mother flounder and drown, helpless to do anything to alter what was happening. Tears filled her eyes, squeezing past closed lids to course down her cheeks. Her grief was suddenly as overwhelming as if she were, truly, watching her mother drown.

"Livvy?" Seth was back in the room with her. She heard him say her name, knew he was there, but was powerless to respond, to stop the tears, to turn off the grief. She cried silently, her head bowed so that her forehead rested on her knees, hoping that he would just leave her be.

"Livvy." He squatted down in front of her, his hands smoothing her hair back from her face, his fingers finding the tears on her cheeks and tracing their path. "Are you *crying?* Look at me."

She wouldn't. She knew it would upset him, and she didn't want to do that. If she could have turned off the tears, she would have. But she was overflowing with sorrow, and there was simply nothing she could do to stop it.

"Damn it, Livvy." He sounded as if he felt as

helpless as she did. His arms came around her, awkward because of her position. He stroked her back through her thin black sweater, and patted it clumsily. "Don't cry. Please. Whatever happened in the past, it's not worth a moment of your tears."

She tried to stop. She really did. She scrunched her eyes up tight and took a deep gulp of air — but the gulp turned into a sob and the tears continued to flow.

"Shit." He stood up, his hands circling her wrists, pulling her up with him. She came to her feet at his urging, limp but unresisting, her eyes still closed as she did battle with the insurgent tears. Her hair swung back from her face as her head tilted back, all except for a few strands that clung to her wet cheeks. He smoothed the stray hairs away with gentle fingers and pulled her against him. His arms closed around her, enfolding her icy body with his warmth.

Olivia buried her face against his chest, wrapped her arms around his waist, and cried as if her heart would break.

"Shh. Shh, Livvy. Don't cry. Please don't cry." Holding her tight, he rocked her back and forth. "It's stupid to cry about something that happened twenty years ago. Please don't cry."

His murmured attempts at consolation reached her, soothing the raw edges of her grief. As her sobs lessened in intensity, she could feel the strength in his arms and the hardness of his chest beneath her cheek. He smelled good, with

some indescribable combination of fabric soft-
ener (his shirt), chlorine (the dunking booth),
and man. He was taller than her, broader than
her, and stronger than her, and she liked that.
But what she liked best was that he was, simply,
Seth.

Her tears lessened and finally stopped, and for
a little while after that she was content to just lie
against him, tired out by the force of the emotion
that had racked her and comforted by being held
in his arms.

There was nowhere else on earth where she
felt safer, Olivia realized. Nowhere else on earth
that felt more like home.

He, in turn, seemed to be in no big hurry to let
her go.

She should unlock her arms from around his
waist, ease out of his arms, announce that she
was all better now, and apologize for the wet
splotch she had made on the front of his shirt.

That was absolutely what she should do. She
knew it as well as she knew her name.

Instead she snuggled closer still, savoring the
feel of him, the smell of him, the feeling of both
safety and danger that he evoked in her now that
the maelstrom of grief that she had been caught
up in had subsided.

He was Seth, her Seth, but she wanted more
than comfort from him now.

Somehow he must have sensed the alteration
in her, because his body changed even as she
held him. The muscles of his back tensed be-

neath her clinging hands. With her ear pressed to his chest, she could hear the acceleration of his heart.

Olivia felt her own heartbeat speed up until it was pounding in her ears. For her own sake, for the sake of their relationship, she needed to move out of his arms now. . . .

She moved all right, turning her head and lifting it away from his chest so that she could look at him. But her arms had a mind of their own, and they weren't letting him go. Her body had a mind of its own, too, and it wasn't separating from his by so much as a millimeter.

His head was bent protectively close to hers. She looked up into his eyes, and found that they were very near. They were dark and turbulent, and as she met them he partially lowered his lids as though to hide what was in them from her. His facial muscles were tense. His mouth was clamped into a hard, straight line. He looked like a man doing battle with his own desire.

"Seth," she whispered, unable to help herself as her chin tilted up and her mouth moved infinitesimally closer to his.

"Better?" he asked, and his voice was hoarse. His gaze slid from her eyes to her mouth and back.

Olivia nodded. Her breathing had quickened, and so, she saw, had his. From her shoulders down her body was so close to his that they were practically fused together. Some of it was her fault — she pressed against him like they were two halves of the same piece of Velcro.

But his arms were wrapped around her, too, and he wasn't letting her go.

"Seth," she said again, her voice a soft breath of sound. Her eyes locked with his, and she saw the hot flicker in their depths, the sudden dilating of his pupils. His arms tightened around her, pulling her closer yet, and she could feel the slight tremor that racked them.

"Jesus Christ, Olivia." His voice was thick, hoarse, almost unrecognizable. This time *he* moved, pulling her up on tiptoe as his mouth came down on hers.

His mouth slanted across hers with fierce hunger. His tongue slid between her lips, touching hers, possessing her mouth. Olivia kissed him back just as fiercely, opening her mouth for his taking, possessing his in turn. She couldn't get enough of him, just as he, it seemed, couldn't get enough of her.

Without ever lifting his mouth from hers he turned her around and edged her a step backward. Olivia found herself with her back against the row of lockers. The metal was slick against her sweater and skirt. She could feel the coolness of it against the backs of her calves. A locker handle dug into her side. She barely noticed, and didn't care.

He pressed full against her, his weight pressing her into the lockers. She could feel the whole long, muscular length of him. Her body was covered by his, flattened by his, aroused by his. One hand slid beneath her hair to cup the back of her skull, tilting her face up to his. His other hand found her breast, caressing it through her thin black sweater and the silky nylon of her bra.

Olivia felt an explosion of desire so hot and primitive that her insides seemed to melt. She made a little mewling sound deep in her throat, and her hands delved beneath the hem of his polo shirt to flatten against the bare skin of his back.

His back was warm, and muscular, the skin silky smooth and faintly damp with sweat. She slid her hands upward, dislodging his shirt in the process, stroking the long muscles with her palms, and he groaned into her mouth.

His hand came under her sweater, moving up over her rib cage and slipping beneath her bra. Big and hard and hot, it closed over her breast, and Olivia went weak at the knees. If his weight against her hadn't been holding her up, she would have sunk bonelessly to the floor.

His thumb swept across her nipple. Quite unable to help herself, Olivia began to tremble. She clutched him tightly, her nails digging into his back. *She wanted him.*

"Seth?" The locker room door swooshed open, footsteps sounded on the tile floor, and Phillip's voice called out urgently, all at the same time.

Seth moved quickly, his head lifting, his body shifting so that his back blocked Phillip's view of her. Her hands flattened on his back, and then were still. Trying to hide the fact that they were underneath Seth's shirt was useless. From where he was standing just inside the door, Phillip would have an unimpeded view of Seth's back, at the very least.

From Phillip's sudden silence, and the lack of footsteps or other sounds, Olivia surmised that he was standing there frozen in shock, staring at them. She couldn't be sure, because Seth's body blocked her from seeing Phillip, too.

"What is it?" Seth turned his head to speak over his shoulder, his voice remarkably cool. His hand slid out from beneath her sweater. Her breast tingled at the withdrawal, and she felt suddenly bereft. She took a deep breath, trying to steady herself. But her body had a mind of its own, and continued to tingle and burn.

"God, I'm sorry. I had no idea. . . ." Phillip's voice trailed off, and he took a deep, obviously embarrassed breath. "Your mother's collapsed. She's been taken to the hospital."

"*What?* What happened?" Seth whipped around to look at Phillip, and Olivia's hands fell away from his back. Shocked at the news, still not quite sure of her knees, she crossed her arms over her throbbing breasts and leaned against the lockers, staring at Phillip over Seth's shoulder. She was frightened for Callie — and she also felt very vulnerable suddenly, and ashamed. There was no excuse for her, either. She'd known from the beginning that getting sexual with Seth was a stupid, stupid thing to do.

"I don't know. She just collapsed. Ira went with her in the ambulance, and Mallory . . ." Phillip's voice faltered, and his gaze slid past Seth to Olivia. He turned beet red as their eyes met, and from the way her face felt she supposed she did, too. "Mallory sent everybody she could find in search of you."

Seth took a quick breath, and seemed to make a conscious effort to get a grip on his emotions. "Where's Chloe?" It was a rapid-fire question.

Phillip shook his head. "I don't think she was with Aunt Callie when she collapsed. I know she wasn't with Mallory." He glanced at Olivia again, as if his gaze was drawn to her almost against his will, then back at Seth. His voice was unhappy as he said, "Mallory got Ira's keys from him, and she's sitting in his Lincoln out in front of the school right now, waiting to drive you straight to the hospital."

Of course, Olivia thought, *Mallory* would be going to the hospital with Seth. He was going to marry *Mallory*. How could she have been so stupid as to let herself forget?

"I'll find Chloe and bring her home," Olivia volunteered. To her surprise, her voice sounded almost normal. Right now, the best thing she could do for Callie — and Seth — was take care of Chloe.

Seth and Phillip both looked at her.

"Take my car." Without arguing, Seth dug in his pocket for the keys. He glanced at Phillip as he handed them to Olivia.

"Give me a second here, will you?" Seth said.

Phillip and Seth exchanged a purely masculine look.

"Oh. Sure." Phillip nodded, the movement jerky, glanced again at Olivia, and withdrew.

Seth turned back to her. His gaze met hers, and his mouth twisted almost wryly.

"You okay?" he asked.

Olivia nodded. "Fine. Go." If he said he was sorry, she thought, she would want to die.

"I'm going" was what he said. Then he leaned over to drop a quick, hard kiss on her mouth. "I'll call you from the hospital. Try not to worry: I doubt if it's anything serious. And don't forget about Chloe."

"No, I won't."

Her lips quivered from that kiss. Even as she spoke, Olivia found that she was talking to his back. Seconds later he was gone, the door swinging shut behind him, and she was left standing there in the boys' locker room, alone.

chapter 33

"No! Go find your own place! You can't hide in here with us! You're too fat! Your big butt will stick out, and we'll get caught for sure!" The two girls giggled, blocking the way into their hiding place — a narrow space between a central air-conditioning unit and the stucco wall of the school — with a flattened cardboard box.

Left alone outside that coveted hiding spot, Sara backed away. Her lower lip quivered, but she bit down hard on it and refused to allow herself to cry. She should be used to it by now, but being called fat really hurt. Especially by Chloe, who was supposed to be her friend.

"Ready or not, here we come!" Eric Albright and Jeff Stolz were "it," and their yell galvanized Sara into looking around for another hiding spot. Not that Eric or Jeff would be looking for her, particularly. She wasn't one of the popular girls. They would be looking for Chloe, and her best friend, Ginny, who was hiding behind the air-conditioning unit with her, or Tiffany, or Shannon, or Mary Frances, or Rachel. *Those* were the girls the boys liked. The thin, pretty girls who had lived in LaAngelle all their lives, and gone to school together since kindergarten. Sara was the only newcomer to this group in two years, and she was *fat*.

Being fat made everything so much worse.

Sara could hear the boys coming, laughing and calling out to each other as they ran to check all the likely hiding places behind the school, where the game was being played. The Fall Festival was going on in the building, and there was lots of activity at the front of the school and on the soccer field, but the kids had the playground to themselves. It was dark, but the boys had flashlights, and anyway there was enough light being thrown off by all the Fall Festival stuff that they would see her if they looked her way.

Panicking, Sara ran to the grove of trees that ringed the school property, and ducked behind one of them. Crouching down, she watched with bated breath as, flashlight in hand, Eric ran in her direction. Eric was really cute, and she wouldn't mind if he caught her. But if he did, then she'd have to try to beat him back to base, and she couldn't run very fast.

Because she was fat.

She hated being fat.

Her mom said she wasn't fat, that she was perfect, but that was just how her mom was. Her mom would never tell her she was fat, even if it was true. And she knew it was. She could look at the other girls' butts and her own butt, and see that hers was a lot fatter than theirs. It wasn't rocket science.

Eric ran around the big snowball bush at the edge of the grove of trees, shining his flashlight under it. Then, finding nothing, he ran back toward the center of the playground. The beam of his flashlight bobbed and weaved over the ground.

"There's Shannon! I see Shannon!"

Jeff's yell came from the opposite end of the playground. The ensuing burst of wild shrieking and laughing told Sara that he was racing somebody home.

A wave of loneliness so intense that she almost cried again washed over her. She missed *her* school, and *her* friends. Even in Houston, though, some of her classmates had started teasing her at the end of last year about being fat. Which told her that it was perfectly true. Everybody wouldn't say it if it wasn't true. She wasn't stupid. She knew that. *She was fat.*

But her *friends* hadn't teased her. Kristen Staffieri had been her best friend since kindergarten. Sometimes — like right now — she missed Kristen and Polly and Grace *so much.*

Why had she ever told her mom she would move to this stinky place, anyway?

Her mom liked it here. Her mom was happy.

There was enough money, and the house was a mansion, and her mom had a good job. Plus she'd grown up here, and all her friends and relatives were here. Her mom belonged here.

Sara did not.

But it was good to see her mom happy. Her mom had always been worried before, about money and things. And her mom was home every day after school here. That was a big plus.

There were a lot of good things about here. Her mom being home and happy was really important. And Seth and Aunt Callie were nice, and Martha was nice, and Chloe was nice sometimes, too, when she wasn't around her *friends*.

And just about the best thing of all was Smokey, her kitten. If she hadn't come to live here, she wouldn't have Smokey.

She guessed the only really bad thing about here was that she was fat. If she wasn't fat, the kids wouldn't be so mean.

But she would be fat anywhere she went.

It was hopeless.

Sara heard something. She didn't know what, a footstep or a rustle or *something* that made her look around.

There was this huge, big *thing* standing beside another tree just inside the grove. It was dark among the trees, really dark, not kind of dark like out on the playground, and she couldn't see whatever it was clearly, but it looked kind of like a person and kind of not. It was too big, taller and bigger even than Seth, with a great big body and long spindly legs and a small bullet-shaped head and — and wings.

It looked like the thing that she'd seen standing at the foot of her bed the night she'd had the really, really bad dream.

About the vampire lightning bug king.

He was looking straight at her. He was *coming* straight at her.

For a second Sara was frozen in horror, watching him glide toward her. Then she jumped up from her hiding place and burst out onto the playground with an earsplitting shriek.

"There's Sara! I see Sara!"

Eric came pounding toward her from behind the swings, the beam of his flashlight drawing crazy arcs of light through the air.

Fresh from her encounter with the vampire lightning bug king, Sara nearly beat him to base. Not quite, but nearly.

"Sara! Have you seen Chloe?"

Suddenly her mom was there, and in all the confusion of finding out what had happened to Aunt Callie and getting Chloe and finding Seth's car and driving home Sara forgot about the figure she had seen in the woods.

Until she fell asleep, that is. Then her subconscious remembered, and she had another nightmare.

And woke up screaming.

Stalking her was surprisingly fun, he thought, as he slid out her window and clicked the latch into place. Exhilarating, really. Walking swiftly along the gallery, he waited only long enough to see the light burst through the windows of Sara's room before ducking into the room two doors along. He'd been watching her tonight, as he watched her lots of nights now, and he hadn't been able to resist appearing in the woods at the school festival when he'd seen her duck into them, alone. Sensing her terror as she saw him, hearing her scream and watching her run away had been a thrill.

He wondered that he had never tried stalking one of them over a period of several weeks before.

Ah, well, he'd just added a new twist to an old game. That's what made life fun.

chapter 34

Callie was sinking fast. An adverse reaction to the chemotherapy had caused her collapse, and the chemotherapy itself had been, of necessity, discontinued. Her cancer was now overwhelmingly aggressive, invading her body like a marauding army of killers. Her only hope of survival lay in a bone-marrow transplant, or in getting accepted for an experimental treatment being studied in clinical trials at several major cancer centers around the country. Her doctors had been frank in saying that she was not an ideal candidate for either. She was already too sick, too weak. Seth refused to accept their verdict. Since early Saturday morning, when Olivia had joined the steadily growing group of family and friends in Callie's private hospital room, Seth had been constantly in and out as he worked the phone and the network of Charlie's doctor contacts, calling specialists in Boston, in Houston, in New York.

"Son, there are some things you just can't fix," Callie told Seth gently from her hospital bed. Dressed in chinos and a deep green polo shirt, bleary-eyed from lack of sleep but freshly showered and shaved, Seth was moving around the room, gathering up the last of her medical records to be faxed to Houston. The specialists at the big cancer treatment center there had agreed to at least look at her case. It was Sunday morning, and even getting people on the telephone was a trick.

Olivia had arrived at the hospital about an hour earlier, after dropping off Sara and Chloe at Sunday school. Martha would pick them up, and watch them until Olivia got home later that afternoon. Olivia had spent a moment with Big John in the Intensive Care Unit on the fourth floor, holding his hand and listening to the whoosh of mechanized breathing that permeated the ICU. He still didn't know her, or anyone, as far as they could tell. Prospects for his recovery were not good, Charlie said.

But Callie's sudden deterioration was the more immediate crisis. Seth was an almost constant presence at her bedside, and Ira was almost as faithful. Otherwise, people were sitting with Callie in shifts, with everyone from Belinda to Keith to friends such as Augusta Blair and Charlotte Ramey taking a turn. Everyone was heartbroken at what was happening, and no one wanted her to have to face it alone. Not even for a minute.

"But we don't know that *you're* one of those things that can't be fixed, Mother," Seth replied just as gently. He stopped striding around the room, and bent over his mother, taking her hand in his. Frail in her blue hospital gown, Callie clutched his hand tightly, her fingers that were now so bony she'd had to remove her wedding ring to keep it safe curling around his.

"Oh, Seth." Her head barely denting the thin hospital pillow on which it rested, Callie smiled up at him. "You're a fighter, just like your father. I've always admired that in both of you. That's one thing I never was."

"You are too a fighter, Mother. You're going to fight this. And you're going to win." Seth bent down to kiss Callie's thin cheek, squeezed her fingers, and, with a quick, unreadable glance for Olivia, tucked the file folder with the gathered papers under one arm and left the room.

Olivia had not spoken to him alone since he had left her in the locker room on Friday night. He had spent the past two nights in his mother's hospital room, sleeping — or not sleeping — in the big recliner that had been placed near the head of her bed. Olivia was sitting in it now. During the day, he'd been talking to doctors, making phone calls, searching the Internet, doing everything he could to find the solution to the problem of saving his mother's life. His attitude was, there was bound to be an answer out there. They just had to find it.

"That's the worst thing, I guess: I know he's going to have a hard time dealing with my being gone, and it just tears me up to think about it." Callie's head had turned toward the door as her gaze followed Seth from the room. Now she was looking at Olivia again, unshed tears bright in her eyes.

"Oh, Aunt Callie, please don't talk about being gone like that," Olivia pleaded, reaching for her aunt's hand. "Plenty of people survive cancer nowadays. The numbers are going up all the time."

"Olivia, honey, I don't think I'm going to be one of them." Callie grimaced and groped for the dial on her tubing that allowed her to self-administer a dose of pain medication. Olivia turned it for her. After a moment Callie took a deep breath and produced a wavery smile. "I've had the feeling since early this morning that pretty soon now I'm just going to slip away. If I had my druthers, I'd really druther stay right here on earth, but I don't have my druthers, so the only thing to do is face the truth, however un-pleasant it is."

"Aunt Callie . . ." Olivia said helplessly, leaning closer. Tears sprang into her eyes as she looked at her aunt. Callie's skin was ashen yellow now, and she was almost completely bald. Olivia realized with a sense of shock that Callie's state closely resembled that of the woman they'd seen being wheeled down the hall in this same hospital when Olivia had driven Callie in to see Big John. Remembering Callie's reaction to the woman, Olivia shivered inwardly. She was sure her aunt had had a premonition even then of what was to come.

"I can't talk like this to Seth, because it upsets him. He's my only child, my son, and I love him more than anything in the world. But he can't deal with this very well. Men don't handle pain as well as women, haven't you noticed? They're babies, even the best of them."

Olivia could find nothing to say to this, so she simply held Callie's hand. Callie glanced past her out the window, where sunshine poured brightly down from a celestial blue sky. A pair of black starlings swooped into view and were just as suddenly gone, flying swiftly one after the other past the small, rectangular peephole onto the world beyond that room, where ordinary things were still important.

"You know what I hate? I just hate it like the dickens that I'm going to miss Christmas. The idea that I won't ever see a Christmas tree again — that really bothers me. That's stupid, isn't it? To grieve over a Christmas tree?"

"Oh, Aunt Callie." The tears that had been swimming in Olivia's eyes overflowed. Her hand tightened on Callie's. "No, it isn't stupid."

"Now you've got me crying, and I've got you crying, and the upshot of it is going to be that I'll wind up spending some of the most precious hours of my life with a stuffed-up nose and a raw

341

throat." Callie took a deep breath, and managed a weak chuckle. "Oh, Olivia, I'm so glad you came home when you did, and brought Sara with you. Your being home again at this time has been a blessing to me, it really has."

"I'm glad I came home, too." Olivia could hardly get the words out around the lump in her throat.

"It's going to be all right, honey, you'll see. In the end, it'll be all right."

Mallory walked into the room then, carrying a huge bouquet of pink roses in a white china vase, her high heels clicking over the terrazzo floor. Olivia released Callie's hand and murmured a polite greeting to Mallory. As usual, the other woman was perfectly groomed, in a gray silk suit and pearls. She looked like she'd come directly from either church or work.

With a quick smile for Olivia, Mallory walked up the opposite side of the bed from where Olivia sat and placed the roses on the bedside table. Their scent perfumed the air, temporarily masking the medicinal smell of the hospital.

"How are you doing?" Mallory asked Callie tenderly, bending over the older woman for a hug. The sunlight flashed on her diamond engagement ring, the ring that was the symbol of her and Seth's love. Olivia was reminded again that Mallory was going to be Seth's wife. No matter how hot it had been, that kiss in the locker room had been an aberration, not a promise, and, she told herself, she would do well to keep that firmly in mind.

"I'm fine," Callie replied, summoning up her usual brisk manner for Mallory. "Now, you just sit right down here and tell the latest news on the wedding. Did you get that caterer you wanted?"

"Well, their estimate was a little bit higher than I expected . . ." Mallory began, availing herself of Callie's invitation to sit, in a metal-framed chair on the other side of the bed.

The three of them chatted about the wedding — which was *not,* at the moment, Olivia's favorite topic — for a little while, and then Ira arrived, along with Phillip and his wife. Olivia had seen Phillip at the hospital twice since he had come upon her with Seth. Not by word or glance had he indicated that he remembered anything about what he had seen. Olivia was grateful for that.

"Olivia." Callie caught her hand as Olivia stood up to leave. She was whispering as the others talked among themselves. "Bring Chloe up to see me later today, would you please?"

Looking down at her aunt, Olivia read the clear message in the now-faded blue eyes. She nodded as if making a solemn promise, and Callie released her with a tired smile.

When she returned with Chloe, it was just before suppertime. The curtain over the window was closed, and the room was only dimly lit. Callie appeared to be asleep, and Father Randolph was sitting beside the bed, reading silently from his Bible. Cute in jeans and a denim vest over a white T-shirt, her blond hair caught back from her face Alice-in-Wonderland style and tied with a blue ribbon, Chloe had been voluble all the way into Baton Rouge. But she fell silent upon entering the hospital room, and her hand found its way into Olivia's. Olivia held that suddenly cold little hand tightly. Father Randolph looked up and saw them. He smiled, coming to his feet and walking over to join them as they stood rather awkwardly just inside the door.

"What have we here?" he whispered, nodding at the object Olivia held in one hand.

"Olivia thought Nana wanted a Christmas tree," Chloe sniffed, regaining some of her spirit. "I don't know why. It's not even Halloween yet."

Father Randolph exchanged glances with Olivia. In his eyes she read an exact understanding of the situation.

"It'll make her a wonderful night-light" was what he said. Taking it from Olivia, he set the foot-tall, fully decorated, artificial pine tree down in the center of the bedside table, moving Mallory's roses to the larger table in the corner in the process. Then he plugged in the cord so that the tree was suddenly resplendent with twinkly red and green and blue and yellow lights.

Olivia had bought it at a garden supply center after leaving the hospital.

In the bed, Callie stirred, awakened no doubt by their voices, and opened her eyes. Her head turned to the side, her attention apparently attracted by the blinking lights on the bedside table. When she saw the Christmas tree her eyes widened, and she went very still for a moment, just looking at it. Her lips trembled, and then a slow smile stretched her dry lips. Looking around, her gaze sought and found Olivia, who was standing with Chloe at the foot of the bed.

"Thank you," Callie said, and then her eyes were all for her granddaughter.

"Chloe." Callie's voice was noticeably weaker than it had been earlier that day. With an effort, she hitched herself up a little higher in the bed and held out her hand to the girl.

"Nana," Chloe said on a sob, and then rushed around the bed to take her grandmother's hand.

Olivia and Father Randolph exchanged glances, and, together, silently withdrew to the hall, leaving the old woman and the young girl to say what Olivia thought would almost certainly be their good-byes.

chapter 35

It poured down rain all the next day and far into the night. Sitting in the big recliner next to his mother's hospital bed, his hand holding hers as she slept the deep, drugged sleep of the desperately ill, Seth thought that the sorrowing dark skies and silvery sheets of water were a perfect metaphor for his mood. His mother would be dead soon, if not today then tomorrow, or the day after that.

Dead. There was surely no more final word in the English language.

And there was nothing he could do to save her. Earlier that day, he'd had to make the heart-wrenching decision, and sign the papers, that would stop them from putting her on life support.

On the front of her medical chart had been placed a little sticker, with the words *No Code* scrawled under it. It was hospital jargon to alert all personnel that the patient had a "Do Not Resuscitate" order.

It was all so matter-of-fact. *He* had been outwardly matter-of-fact when signing the papers, when he had felt like his heart was being ripped from his chest.

He was a thirty-seven-year-old grown man, a father himself, and yet the thought of his mother dying made him feel like a scared little boy.

Just before he had left with Ira at about eleven P.M., Father Randolph had pulled Seth aside and counseled him to pray.

"I think it's time to ask for God's help for your mother, Seth" were Father Randolph's exact words. They'd been in the hall outside his mother's room. The nurses had warned them all that whether she appeared unconscious or not, Callie might still on some level be able to hear everything that was said in her presence.

Seth had snorted. "Hell, Father, you think I *haven't* prayed? I've prayed until my knees were numb, and she's still suffering. It's the damnedest thing. My mother never harmed a living creature in her life, and she's suffering."

Father Randolph looked at him with compassion. "You prayed for her to get well, didn't you?"

"Of course I prayed for her to get well. What else would I pray for?" Seth was scared, and angry with it. "In there is living — no, make that dying — proof that God doesn't answer prayers."

Father Randolph's voice was sorrowful. "Seth, I firmly believe that God does answer all prayers. But one of the hardest things that we, as people of faith, have to learn is that sometimes, when He answers, the answer is no." He put a hand on Seth's shoulder. "When I pray for your mother, I ask God to wrap her in His love, and take her into eternal life with Him in His own good time."

Then Father Randolph bade him good night, with the promise that he would be back first thing in the morning.

Now Seth twisted and turned in the vinyl chair, trying without success to get comfortable, unwilling to let go of his mother's hand in case she should somehow be able to sense his touch. It was around one A.M., and the hospital had settled down for the night. The room was illuminated only by the glow of the monitors and the incongruously cheerful lights on that damned little Christmas tree that Olivia, seconded by Father Randolph, had insisted be kept lit. The atmosphere was hushed, and except for the occasional squeak of a nurse's shoe or the rattle of a cart in the hall, all was quiet outside the room. But inside was a different matter. Every sound seemed to be magnified: the drip of medicine from the IV bag into the tube that led into his mother's arm, the whir and pulse of the machines that monitored her heart and breathing, the restless shuffling of her feet as they shifted almost constantly beneath the bedclothes.

She'd been moving her feet like that for almost half an hour.

The convulsive way her feet moved scared him almost as much as the rattle of her breathing. Both were something new.

He looked at her face, drawn by some sixth sense, to find that her eyes were open and she was looking at him. Seeing her awake, and apparently aware, for the first time all day so surprised him that for a moment he blinked at her without speaking.

"Hey," he said softly, recovering. She smiled at him, tightening her fingers around his hand. Once a sturdy woman, she was now so frail that her body made only the smallest of mounds in the bedcovers. Her eyes were sunken, her face skeletal beneath dry, yellowing skin. To his knowledge, she had not eaten solid food since being admitted to the hospital. He was conscious of a sudden strong urge to feed her, to run out to the vending machines in the hall and buy candy bars and sodas and force her to eat.

As if he could save her like that.

Her gaze moved over his face as if she would memorize every feature. Her voice, when she spoke, was scarcely louder than a whisper. "Remember when you were little, how you used to like to pick me flowers all the time? We had all those gardens, all those flowers — roses and amaryllis and peonies, all so lush and beautiful — and what you'd always pick were the dandelions out of the yard. You'd come and give me this handful of scraggly weeds, which you thought were the most beautiful flowers on earth. And you know what? I thought they were the most beautiful flowers on earth, too, because you gave them to me." Her eyes smiled into his.

"I remember," Seth said. He leaned forward so that his face was close to hers. His hand clasped hers strongly. "You always used to put them in a washed-out jelly glass in the center of the kitchen table."

"That's right." She gave a little choked laugh, then looked at him intently. "Seth — I want you to know, you've been the joy of my life. I have loved you from the moment you were born, and I will love you forever. I couldn't have asked for a better son. You've done me proud."

"Mother." Seth choked on the word. His throat closed up, and his eyes filled with tears. "Mother."

She looked at him — and then beyond him, past his shoulder toward something in the corner of the room. Her face lit up all of a sudden, like she'd had a wonderful surprise. Seth even looked around to see who was there, but there was no one. Nothing. Just a round table crowded with plants and flowers.

"Why, Michael!" she said, still looking beyond him, her voice stronger than it had been before, almost normal, in fact, and smiled. Then she took a long, slow, deep breath that rattled audibly, closed her eyes, and seemed to sleep.

He never heard her exhale.

"Mother!" he said, alarmed, coming to his feet to lean over her. Then, urgently, "I love you, Mother!"

At almost the same moment, a monitor sounded an alarm, and there was the rush of footsteps in the hall leading toward the room. Seconds later, the door burst open, and the room began to fill with medical personnel.

chapter 36

The bedside clock read 3:32 A.M., and Olivia was wide awake. She lay in her bed, in the room next to Sara's that had once been Belinda's but now was hers, breathing in and out with quiet concentration, struggling to banish the last fragments of horror left over from the dream.

The scent of White Shoulders was elusive, as it always was when the dream woke her in the middle of the night. She could never be sure whether it was really present, or whether the scent was just her imagination working overtime.

Was it possible to *imagine* smelling a long-out-of-date perfume?

It was not pitch-black inside the room, but near enough to make little practical difference. The pouring rain outside precluded any moonlight from creeping through the curtains, and the only illumination was the digital clock beside the bed. If she lifted her hand and placed it between her eyes and the clock she could see it. Otherwise, she could not.

The dream had come to her the last three nights, each time with increasing intensity. She was starting to dread falling asleep. She knew why it came, of course.

Because she could not get out of her mind the dreadful images conjured up by the story that Seth had told her: her mother, young, healthy, with a beloved child, committing suicide by drowning herself in the lake.

Oddly enough, in the dream, the drowning did not *feel* like a suicide. The emotion that came through was fear, not sorrow.

In the wake of Callie's hospitalization, the atmosphere in the house was enough to make anyone have bad dreams, Olivia thought, being purposefully rational. Chloe was cranky and manic by turns, Sara was withdrawn, Martha was distracted, and she herself had been hit with so many emotional whammies over the last few days that she felt shell-shocked.

To make things worse, Sara, too, was having bad dreams: The vampire lightning bug king was back. It had apparently exercised such a powerful grip on her imagination that on Friday night she had woken up screaming that it was coming to get her. Last night she had dreamed that it was in her room.

Tonight, though, all had been quiet. Except for

her own nightmare, nothing had occurred to disturb her rest. Still, Olivia had found it difficult to sleep.

It did not help knowing that tonight there were only four people in this vast pile of a house: she and Sara in this wing, Chloe and Martha in the other.

The house felt surprisingly empty without Seth and Callie in it.

Olivia took an exploratory sniff, and realized that the scent of White Shoulders, if indeed she had ever really smelled it, had dissipated.

At about that same time, she heard what she was almost certain were footsteps on the gallery. Firm, heavy footsteps that could not by any stretch of the imagination belong to Sara, or Chloe, or even Martha.

A man's footsteps.

She listened again, carefully, straining to hear over the steady rush of the pouring rain.

But try though she might, she heard nothing more.

Olivia lay in her warm, comfortable bed a moment longer, flat on her back, her hands curled around the topmost edge of the sheet and quilt that covered her, staring toward the curtained windows, listening so hard that her head ached.

She had not imagined those footsteps, she was certain. But who could be out on the gallery in the middle of the night?

Olivia could not have put a name to the fear that suddenly took root in her mind, but it galvanized her. If someone — some man — was on the gallery, she wanted to know who it was.

Three times since moving into this house, Sara had woken up crying that something or someone was in her room.

From the depths of Olivia's subconscious, a memory stirred. Had *she* not dreamed something similar once? Something about a man standing at the foot of her bed? Or had she? The memory, if memory it was and not just a sympathetic projection of what Sara had experienced, slithered away like a snake sliding back down its hole, too elusive to be grasped.

But it left an unpleasant residue behind.

Maybe, just maybe, something — someone — really *was* sneaking into Sara's room as she slept. Maybe the vampire lightning bug king wasn't as fanciful as it sounded.

Just considering the possibility made Olivia's blood run cold.

Throwing back the covers, she got out of bed. Leaving the light off so as not to warn away anyone who might still be outside, Olivia crept into the hall and opened the door to Sara's room to check on her. Without taking more than a step inside, she could hear her daughter's regular breathing, and, by the faint, orangeish glow of the small night-light that now burned all night beside her bed, see her huddled shape under the bedclothes. Her kitten — Smokey — was curled up on the quilt next to Sara's legs, also soundly asleep.

Olivia smiled, looking at that kitten. Sara was so happy to have it, Olivia found herself treating it like a cherished member of the family.

Sara was safe. Olivia's stomach settled, and only then did she realize that it had been *un*settled, with that funny feeling she got sometimes when she stepped into an elevator and it started to drop too fast.

Okay, so there was nothing in Sara's room. But she still didn't think she had imagined those footsteps on the gallery.

Closing Sara's door behind her, she returned to her own room, crossed to the nearer of the two windows and pulled the drape aside just enough to permit her to see outside.

All that met her gaze was a wall of charcoal gray. Of course, with the rain falling like it was, what else had she expected to see? Unless someone stood right in front of her window, she was not going to be able to see him unless she stepped through the window.

At the thought, a little shiver of fear ran along her spine. If someone *was* on the gallery, was going out to take a look really a good idea? Olivia hesitated. On the other hand, she was never going to be able to get back to sleep unless she *knew*.

Moving as silently as she could, Olivia unlatched the window, opened it partway, and stepped out onto the gallery.

A rush of rain-cooled air scented with honeysuckle and sodden earth greeted her. Folding her arms across her chest in defense against the un-expected gust, Olivia looked cautiously up and down. The gallery was alive with shape-shifting shadows, its far ends obscured enough to pro-vide dark and secret concealment for all manner of possible intruders. From somewhere to her right came a series of soft, repetitive sounds, the origins of which were lost in the gloom. The mysterious squeaks or creaks or even moans were muffled almost to the point of extinction by the gentle roar of the falling rain.

It occurred to Olivia then that this late at night, with the rain cutting them off from everything around it, the Big House was as isolated as if a hurricane had picked it up and set it down again smack in the middle of the Atchafalaya Swamp.

She should go back inside, right now, and lock her window tightly behind her.

Olivia was just about to take her own advice when she perceived that one of the rocking chairs at the far end of the gallery was moving. Her eyes widened and her lips parted as she real-ized that the chair was being rocked slowly back and forth. The grating of its rockers against the gallery's plank floor was the mysterious sound she had heard.

Someone was rocking in the rocking chair.

She could just make out a dark form blotting out the whiteness of the seat and back and arms of the chair. Thoughts of ghosts and zombies and all kinds of freaky possibilities whirled through her mind, but then she realized that there was something familiar about the sitter's sprawled posture.

"Seth?" she whispered, staring.

There was no answer. The rocking chair continued to move without pause. But somehow, without being sure why it was so, she was certain it was he.

"Seth?" She walked toward him, forgetting that she was clad only in her nightgown, her arms crossed over her chest, her bare feet making no sound at all as she padded over the smooth-painted wood. She did not think he was aware of her, because the chair never varied the rhythm of its slow rocking.

Beyond the porch eaves, the rain fell in a dark, translucent curtain. The intermittent gusts of rain-scented air set her blush-pink nylon gown to fluttering about her ankles like wings.

"Seth?" It *was* him. Olivia drew near enough to be sure, frowning as she traced with her eyes the hard-set lines of his profile. He was staring out into the darkness where there was nothing to be seen, his fingers curled around the squared wooden edges of the armrests, his feet flat against the floor as he pushed the rocking chair rhythmically back and forth.

Something was wrong. Olivia knew it before she ever reached him.

Resting a hand atop the intricately woven chair back, she looked down at him.

"Aunt Callie?" she asked in a dry, constricted voice.

He looked up at her then. His eyes glinted at her through the shadows.

"Mother died at one seventeen." His voice was utterly calm. Preternaturally so.

Olivia gasped, her hand flying to cover her mouth.

"Oh, no," she said when she could speak. Tears sprang to her eyes, and began to trickle down her cheeks. "Oh, Seth, I'm so sorry!"

"I decided to wait and tell Chloe in the morning." He still spoke in that detached voice. His gaze slid away from her, and the rocking chair began to move again, back and forth, back and forth, in a terrible rhythm of sorrow and control. "I can't decide whether I should go ahead and send her to school tomorrow, though. Maybe it would be best to keep on with her normal routine. What do you think?"

"I think she should stay home. Oh, she'll be heartbroken. Aunt Callie loved her so." Olivia felt like she had been punched in the stomach herself. She suspected that shock was cushioning the worst of the blow, just as it must be for Seth.

He grimaced. It was the only sign of emotion she had seen from him so far. Olivia knew how close he had been to his mother, knew that he, too, was heartbroken, far more heartbroken even than Chloe would be. As much as Callie had loved Chloe, she had loved Seth more. But being the man that Seth was, the man he had been brought up to be, he was going to try to tough it out.

He would know no other way than to be stoic in the face of grief.

"I stayed until they came to take her away. Walking out of there and leaving my mother in that room with strangers was the hardest thing I've ever done in my life." He spoke to the rain, the wind, the night. He never looked at her at all.

"Oh, Seth," Olivia said again, helplessly. She leaned down to hug him, her arms sliding around his shoulders as she pressed her wet cheek to his in a gesture of wordless comfort.

"Livvy," he said. Hooking an arm around her waist, he pulled her down onto his lap. She went without protest. His arms slid around her, then tightened almost convulsively. She wrapped her own arms around his neck and buried her face against his shoulder as tears poured from her eyes like the rain beyond the gallery. She cried for him, because he would not. And for Aunt Callie, and herself, and Chloe, and Ira, and for all the others who had loved Callie Archer and would grieve for her, too.

Seth held her while she cried. She could feel the steady rise and fall of his chest as he breathed, the hard muscles of the arms that pressed her close and the thighs upon which she sat, the solid strength implicit in the breadth and length of him. His body was warm and she was freezing. She huddled closer, curling around him, and he patted and rocked and soothed her as if doing so helped comfort him, too.

"She talked to me, a little," he said eventually.

"Just before she . . ."

His voice broke off, and he inhaled sharply. It was obvious that he could not go on.

Olivia lifted her head from the cradle of his shoulder and looked at him. She was so close — just inches away — that even in the shifting darkness she could tell that his face was taut with sorrow, and his mouth was tight with it. But it was his eyes that were the worst. They were dark and liquid, gazing not at her but out into the night, with the glazed look of a creature in terrible pain.

"Seth," she whispered, and kissed him softly, gently, full on the mouth, meaning to distract him, to offer an antidote to his sorrow. But his reaction caught her by surprise.

His gaze slanted sharply down so that he was looking full into her eyes. One hand came up to cradle the back of her head, and then he kissed her, deeply, ravenously, as if he couldn't get enough of the taste of her mouth. Her eyes closed, and she made a wordless sound of assent, her arms tightening around his neck as she kissed him back. His fingers burrowed deep into her hair, finally fanning out against the base of her skull. He shifted her so that her head was pillowed against his shoulder, and his kiss deepened until she thought he must be trying to draw her very soul into his mouth. Her body quickened, throbbed. Her pulse kicked in, pounding in her ears. His hand found her breast through the thin nylon of her gown, flattening over it, squeezing, caressing. Her nipple hardened in instant response. Hopelessly on fire for him now, she quivered and gasped her pleasure into his mouth. All thoughts of loss, of grief, of before and after faded, to be replaced by the now.

Now Seth was kissing her, now his hand was on her breast, now her body was quaking with desire. There was nothing beyond this.

His mouth lifted away from hers, and he moved, standing up abruptly with her in his arms. The chair rockers made a scraping sound as they were pushed back across the floor. Seth turned with her, carrying her with one arm around her back and the other beneath her knees, and walked with long, deliberate strides toward the window that she had left open. Her arms were looped around his neck. Her bare feet dangled free.

He took a deep breath as he reached the open window and stopped, looking down into her face.

"Livvy," he said, his voice very quiet and not quite steady. "If you don't want me to make love to you, now is the time to say so."

She lifted her head from his shoulder and met his gaze. With the sound and smell of the rain adding exotic texture to the darkness all around them, they could have been alone on a deserted island.

"I want you to," she whispered, her hands tightening around his neck. His eyes gleamed down at her, and the corners of his mouth tightened briefly in acknowledgment.

Then he shouldered through the window, took the few strides he needed to cross the room, and laid her down very gently on her bed.

chapter 37

Seth came down beside her, his mouth on hers again almost before Olivia had time to draw breath. Hers was a double bed with a thick, too-soft mattress, a mahogany four-poster that was not an antique but merely old. It creaked as his weight joined hers, and creaked again as he kicked aside the covers that Olivia had left already partially thrown back. Except for the faint greenish glow of the digital clock, there was no trace of light in the room. Even the French window, which still stood partially open, let in only a wedge of rain-tinged charcoal that blended almost unnoticed into the darkness.

His hands went under her nightgown, stroking over her skin, caressing her thighs and stomach and breasts. Then, in a single, swift movement he pulled the flimsy garment up over her head and off, tossing it out of his way. She was naked while he was still fully clothed in the khaki pants and blue button-down dress shirt he'd apparently worn home from the hospital. She thought he even still wore his shoes. The feel of his hard, clothed body pressing against her nakedness made her ache. She reached for the buttons on his shirt, determined to strip him, too. Then his fingers slid between her legs, staking quick, intimate claim to her body, and his mouth trailed down over her neck to find her breasts.

Olivia gasped, shuddering, her body instantly catching fire as his hands and mouth took thorough and complete possession of her. After that, all she could do was cling to him and respond. He was urgent with passion, his mouth and hands faintly rough as they molded her to his will, his lovemaking selfish with need.

This was Seth, she kept reminding herself. *Seth* . . . Anything he wanted to do to her, he did with her goodwill. She was pliant as quicksilver beneath his hands, too aroused to do more than clutch the sheet upon which she lay and writhe in mounting ecstasy beneath his caresses. He staged a predatory assault upon her senses, determined, ruthless, driven by a fierce passion that overwhelmed every inhibition she had ever had.

By the time he got naked himself and pushed inside her, she was begging for it, gasping her need into his ear, cajoling him with her hands and her body. The joining felt so good, so right, that she came almost instantly, stiffening and gasping out his name as he filled her. But he didn't stop, didn't wait. He pulled back out and drove in again, then kept going, his strokes violently hard and fast, his mouth finding hers and taking it, too. Kissing him back with passionate abandon, Olivia wrapped her arms around his neck and her legs around his waist and moved with him, matching him stroke for ruthless stroke, her body catching fire once more.

He shuddered when he came, and she shuddered, too, then came again herself. For a moment afterward he was still, lying on top of her, his weight pushing her down into the mattress, his body hot and damp, his breathing labored. Then he shifted, rolling to one side and pulling her with him. He ended up flat on his back with his head on her pillow, his arms holding her loosely as her head rested on his shoulder.

"Livvy." His breathing had slowed, and his voice, though still husky, was almost back to normal. "God, Livvy. I never meant to do that."

Her right hand, which had been working its way through the surprisingly thick wedge of hair on his chest, stilled. Her head lifted from his shoulder as she tried, and failed, to read his expression through the darkness.

"If you're getting ready to apologize, Seth Archer, let me warn you that I've always greatly admired Lorena Bobbitt."

"You're scaring me to death." There was the suggestion of a smile in his voice. "Actually, I'm not sorry. Or, at least, I'm only sorry if you're sorry."

"I'm not sorry."

He took a deep breath, and went very still suddenly. Olivia sensed that the memory of his mother's death had come crashing down on him without warning. For a moment the weight of his grief was almost palpable.

She closed her eyes, hurting, too, for him and for herself. But hurting served no purpose. It would not change a thing, right a wrong, bring the dead back to life. And she could not bear the thought that he was suffering. Opening her eyes, she wriggled on top of him, her naked front lying full against his, and tilted her head to press a softly titillating kiss on his mouth.

"For the rest of the night, we're not going to think about anything but this," she whispered, reaching down between their bodies to find and hold his already hardening member. "Nothing but this."

Then she kissed him again, and, after the briefest of hesitations, he kissed her back. This time, when they made love, she was the aggressor, her hands and mouth learning all there was to know about him. In the end, though, they reached the same peaks as before, and she had to press her mouth hard against his shoulder to muffle her cries.

Eventually they fell asleep, wrapped in each other's arms.

When Olivia opened her eyes pale morning

light was pouring through the window Seth had left ajar, spilling over the bed — and her alarm clock was jangling with shrill urgency.

"Reality intrudes," Seth muttered, as Olivia lunged across the bed to shut the thing off.

For a moment she lay on her stomach, naked, blinking, her upper torso supported by her elbows, her hair falling forward over her shoulders. Then she tossed the curtain of coffee-colored hair back from her face and looked at Seth.

She'd slept with Seth. Just putting it into words in her mind made her feel tingly all over.

His eyes were closed. His short, sandy hair was mussed so that the longer top part stood up in spikes. A dark stubble of five o'clock shadow roughened his cheeks and jaw. The tiny lines radiating from the corners of his eyes and the deeper ones bracketing his mouth were all too visible in the unforgiving morning light. And still, she thought, all she had to do was look at him lying naked in her bed and her pulse picked up and her body melted.

She had slept with Seth.

He was sprawled on his back with the sheet pulled up over his body almost to the waist. His chest was paler than his arms and neck and face, which Olivia knew was because he did not often go shirtless in the sun. One arm was folded beneath his head, revealing a shock of ash-brown hair in his armpit. Olivia took just an instant to admire the corded muscles in that bent arm. Then her gaze moved appreciatively over the powerful-looking width of his shoulders, his broad chest with its triangle of ash-brown curls and flat male nipples, and what she could see of his sinewy abdomen. Finally her gaze rose again to his face. She expected to find that by now he was looking at her with the same interest she was according him, but he was not. His eyes remained closed. The tautness of his facial muscles and the thin, compressed line of his mouth told her that he was once again experiencing the pain of his loss.

Reality intrudes, he'd said. Ah, yes. Olivia felt the heavy weight of grief begin to settle over them both, over the house. With the coming of day, there was no longer any way to ward it off.

"I've got to make some phone calls, and tell Chloe," he said heavily, opening his eyes and meeting her gaze. "Jesus, I'm no good at this."

His gaze swept down her body, lingering in obvious appreciation of the lush curves of her breasts, the feminine indentation of her waist, the roundness of her bottom, the shapeliness of her legs. The tawny cast of her skin stood out sharply against the whiteness of the sheets, and she thought from his expression that he admired that, too.

His eyes met hers again when he had finished looking, and this time he smiled crookedly at her, the somberness that now darkened his expression lifting briefly.

"Last night, did I remember to tell you how beautiful you are?" he asked.

Olivia shook her head without speaking.

"The most beautiful thing I've ever seen in my life," he said, leaning sideways to kiss her mouth.

Her mouth softened responsively under his, but before she could do more he straightened, swung his legs over the side of the bed, and stood up.

He seemed totally unself-conscious about his nudity as he reached for the clothes he had dropped on the floor the night before. The idea that she was seeing Seth naked entranced Olivia. She silently admired his tall, muscular athlete's build, his firm butt, and his other very male parts. She was an interested spectator as he pulled on his clothes with swift efficiency, stepping first into his briefs — he wore briefs, plain white Fruit of the Looms — and then his pants, which he buttoned and zipped. Pulling on his shirt, he buttoned only a couple of buttons and left the tails hanging, stuffed his socks in his pants pockets, and thrust his bare feet into his shoes.

Then he looked at her again. By this time, she was in a sitting position, propped up by pillows against the headboard. The sheet was anchored firmly beneath her armpits so that her body was now modestly hidden from his view.

"What do you think I should tell Chloe?" he asked, pain obvious in the narrowing of his eyes and the hard set of his jaw. "That Nana died last night? Isn't that kind of blunt for an eight-year-old to hear? That Nana went to

370

heaven to be an angel? What?"

Olivia hesitated. Breaking the news to a child of the death of a loved one was new to her, too. She thought of what she would say to Sara under such circumstances. She thought of the very little she could remember of what had once been said to her.

"I think I'd tell her both of those things," she said slowly. "And tell her that her Nana loved her and will always be watching over her. If it's possible, I'd let her help in planning the funeral. She needs to be a part of this, Seth. It'll help her come to terms with the reality of what's happened."

Seth nodded, then grimaced. "I'm having a hard time grasping that Mother's gone myself. Until yesterday, I never really believed she was going to die."

He turned away and started for the window. Before he stepped through it, he turned back to look at her.

"Livvy, thank you," he said quietly. "Without you, I don't think I could have made it through last night."

She made a face at him. "Please, think nothing of it," she said, too politely. "I'm glad I was able to help."

That earned her a half smile.

"God, I'm glad you're home," he said, and stepped through the window, pulling it closed behind him.

Olivia simply sat and looked at that closed window for a long time.

chapter 38

The few days until Callie's funeral passed in a blur for Olivia. From almost the moment she left her room that first morning, she was busy. Which, she decided, was a good thing, because it left her no time to think or feel or do anything but *do*. There were phone calls to be made, houseguests to be seen to, and Sara and Chloe to be taken care of, as well as a thousand and one other chores.

Seth was even busier than she was, and, she suspected, he welcomed the constant activity for the same reason she did: It kept him from having to deal with his own emotions. She scarcely saw him, and never alone, which was just as well, because every time she remembered the intimacy of the things they had done together in her bed she wanted to blush. That she could have done this or kissed that or permitted the other with her big cousin — in the cold light of day, it seemed almost impossible.

Clearly he had put that night behind him. Not by word or gesture did he indicate to her that he saw her any differently than he had before. Once he walked out of her bedroom, it was as though nothing between them had changed.

He was busy, she told herself. Very busy. Besides making the arrangements for his mother, he still had the Boatworks to run, Big John to check on and make decisions for, and everybody in town coming by the house and funeral home and stopping him everywhere he went to offer condolences.

Theriot's Funeral Home on Cocodrie Street, where Callie's body had been taken, was packed, as the entire population of the town of LaAngelle came by during visiting hours to pay their respects. Everyone had loved Callie Archer, and Olivia got the sense that her death was felt to be the community's loss as much as the family's.

Callie's sister Ruth and two elderly aunts were staying at the Big House until after the funeral. In addition to those overnight guests, the house was filled with people day and night. They went to the funeral home for visiting hours in droves, and they returned to the house afterward in droves. Martha and Keith cooked from dawn until midnight, and casseroles were dropped off almost hourly by those expressing their sympathy in the most practical way they could think of.

The atmosphere at the house, and, to a lesser extent, at the funeral home, was surreal. It was almost that of a party, with relatives who had not seen each other for months or years catching up on their lives, and friends and neighbors gathering in little groups to gossip about everything from the state of their jobs to the state of the country, to the fashions the mourners were wearing, to the love lives of those assembled. Children were everywhere, running in and out as if they had been brought together for a play date rather than a funeral. Besides Sara and Chloe, there were Phillip's four, Belinda and Charlie's daughter Angela's two, and a whole passel of ever-changing children from the town. They ate and drank, played and squabbled, and in general served as counterpoint to the true somberness of the occasion.

Savory smells emanated around the clock from the kitchen, where the counters and table were loaded down periodically with a buffet feast. In the dining room, urns full of coffee and tea had been set up, along with a constantly changing variety of tempting desserts (Keith's specialty). So many flowers were delivered that Olivia eventually ended up massing the overflow at either end of the veranda. Their sweet perfume lay heavy on the air, a constant reminder of both life and death.

As Seth's fiancée, Mallory was very much in evidence, standing with the family at the funeral home, giving directions to Martha and the other help hired for the occasion, and acting as hostess at the house. She also bought a beautiful black taffeta dress with a white lace collar and a white petticoat at an exclusive store in Baton Rouge and brought it out for Chloe to wear to the funeral, with matching white lace stockings and shiny black patent leather shoes.

Chloe, of course, when presented with the gift, refused to so much as try the dress on. Summoned to the scene of the crisis by an alarmed Sara, and fearing an imminent explosion that would be made doubly dreadful with so many people in the house, Olivia hastily distracted Chloe by telling her that Martha needed both her and Sara urgently in the kitchen to help make brownies for the visiting youngsters, which both girls loved to do. Then Olivia placated Mallory by promising to do her best to get Chloe to wear the dress to the funeral.

With Callie no longer with them to see to Chloe's needs, and since no one wanted to intrude on Seth with petty annoyances at such a time, Olivia quietly oversaw Chloe as well as Sara. Since figuring out the cause of Chloe's bouts of misbehavior, she had developed a very real sympathy for the child, and a growing fondness for her as well.

Besides dealing with her own grief over Callie's death, the hardest thing for Olivia was watching Seth with Mallory. Chic in black, her blond hair elegantly styled, her makeup flawless, Mallory was never far from Seth's side during those difficult days. She clung to his arm, whispered in his ear, hugged him, dropped light kisses on his cheek or mouth when she entered or exited a room where he was present. Seth made no effort that Olivia could detect to repulse her. On the contrary, he seemed perfectly accepting of her attentions. Which, of course, was understandable, given that Mallory was Seth's fiancée. But watching them made Olivia burn with what she was finally forced to acknowledge was a case of acute jealousy. She had to keep reminding herself that Seth was no more hers now than he had ever been. Just because they'd spent the night together did not mean that he belonged to her. He belonged to Mallory.

The sad truth of the situation was, she had simply helped him make it through one really difficult night. He was going to *marry* Mallory.

She had known better than to have sex with Seth. She had warned herself against it from the beginning. But she had gone ahead and done it anyway, and look where it had landed her: She seethed with jealousy whenever Mallory was near, she burned with resentment when Seth treated her no differently than he ever had, and she ached for him to wrap his arms around her and kiss her senseless and carry her off to bed again.

None of which was a pleasant state of affairs, and all of which she had brought on herself.

The strain of juggling so many emotional balls must have shown on her face, because on the night before the funeral — it was to be held at eleven o'clock Thursday, at St. Luke's — Charlie came up to her as she was refilling the coffee urn in the dining room and asked with some concern how she was holding up.

"You look pale," he said, his hazel eyes kind as they moved over her face. "And you have big dark circles around your eyes. Are you getting enough sleep?"

Olivia smiled affectionately at him. The short answer was no. So that Chloe would not be alone at night — the time, as she knew from experience, when grief weighs the heaviest — she had set up Sara's room as slumber party central. She, Sara — a willing helper in the plan to keep Chloe occupied — and Chloe had constructed a tent from quilts, furnished it with sleeping bags, and brought in a TV with a VCR, eight-year-old-friendly tapes, books, and snacks. That was where the two girls and their three cats had been sleeping, while she slept in Sara's bed in the midst of the nightly circus to keep an eye on them and be there if she was needed. As she had fully expected, the girls kept her awake till midnight or later every night. After exhaustion finally claimed them, thoughts of Seth with Mallory plagued Olivia (were they having sex even at that moment?) enough to penetrate even the weight of her ever-present grief for Callie. Then, when she finally did manage to fall asleep, her mother's death haunted her dreams, in ever more excruciating detail.

She woke up every night about three thirty A.M., bathed in sweat and terrified, to the scent of White Shoulders perfume. And that wasn't all. One night just as she was about to close her eyes she could have sworn she saw the rocking chair in the corner move as if someone were rocking there. Another time, right after the girls had gone to sleep, she'd looked into the gilt-framed mirror that had been hers as a child and gotten the uncanny sensation that the face looking back at her was not her own, but her mother's. There was the slightest difference in the angle of the jaw, and the shape of the nose. . . .

The sense that she was looking at her mother's ghost had so unnerved her that she'd dropped the hairbrush she had been holding. She'd glanced down in automatic reaction to the falling brush, and when she'd looked in the mirror again the face she'd seen reflected there was definitely her own.

As had the first one been, of course. Any other interpretation was ridiculous. Her mother was not trying to communicate with her from beyond the grave. That was *X-Files* territory.

The more she thought about it, though, the more convinced she grew that the suicide scenario just did not fit with what she saw in her dreams. Of course, dreams were not reality, but still . . . She had a gut feeling about it: What she had been told about her mother's death was somehow wrong.

"No," she said impulsively, in reply to Charlie's

question, turning to face him and placing a hand on his arm. Never a particularly handsome man, he was now balding and florid-faced and sporting a considerable spare tire around the middle. In a navy-blue suit with a white shirt and red tie, he looked hot and uncomfortable. "I'm not sleeping well. Seth told me not long ago that my mother — committed suicide, when I always thought her death was an accidental drowning. I've been having nightmares about it, and they've been keeping me awake. Seth also said that you tried to revive her the night she died, and you'd been treating her for depression prior to that. Is that true?"

Charlie looked taken aback, but he nodded slowly, his gaze keen on her face. "I don't know why he told you that. But yes, it's true."

Olivia glanced around as a couple of neighbors wandered in for coffee and dessert. She lowered her voice. "In my dream, I can see the whole thing happening. My mother in the lake, and — and everything. It doesn't *feel* like she's committing suicide. I think that's what's really bothering me."

Charlie, too, glanced at the people behind them. "If you really want to talk about it, stop by my office next week," he said quietly. "I'll be glad to tell you everything I know."

Olivia nodded and would have said more, but at that moment Mallory appeared in the doorway, her gaze going straight to Olivia, her mouth thin-lipped with rage.

chapter 39

"She cut it up." Mallory spoke under her breath, but her fury was obvious when Olivia, in response to an imperious gesture, joined her in the front hall. At Olivia's questioning look, Mallory was more specific. "Chloe. Took scissors and cut up the dress I bought her to wear to the funeral. It's hanging in her closet in tatters."

"Oh, no," Olivia said, shocked. "Oh, dear. Are you sure *Chloe* did it? Maybe the kittens clawed it, or something."

This attempt to shield Chloe earned Olivia a black look.

"I asked Chloe if she'd tried on the dress I bought her yet. She said right to my face that she wasn't going to have to wear it, because she had turned it into rags. I didn't believe her — I thought surely no child, not even Chloe, could be that deliberately destructive — but I went to her closet and looked. She was telling the truth. The scissors were right there on the floor under the dress, with threads from the dress still clinging to the blades. She cut it up!"

Olivia sighed. Even without viewing the damage for herself, she had no trouble believing that Mallory was telling the truth. Chloe's behavior had been much improved lately, but Chloe was still Chloe. And she was no fan of Mallory's.

"I'll talk to her," Olivia said. "She was very wrong to do it, and she'll apologize, I'm sure. But —"

Mallory cut her off furiously. "I don't know why I'm even talking to you. The person to handle this is Seth. He's the only one with any degree of control over that little — girl. He's going to have to exercise it."

Turning on her heel, Mallory stalked away, passing through the open pocket doors into the large, antiques-filled living room, where Olivia located Seth with a glance. Dressed in a navy sport coat and khaki pants, he was leaning a shoulder against the far wall as he talked with about half a dozen guests. He looked tall and impossibly handsome as the lamplight cast a warm glow over his grief-shadowed face, and Olivia's chest ached just looking at him. As Mallory walked up to him and curled a proprietary hand around his arm, she could no longer watch. Olivia abruptly turned her back, heading in search of Chloe. Martha, who was busy chopping onions, directed her to the children, on the back veranda just outside the kitchen, adding that she'd been keeping an eye on them through the windows. Keith, who was sipping a glass of white wine as he stirred something on the stove, remarked that they were all actually behaving rather well. Leaning against a counter nearby, David made a skeptical face, but said nothing to contradict Keith.

Chloe was indeed on the back veranda. Sara and several other children were with her, and they were crawling around on the floor apparently pretending they were dogs. Ginger the cat watched from the railing with tail-twitching disdain. Smokey and Iris, the kittens, played with a moth nearby. The only overhead fixture on either porch had been affixed to the veranda ceiling just outside the kitchen door. It had been switched on, attracting swarms of insects and bathing the children in its yellowy light. Olivia could only hope that they all wore insect repellent, as she did not.

Beyond the porch, it was a lovely, moonlit night. Mouthwatering aromas from the kitchen blended with the perfume of flowers to scent the warm, moist air.

Sara greeted Olivia with a bark, and a shake of her blue-jeaned bottom that was supposed to pass, Olivia guessed, for a wag of her dog's tail.

"Hi, pumpkin." Olivia ruffled her daughter's hair as Sara clambered over to her. Sara looked up at her reproachfully.

"Mom, I'm a dog," she protested.

"Oh. Good dog." Olivia patted Sara's head instead of ruffling her hair, and Sara panted happily. Olivia looked for Chloe. She and another little girl were near the steps that led down to the parking area. On all fours, they were busy making digging motions with their hands. With the knowledge gleaned from some years' acquaintance with such games, Olivia guessed that they were supposed to be burying their bones beneath the plank floor.

"Chloe, could I speak to you for a minute, please?" Olivia called.

Sara stopped her pretend burial of a bone at her mother's feet to look up at Olivia worriedly.

"Is Chloe in trouble?" she whispered, apparently recognizing a certain tone in Olivia's voice.

Glancing down at her daughter, Olivia stifled a sigh. Sara knew her too well. Placing her finger against her lips, she shook her head, their signal for *if you'll be quiet for now, I'll tell you everything later.*

Sara said nothing more, but gazed up at Olivia wide-eyed, her doggy game forgotten.

Chloe ignored Olivia's summons, continuing with her game. The other little girl crawled awkwardly down the steps, still in game mode. When Chloe would have followed, Olivia called her again, more sternly this time. Chloe threw her a dirty look, but this time she came, bounding over to Olivia on all fours, still in her doggy persona.

"What?" Chloe asked, borderline rude, tilting

her head back so that she could see Olivia's face. Like Sara, she was wearing blue jeans, with a long-sleeved yellow T-shirt and a yellow ribbon tying up her ponytail. She looked angelic, which she definitely was not.

Now that an adult was present to spoil their game, the other children scampered down into the backyard. They stopped crawling and took off whooping across the grass in two-legged pursuit of each other. The night was bright with moonlight and stars, and Olivia thought that they could come to no harm in the backyard.

She turned her attention to the problem at hand. With only Sara still within earshot, Olivia asked Chloe quietly, "Did you cut up that beautiful dress Mallory bought you to wear tomorrow?"

While Sara did not quite succeed in muffling a gasp, Chloe met Olivia's gaze defiantly.

"I told her I wasn't going to wear it, and I meant it."

Seriously concerned by what the destructiveness and defiance of the act said about the little girl's state of mind, Olivia hunkered down in front of her. She was wearing her short-sleeved black sweater, a charcoal knee-length skirt, hose, and black heels, and getting down to Chloe's eye level required some care in case she should rip her hose or reveal too much thigh, but she managed.

"Chloe, honey, why on earth would you do such a thing?"

"That's exactly what I want to know." Seth spoke without warning, making them all — Olivia, Sara, and Chloe — jump. A glance back told Olivia that he was standing behind her, frowning at his daughter, holding the mutilated black dress in one hand. One horrified look showed Olivia that the garment had, indeed, been ruined. The skirt and petticoat had been cut into ragged strips that fluttered like kites' tails from the ribbon waistband.

"Well, Chloe?" Seth asked when Chloe didn't say anything. Olivia stood up, smoothing her skirt and folding her arms over her chest, acutely aware of Seth. Abandoning her game, Chloe plopped on her bottom and crossed her legs in front of her, rested her hands on her knees, and gazed up at her father mutinously.

"I don't have to wear what Mallory tells me. She's not my mother!"

Seth's mouth tightened. Observing that, and knowing it for the storm warning it was from long experience, Olivia put a quick, cautionary hand on his upper arm. It was the first time she had touched him since he had walked out of her bedroom, and if she'd had time to think about it she wouldn't have done it. Sex had changed everything between them, just as she had known it would. They were no longer simply family to each other. Undercurrents upon undercurrents had been added to their relationship, making even the most innocent touch suddenly awkward.

Seth looked at her, and for a moment their eyes met and held. She thought his expression softened for her, and then he looked back at Chloe and his face grew hard again.

"You're right, Chloe. Mallory is not your mother. But that is no excuse that I can see for the deliberate destruction of a perfectly beautiful dress that she gave you." His voice was grim despite what Olivia had hoped would be the moderating influence of her hand on his arm. Chloe was grieving, too. He — they all — needed to take it easy with her.

Chloe glared at him. Then her lower lip began to tremble and her eyes filled with tears.

"You hate me, don't you?" she cried, jumping to her feet. "Everybody hates me now that Nana is dead! Everybody!"

Bursting into tears, she turned and ran down the back steps, then disappeared into the dark around the side of the house.

"Chloe!" Seth yelled after her. Then, bitterly, as it became obvious that Chloe was long gone, he added, "Goddamn it!"

His gaze met Olivia's, who looked significantly down at Sara. Still crouched at Olivia's feet, Sara was looking up at him wide-eyed.

"Oh," Seth said. To Sara he added, "I'm sorry. I shouldn't have said that."

"That's okay," Sara said gravely. "You don't have to worry that I'll repeat it in school or something. I know better than to say bad words."

"At my age, I should know better, too," Seth

said, placing a hand briefly on the top of her head in an affectionate gesture. "You're a good girl, Sara." Then he looked at Olivia with a weary sigh. The glow from the yellow porch light made his hair gleam gold. His face was all hard planes and angles. "Should I go after her? Or leave it alone?"

"Go after her," Olivia advised quietly. "She's hurting, too."

Seth looked at her for the briefest of moments, then picked up her hand that had dropped away from his arm when Chloe ran down the stairs. He carried it to his mouth, pressing the back of it to his lips. The heat of his mouth on her skin sent a shiver snaking all the way down to her toes. He turned her hand over and kissed her palm, while Olivia looked at him with, she feared, her heart in her eyes.

Seth. Her body ached. Her heart pounded.

"I'm glad you're home," he said, as he had before. "I don't know how any of us would get through this without you."

Then, before Olivia could say anything, he released her hand, handed her the mutilated dress, and ran lightly down the back steps in pursuit of Chloe.

"Why did Seth kiss your hand, Mom?" Sara asked curiously when he was gone.

Olivia had forgotten they'd had an audience. Feeling hideously self-conscious all of a sudden, she glanced down at her daughter.

"To thank me for helping him out with Chloe,"

she said as lightly as she could, and was thankful that Sara apparently accepted her explanation at face value.

What made it even worse was, Olivia feared that her explanation was the truth.

chapter 40

Walking through the front yard calling softly for his daughter, Seth cursed under his breath. He didn't need this. He really didn't need this. Just getting through this thing, hour by hour, day by day, was taking every bit of fortitude he possessed. He didn't need any more problems. Not right now. He knew his approach to Chloe's misdeed had not been exactly sympathetic. But when Mallory had told him what Chloe had done, and then shown him the ruined dress, he had lost his patience and his temper at the same time.

During this time of family crisis and mourning, was it too much to expect his daughter to behave?

But as he kept reminding himself, Chloe was only eight years old when all was said and done, and she was grieving, too. It was possible that her latest bit of acting out could even be laid at his door. He hadn't been very sensitive to her needs during this difficult time. In fact, he'd been downright insensitive, too caught up in his own pain to reach out to her in hers.

Poor little girl, he'd better remember that he was all she had left. And right at the moment he wasn't sure if he was a whole heck of a lot better than nobody.

For all his awkward attempts to parent her — the school visits, the bedtime stories, the stilted conversations about her interests, all undertaken at Olivia's prodding — he and his daughter just didn't seem to be able to connect. He could, and did, provide well for her materially. As far as providing for her emotionally, well, he had to admit that despite all his efforts so far he'd been pretty much of a dud.

Thank God for Livvy. She was helping Chloe get through this, keeping her busy, watching out for her, even sleeping in the same room with her. He should have been the one to be there for Chloe, he knew. But he just didn't seem to have the knack.

Livvy was helping him get through this, too. Without her, the night of his mother's death would have been, for him, the proverbial dark night of the soul. Even now, he would be lost if he did not have the memory of their lovemaking to sustain him. Just the knowledge that Livvy was going to be there when this was all over gave him a light to steer for through the fog of his grief.

If he could only get through the next few hours, through tonight and his mother's funeral tomorrow, then he could turn his attention to sorting out the rest of his life.

Chloe was huddled on the top step of the gazebo. Seth would never have seen her if she hadn't sniffled loudly as he walked by. He turned his head in response to the sound and there she was, her knees drawn up to her chin, her arms wrapped around her blue-jeaned legs. It was a bright night, with a sky full of stars and a moon as big and round as a frosty eyeball. The moonlight made Chloe's pale hair seem to glow. The gazebo, an elaborate Victorian-era structure, looked like a birdcage dropped down in a corner of the lawn. Chloe was the bird perched inside it.

In the second before Seth headed toward her it struck him how small she was. Like Jennifer, Chloe had a delicate build with fragile bones. She looked a great deal like Jennifer, too. Seth wondered suddenly if it would have made any difference to their relationship if she had looked like him instead of her mother. Maybe she would have felt more like his child than Jennifer's, then.

"Hey," he said softly, mindful that, under the circumstances, his approach had probably been too harsh before. He wished he had some pet name for her that he could use to kind of warm things up, like he'd heard Livvy call Sara *pumpkin* more times than he cared to count, but he couldn't think of one and it would be too artificial-seeming to just come out with something cutesy out of nowhere. "We need to talk."

He climbed the steps and sat down beside her, his size eleven shiny black moccasins planted firmly a step below her much smaller feet in their yellow-trimmed sneakers, his arms crossed loosely over his khaki-covered thighs as he leaned slightly forward and laced his fingers together between his knees. He hesitated, feeling ridiculously ill at ease. It was sad, he thought, that he should not know what to say to his own child, but there it was: He didn't.

Tightening her arms around her legs, Chloe cast him only a single glance before looking away. But at least she didn't cut and run.

In the annals of his relationship with his daughter, that, Seth thought with a touch of gallows humor, was a positive sign.

"Nana told me I should wear my blue dress with the daisies on it to her funeral," Chloe disclosed before Seth could say anything. "She said that it was her very favorite, and if she looked down from heaven and saw me wearing it that would be like a secret message between us. So that's the dress I'm going to wear, not some stupid fancy black one that *Mallory* bought me."

Seth ignored the belligerence of that speech, and the nasty tone in which she said Mallory's name, too. He zeroed in on the really important part.

"*Nana* told you that?" he questioned carefully. "When?"

"When Olivia took me to the hospital to say good-bye. Nana told me to wear my blue dress, and that's what I'm going to do."

"Olivia took you to the hospital to say good-bye to Nana? When?"

"Sunday afternoon." Chloe shot him a quick, almost wary glance. "Nana said I shouldn't tell you, because it would make you too sad to know we had to say good-bye. But I thought you better understand about the dress."

Seth felt unexpected tears sting his eyes. His throat tightened at the idea of his mother and daughter conspiring to shield him from pain. It was eye-opening that, in his mother's view, Chloe rather than himself had been the one who was strong enough to face the truth.

"Now that you know, are you still mad about the dress?" Chloe asked in a small voice, shooting him that wary glance again.

Seth shook his head. He didn't try to speak.

"You miss Nana a whole a lot, don't you?"

Seth nodded.

"She said you were going to be really sad after she died. She said that I would be sad, too. But she said she'd still be with us, all the time. She said it would make her happy to know that we were happy. And she said that if we wanted to talk to her, all we had to do was come outside on a night when there was lots of stars, like tonight, and pick the star that twinkled the most, and that would be her, waving at us." Chloe looked up into the sky and pointed. "See that star over there? The blinky one. I bet that's her. I already waved."

Seth looked where Chloe pointed, and saw, in the company of dozens upon dozens of stars in a star-filled sky, a large, bright star not too far above the western horizon that did indeed, when seen through tear-filled eyes and a rapidly dispersing cloud cover, seem to blink. With Chloe's eyes on him, he waved, too.

"So don't be sad, Daddy," Chloe said softly, her gaze earnest as she turned it on his face. "Nana's still with us. We just can't see her anymore."

Seth felt as though a huge hand was squeezing his heart. Here was his little girl, all of eight years old, trying to comfort *him*. He didn't deserve her.

"Chloe," he began. Suddenly the name that he had called her as an always smiling toddler, before things had started going wrong between him and Jennifer and Jennifer had taken Chloe away, came back to him. "Honey-bug, I love you. I know I don't say it much, but I do. You and me, we're a team. If we stick together, we can get through this thing all right."

Chloe looked at him again, her eyes bright with tears as they searched his face. Seth wrapped both arms around her, pulling her close. Suddenly hugging her didn't seem awkward at all. It felt right.

"I love you, too, Daddy," Chloe said. "You haven't called me honey-bug for a long time."

"I just remembered," he answered truthfully.

The two of them sat there together in the moon-washed darkness, talking and looking up at the one blinky star in a star-filled sky.

chapter 41

Savannah De Hart was too excited to sleep. It was long after midnight on the morning of the Fourth of July, which was, after Christmas, her very favorite holiday. It was even better than her birthday, because she had to share her birthday with her twin, Samantha. They would be nine years old on their next one, August sixth. But Fourth of July — *this* Fourth of July — was special. Yesterday she had been crowned Little Miss Rice at the Old Crowley Rice Society Celebration, and today she got to ride on the very top of the Rice Society float in the town's Fourth of July parade, wearing her crown and her sash and waving at the crowd as she passed.

Samantha had been first runner-up. With the other three runners-up, she would ride on one of the Rice Society float's corners.

Savannah was glad Samantha had been first

runner-up. She felt her sister's triumphs and defeats almost as keenly as she did her own. She *wanted* Samantha to do well, always.

Only sometimes, maybe, not quite as well as she did herself.

When they had announced the winner, Mommy had been so proud of her. She had laughed and hugged Savannah first when she ran up on stage, and called Savannah her beautiful girl.

Since she and Samantha were identical twins, that didn't really give her an advantage over her sister. They were both small for their age, with long black hair that they wore in ringlets down their backs for the pageants, bright blue eyes, and such pale skin that Mommy had to use a whole lot of blush on them to give their faces *definition*. But she could sing and dance a little better than Samantha, and that, plus her *sparkly personality,* as Mommy called it, was why she had won.

Samantha was quieter. Samantha didn't have a *sparkly personality.* Samantha didn't really like competing in pageants. But Savannah loved it. She loved the attention, she loved the beautiful costumes she got to wear, she loved the trophies, and most of all she loved making Mommy smile.

Samantha had cried herself to sleep tonight. Savannah felt bad about that. She'd gone in to comfort her sister, crawling into bed with Samantha and staying there until Samantha had fallen asleep. She hated for Samantha to feel bad, and Samantha felt bad because she hadn't won. Samantha hated letting Mommy down. They both did.

Their brother, Samuel, who was two years younger, didn't ever have to worry about letting Mommy down. He was just a dumb boy, and no one ever paid much attention to him.

Sometimes Savannah thought Samuel was lucky.

She and Samantha had their own rooms, which were connected by a bathroom. Samuel was across the hall from Samantha, and Mommy and Daddy — when Daddy was home, which wasn't often; he traveled a lot in his job with the oil company — were across the hall from her. Their house was nice. It was something called a split-level, in a subdivision with lots of other houses just like it. What made theirs special was that Mommy had planted lots of flowers all over the yard, and had decorated it really pretty inside. Her room had pink walls with yellow curtains and bedspread. Samantha's had yellow walls with pink curtains and bedspread. Samuel's was just dumb old blue, with baseball stuff everywhere. Samuel loved baseball.

He was one weird little kid.

Savannah turned onto her side and curled up into a ball, trying her best to go to sleep. If she didn't, she wouldn't look her best for the parade tomorrow. She lay still for a while, concentrating fiercely on going to sleep — but finally she couldn't resist turning back over and taking one more peep at her crown and sash and pageant dress that were all laid out on the chair by the dresser, ready for her to put them on for the parade.

There was something in front of the chair, blocking her view. Even as Savannah squinted at it, trying to make out what it was through the darkness, it moved toward her.

"Samantha?" she asked uncertainly, sitting up. But even as she said it, she knew it wasn't Samantha. Knew it as certainly as she always knew everything about her twin.

She knew, too, that she was in danger, with a dead-on instinct as old as humankind. Terror raced down her spine, and she screamed, only to have the cry immediately choked off by something wet and smelly that was shoved into her face, choking her, at the same time that a hand grabbed the back of her head, keeping her from pulling her face free.

Mommy, she cried, but only in her mind, as she plunged down into a darkness from which she knew, even as she succumbed to it, there would be no escape.

Picking victims was both an art and a science, he mused, suppressing the urge to whistle cheerfully as he let himself out the front door of the house, child, crown, sash, and dress slung together in the laundry sack he carried over his shoulder. Really, it was getting ridiculously easy. Breaking into houses was almost child's play for someone with a little know-how and the proper tools. The funny thing about it was, they felt safe in their houses.

The mommies all slept like rocks while he broke in and stole their babies, because they thought their sweet little darlings were all tucked up in bed and so safe.

Just thinking about it amused him.

He took great care in making his selections now. He didn't take just any little girl who happened to catch his eye. Oh, no, he had to give himself credit for more discrimination than that. They had to meet certain criteria — and he had to scout out where they lived, making sure that it was possible to acquire them with relative ease. About a month ago, he'd been on the verge of taking a cute little thing with hair so blond that it was almost white. But when he'd followed her home, he'd discovered two negatives that had, in the end, scuttled the plan. The first was the family pet, which was a very large, unfriendly German shepherd, who'd actually tried to leap the fence to get at him when he had only, in the act of casing the place, walked casually by. The second was the size of the house. Obviously the girl's family was wealthy, and taking the child of a wealthy family would attract more attention than he cared to have focused on his activities. He'd learned about the pitfalls of too much publicity with Missy Hardin. He still felt bad that her father had been the one to take the fall for that.

But he hadn't known what he was doing then.

He'd refined his technique considerably since. He found them, watched them for a while, checked out their houses, then went in and got them. It was as simple as that.

He'd seen Little Miss Rice at the pageant yesterday, for example, and known instantly that she was perfect for him. Her house was no problem. A five-year-old with a screwdriver could have broken in. And the family pet was a cat. Soft, fluffy, and definitely not a threat.

Acquiring Little Miss Rice more than made up for losing the blonde. Actually, he was amassing quite a collection. There was Becca, who he had to admit was kind of nondescript, because he'd taken her before he'd really known what he was doing. But still, he valued her because she was the first. His muse, if you would. Then there was Maggie, with all that short, frothy yellow-blond hair — a definite improvement. Kathleen, with her masses of flaming red hair, was a real conversation piece — except, of course, he had no one to converse about her with. And this one, who looked like a little Snow White — she would be the centerpiece, with her crown and sash and dress.

Perhaps, he mused, as, cargo loaded, he drove away down Route 13, he should consider branching out. Go for something a little more ethnic next time . . .

chapter 42

Callie Archer was laid to rest beside her long-dead husband in the family cemetery above the lake. It had been her wish, but a special permit from the town had been required to see it carried out, as burials in private ground were no longer routinely allowed. When the time came for Big John to be buried, he would join her there, in the remaining half of the grave site now occupied by his wife, Marguerite. With the addition of those two, the cemetery would be out of room. The remaining Archers would be buried in the graveyard beside St. Luke's.

It had rained during the night, but the weather was good for the burial. The heavy ground fog that had covered the landscape during the morning had, for the most part, been burned away by the noonday sun. It was warm, but not with the suffocating humidity of summer. The heat was pleasant rather than baking, and only a little sticky. The sky was a clear, almost cloudless blue. Birds sang and swooped; insects droned.

Set on approximately an acre of once-lush but now faintly scraggly-looking grass on a bluff overlooking Ghost Lake, the cemetery was surrounded by a four-foot-tall black wrought-iron fence, now slightly rusty. The funeral cortege approached along the access road from the rear, and stopped. Pallbearers carried the coffin over the bumpy ground from the hearse to the bier beside the grave, which had been dug the day before. The motorcade of mourners parked in the grass alongside the narrow gravel road, and, except for the crunch of their feet on the gravel, followed the coffin to the grave site in near silence.

Olivia had not been near the cemetery in years. As a child, she had been a fairly frequent visitor, moving from monument to monument, always seeking one particular name. She had never understood why her mother wasn't there, beside her stepfather. Once, when she had asked, what they told her made no sense: Her mother had been *cremated*. Now, of course, she understood what that word meant, and she knew, too, with her fresh, terrible knowledge, why it had been done: As a suicide, Selena Archer would not have been permitted to await eternity in hallowed ground.

The pain of that truth was so intense that

Olivia immediately strove to banish the thought from her mind.

"Mom, you're squeezing my hand too tight," Sara whispered from beside her, tugging to free her fingers. Wearing a forest-green dress with lots of smocking on the bodice and a white Peter Pan collar, white stockings, and black mary janes, Sara looked adorable — and very grown up.

"Oh, sorry." Loosening her grip with a quick, apologetic smile for her daughter, Olivia felt some of her pain ease. Sweet Sara, with her wide brown eyes and earnest face, was the present and the future. Olivia's mother belonged to the past, and for today, at least, should be left there.

The Archer family cemetery had been designed to honor the original owner of LaAngelle Plantation, Colonel Robert John Archer, and his wife and descendants. His mausoleum dominated the graveyard. Built of white marble, turned creamy yellow with age, it was fashioned like a miniature Greek temple, with an elaborately carved portico, a quartet of fluted columns, and twin life-size marble angels guarding the long-closed door. Votive candles set in holders carved into the angels' hands burned brightly to welcome the cemetery's soon-to-be newest resident. Other life-size stone angels — there were six, to mark the graves of each of the colonel's children — stood sentinel around the mausoleum. Later residents of the cemetery had apparently not shared their ancestor's appreciation for angels. The markers for subsequent Archers leaned toward five-foot-tall monoliths and simple stone crosses. The most touching, in Olivia's opinion, was a small pink marble cross set atop a stone pedestal. Inscribed simply ABIGAIL, above the dates of birth and death, it was a tribute to a long-ago Archer six-year-old. As a youngster exploring the cemetery, Olivia had merely found the old cross interesting. Now, setting eyes on it again as a mother, she felt a thrill of grief for that lost little girl, and in consequence gripped Sara's hand too tightly again as they walked across the grass.

"Mom!" Casting her a disgusted glance, Sara disengaged her fingers.

The group assembled for the graveside service was considerably smaller than the crowd that had thronged to the funeral service proper in town. St. Luke's had been full to overflowing. People who couldn't get inside the church had stood outside, on the grounds and in the parking lot, in respectful silence.

But this final farewell before Callie's body was committed to the earth was limited to her family and very close friends. They gathered around the polished walnut coffin, which was covered with a blanket of white lilies; more flowers were massed on the grass just beyond the open grave. Seth and Chloe, he in a black business suit and she in an incongruously cheerful blue dress with white and yellow daisies appliqued around the hem, stood hand in hand before the casket. Seth's face was pale and haggard, his eyes red-rimmed, but he was outwardly composed. Chloe showed fewer overt signs of grief than he did. The impression one got, watching them, was that it was she who was consoling him, instead of the other way around. Mallory, in a form-fitting black knit dress, stood on Seth's other side clutching a prayer book, her engagement ring glinting in the sun every time she moved her hand. Olivia tried not to think about that engagement ring, or, for that matter, about the engagement. But the stab of jealousy she felt whenever Mallory leaned against Seth, or took hold of his arm, or tiptoed to murmur something in his ear, pierced even the dark cloud of her grief.

Despite the wild night of passion they had shared, *Seth was going to marry Mallory.* Them was the facts, as the saying went, whether she wanted to face them or not.

When Father Randolph, who was officiating just as he had at the church, intoned the traditional ". . . ashes to ashes, dust to dust," Ira burst into noisy sobs, and turned away, hiding his face in his hands. Answering tears flowed down Olivia's cheeks. To think that Callie had finally found love again after so many years, only to lose it so soon to death, added another degree of sorrow to her feeling of aching loss. She stood with her head bowed, clutching Sara's hand again in the midst of a weeping crowd of relatives and friends, listening with numb grief to Father

406

Randolph until the service ended.

Then she looked up just in time to see, through the film of her tears, Mallory step into Seth's arms, where she was warmly embraced as his head bent over hers.

Obviously Seth didn't need any comfort Olivia might have to offer. She turned away, only to find herself enveloped in a bear hug by Keith, who stood with David on her right. Keith, the tenderhearted, was crying while David, a typical Archer stoic, was not. Olivia hugged Keith and cried, too. When at last neither of them could cry any more, they turned, and, together with David and Sara, followed the rest of the mourners back to the Big House for the traditional after-funeral feast.

By the following Monday, life at LaAngelle Plantation had more or less resumed its usual rhythms. If there was a sense of profound loss in the air, they all labored to ignore it. Meals still had to be eaten, children had to be cared for, wages had to be earned. In short, life had to go on.

David and Keith had flown to California immediately after the funeral. They were scheduled to return on Monday afternoon. Chloe was once again sleeping in her own room, with Seth next door and Martha, who was going to continue to stay on in the house until Seth's wedding, across the hall. Olivia and Sara stayed where they were. Callie's room remained as it was on the evening she had left it, although going through and packing away her possessions was a looming job that no one seemed quite ready to face.

As was her routine before Callie was hospitalized, Olivia got the girls ready on Monday morning and drove them to school, then went on to the Boatworks. Seth had left the house shortly before seven, so he had been at work for nearly two hours when Olivia arrived. The door to his office was closed, and she assumed that he was inside, although he could just as easily have been anywhere about the place. She knew he hadn't been sleeping well: Twice since the funeral, she had heard him in the wee hours of the morning walking up and down the gallery. She had not gone outside to comfort him. Doing so once had already done far too much damage to their relationship — and her heart.

Since the funeral, they'd seen each other only in company. Although he had gone in to work Friday, Saturday, and part of Sunday, and driven to Baton Rouge to check on Big John in the hospital every day, Seth was making an obvious effort to be home in the evenings for Chloe. Twice they had all shared supper, and Olivia had found herself thankful for the presence of Martha and the little girls at the table. On other occasions when Seth was present, Olivia left him with his daughter while she and Sara did their own thing. For the four of them to do things together smacked too much of a family group, which wasn't good for anyone under the circumstances. The really hurtful thing about it was, Seth no longer seemed comfortable in her presence. Once or twice, Olivia got the impression that he had something he wanted to say to her, but, if so, he never spoke out.

An apology coupled with a hearty *let's put that unfortunate night behind us, dear, shall we?* was heading her way. She could feel it.

It was going to crush her like a brick dropped on a bug.

She and Sara and Chloe had stayed home on Friday, so Monday was Olivia's first day back. It felt good to be at work, good to be busy, good to talk to people about the normal, everyday minutiae of life. After spending the first hour or so of the workday being very quiet and low-key out of deference to the family's loss, Ilsa was, by midmorning, chattering away about her baby and her upcoming maternity leave, to which she was looking forward very much. Everyone Olivia talked to was pretty much the same way, from the people delivering supplies to the clients on the telephone: a few minutes of respectful decorum, and then business as usual.

Looking unbelievably slender in a navy-blue skirted suit, three-inch heels, and pearls, Mallory came breezing in about fifteen minutes before lunchtime, carrying an embossed white folder in one hand. Her presence was not unusual, or at least it hadn't been in the weeks before Callie's death. Mallory had always stopped in to see Seth nearly every day for one thing or another. But things had changed since then.

Or, at least, things had changed for *Olivia* since then.

She'd sooner see a rabid polecat than Mallory, she discovered.

"Hello, Olivia! Hi, Ilsa!" Mallory greeted the two women in the outer office with a breezy smile. As she was wrestling with the balky computer at the time, Olivia reasoned that she had a perfectly acceptable excuse for not returning Mallory's greeting with much enthusiasm. Undaunted, Mallory stopped by the workstation where Olivia was trying everything she could think of to get the stupid machine to display the data she had loaded into its memory bank only two weeks before, leaned a hand on the desk, and asked confidentially, "How's he doing?"

Knowing that *he* referred to Seth, Olivia smiled with as much affability as she could muster, which wasn't too much. "As far as I know, he's doing fine."

"I'm glad to hear it. The invitations finally came in, and I wanted him to take one last look at them before I have them addressed and sent out. I know the timing's a little insensitive, but the wedding's in six weeks. We're running late as it is. And Callie *did* say she didn't want us to postpone it or anything because of her." Mallory straightened with a smile, opened the folder, and scooted it across the desk so that Olivia could see. "What do you think?"

Mallory Bridgehampton Hodges
and
Michael Seth Archer
Request the Honor of Your Presence
At the Celebration of Their Marriage . . .

Olivia couldn't stand to read any more. "They're lovely," she said, looking back at the computer. The invitations *were* lovely, with black engraving on thick white vellum paper — but they made Seth's approaching nuptials seem hideously real.

He's mine, she thought fiercely, but of course it wasn't so. It was written right there in front of her nose in black and white: Seth belonged to Mallory.

And she'd better get used to it.

Getting sexually involved with her big cousin had been the biggest mistake of her life. She'd known it was stupid from the beginning. But she'd gone ahead and done it like the heedless fool she was, and now it was too late to take it back. She needed to accept that night for what it was, nothing more or less than a desperate reaching out for comfort on Seth's part. She'd been present, and willing, and female, and that was all it had taken. The sensible thing to do now was to pretend, to herself and Seth and everybody else, that it had never happened; to go back to being loving cousins, and good friends.

But when had she ever done the sensible thing?

She was in love with Seth. The knowledge jumped out at her without warning, and as Olivia absorbed it she became physically ill. She felt light-headed, short of breath. She didn't want to be in love with Seth. She refused to be in love with Seth.

Being in love with Seth when he was going to marry Mallory was the quickest route she could think of to a broken heart.

Oh no, oh no, oh no, Olivia thought in a panic, pushing her chair back from the desk. Its ancient casters moved with a protesting squeak, but Olivia barely heard it. Jumping to her feet, she managed a tight smile for Mallory, who was watching her with some bewilderment, and a glance for Ilsa.

"I'm going to the rest room," she announced, and fled.

When she came back, having bathed her face and held her wrists under cold running water until the light-headedness subsided, Ilsa was alone in the outer office.

Thank God. Olivia wasn't up to any more of Mallory at the moment. Or Seth, either, for that matter, although she had hardly seen him all day.

"You okay?" Ilsa asked with concern. Olivia nodded, sitting back down in front of the computer screen. Ilsa seemed to take her at her word. Still, Olivia was glad of the distraction when Phillip and Carl walked into the office together moments later.

Tall, dark-haired and stocky, dressed almost

identically in the gentleman's uniform of navy sport coat and khaki slacks, they could have passed for twins. They were scowling at each other, their bushy black eyebrows meeting over nearly identical pugilistic noses, and it was obvious that brotherly relations were not at their warmest.

"Not before June fifteenth," Phillip said to his brother in a firm tone. "It'll take us at least that long to finish it up."

"But I promised him April first." Carl looked belligerently at Phillip.

"Well, *un*promise him. Archer Boatworks doesn't make promises we can't keep. That's why we've been in business so long."

"You sound like a paid advertisement," Carl groused. "This is an order for a five-million-dollar yacht we're talking about. I don't see why we can't hurry things up."

"Because it *is* a five-million-dollar yacht, you dummy." Phillip sounded exasperated. The two brothers paused by the desk where Olivia worked at the computer, glaring at each other.

"Boys, boys," Ilsa said mock-reprovingly from across the room. "Why can't we all just get along?"

"Because my brother's an idiot," Phillip and Carl said at the same time. They looked at each other in surprise, then burst out laughing.

Even Olivia had to smile.

"He in?" Phillip asked, nodding toward Seth's closed door.

413

Ilsa shook her head. "He and Mallory went to lunch."

"Speaking of lunch." Carl grinned down at Olivia. "How about letting me buy you a sandwich? Chicken salad's on special at the inn today."

Carl had been asking her out for approximately as long as she had been back in LaAngelle. Olivia just as regularly turned him down. Automatically she started to refuse again, but then she caught herself.

If she was going to cure herself of her hankering for Seth, she was going to have to find somebody else to hanker after. Carl wasn't exactly the man of her dreams, but he would do in an emergency. And this qualified as an emergency.

"Sounds good," she said, smiling warmly up at him. He, Phillip, and Ilsa looked equally surprised as Olivia got to her feet.

chapter 43

By the time Olivia returned to the office, it was fifteen minutes until two o'clock and she was seriously considering Carl's invitation to go dancing in Baton Rouge on Friday. After all, she was fond of Carl, even if she wasn't wildly attracted to him. Every date didn't have to be a deathless romance, after all. There was really no reason at all why she shouldn't go out with him. If Belinda didn't like it, too bad.

Of course, going out with Carl would encourage him to like her more than he should. He'd already, during the course of a single lunch, sat beside her in their booth, draped his arm "casually" about her shoulders, and held her hand. In other words, he had made it abundantly clear that his interest in her was sexual, and there, she feared, lay the problem.

She had absolutely no intention of sleeping

with Carl, and he seemed to have every intention of sleeping with her.

So going dancing on Friday was probably out.

Seth was seated in Olivia's chair behind the computer when she and Carl walked into the outer office. Wearing a button-down blue shirt with a yellow silk tie and navy slacks, his long legs sprawled out in front of him, his hands folded on his chest, Seth looked thoroughly put out about something. If he was trying to operate the blasted computer, Olivia thought, she could certainly understand his ill humor. Or maybe — and this was cheering — maybe Mallory had done something to make him cross.

Ilsa, who was filing papers on the other side of the room, looked around and widened her eyes at Olivia in silent warning.

"Did you two have a nice lunch?" Seth asked, too politely, his gaze raking Olivia before moving to fix on Carl.

"Very nice." Choosing to ignore Ilsa's signal — if Seth was in a bad mood, she for one didn't care — Olivia smiled brightly at him as she slipped her nubby gold blazer off her shoulders and hung it in the closet near the door. The gold T-shirt that she wore beneath had not come with the blazer, but the color was close and the pair made a nice outfit when worn with a slim black skirt and heels. Certainly it was nowhere near as expensive, or as chic, as the outfits Mallory habitually wore, Olivia thought, as she moved to take possession of her desk, but it suited her budget and *her* just fine. "So nice, in fact, that we're going to Baton Rouge on Friday to go dancing."

"Oh, really?" Seth's eyes narrowed at her as she came around the desk toward him. Olivia met his gaze with a challenging look of her own, and pointedly stopped beside her chair, which he occupied. She was putting him on notice that she, too, could put their brief romantic interlude behind her.

Whether she really could or not.

"Hey, hey, hey, that's great! I could've sworn you were gonna say no." Carl was all affable charm as he grinned at Olivia from the opposite side of the desk. Olivia, still standing, smiled back at him, knowing that she was probably making another mistake by encouraging Carl and, at the moment, not particularly caring. Seth, still seated in her chair, did not smile.

"Correct me if I'm wrong, but didn't you have a meeting with a client at one?" Seth's gaze was fixed on Carl now, and there was a definite edge to his voice.

Carl's expression changed ludicrously. "Oh — my — God!" He slapped his forehead, glanced at Olivia, and looked guiltily back at Seth. "I completely forgot."

"I gathered that." Seth, too, glanced at Olivia, as if he knew precisely where to place the blame — on her. He stood up, his attention shifting to Carl again. "Apparently Mr. Crowell waited for about thirty minutes, then stormed out. I don't

417

think we'll be building a boat for him anytime soon."

"Oh, man, I'm *sorry*." Carl groaned. He leaned both hands against the desk and shook his head. "I don't know how I came to forget about it. That meeting's been in the works for two months."

"I know how you forgot about it. You were out chasing around after Olivia." Seth's gaze shifted to Olivia again, his expression grim. His next remark was addressed to her. "There's a reason lunch is set for *an hour,* from noon until one."

"Does that time limit apply to everyone?" Olivia asked, sweet as pie. If Seth was going to be unpleasant, she was going to give as good as she got. No matter how busy they were, he always found plenty of time for *chasing around after* Mallory. "Obviously *you* weren't back from lunch until after Mr. Crowell had left, or you would have taken care of him yourself."

Seth's eyes narrowed on Olivia's face. Carl looked horrified. From behind Seth's back, Ilsa shook her head in a frantic *no.* Olivia didn't care if she *was* antagonizing Seth. She had finally reached the point where she was well and truly mad at him. Her heart was breaking, it was all his fault, and he didn't care. Worse, he'd obviously taken a long lunch with Mallory. During the course of which eating lunch was probably the least of what they'd done.

Carl rushed hurriedly into speech before Seth could say anything. "I'll call Mr. Crowell back

418

right now and apologize. I'll tell him — I'll tell him — I'll think of something."

"You won't reach him today. He's already checked out of his hotel. Face it, lover boy. You've blown this one big-time."

Olivia glared at Seth. Carl, clearly more concerned about the lost sale than Seth's uncharacteristic nastiness, headed toward the door.

"I've got his cell phone number in my office. I'll tell him I had a flat tire." His voice dropped to a mutter. "In LaAngelle? Hell, I could catch a ride from anyone in town. That won't wash." It was obvious that Carl was now talking to himself. As he exited he called over his shoulder in a louder voice, "Thanks for lunch, Olivia! I'll get back to you with the arrangements for Friday!"

There was a moment of silence. Then Ilsa ostentatiously turned back to her filing. Olivia, with a fulminating glance at Seth, sank down in her chair. Seth, after returning Olivia's look with an equally charged one of his own, headed for his office.

At the door he paused. In a carefully neutral voice he said, "Would you come into my office for a minute, please, Olivia?"

Olivia looked up from the blue glow of the computer screen. Oh, yes, she would come into his office. She positively welcomed the chance to speak her mind to him without any witnesses.

"Certainly," she answered as coolly as he had spoken. In the corner, Ilsa rolled her eyes in silent sympathy. Olivia lifted her chin, and straightened her spine. Seth was politely holding the door open. She sailed by him without so much as a sideways glance. He closed it behind her.

His office was an advertisement for the Boatworks' expertise with fine materials. Teak paneling, hand-rubbed to an expensive glow, shone in the sunlight admitted by the single large window. Built-in bookshelves, also of teak, rose floor to ceiling behind his desk, and to chair-rail height around the rest of the room. His desk was large and impressive, a polished mahogany antique, with a brass desk lamp and leather accessories. The black leather chair behind it was large and authoritative. Clustered around a gleaming brass and glass coffee table, a couch and two more chairs upholstered in black leather completed the room's furnishings. Scale models of yachts were everywhere. Paintings of ships at sea hung on the walls. The carpet was a tasteful charcoal gray. The smell of Lemon Pledge and Armor All hung faintly in the air.

"I don't want you dating Carl," Seth said abruptly, leaning back against the closed door as Olivia turned to face him. Olivia noticed, and wished she hadn't, that his shoulders were almost as broad as the door frame. His blond hair was longer than he usually wore it, and she guessed that, with all that had happened, he had not found time for his usual haircut. His face was drawn in the aftermath of his mother's death, with the lines around his eyes more pronounced than they had been before. The eyes themselves were a deep, penetrating blue as she met them. His mouth was a straight line.

"Oh, really?" she asked, her eyebrows lifting. Resting a hand and her hip on his desk, she gave her head a toss so that one glossy brown wing of her hair swung away from her face. "And why is that?"

"Because it will only cause trouble. A lot of companies have policies that prohibit employees from dating each other. So does Archer Boatworks."

"We do not! Since when?"

"Right now."

"You can't do that!"

"Sure I can. I'm the boss. I can do any damn thing I please, if I think it's for the good of the company."

Olivia simply stared at him for a moment as words failed her. When she could talk, she asked carefully, "And just how is my going dancing with Carl going to harm Archer Boatworks?"

Seth's gaze moved slowly over her, from the top of her head to her high-heeled shoes. Bosom swelling with indignation under the thoroughness of that look, Olivia was nevertheless thankful that she'd taken time to brush her hair, powder her nose, and put on fresh lipstick before returning from lunch. She might not be as chic as Mallory, and her clothes might shriek Kmart rather than Saks, but she was, at least, minimally well-groomed.

"To begin with, it's going to piss me off, and I have enough on my plate right now without worrying about what's going on with you and Carl."

"I can't go dancing with Carl because *it's going to piss you off?*" Talk about dog in the manger! Olivia couldn't believe it. Her temper heated, and she glared at him. "Well, guess what? I don't *care* if it pisses you off! Too bad, so sad!"

"I broke up with Mallory today," he said mildly, catching her by surprise.

Olivia's eyes widened as his words penetrated. Her indignation fizzled out like a deflating balloon. "You broke up with Mallory? You broke your *engagement?*"

"That's what I said." He came away from the door, moving toward her.

"But — she had the wedding invitations with her." It was stupid, she knew, but she was having a hard time grasping the reality of what he was saying. "They were all printed up."

"I know. I felt — feel — pretty bad about it, I must admit. But the only alternative was to marry her, and I finally figured out that I don't want to do that."

He was standing in front of her now, not touching her but close, a smile lurking around the corners of his mouth. Still leaning against his desk, Olivia looked up into his eyes. She thought they were almost — tender, as they met hers.

Still, she would not allow herself to believe.

"And this is supposed to interest me — why?" Her tone was frosty.

This time he really did smile. "I don't know," he said. "I thought we might kind of pick up where we left off."

"Where we left off?" Her heart was thudding in her breast. She couldn't move her gaze away from his.

"Unless you just went to bed with me to be kind." He picked up her hand and carried it to his mouth, where he pressed his parted lips to her palm. Olivia felt the moist heat of his lips on her skin with every fiber of her being. "*Were* you just being kind to your grief-stricken cousin, Livvy?"

"You're not my cousin," Olivia said fiercely, and threw herself into his arms. Her hands locked behind his neck, and his arms wrapped around her waist.

"No, I'm not, thank God," he said, and kissed her.

The phone on his desk shrilled, interrupting.

"Shit," Seth muttered, pressing Olivia back against the desk as he groped for the ringing instrument without releasing her. Only as he punched a button and growled "What?" did she realize that he was speaking over the intercom.

"Mr. Archer, your two thirty appointment is here." Ilsa's voice sounded disconcertingly clear, almost as if she were in the room with them.

"Give me one minute." Seth punched the button to turn the intercom off. Olivia was leaning against him, her arms around his neck, her mouth pressed to the warm, prickly skin just below his jaw. The hard edge of his desk cut into her bottom as his weight held her against it, but she didn't care. All she cared about was Seth.

Her Seth, now.

He found her mouth, kissed her again, then slid his lips along her cheek.

"How about dinner tonight?" he asked, with his mouth at her ear.

"Are you asking me for a date?" The idea charmed her. Dating Seth — she would never, in all the years she had known him, have foreseen herself doing such a thing. She reared her head back so that she could look at him. Her expression turned mock severe. "I thought you said that Archer Boatworks has a policy about employees dating each other."

"I must have forgotten to mention that our policy specifically excludes the general manager." He smiled down into her eyes. "So how about dinner?"

"Sara. Chloe . . ." She could hardly think when he looked at her like that. Being in his arms felt so good, so right. Joy fizzed inside her like bubbles in champagne.

"Martha can baby-sit. We won't be late. I want to take you out."

"Seth." Olivia strove to keep a cool head. She was so happy, so deliriously happy, that all she wanted to do was be with him every moment for the rest of her life. But there were difficulties that had to be faced. "Chloe might not like the idea that we're — involved. She likes me now, but . . ."

"Involved? Good word. I like it. Much better than dating." Seth kissed her again, quickly and deeply. Responding, Olivia almost lost her train of thought. When he lifted his head, she remembered, and doggedly persevered.

"I think we should be discreet in front of the girls. I . . ."

The telephone shrilled again. This time, when Seth answered it, Phillip's voice came over the intercom, all pleasant and jolly for the benefit of the audience in the other room, but with an unmistakable subtext.

"Seth, buddy, *Niko Terezakis* is here."

Niko Terezakis, Olivia knew, was one of the Boatworks' wealthiest clients. The new yacht he was thinking about ordering would be in the ten-million-dollar-or-more range.

"I'll be right with you," Seth said into the intercom, and turned it off. "Don't worry about Chloe. She likes you. She never did like Mallory. She told me Mallory was only nice to her because she was trying to hook me."

"Chloe has her moments, but no one can say she's not smart." Olivia pulled out of his arms. "You need to get back to work. And I need to go pick up Sara and Chloe. We can talk about this later."

"Wait a second." He put his hands on either side of her face, tilted it up to his, kissed her mouth, and looked down at her consideringly. Then he grinned. "You were mad as fire at me when you marched in here, and now you're smiling and your eyes are glowing and your lip-stick's all gone — what's Ilsa going to make of that, I wonder? And Phillip?"

"This is going to be embarrassing." Olivia groaned as the truth of what he was saying hit her. Pulling away from him, she smoothed her hair with her hands as best she could, and bit her lips so that the absence of lipstick might be less noticeable.

Seth laughed. "Look at it this way: We'll give them something to talk about."

"There's a happy thought," Olivia muttered, and headed for the door.

Seth was right behind her, reaching around her to open the door for her.

"Try to look as grouchy as you did when you came in," he whispered teasingly in her ear, his hand on the knob. "And remember to tell Carl that going dancing on Friday is *out*."

Before Olivia could reply he pulled the door open, and she suddenly felt like the leading lady on the play's opening night: All eyes were on her.

Olivia was flustered, and she knew her cheeks pinkened as both Ilsa and Phillip looked her up and down. Ilsa's eyes held compassion at first — obviously she thought Olivia had just endured a major chewing out — then widened with growing surprise. Phillip's gaze was dark with disapproval from the beginning. Of course, he'd surprised her with Seth before, and must have had an inkling about what was going on behind Seth's closed office door.

The third occupant of the room, a black-haired, swarthy-skinned man who was not quite as tall as Phillip but had an air about him of one who expected everyone around him to jump to his bidding, merely had appreciation in his gaze as it ran over Olivia.

"Niko!" Seth said affably, moving around Olivia to shake the client's hand. "Sorry to keep you waiting. Come on into my office, and I'll show you the plans we've drawn up for the *Athena*. She'll be magnificent. . . ."

With Phillip trailing, the three men went into Seth's office and closed the door.

Olivia was left alone with Ilsa, who was still looking at her wide-eyed, her work suspended as she stood beside the file cabinet with a folder forgotten in her hand.

But whatever Ilsa might have been thinking, she had too much tact to put it into words.

Olivia escaped with a smile and a quick goodbye, grabbing purse and blazer and hurrying out the door to pick up Sara and Chloe from school.

chapter 44

Seth got home at a little after five, which was extremely early for him. Olivia was sitting at the kitchen table surrounded by seven little girls in brown uniforms, all busy gluing Popsicle sticks together to make bird feeders. She was wearing ancient jeans worn thin enough at the knees to be turned into next season's shorts, a baggy olive-green T-shirt, and sneakers without socks. Her hair was twisted up in a knot at the back of her head, and secured with a pencil. Tendrils escaped to straggle around her face. Her makeup had long since worn off, and she had glue on her fingers and her right cheek. When Seth stepped through the back door, she looked up to see who it was and her breath caught.

He'd added a camel sport coat to the navy pants, blue shirt, and yellow tie he'd been wearing earlier, and he looked good enough to eat.

He paused just inside the door, looking surprised to find a gaggle of chattering girls around his kitchen table.

"Brownie troop," Olivia said by way of explanation as he met her gaze, and smiled at him.

"Oh," he said, and smiled back. His eyes were dazzlingly blue, she thought, and his mouth . . . She had to fight the urge to stand up, walk to the door, throw her arms around his neck, and kiss that curved-into-a-smile mouth.

Not in front of the girls, she reminded herself.

"Daddy!" Looking up from her bird feeder at last, Chloe greeted him with a smile. "You're home early!"

"Yup." He strolled over to where she was sitting, placed a hand on her shoulder, and looked down at her Popsicle-stick creation. "Great job, honey-bug. Uh, what is it?"

The girls all giggled at his ignorance.

"A bird feeder!" Chloe said indignantly. "Olivia showed us how to make them. We're going to sell them at the carnival."

"Oh." Seth nodded as if he knew just what she was talking about, which Olivia was willing to bet dollars to doughnuts he didn't. "Hello, Sara."

"Hi, Seth." Sara, whose bird feeder was further along than anyone else's because of her diligence in the face of distraction, glanced up at him, focused, and awarded him a beaming smile.

"The Christmas carnival at school," Olivia clarified, standing up and wiping her hands on a

429

damp paper towel. "The Brownies have their own booth this year."

"And we're going to have the best stuff there, and make a ton of money to pay for our spring camping trip," Ginny Zigler boasted. Tall and bone-thin, with glossy dark blond hair pulled back from her face into a curly ponytail, Ginny was, as Olivia had already figured out, Chloe's best friend. Like Chloe, she had a strong personality, and Sara tended to be subdued in her presence.

"You know all the girls, don't you, Seth?" Olivia asked casually. To tell the truth, she doubted that he did. In any case, without waiting for his answer, she introduced them, gesturing at each one in turn.

"Katie Evans, Tiffany Holt, Mary Frances Bernard, Shannon McNulty, Ginny Zigler. Say hi to Mr. Archer, girls."

"Hi, Mr. Archer," they chorused dutifully.

Seth smiled and nodded. And looked at Olivia again.

"We'll be finished here in a few minutes. The girls get picked up at five thirty."

"Oh." Seth's eyes met hers, slid down to her mouth. "Where's Martha?"

"Gone into town to visit her daughter. She'll be back about six."

"Mrs. Morrison, can you help me with this? My fingers keep getting stuck to the roof." Shannon's voice was plaintive. Olivia moved around to help her, smoothing the glue out with her fingertips. Wiping her hands on the paper towel again, she looked up to find Seth's eyes on her.

"I'm going to go up and change clothes. I'll be down again in a few minutes."

"We'll be here," Olivia said, smiling at him again. She just couldn't seem to *not* smile at him.

"Mrs. Morrison, are we going to paint them today?" Mary Frances asked.

"No, not today. We have to let the glue dry really well first. We'll paint them next week." Seth left the room as Olivia answered. Her gaze followed him until she realized what she was doing. Then she forced her attention back to the girls and their project.

By the time Seth came back downstairs, the bird feeders were lined up on the kitchen counter to dry, and the girls were playing in the backyard.

He was wearing chinos that looked almost as old as her jeans, a faded denim shirt with the sleeves rolled up, and boat shoes. The casual clothes suited his athletic build, and the denim shirt made the blue of his eyes seem very bright.

"Where is everybody?" Seth asked, looking around as he came through the swinging door.

"Outside." Olivia was washing her hands in the kitchen sink. He came up behind her, wrapped his arms around her waist, and kissed the back of her neck, which her casual upsweep had bared. A shiver of pure pleasure raced down Olivia's spine. She finished drying her hands, turned, and slid her arms around his neck, smiling up into his eyes.

"I came down to help," he said in a complaining tone, as he pulled her close.

"Too late," Olivia murmured, going up on her toes to kiss him. His mouth was hot and hungry as he kissed her back, and Olivia felt herself go weak in the knees.

"Did I tell you that you're nice to come home to?" he murmured against her mouth a moment later.

Nice to come home to. That had such a wonderful ring to it. A cozy, permanent ring.

Smiling a little, she shook her head.

"You give this place a heart," he said, kissing the corner of her mouth. "I don't think I could face this house right now, if you weren't in it."

She saw the pain flare in his eyes.

"Oh, Seth, I know you're hurting," she said, and turned her head so that her mouth found his. She kissed him softly, gently, a lover's kiss, filled with exquisite tenderness. "We're all hurting, everyone who loved your mother. But I know you're hurting most of all. I wish I knew something that would take away the pain."

"Livvy . . ." He took a deep breath when she slid her mouth along his bristly cheek to nibble at his earlobe. She could feel his chest expand against her breasts, his arms tighten around her waist. "You take away the pain."

He kissed her again, his mouth hard and hot. When he lifted his head, they were both breathing hard, and his body was pressing hers

432

back against the counter. The evidence of his arousal was unmistakable between them.

"Okay, I think we'd better call a halt," he said after a second, lifting himself away from her with obvious reluctance. He turned so that he was leaning back against the counter beside her. His hands curled around the beveled edge on either side of his body as he looked at her. "I have a great idea: How about we all, you, me, Sara, and Chloe, go out for pizza?"

Olivia took a deep, steadying breath. Her pulse was racing and her body tingled and ached. But overriding her desire to drag him off to bed immediately was delight that he had thought of taking Chloe and Sara on an outing. As a father, he was making giant strides. The smile she gave him sparkled. "That sounds wonderful! The girls will love it. But I have to clean up a little bit first. I can't go anywhere like this."

His eyes moved over her. He didn't have to say it for her to know he found her beautiful. It was there in his eyes.

"Go wash your hands and face, and put on some lipstick, or whatever it is you women do, and come back. Don't change clothes. I like the way you fill out those jeans."

He grinned wickedly at her, and Olivia couldn't help it: She leaned toward him, dropped a quick, heated kiss on his mouth, and fled before he could grab her.

chapter 45

Seth was smiling as he went out the kitchen door to watch the girls at play. They shouted and ran, paying no heed to him at all. Birds twittered, frogs and insects traded insults back and forth, peacocks trolled the hedge line for grubs. The late afternoon sunlight was beautiful, he thought, and realized with a sense of shock that he rarely saw it. He'd been working such long hours for so long that the softly diffused golden light that spilled over the backyard was a novelty to him. He sat in the rocking chair that his mother had favored, took an instant to acknowledge both the pain and the comfort that sitting in her chair brought him, and then deliberately moved his thoughts on to something else.

Livvy. Just thinking of her made him smile, and burn at the same time. Who ever would have thought that the plump little girl who used to

434

follow him everywhere would grow up to claim such a big chunk of his heart?

Not he. Never in a million years.

Like this impossibly big, run-down old house, and the Boatworks, and his family, and, in fact, the entire town of LaAngelle, Livvy was part of the fabric of his life. She fit into it seamlessly, and she always had. Maybe that was why it had taken him so long to realize the truth: He didn't just want to take her to bed and keep her there for a month of Sundays. He was in love with her.

Whoa, he cautioned himself as the full force of that hit him. He loved Livvy, of course. He had always loved her, from the time he had first set eyes on her as a chubby-cheeked baby through her maddening metamorphosis into a teenage sexpot, and beyond. He'd loved her when he'd quarreled with her the night she'd run away with that bastard Morrison, he'd loved her the whole time she was gone, and he'd loved her when she came back to LaAngelle. But that was a different kind of love, a careless, familial love, a protective, big-brother sort of love that had only now and then been marred by transient feelings of lust.

What he felt for her now was all that, and more. A whole lot more.

He loved her, and he was in love with her. Truly, madly, deeply, as the saying went.

Just the thought of his life without Livvy in it made him go cold with fear. It would be like someone suddenly extinguishing the sun. He

435

wanted her to love him back, to lavish love on him like she did on Sara, like she seemed ready to do on Chloe. He wanted her for himself, and he wanted her for Chloe. Livvy and Sara, he and Chloe: a family. The *start* of a family. There'd be more. Livvy was made to raise children. She was as loving and giving a person as he had ever known.

He wanted her forever.

The knowledge scared him a little. Go slow, he cautioned himself. He'd been married once, and divorced. Chalk up one colossal mistake. Until shortly after noon today, he'd been engaged to be married a second time. Chalk up another mistake, not quite so big because he'd aborted in time but with the potential for major disaster. Now he was in love with Livvy. *Really* in love, which, with the wisdom of hindsight, he could see he had never been before. Livvy was not a mistake. What he felt for her was fundamentally different than what he had felt for Jennifer, or Mallory. He knew it as surely as he knew the sun would rise in the morning. But still, it couldn't hurt anything to just go slow.

For Chloe's sake, and Sara's sake, as well as Livvy's and his own.

Give them all time to get used to being a family together, before he said or did anything that would make it official.

There was no rush, after all. He could take weeks, or months if need be. The one thing he and Livvy had was plenty of time.

As long as Carl, and every other man, stayed out of the picture. Seth half smiled as he remembered how violent he had felt toward his younger cousin when Livvy had announced that he was taking her dancing on Friday. Over my dead body, was his first thought. His second? No, over Carl's.

He was going to take his time, but he was going to make sure that Livvy stayed exclusively his while he did it. Which shouldn't be a problem, he thought. From now on, he was going to keep her busy day and night. Especially night . . .

"Fatty, fatty, two by four, can't get through the kitchen door!"

That childish taunt, repeated twice, broke through Seth's reverie like a bucket of cold water. Startled, he looked out over the backyard to find that Chloe and her friends had scrambled up the old rope ladder that hung down from the tree house he'd built as a boy high up in the ancient live oak near the perennial garden. Apparently unable to make it up the ladder, Sara clung precariously halfway up, her body and the ladder bent into an L-shape. As he watched, she slowly and clumsily managed to climb back down to the ground.

"Fatty, fatty, two by four . . ."

"Whoa!" he yelled, shooting up from the rocking chair like a rock from a catapult and striding to the porch rail. "Just one darn minute there! Sara, come here. The rest of you, Chloe, you and your friends, you come here, too."

437

There was instant silence, and then they scrambled to comply. Sara, her face miserable, was the first to reach him. He waited for them on the bottom step, arms crossed over his chest, a frown on his face. The other girls, his guilty-looking daughter included, after climbing one after the other down the ladder in apprehensive silence, came toward him in a group. For a moment Seth wished vainly for Olivia, and even glanced around to see if, perhaps, she might be somewhere in view. But she was not. He was going to have to handle this as best he could himself.

"It's all right, Seth. Really. It doesn't matter," Sara muttered as she reached him, her face miserable. Looking at her, Seth felt a shaft of real anger shoot through him. Maybe it was true that kids were cruel, but they weren't going to be cruel to Sara if he could help it. She was a sweet kid, with a kind heart, and he was fond of her for her own sake quite apart from the fact that she was Livvy's girl.

"It's not all right," he told her firmly, stepping down onto the concrete walkway that connected the back steps with the parking area. He put his hands on her shoulders, and turned her to face the other girls, who approached en masse, looking faintly scared. Shooting Chloe in particular a reproachful glance as the whole group stopped just a few feet away, he tried to do his best for Sara.

"Okay, I heard you all calling Sara fat," Seth

began. He could almost feel Sara cringing beneath his hands, but he kept them on her shoulders and held her in place, facing her tormentors. The other girls — his own darling daughter, the other pretty little things who looked like butter wouldn't melt in their mouths — looked up at him wide-eyed.

"Ginny said it first," said one. She had dark hair that tumbled around her shoulders and pale skin, and was not particularly skinny herself.

Not knowing for sure which one Ginny was, Seth let that pass. Besides, it was irrelevant.

"It doesn't matter who said it first," he said ruthlessly. "What matters is that it was said at all. The point is that you hurt Sara's feelings. I want you to apologize, all of you, right now."

A chorus of sweet little voices murmured various versions of "I'm sorry." Seth's mouth twisted. He didn't know why, but his gut told him that just getting them to apologize wasn't going to get the job done.

"All right, I want all of you to line up," he said. "Side by side, shoulder to shoulder. You, too, Sara." He gave her shoulder an encouraging pat.

When they were more or less lined up — he had to reposition a few of them — he walked back and forth in front of them, hands clasped behind his back like a drill sergeant. Except for small matters of size and shape and hair color, they all looked so alike in their brown dresses that trying to tell them apart seemed hopeless. Except, of course, that he knew Chloe and Sara.

Chloe was already starting to frown at him, but the other girls, including Sara, were big-eyed as they watched him.

"Okay, you're the tallest." Abruptly he pointed at a little girl with a glossy brown ponytail.

"That's Ginny," one of the others piped up.

Seth nodded solemnly. "Ginny's the tallest — but you" — he pointed at another girl — "are taller than she is" — he pointed to a third — "and you" — he pointed to a fourth — "are the shortest. Okay, let's line up according to height."

Looking surprised, the girls all shifted positions until they were lined up from tallest to shortest.

"Okay, sing out," Seth directed. "I want to hear your names. In order." He pointed.

"Ginny," said the first one.

"Shannon," said the next.

"Mary Frances."

"Chloe."

"Katie."

"Sara."

"Tiffany."

"Very good." Seth surveyed them again. "Now everybody stick out her right foot." The girls, giggling a little now, complied. Seth looked at the extended feet with a frown. "Okay, let's line up by foot size. Biggest first, all the way down to the smallest." The girls complied, with much measuring of feet to see who stood where. "Okay, sing out." He pointed.

"Ginny!"

"Mary Frances!"

"Shannon!"

"Katie!"

"Sara!"

"Chloe!"

"Tiffany!"

"Good job," Seth approved. "Now let's try — hair color. From lightest to darkest."

This time the girls were really giggling as they lined up.

Seth pointed.

"Chloe!"

"Tiffany!"

"Ginny!"

"Katie!"

"Shannon!"

"Mary Frances!"

"Sara!"

"You're doing great," Seth said, encouraged. "Let's try one more thing. Let's line up by — noses. Who's got the biggest nose?"

The girls were giggling hysterically as they pressed their faces together to measure nose size. When at last they were in order, Seth pointed at the first.

"Ginny!"

"Mary Frances!"

"Tiffany!"

"Katie!"

"Shannon!"

"Sara!"

"Chloe!"

"Okay," Seth said, knowing he had to sum up his little exercise so that they would get the message. "I hope you ladies noticed that every time you lined up, the order changed. Some of you are tall, some of you aren't so tall. Some of you have big feet." This produced a chorus of encouraging giggles. "Some of you have big noses." More giggles. "The point is, you're all different. Each one of you is like a snowflake. You're unique and beautiful in your own way. So it's silly to tease somebody for being taller than somebody else, or having a bigger foot than somebody else, or being fatter than somebody else, and I don't want to ever hear of it happening again. Every one of us has special things about us. That's what makes us snowflakes and not" — here his inspiration failed — "mashed potatoes."

"Daddy, that's dumb." Chloe groaned, while the other girls, Sara included, giggled.

Seth shrugged apologetically. "I know, but I mean it anyway. No more teasing. Now go back and play."

They scampered off. Sara hung back a little.

"Thanks, Seth," she said, smiling shyly at him. Then, to Seth's surprise, she gave him a quick, fierce hug. Before Seth could react, she was running off to join the other girls.

With that hug, Sara cemented her place in his heart. Like Chloe and Livvy, Sara now belonged to him, too.

chapter 46

Going out for pizza was fun. The four of them sat in a booth in Guido's, which had just opened in a storefront on West Main that had once housed a shoe repair shop. The surroundings were Spartan — faux wood paneling, linoleum floors, a counter scavenged from a defunct bar. But the pizza — actually made by Emily Marsden, the fortyish wife of a Boatworks' employee, who owned and operated the restaurant and had chosen the name simply because she liked it and it sounded Italian — was great.

Apparently half the town agreed. The place was packed with diners by seven, and people were coming in and out constantly to pick up carry-out pizza. Everyone knew Seth, of course, and most everyone knew Olivia. Greetings were exchanged right and left, and speculative looks were cast their way as they ate. She and Seth and their daughters going out for pizza should not have provoked any comment — it was a perfectly innocent activity. But in LaAngelle, whenever members of the opposite sex who weren't father and daughter, mother and son, or brother and sister were seen eating out together, there was always a buzz. Given Seth's stature in the community, there was going to be a lot of buzz. Once it was learned that he was no longer engaged to marry Mallory, the buzz would turn into a roar.

But that was something that could be held off until another day, Olivia thought with relief, as she and Seth exchanged a few smiling words with Sharon Bishop, the nosy high school principal, and her husband on the way out. For now, Seth's broken engagement was not generally known, and she and Seth were protected from the worst of the talk by their stepcousin status.

Of course, that selfsame stepcousin status would simply be one more thing for the gossips to talk about once their new relationship became generally known.

Olivia wasn't exactly looking forward to that. But when she considered the alternative — Seth's being involved with anyone except herself — she decided, on balance, that she could live with it.

Martha was at the Big House when they got home. She was in the kitchen gossiping with Keith, who'd flown into Baton Rouge with David not long before, and driven on out to LaAngelle Plantation while David stopped off at the hospital to visit Big John. Martha and Keith had gotten to be good friends over the course of the last few weeks. Like army buddies, they joked with ghoulish humor, they'd shared a lot of KP duties.

As usual, Olivia supervised homework at the kitchen table. Both girls had the same assignments, but most of the time they worked at different paces. Sara, the diligent, plunged right in and kept plugging away until she was finished. Chloe, bright but rebellious, tended to put off whatever she could until the last moment, and then complete only what she had to under the threat, delivered by Seth, of major sanctions. Fortunately, there wasn't much tonight, and homework was completed without any undue difficulties.

Still, by the time the girls had finished, picked out what they were going to wear the next day, had baths and fallen asleep, it was after ten.

Routines were good in that they lent an aura of normalcy to day-to-day living, even when the household could never, in the wake of Callie's death, be the same as it was, Olivia reflected as she slid into the bathtub herself. The thought of her aunt brought a cloud of sadness with it. As she soaped herself, Olivia said a heartfelt prayer for the repose of Callie's soul, and then surprised herself by yawning hugely. She was *tired*. She had listened to Sara's prayers, read aloud a chapter from *Little House in the Big Woods*, tucked her daughter in, and kissed her good night, while

Martha and Seth, between them, performed essentially the same ritual for Chloe. Now that Sara had Smokey to sleep with her, she was usually content to fall asleep on her own. Leaving Sara to do so when she had always lain down with her daughter until she fell asleep was a transition point in their relationship, underlining to Olivia that Sara was growing up. She supposed that was why walking out of that bedroom and leaving Sara alone in it at night had lately caused her a pang of discomfort. Certainly there was no other explanation for her recent urge to crawl into bed with Sara and stay there until the sun broke the eastern sky in the morning.

Call her overprotective, but lately Olivia even had been getting up once or twice to check on Sara during the night. The vampire lightning bug king had not made an appearance in Sara's dreams since Callie's death, but still . . .

Every time she thought about those dreams, Olivia grew uneasy. Was it just coincidence that she had once had similar nightmares herself?

Maybe it was simply that both she and her daughter were prone to bad dreams, she mused. After all, she had been plagued by nightmares about her mother ever since returning to live at LaAngelle. Maybe there was something in the atmosphere here that both she and Sara were sensitive to, Olivia thought almost hopefully. Certainly the notion made more sense than anything else she could come up with.

But tonight, she was not going to think about

nightmares, either hers or Sara's. Tonight she was going to think about Seth.

Finishing her bath, she reapplied her makeup, brushed out her hair until it shown, applied a strategic dab or two of perfume, and dressed again, in a fresh pair of jeans and a white rayon camp shirt, which she tucked in at the waist. Then she went downstairs again.

Seth had said he would be waiting for her in the den. Olivia smiled with anticipation.

He was indeed waiting for her in the den, Olivia saw as she stepped through the pocket doors. He was sitting on the yellow chintz couch, long legs stretched out before him, hands locked behind his head as he talked to David, who was sitting in the comfortably shabby leather armchair to his right. On the other side of the couch Keith sat in the matching leather armchair, talking to Martha, who had pulled up a rocking chair. They all faced the TV, which was on, but no one seemed to be watching it.

Taking in this group with a glance, Olivia had to smile. So much for being private with Seth.

He must have thought the same thing, because when she walked into the room he looked up, met her eyes, and gave her a rueful smile.

"Oh, Olivia, Carl called for you. Something about Friday. I left the message on the blackboard in the kitchen," Martha said.

Seth's smile soured and died, and his eyes narrowed.

"Thanks, Martha." Conversely, Seth's reaction

widened Olivia's smile. She was, of course, going to tell Carl that she couldn't go out with him on Friday. But she liked the idea that Seth didn't like Carl's call, nonetheless. It made up, a little, for what she had suffered over Mallory.

Olivia looked around the room and hesitated, not sure whether or where to sit down. All the chairs were taken, and she wasn't really comfortable about the idea of sitting on the couch beside Seth. Their involvement wasn't ready for public consumption yet. It was still too new.

Seth solved her dilemma by standing up.

"If you think he ought to be transferred to another hospital, I have no objection," Seth said to David. "Charlie doesn't seem to think it's a good idea, though."

"He's not showing any improvement where he is," David said.

"We can talk about it some more tomorrow." Seth shifted his attention to Olivia, and smiled. "Feel like getting some fresh air?"

Olivia nodded, too conscious of suddenly being the cynosure of all eyes to speak. Out of the corner of her eye, she saw Keith look significantly at David, and David nod discreetly in turn. Martha's eyes widened.

"Good night, all," Seth said over his shoulder, and followed Olivia out of the room to an answering chorus of good-nights.

Once outside on the veranda with the front door shut behind them, Olivia stopped and took a huge gulp of warm, honeysuckle-scented night air. Seth, standing beside her, grinned down at her.

"Think they're talking about us?"

"Oh, yeah."

"It's going to get worse before it gets better."

"I know."

"Can you take the heat?"

Olivia shrugged fatalistically. "Considering the alternative, I guess I can."

"And the alternative is . . . ?"

"Giving you back to Mallory." She shook her head, and slanted a smiling look up at him. "Nope. Not an option."

Seth turned her around to face him, his hands on her arms just above her elbows. His eyes met hers, a trifle narrowed even as a faint smile flickered around the corners of his mouth.

"By the way, when you talk to Carl, you had better explain exactly why you won't be going out with him, because if he continues to come sniffing around the front office every day like he has been I'm liable to break his nose."

Olivia grinned. "You wouldn't."

"I might. He's been in my damned office three times a day for the past month, and I'm getting tired of seeing his ugly face. Before you came to work for us, if I saw him twice a week it was a lot. When you were turning him down, the situation was just barely tolerable. Once you said yes to him, the potential for violence rose considerably."

"Jealous," Olivia said reprovingly, and shook

her head at him. Her arms slid up around his neck.

"Damn right." He looked down at her, his hands at her waist, and his gaze slid from her eyes to her mouth. But he didn't kiss her, as she had expected, and he seemed suddenly restless. "Want to go for a walk?"

Olivia shook her head. "Not really."

"We could sit out here for a while and talk."

"Yeah. We could." Her lack of enthusiasm was clear from her tone.

"What do you want to do, then?" He sounded faintly impatient.

"Oh, I don't know. I thought we might — go to bed." Her eyes twinkled up at him.

Seth began to grin. "Here I am, trying to court you, trying to inject a little romance into what's left of our evening, and all you can think about is rushing me into bed. If you're not careful, you're going to make me think you don't respect me."

Olivia's hands slid down over his shoulders, and she began to undo the top button on his shirt. "Oh, sure, I respect you. But what I really want to do is see you naked."

"That's it." Seth's hands closed over hers as she undid the second button, stilling them and holding them against his chest. She could feel his body heat radiating through the thin denim. His eyes gleamed down at her. "Let's go upstairs."

They turned as one toward the door, and stopped dead, exchanging bemused glances.

"They'll see us going up the stairs," Olivia said hollowly.

Seth ran a hand through his hair, and stared at the closed door in frustration. "Hell, I feel like a teenager."

"Want to go make out in your car?" Olivia asked, and began to giggle.

"Hush, they'll hear you." He gripped her hand, pulling her along the front of the house. "I've got a plan."

"What?"

"We'll sneak up the outside stairs, and go through the French windows."

"Lover, I don't know about you, but I keep my French windows locked."

Seth stopped on the first rung of the metal stairs along the side of the house that led up to the gallery, and looked down at her.

"What did you call me?"

Olivia was suddenly self-conscious as she remembered. "Oh — lover?"

He came back down the stairs to slide a hand under her hair and tilt her face up to his. "I like the way you say that," he said, and kissed her.

When he let her go, Olivia's head was spinning.

"Come on." Seth pulled her ruthlessly up the stairs behind him, then along the gallery. "Your room or mine?" he asked over his shoulder.

"Mine's locked," Olivia reminded him in a hushed tone. Her lips still throbbed from that kiss.

"So's mine." He paused to fish something out of one of the hanging fern baskets. "Yours is closer," he decided.

"What is that?" Her gaze was rivetted on the object he held in one hand.

"A file. I guess it's been in that basket for decades. I haven't used it often, but when I do I always put it back. It's pretty handy, actually. If you just slip it between the windows, you can jimmy up the latch, and — presto — you're in." He demonstrated on her window as he spoke. Olivia was appalled at how easily he gained access to her room.

"You mean that thing's been out there all this time?" she demanded accusingly even as he drew her inside and closed the window behind them. She'd left the bedside lamp on, and its warm glow made the room seem welcoming. "*Anybody* could have done that! I want that thing — and I want those latches replaced with something more modern that can't be jimmied! Tomorrow!"

As she considered the possibilities, Olivia's blood ran cold.

"If it bothers, you, sure," Seth said, putting the file down on her dresser and sounding faintly surprised. "I guess I never thought about it from a woman's point of view. It always just seemed kind of convenient to me. In case I was out late, and forgot my key."

"It would." Olivia was already being distracted by his arms sliding around her waist. His arms

452

were solid with muscle, and his body as he pulled her against it felt rock hard. She loved the way he felt. His blond head bent over her dark one, and she looked up at him. His face was bronzed and hard-planed, with tiny lines radiating out from the corners of his eyes. His mouth was long and firm and just faintly smiling. Her gaze traveled over his firm chin and down the strong column of his throat to the buttons she had unfastened on his shirt. Making a mental note to call a locksmith first thing in the morning, she turned her attention to unfastening the remaining buttons.

chapter 47

"You're beautiful," Seth said, as her fingers worked at the buttons. Glancing up at him, Olivia discovered that he wasn't smiling any longer. His eyes were intent on her face, and something about the way he was looking at her gave her the shivers. She finished with the buttons and his shirt fell open, exposing a long rectangle of hard-muscled flesh liberally covered with hair.

"So are you," she replied cordially, and he responded, she thought, involuntarily, with the ghost of a smile.

Her hands slid up over his chest, savoring the warmth and feel of his bare skin. He caught her hands, flattening them against him. When she looked up at him inquiringly, he shook his head at her. Heat flared at her from the depths of his eyes.

"Stop right there," he said, his voice husky. "Or this is going to go way too fast."

"I want to see you naked. I told you." Olivia was teasing him, flirting with him, but at the look in his eyes she caught her breath, and suddenly she wasn't teasing anymore. He let go of her hands to pull her into his arms, and she slid her hands up under his shirt, over his broad shoulders, and clung. Beneath her fingers she could feel his shoulders tighten. One hand slid down her back, found the curve of her bottom in the ancient jeans, and splayed over it, pulling her hard against him.

Then he kissed her.

Olivia clung to his shoulders and pressed her body against his and rose up on her tiptoes as she kissed him back. Then she reached between them for the button securing his pants. As she freed it he made a sound like a groan under his breath and lifted her off her feet, carrying her the few steps to the bed.

"You're strong," she said admiringly, batting her eyelashes at him playfully.

The merest shadow of a smile touched his mouth. "You're light."

He laid her down, and shrugged out of his shirt. Olivia had just a second to admire the sheer masculine beauty of his chest before he came down beside her, his broad shoulders blocking the light of the bedside lamp. Not bothering with the buttons, which Olivia thought commendably efficient of him, he lifted her loose white camp shirt over her head and threw it aside. For a moment he looked down at her, his eyes admiring the silky pink bra that she had taken pains to wear for him.

"Pretty," he said, and bent his head to press his lips to her nipple through the thin layer of rayon.

Olivia shuddered as the moist heat of his mouth burned through to her flesh, and buried both hands in the short spikes of his hair. After a moment he lifted his head, then reached around behind her back to unhook her bra. Removing it, he simply looked down at her for a moment, his gaze devouring the full, strawberry-tipped globes of her breasts.

While she watched him, he bent his head again. Warm, moist, and just faintly rough, his tongue ran over her already distended nipple. Desire shot through her like a lightning bolt. She gasped, pulling his head down harder against her breast. Obediently he drew her nipple into his mouth, nibbling and tugging. Even as his mouth moved to her other breast, his hand found and freed the snap of her jeans. As she heard the sound of her zipper being lowered, he lifted his head away from her breast. His gaze fixed on her face. Their eyes met for a moment, and then Olivia's attention shifted. She watched, fascinated, as his hand, long-fingered and bronzed, disappeared inside her open zipper. His palm was warm and faintly rough as it slid over her stomach and delved inside her pink bikini panties.

Then he made her wait.

Olivia squirmed, silently pleading with him to continue as his fingers found and caressed the sable triangle of curls, while refusing to go lower. He was teasing her deliberately, she knew. He knew what she wanted. She glanced up at him, half annoyed, half on fire, to find that he was watching her still.

"Seth." Desperate, she gasped out his name. Her hands dropped from his shoulders, slid down his arms and back up again, her nails faintly scoring the hard muscles there in supplication.

At that he relented, pushing her jeans and panties down almost to her knees and sliding his fingers between her thighs. He touched her where she most wished to be touched, watching her face as he pressed and stroked and finally slid inside. Olivia closed her eyes against his heated blue gaze and dug her nails into the mattress and gave herself up to the mind-blowing pleasure of it, writhing desperately under the ministrations of that knowing hand until finally, without warning, it withdrew. She made a faint sound of protest, and her eyes opened. Her gaze met his for one electrifying instant as he stood up to shuck his pants, and then he jerked her jeans and panties the rest of the way off and replaced his fingers with his mouth.

By the time he slid up her body, heatedly kissing her belly button and breasts on the way and then burying his mouth against her throat,

Olivia was on fire, trembling with need as she wrapped her legs around his hips. She felt the fine tremors that shook his arms as they crushed her to him, and realized that he was trembling, too. Then he was inside her, plunging deep, and she cried out.

All thoughts of playing were forgotten now. He took her fiercely, driving into her with an urgency that made her strain and buck and writhe in frenzied response. Her hips arched up off the bed to receive him. She shook, and clung, and at the end, when the firestorm took her, cried out his name.

"Livvy," he groaned in response, huge and hard and hot as he thrust into her trembling body. "Ah, Livvy."

Then he shuddered, and was still, holding himself throbbing inside her. After a moment he went limp. His big body sprawled atop her, damp with sweat.

Olivia wrapped her arms around his back, kissed his shoulder, and closed her eyes. Within seconds she was fathoms-deep asleep.

"Livvy! Livvy, wake up! Olivia!" His voice pulled her out of it, dragging her from the darkness, from the shore of the moonlit lake where her mother struggled in the water. Olivia moaned and flailed, hitting something warm and resilient and then gasping as a brilliant burst of light shone full on her fluttering lids.

"Livvy!"

Seth's voice. She would know Seth's voice any-where. Gasping as though she had run a mara-thon, she opened her eyes a slit. Seth was leaning over her, his blond hair wildly disordered, five o'clock shadow darkening his cheeks and chin, his blue eyes narrowed with concern for her. His broad bare shoulders and the tapered width of his chest loomed in front of her, and Olivia saw with a glance that he was propped on one elbow, his chest and arms naked above the quilt that cut him off at the waist. A second, sweeping glance showed her that they were in her big four-poster bed, in the bedroom she had inherited from Belinda.

They had made love. She had fallen asleep. Seth must have tucked them both in — and he had stayed with her. As the knowledge that she was sleeping with Seth percolated through her terror-dulled brain, Olivia took a deep breath, and some of the tension that held her in thrall seeped away.

"Seth," she murmured. Taking further stock of the situation, she realized that they were both naked — and then she smelled it: the elusive hint of White Shoulders perfume. Glancing quickly at the clock, she saw that the time was 3:29 A.M.

Seth had dragged her from sleep before the dream ended.

"Do you smell it?" she asked him, not very co-herently, looking wildly around. The light was on. Except for the part Seth's body blocked from view, she could see the entire room perfectly. No one was present except the two of them. No ghost, and no living human being.

Only that trace of perfume.

"Smell what, baby?" The frown that had been lifting from his face settled back down again. Furrows marred the skin between his brows. His eyes moved over her face.

"Anything. Sniff!" Fully awake now, Olivia hitched herself up on the pillows, taking the sheet with her and securing it with an arm above her breasts. She glanced around the room again as she followed her own instruction. Looking at her like he thought she'd lost her mind, Seth nevertheless sniffed the air.

"Well?" she demanded.

"All I smell is your own sweet skin," he said with a humorous glint, lowering his nose to her arm and ostentatiously sniffing. "Very nice."

"I'm serious." She smacked his thickly muscled shoulder with her palm, and he straightened. Another glance around the room convinced her: She and Seth were alone. The smell of the perfume was fading, too.

"What am I supposed to smell?" he asked cautiously, glancing around, too. "Gas or something?"

Olivia sighed. "My mother's perfume," she admitted, knowing that it sounded outlandish even as she said it. "She wore White Shoulders a lot. I remember how it smelled. Every time I wake up from having the nightmare, the smell is in the room."

For a moment Seth said nothing. He simply regarded her narrowly from under frowning brows. Then he flopped back down on his pillow, slid an arm behind his head, and looked at her again.

"And you believe your mother is haunting you." It was a shrewd guess. Seth knew her well.

"Yes. No. I don't know. What am I supposed to think? I keep having this nightmare, and every time I wake up I smell her perfume."

Seth sighed. Reaching over, he slid an arm beneath her and pulled her against him. Nothing loathe, Olivia snuggled close, ending up with her head on his shoulder and one hand splayed across the warm breadth of his chest. Before they were settled, her leg was draped over his thighs.

"So talk to me," he said. "I take it you've been having nightmares ever since I told you about your mother's suicide. You should have told me."

"Actually," Olivia said, her fingers idly tracing the outlines of the hard muscles beneath the gold-tipped hair on his chest, "I started having this nightmare — this same nightmare — before I knew anything about that. I've been having it ever since I came home again. And — and that's not all. In my dream, my mother — it doesn't seem like she's committing suicide. It's more as if something is pulling her under the water against her will. Every time I dream about it, the details get more vivid, but it's the same thing. Her drowning is not a suicide."

"Hmm," he said, and thus encouraged, Olivia ended up telling him about everything: the voices that seemed to call to her from the lake, her odd, almost physically ill reaction to her mother's picture, even the face that was so like her own but wasn't quite hers in the mirror in the bedroom where Sara now slept. She didn't leave anything out, and by the time she got through she felt several degrees better.

Seth said nothing for a moment, just lay there with a meditative expression on his face.

"So I'm a total nutcase, right?" she asked, feeling almost cheerful. The improvement in her mood had something to do with getting the whole thing off her chest, she knew. But it had more to do with the fact that she was naked in bed with Seth, had been sleeping with Seth, and now considered him irretrievably hers. She was ready, willing, and able to take on all challengers.

"I'd say you were more traumatized than nuts," Seth said slowly. "Livvy — I think you ought to talk to someone about it."

"I just told *you* the whole thing." There was the faintest touch of indignation in her voice.

He slanted a look down at her. "I mean a professional. A psychiatrist. Like I said, I think your mother's death traumatized you. Moving back home after all that time away must have jolted loose all kinds of emotions that you've been suppressing for years."

Olivia thought about that for a moment. "Is that what you think is happening?"

"I don't see any other explanation."

Olivia peeped up at him. "You don't think — my mother's haunting me, trying to tell me that her death *wasn't* a suicide?"

One corner of Seth's mouth quirked up in a wry smile. "Livvy, seriously, do you?"

"But what about the perfume? I keep smelling it every time I have the dream. And the face in the mirror, too. I'm — I'm almost sure it was my mother's face I saw, not mine."

"I didn't smell anything, Livvy." His voice was gentle.

Olivia grimaced. "You're saying it's my imagination."

"I'm saying you ought to talk to somebody. Get Charlie to give you the name of somebody good."

"Seth."

"Hmmm?"

"I'm glad you were with me tonight when it happened. It's been horrible, having that dream night after night and waking up terrified and all alone."

A spark of humor lit his eyes. "You should have come and crawled in bed with me. I wouldn't have kicked you out, guaranteed."

Olivia smiled. "I wish now I had, just to get your reaction."

"Baby, believe me, there's no doubt about my reaction. I've been wanting to take you to bed since you were seventeen years old."

Olivia's hand stilled palm-down on his chest.

She propped her chin on her flat hand and stared at him. "You have not."

"I can still remember the dress you wore the night you eloped. It was bright red, had little skinny straps and ruffles around your knees, and made your tits and ass look good enough to eat."

"How vulgar." Olivia chided him for his choice of words with a grin.

"Yeah, well, when I caught you making out with that lowlife Morrison — right before we had our fight and you ended up slapping my face —"

"Sorry," Olivia mouthed with a little moue of apology.

"What I really wanted to do was kiss you myself. Actually, take you to bed myself. I knew you were sleeping with him." Seth's voice deepened into a growl at the end.

Olivia's eyes widened on his face. Her breath caught in her throat at the look in his eyes, and her pulse picked up its pace.

"I wish you had," she said softly. "Kissed me, I mean, and taken me to bed. That night. It would have saved us both a truckload of trouble."

"I was a twenty-eight-year-old man then, and you were a wild little girl of seventeen. We might have been legal together, but we sure as hell wouldn't have been moral. Besides, you thought of me as a sort of big brother. If I had touched you then, I would have been a bigger lowlife even than that loser Morrison."

Olivia looked at him for an instant. "I'm glad I grew up."

She wriggled on top of him, and lay there, her arms folded on his chest, her chin resting on her hands. His eyes twinkled and darkened at the same time as he looked down at her. "Me too."

Then his arms came around her and he rolled, pinning her beneath him. After that, neither of them spoke again for a very long time.

chapter 48

After dropping off the girls at school the next morning, Olivia decided on impulse to stop by Charlie's office. Seth's suggestion of seeing a professional had merit. She wanted the name of a psychiatrist — and, she thought, a hypnotist. All Seth's logic had not completely convinced her that her mother was not trying to get a message to her from beyond the grave. Maybe a hypnotist could take her into the dream, and elicit information that faded away when she woke up. She had the feeling there was something she wasn't quite grasping, something that was floating maddeningly just beyond her reach.

If so, she had to know.

Charlie's office was on Chitimacha Street, in a single-story brick building that had once been a house. He had paved the front yard, hung a shingle on the door that said CHARLES VERNON, MD, and listed his office hours, but otherwise the house remained essentially unchanged.

His office hours officially began at eight thirty, but Olivia knew he was in when she drove by because his Lexus was parked in the space beside the office reserved for his exclusive use. Praying that Ira and his deputies were occupied elsewhere — a traffic ticket was something she didn't need — Olivia made a U-turn and pulled into the parking lot. Getting out of the car, she smoothed her hair and dress — she was wearing a new camel-colored knit with a self-belt and a slim skirt that did great things for her figure, bought with Seth in mind — and headed for the door. Knocking loudly, she turned the knob and walked into the reception area.

"Uncle Charlie?"

Charlie was nowhere in sight. He was probably in the private office in the rear, Olivia surmised. She knew that he liked to come in early and read the newspaper. There was a small bell to ring for service on the counter that separated the reception area from the business office. Olivia hit it twice, sharply, and then waited.

The reception area was the house's former living room, and it was generously proportioned. Grass cloth in a tasteful shade of tan covered the walls, and a tan and gray mottled carpet was on the floor. The chairs — there were a dozen of them, ranged against the wall — had gray vinyl backs and seats with pale wood arms. A matching coffee table in the center of the room held a selection of magazines. What was most unusual about the reception area, and indeed the whole office, were the accessories: Skilled taxidermist Charlie had made use of his talents to enliven corners and other odd niches with his work. Olivia found herself staring at a stuffed black bear in the corner of the reception room. The creature, taller than she was, was rearing on its back legs, its front paws extended. It looked so real that she had to resist the impulse to back away from it. Even its eyes looked real.

"Who's there? Oh — Olivia!" Dressed in a white lab coat with a pen protruding from his breast pocket, Charlie looked delighted to see her. "Come in, come in!"

He held open the bottom half of the Dutch door that led into the business office, and Olivia walked inside. A stuffed squirrel had pride of place on the file cabinet, she noticed as she followed Charlie on down the hall. He led the way into his private office, and settled himself behind his desk, motioning Olivia into a chair across from him. Sitting down, Olivia found herself staring at the huge stuffed bass mounted on the wall just above Charlie's head.

"What can I do for you, Olivia?" Charlie asked, leaning back in his chair and surveying her keenly. "That is — I'm assuming this is not a social call."

Olivia shook her head. "Remember the nightmares I told you about? About my mother's death."

"I do, yes."

"I'm still having them. Actually, they're getting more and more vivid all the time." Olivia looked at him almost pleadingly. "Uncle Charlie, what happened that night?"

He looked at her for a long moment without saying anything. Then he leaned forward, placing his forearms on the desk and steepling his fingers as he looked at her. "There's not a lot I can tell you. I was only there at the end. We'd all been looking for your mother because James was concerned when he came home and couldn't find her anywhere in the house. It was late, after midnight, I forget the time exactly but late. Big John somehow spotted Selena floating in the lake, and started yelling. I came and pulled her out and tried to revive her. It was no use. She was dead when I pulled her out of the water."

"Was she wearing a nightgown — a white nightgown, ankle-length, with wide lace straps?" Olivia's question was impulsive. She merely wanted to verify any of the dream's details that she could.

Charlie stared at her, then blinked. "Why — yes, I believe she was. A white nightgown, in any case. Long, because it covered her legs."

Olivia closed her eyes for a moment, then opened them again. "Did you see any indication — is there any reason to think that it might not have been suicide?"

"Olivia, I'm sorry, but no. No, there's no reason to think that."

Olivia sighed. "I guess what I need from you

next is the name of a good psychiatrist. And a hypnotist."

Charlie blinked at her. "The psychiatrist I can understand, if you're having nightmares and they're troubling you. But a hypnotist?"

"I want to see if there are any details in the dreams I'm having that I'm forgetting when I wake up. I keep getting the feeling that I'm missing something. I thought maybe a hypnotist could help."

Charlie nodded. He reached for his prescription pad, and pulled the pen out of his pocket. Scratching something on the top sheet, he tore it off, then started writing on the second sheet. "A psychiatrist is no problem. I've known John Hall for years, and he's right close in Baton Rouge. A hypnotist — well, I'll have to look into that. When I come up with somebody, I'll let you know."

"Could you try to find somebody soon?" Olivia hated to be pushy about it, but there was a sense of urgency driving her now. Probably because, knowing Seth, if she didn't fix herself soon, he'd be working on a way to fix her himself. Seth was like that.

"Soon as I can, I promise." Charlie pushed the pieces of paper across the desk at her and stood up. "I've written down John Hall's number — when you call him, tell him I referred you. And the other's a prescription for medication to help you sleep. If you can't beat those nightmares one way, you can beat them another. In fact . . ." He walked around the desk as Olivia stood up, too. "I think I've got some samples. Go on out to the reception room, and I'll bring them out to you."

Olivia did, and he joined her a few minutes later, handing her a small white bottle with a yellow label. "You take two of those at bedtime, and you won't have any more problems with nightmares, even without the psychiatrist."

"Thank you, Uncle Charlie." Olivia smiled warmly at him, and started to pull out her checkbook. He waved her on out the door.

"You're on the family plan," he told her. "Now, go on to wherever you were going. And let me know how things work out."

Olivia was left with nothing to do but thank him again, put the pills in her purse, and head to work.

It was probably a good thing that Seth was busy with clients all morning, Olivia thought. She had work to do, after all, and he was a definite distraction. She called a locksmith about the French windows, then got busy with the computer. Ilsa eyed her a little askance at first, but Olivia said nothing, and over the course of the morning Ilsa seemed to forget any suspicions that the events of the previous day might have aroused. Shortly before lunch, though, a woman walked in carrying a huge bouquet of deep red roses arranged in a tall glass vase. Olivia and Ilsa both stopped work to stare at the delivery in surprise.

"These are for you, Mrs. Morrison," the

woman said cheerfully, and Olivia recognized her as Dana Peltz, owner and operator of Blooming Blossoms, LaAngelle's only florist. "Two dozen of my very best. I almost didn't have enough. Where do you want me to put them?"

"On — on my desk," Olivia said, trying to hold on to her composure. Of course they were from Seth, she thought, and her heart warmed along with her cheeks.

"You enjoy." Dana Peltz put the roses down, gave her a warm smile, and left. Ignoring Ilsa's wide-eyed gaze, Olivia moved to her desk and bent to sniff the roses. Their scent was heavenly.

"Who . . . ?" Ilsa began, then broke off as Carl walked into the office, wearing a navy sport coat that looked new, with pale gray slacks, a blue shirt, and a yellow tie. His dark hair was neatly brushed, his shoes were shined, and it was obvious that he had taken more pains with his appearance than he usually did.

Olivia immediately felt bad.

"Did you get my message . . . ?" Carl began, only to break off as he saw Olivia bending over the roses. "Nice flowers."

The awful thought had occurred to Olivia, in the few seconds between when he appeared in the doorway and commented on the roses, that *Carl* might have sent them. But from the way he was eyeing the flowers, such was not the case. She fumbled for the card, opened it. *Love, Seth* was what it said.

She breathed an inward sigh of relief. "Thank you," she said to Carl. Ilsa, meanwhile, was eyeing Olivia with open speculation.

"So are we on for Friday night?" he asked. "I'll pick you up at six, and we'll drive into Baton Rouge for dinner, and then go on to —"

Olivia was already shaking her head regretfully, interrupting him. "Carl, I can't."

He frowned at her. "Why not? I thought we had fun over lunch."

Olivia took a deep breath. "We did, but — I'm seeing somebody else."

Carl's frown deepened. "Somebody else? Since yesterday? Who?" His gaze moved suspiciously to the roses.

Out of the corner of her eye, Olivia could see Ilsa's eyes widen.

"Well, that's it for the morning." Seth walked into the office and stopped, looking from Carl to Olivia to the roses, and then back at Olivia again. He was wearing a well-cut navy suit with a white shirt and a red tie, and looked so tall and strong and handsome that Olivia's heart beat faster. As their eyes met Olivia couldn't help it: She had to smile. Seth smiled back at her, then glanced at Carl with disfavor.

"It's you!" Carl burst out, staring at Seth. "Isn't it?"

"What's me?" The look he gave Carl was definitely uncousinly.

"You're putting the moves on Olivia! That's low! That's so low! I can't believe you'd do something like that! Mallory . . ." Carl seemed to choke with indignation. He glared at Seth with open belligerence.

Olivia came quickly out from behind the desk, just in case either party should start to lose his cool. As she stepped between them, shaking her head warningly at Seth, Seth grimaced, then looked over her head at Carl. Next Seth glanced at Ilsa, whose eyes were now as wide as saucers.

"Okay," he said, looking from Ilsa to Carl again, "here's the deal. You can spread it around the whole company, the whole town, and get this over with. Mallory and I are no longer engaged. Olivia and I are seeing each other. End of story."

Carl's gaze riveted on Olivia. "You're going out with Seth?"

Olivia nodded.

"Well, that's fine, then." Carl didn't sound like he believed it, but at least the words were dignified. "You're certainly free to see whomever you choose." His gaze still held a certain belligerence as it shot to Seth. "Fast work, cuz," he said, and turned on his heel, leaving the office.

Olivia let out her breath on a slow sigh. Her eyes met Seth's.

"I have to drive to Baton Rouge to check on Big John during lunch," Seth said, as calmly as if nothing had happened. "Want to come with me?"

"I'd love to," Olivia answered.

Seth nodded. "Give me a minute, and we'll go." He walked into his office and shut the door.

Ilsa looked at Olivia. "Wow!" she said.

Olivia gave up. "I'm crazy about him," she confessed. "Does it show?"

"Like a spotlight in a cave." Ilsa clasped her hands together. "I'm so happy for you! I always thought he was way, way too good for Mallory!"

Seth's door opened again, and Ilsa immediately turned back to the file cabinet. But she sneaked a grin over her shoulder at Olivia as they left.

chapter 49

Olivia was just starting to read aloud their nightly chapter of *Little House in the Big Woods*, when a knock sounded on Sara's closed bedroom door. She and Sara exchanged a quick glance before Olivia put the book facedown on the bed and went to see who was there.

It was Seth. She'd last seen him in the kitchen about an hour earlier, drilling a balky Chloe on her multiplication tables. Sara, who'd had the same assignment, had learned hers in their free period at school, so Olivia had left Seth and Chloe to it and taken Sara upstairs. Dressed in casual khakis and a white T-shirt, Seth still looked faintly harassed. She smiled at him.

"Sorry to interrupt," he said, smiling back. He looked at Sara, who was tucked up in bed with Smokey nestled beside her, over Olivia's shoulder. "Hi, Sara." Then, to Olivia in a lowered voice, "Come out into the hall a minute."

"I'll be right back," Olivia said to Sara, and stepped out into the hall, pulling the door almost closed behind her.

Seth slid a hand along the side of her neck, and dropped a quick kiss on her mouth. "I just got a call from the hospital," he said. "Big John's having trouble breathing, and I've got to go. David's already there, and Belinda's on her way."

"Oh, no!" Olivia said, grasping his arm. "Do you want me to come with you?"

He shook his head. "It's better if you stay here with the kids. I just wanted to let you know so you wouldn't wonder where I disappeared to."

Olivia smiled at him again, her eyes soft. "I'll miss you."

His gaze moved over her face. "How about if I come and crawl into bed with you when I get back?"

Her smile widened. "That'd be good."

"Livvy . . ." He broke off whatever he'd been going to say, leaned down, and kissed her again, brief and hard. "See you later," he said, and headed down the hall.

Olivia turned and went back into Sara's room, to find herself instantly under the microscope of her daughter's all-seeing eyes.

"Mom," she began, before Olivia had even reached the bed. "You really like Seth, don't you?"

Taken by surprise, Olivia looked at Sara carefully. "Of course I like him. What's not to like?"

"Mom." Sara's voice was reproachful. "I mean *really* like him. Like for a boyfriend, or something."

"Sara," Olivia began, then decided to tell the truth. "Yes, I guess I do. Would you mind if he was my boyfriend?"

Sara shook her head. "I like him, too. Only — are you going to marry him?"

Olivia's eyes widened. She hadn't even let herself look that far ahead. "Nobody's said anything about marriage."

Sara made a face. "If you do marry him, would that make Chloe and me sisters?"

"So far, he hasn't asked me to marry him, so I wouldn't worry about it."

"But would it?"

Olivia sighed. "Yes, I guess."

"That's what Chloe said."

"*Chloe* said that you and she would be sisters if her dad and I got married?" Olivia stared at her daughter. "Does she think her dad and I are going to get married?"

Sara shrugged. "She just said that if you and her dad got married, that would make her my big sister, so I'd have to do what she said, so I better get used to it. It was at recess, when she needed somebody to hold the rope for jump rope and I didn't want to."

"Sara." Olivia sat down on the edge of Sara's bed and looked earnestly at her daughter. "Seth is just going to be my boyfriend for right now. *If* we decide to get married, and you notice I say *if,*

478

we'll let you and Chloe know, and we'll all work things out together then. Okay?"

"Okay," Sara said. "I don't mind having *Seth*, but I'm going to have to think about Chloe."

"Well, don't start to worry about it yet," Olivia advised, and picked up their book.

By the time she left Sara's room, had a bath, put on her nightgown — her prettiest, a deep pink nylon number with little cap sleeves and a sweetheart neckline — and checked to make sure Sara was asleep, it was after eleven. Seth still wasn't home — she knew he would come to her when he was — and as idiotic as it seemed, she was lonesome for him as she climbed into bed. It was amazing how fast she'd gotten used to the feel of his arms around her as she slept, to the solid warmth of his body next to hers, to the sound of his breathing.

She was so in love with him it was ridiculous, Olivia thought, smiling to herself. And she was still smiling when she fell asleep.

The sound of the door opening roused her, whether minutes or hours later Olivia couldn't be sure. Seth crept quietly into the room, a large, shadowy presence in the dark, closing the door softly, being careful not to disturb her. Olivia cast a glance at the clock: 1:22 A.M.

"Hi," she said sleepily, turning to smile at him. He froze, then without any warning at all leaped at her with the agility of a gorilla. Grabbing her head painfully by the hair, he jerked her head back and shoved a soaked, smelly rag in her face when she tried to scream.

He was not Seth. He was not Seth!

Olivia's last shocked thought, as she flailed and choked and tried to fight off the intruder, was that it couldn't be happening again.

chapter 50

She remembered. She remembered. She remembered being carried like this before, wrapped up like a mummy, unable to move, barely able to breathe. She remembered the terror, icy-cold terror that tasted like medicine in her mouth and sent tremors chasing each other down her spine. She remembered being jostled, remembered the sounds of the night penetrating faintly through whatever it was that was wrapped around her head, remembered the sounds of a man's heavy breathing.

She remembered. Oh, God, she remembered.

This had happened to her before, long ago, when she was a little girl, younger than Sara. Someone had come into her room in the middle of the night, and grabbed her when she was asleep in bed, shoving a wet, smelly rag into her face. It had knocked her unconscious, and when she had come to, a woman had been screaming.

Her mother had been screaming. In her mind, Olivia could hear her mother screaming as plainly as if it were all happening again, right this very minute. She'd been little, and she'd been lying on the ground inside some sort of cloth bag, and she'd woken up to hear her mother screaming. She crawled out of the bag, to see her mother and a man struggling by the shore of the lake. Ghost Lake. The moon had been shining, painting a line of white across the water like a stripe along a skunk's back. The night had been hot, and muggy, and the insects had been singing and the tree frogs had been piping and fog had been rising like bony fingers stretching up from the water.

She tried to stand up, to go to her mother, to help her, but her knees were wobbly and wouldn't hold her, and her head felt really weird and her stomach heaved like she had to throw up.

Then her mother stopped screaming, just like that, like something had cut off the sound. She lifted her head, looked up, and saw that her mother was in the water now, in up to about her waist, and the man was pushing her face down, holding it under the water so that her mother's dark hair floated like oil on the surface.

He was hurting her mother.

She had to save her mother. She got to her feet, grabbing on to the trees for support, just as her mother's face came up, just as her mother choked and gasped and seemed to break free of the man and turned, arms outstretched, trying to make it back to shore.

Her mother saw her then, standing there under the trees, and screamed at her. *Run away, Olivia! Run! Run away! Run away!* And then the man caught her mother around the waist and dragged her back out into the lake, and her mother's scream turned into a gurgle as he pushed her face down beneath the water again.

Run away! Run! Run away! Her mother's scream echoed in her ears, and she turned and ran, lurched really, from tree to tree until she got to the path and then she turned back to look.

Her mother was in the middle of the lake, her face turned toward shore, her eyes wide and terrified, her mouth open as she screamed. She wore her white nightgown, the one with the lace straps that Olivia thought was so pretty, and she stretched her arms out toward shore as she fought to escape the water. Then the man surfaced behind her, grabbing her around the waist, disappearing under the surface with her, forcing her down.

The last thing Olivia saw was her mother's hand stretching skyward above the surface of Ghost Lake. Then the hand, too, disappeared.

Olivia turned and stumbled along the path through the woods, heading toward the Big House, dizzy and sick and so, so scared. He was coming after her, she knew he was. He would get her; the lake would get her. . . .

He was behind her, soaking wet and panting and reaching out for her. Olivia could hear his slogging footsteps, hear his labored breathing, and hear, too, voices coming from ahead of her, from the direction of the house. She screamed, only it came out sounding more like a squeak. Then something slammed hard into the back of her head.

When she'd awakened again, it was days later, her mother was dead, and her uncle Charlie was treating her for shock and talking her through the terrible nightmares that plagued her.

And after she'd gotten up, gotten well, life at LaAngelle Plantation had gone on. Day in, day out, for weeks and months and years. She'd had no memory of that night. She had buried it deep inside her mind as too terrible to remember. And gradually, even her subconscious had forgotten, until coming back to LaAngelle Plantation had stirred the memories again.

How was it possible that it was happening to her a second time? As the dream coalesced into memory, and the memory solidified enough to be shoved aside so that her mind could function, Olivia realized that what she was experiencing now was no flashback, no dream. She had been drugged, taken from her bed, and was now bound and gagged and wrapped in folds of cloth that prevented her from moving. Blinded by whatever swathed her face, she had to use her other senses. She was being carried over someone's shoulder. She could feel the squishy musculature of the shoulder pressing into her abdomen. A man, from the size and shape of him. Her head was hanging down his back, bobbing slightly as he walked. His arms were clamped over her thighs and the backs of her knees. He was struggling under her weight. She could feel his labored breathing, hear him panting, sense his steps slowing. His smell — she got a faint whiff of sweat, something medicinal, all mixed up with the lush scent of the night. He stepped from gravel to grass, and the sound changed from a crunch to a soft swish.

Where was he taking her?

Bound and wrapped as she was, she knew she had no chance of escape even if she tried to struggle. She forced herself to remain limp, to feign continued unconsciousness.

Then a horrible thought occurred to her: Oh, God, would he throw her into the lake?

It was all she could do not to panic, not to fight, to lay still and quiet and keep her breathing calm. If he suspected she was conscious, he would knock her out again, she was sure, and there would go her last hope, her only hope, of survival.

Breathe in. Breathe out. Keep muscles relaxed.

She heard the faint rasp of metal on metal, and then he turned sideways with her, as if he was having trouble fitting through an opening or a doorway. The side of her head smacked into something hard without warning, and she couldn't help it, she made a sound, a small sound, but he heard.

"So you're awake," he said, and the voice was familiar, shockingly familiar, so familiar she couldn't, wouldn't believe it until he dumped her down without warning on a hard, slick surface and pulled some of the wrapping away from her face.

chapter 51

Seth was tired. So tired he could barely climb the stairs. It was an effort just dragging his feet from one step to the next. If he hadn't known Olivia was waiting for him in her nice warm bed on the second floor, he thought with a faint glimmer of humor, he would have sacked out on the couch in the den.

But the knowledge that Olivia was waiting for him was a powerful incentive. It got his feet up the rest of the stairs.

He would go to her room, strip, fall into bed beside her, wrap his arms around her, and sleep until morning. It was a terrible thought that tonight he was too tired to make love, but he just might be. The events of the last two weeks must be catching up with him, he decided, because he felt totally whacked.

His mother's death was a blow from which he

was never going to recover. The pain of it would be with him until he died. If it hadn't been for Olivia, he didn't think he would have slept a wink since the night she died.

Olivia was his port in a storm-tossed sea. His shelter on a cold winter's night. And all those other poetic things he might think but would never actually be so sappy as to say out loud.

Now it looked like Big John was going to go, too. He'd always thought the old man was too damned stubborn to die. Tonight's crisis had been some kind of mix-up with the medicines, caught by the new doctor David had insisted take over the case. It was not immediately life-threatening, since it had been reversed in time. Charlie hadn't liked the idea of somebody else taking over. He was nowhere to be seen at the hospital tonight. But if he was going to make mistakes with medicine, then he needed to be replaced.

Losing Big John would be a huge blow, especially coming, as it seemed likely to, on top of losing his mother.

The only way he was going to get through it was just to grab Livvy, and hold on tight.

He reached her room, turned the doorknob, let himself in. The upstairs was black as pitch, as always, but he could just faintly see her bed by the greenish glow from her clock.

The clock read 1:59 A.M. The bed looked empty.

"Livvy?" he said softly. No answer.

Waking up fast, Seth groped around on the wall for the switch and turned on the overhead light.

The bed was empty, although it had obviously been slept in. The room was empty. The French windows were closed.

"Livvy?" His voice was louder now.

Of course, she must be with Sara.

He turned on his heel and went next door. There was a lamp on in Sara's room, a little night-light that Olivia allowed to burn all night. By its light, even before he switched on the overhead fixture, Seth saw that Sara's bed was empty, too.

Her covers had been tossed onto the floor, like somebody had thrown them aside in a hurry. It didn't look like something Olivia, or Sara herself, would do.

The kitten, her gray kitten, he couldn't remember its name, came running in from the hall, and leaped onto the bed.

Sara always slept with that kitten. He remembered seeing it on her bed earlier when he had come to tell Olivia that he was going to drive in to Baton Rouge.

Seth's blood ran cold. Even before he awakened Martha, even before he awakened Chloe, even before he rousted Keith from the *garçonnière* behind the house, he knew something was wrong.

Terribly wrong.

While Martha and Chloe huddled in the den,

and Keith ran from room to room in the huge pile of a house turning on light after light after light, Seth got on the phone to Ira. He wanted the sheriff and his deputies out at LaAngelle Plantation, right now.

chapter 52

Uncle Charlie. Olivia couldn't talk, of course, with the gag in her mouth, but her mind shouted his name. She knew him instantly, even through the tan mesh of the stocking he had pulled down over his face. He grimaced beneath the mask and peeled it off, stuffing it in the pocket of the black trench coat he wore, looking down at her almost sorrowfully.

"Well, now, Olivia, you've gotten us both in a fine mess," he said. She was in a bag, a white canvas bag, and he began pulling it off her, easing it down over her shoulders, wiggling it out from under her hips. The shiny silver metal surface she was lying on felt slick and cold against her skin. It was outfitted with straps, inch-wide black mesh straps that he fastened across her waist, securing her to the metal surface. She was bound with duct tape, she saw. The silvery bands were wrapped around her ankles and knees over her pink nightgown, and bound her arms to her body from just above her elbows to her wrists.

Without the bag to shield her from it, the air smelled foul, and Olivia wrinkled her nose instinctively, glancing around to see what could be causing such a stench.

"Yes, it does smell a little ripe in here, doesn't it?" Charlie said, as if he could read her mind. "Next time I come, I think I'll bring some air freshener."

He was busy rolling up the canvas bag, and tending to other things down near her feet. Olivia was so horrified by her surroundings that she paid him little mind.

They were in a crypt. The Archer family crypt, to be precise. She knew it was, because of the inscriptions on the four tray-sized brass plaques set into the marble walls. The plaques commemorated Colonel Robert John Archer, his wife, Lavinia, and two infants. They were only slightly tarnished, and she wondered if they had been coated with something years ago to keep them bright. Each plaque was engraved with a name and dates of birth and death, with several sentences in a flowing script underneath that Olivia could not read, although she was close enough to the plaques to see her own wavery reflection in them.

The reflections provided the first horror. They showed her that she was lying on her back on a makeshift tabletop of bright silver metal with scooped-out channels along the sides that looked as though they were designed to catch liquids. Olivia immediately thought of autopsy tables and blood, and shuddered. The tabletop had been secured with straps to the tops of two adult-sized stone coffins that most likely contained the remains of the colonel and his wife.

But the real horror looked at her from the corners. Olivia's eyes widened as her gaze moved from one to the other. Four of them. Life-size mannequins of four little girls, each of them dressed with exquisite care, their hair — medium brown, blond, red — such beautiful red hair! — and black — lovingly curled. They were standing upright, their arms slightly bent and held a little away from their bodies. Their skin was the only false note. It had a leathery, thick texture. Their eyes gleamed faintly in the light of the battery-operated camp lantern Charlie had set down on the tabletop near her feet. Olivia thought, hoped, guessed, that the eyes were of glass. They looked all too real.

"Are you admiring my girls?" Charlie plucked the wadded rag from her mouth so suddenly that Olivia felt as if half the skin of her lips and tongue had been torn away with it. She tried to swallow, but couldn't because her throat was too dry. She coughed, choked, tried again. This time she succeeded, and she used her newly moist tongue to wet her parched lips.

"Are they — mannequins?" she croaked. Charlie shook his head at her reproachfully.

"No, dear, they're just what they look like. Little girls, well preserved. Meet Becca, Maggie, Kathleen, and Savannah. I'm particularly proud of Savannah. She was Little Miss Rice, you know."

"Oh, my God." Olivia's stomach heaved. She felt sick, horribly sick to her stomach, and dizzy, too. They were *children,* or they had once been, and her uncle Charlie, her kindly doctor uncle had — had . . . "You *killed* them."

"Yes, well, unfortunately that's part of the process. You were almost number five, you know. I chose *you* to come after Savannah, but your mother . . . your mother . . ." His face darkened.

"You drowned my mother, didn't you?"

There was a narrow metal cabinet against one marble wall near her head, and Charlie was busy extracting something from it as he talked. He looked at her over his shoulder.

"I knew you would remember, sooner or later." His voice was resigned. "I had no choice, you know. I don't know how — she was the only mommy who ever did — but she heard me that night. Selena heard me. Or she saw me. I never did know. But she came running after me as I was walking away from the house, and she wanted to know what was in my bag. Well, it was you, of course, but I couldn't tell her that. So I slugged her, and chloroformed her, and carried her and you away from the house. It was a difficult trip, as you may imagine. The pair of you were extremely heavy! But she woke up and

494

started to fight me down by the lake, so I had to drop you and deal with her. By the time I got finished with her — she was a scrapper, your mother! — you were hightailing it back toward the house. I knocked you unconscious, but I didn't have time to do anything with you before Big John was on the scene. By the time I got finished dragging Selena out of the lake and doing my bit with CPR, you had managed to get back to the house. I kept an eye on you for a while after that, but except for a few nightmares you didn't seem to remember anything. I don't know if it was because I hit you so hard on the head, or because you had hysterical amnesia. I'm inclined to go with hysterical amnesia, but that's just an opinion. Of course, when you came to me this morning, and told me you wanted to go see a psychiatrist, and a hypnotist, of all things, I had no choice. I knew you would remember, sooner or later."

Olivia took a deep breath. It was hot in the crypt, and the smell was getting to her. Sweat was breaking out on her forehead, and her body was beginning to stick clammily to the metal on which she lay. But she had to keep her mind clear, had to think. Otherwise, she knew, she was going to die.

Sara. Seth. Their names were almost a scream in her mind. She didn't want to leave them. Not now. Not like this.

But she would not think of them. Could not, if she wanted to stay calm.

"I always thought Big John suspected something," Charlie continued conversationally. "I was already soaking wet, you know, when the two of us went into the water after Selena. I never knew if he noticed or not. But he questioned me pretty sharply afterward. Made me nervous. Turns out that Belinda had thought I was having an affair with your mother, because I was hanging around the Big House so much at night — waiting for my chance to grab you, don't you know — and confided in her father." He chuckled. "I was able to shoot that one down. But I still thought he suspected that something was wrong about Selena's death. I quit collecting after that, you know, and moved my girls up here, just in case Big John was suspicious enough to really start looking into things. But he never did. I thought he'd put the whole matter out of his mind. Then when he saw you again, and had that heart attack, I knew. Guilty conscience got him, for not speaking up all those years ago. But he started to babble about Selena to the nurses in the hospital, and I was afraid of what was going to come out. I had to calm the old boy down. Tonight, when I get done here, I'm going to have to take care of him for good. It's a shame. I've always liked him. Just like I like you, Olivia. I wouldn't be doing this if you'd given me any other choice."

He took something else out of the cabinet, and closed the door.

"Are you planning to turn *me* into — one of

them?" With a nod she gestured at the preserved body of the little girl with the red hair.

Charlie shook his head. "Oh, no. No. You're going to drown yourself in the lake, like your mother. Despondent, I imagine, because you're in love with Seth — Phillip told me that he saw you kissing him, so that will bear that theory out — and he's going to marry Mallory."

"But — but he and Mallory broke their engagement. Yesterday." Olivia was grasping at straws, trying to latch on to anything that might change his mind.

Charlie shrugged. "Doesn't matter. Who knows what might drive a troubled young woman to kill herself? After all, you've been having nightmares about your mother drowning herself in the lake, and just today you came to me and asked me for the name of a psychiatrist. You were quite depressed, too. I'll swear to it."

He smiled kindly at her, and held up his hand. Olivia was horrified to see that it held a syringe half filled with a golden liquid.

"You needn't be afraid that it's going to hurt. I never hurt anyone. For my girls, when I'm ready for them to go — I like to play with them for a while first, but all good things must come to an end — I inject them with five grams of sodium Pentothal to put them to sleep, then give them fifty ccs of pancuronium bromide, which paralyzes all their muscles except the heart, then finish up with 50 ccs of potassium chloride to stop the heart muscle itself. They never feel a thing. For you, tonight, I'm going to put you to sleep with the sodium Pentothal, then throw you into the lake. You'll die from drowning. The signs will be unmistakable. You'll even have lake water in your lungs. And since I'll be signing the death certificate, we won't have to worry about little things like toxicology reports. But you don't have to be afraid. You won't feel one minute's pain."

"Uncle Charlie — please . . ." Pleading with him was useless, Olivia knew. If the man had an ounce of compassion anywhere in his body, she would not now be staring at the near-mummified remains of four little girls. But she had to try. She had to. She wanted to live. . . .

A mewling sound from somewhere behind her head made Olivia's eyes widen.

"Oh, now you've woken Sara," Charlie said reproachfully. "She's going to be my number five girl, you know. Wait just a minute while I put her in her cage."

chapter 53

"Daddy, has something happened to Sara and Olivia?"

At Chloe's question, Seth turned to look at her. Huddled next to Martha on the couch in the den, Chloe had a lightweight blue blanket wrapped over her yellow nightgown. Her face was pale and her eyes were scared. He was in the front hall, giving Ira a quick, tense rundown of the situation. On his say-so, deputies had already been deployed to search the grounds of the estate. In the first frantic minutes after he had discovered Olivia and Sara were missing, he had already determined that there were no cars gone from the garage. They had to be somewhere nearby.

Please God let them be safe.

"Honey-bug, I don't know. You stay right where you are with Martha, and Ira and I will do our best to find them."

"They're dead, like Nana, aren't they?" Chloe began to sob. "I don't want them to be dead, Daddy. I don't want any more blinky stars to wave at. I want them right here on earth."

"Chloe." Giving Ira a helpless look, he took the few quick strides needed to bring him to his daughter's side. He wrapped his arms around her, hugged her tight, kissed her cheek. "They're all right. We'll find them. Don't cry. Martha, take her. Chloe, I have to go look for them. You stay right here with Martha. Martha, don't let her take one step away from your side."

"I won't, Mr. Seth. Don't you be a-feared of that." Martha's reply was fervent. Like Chloe, like himself, she was scared to death, both by the reality and the possibilities.

Please God let them be safe.

Seth disengaged himself from Chloe, who turned to Martha with a sob, and walked back into the front hall, where Ira waited. Ira had bags under his eyes that hadn't been there when his mother was alive, and he'd lost weight.

"If they're on this property, we'll find them," Ira promised grimly as Seth joined them. Seth nodded. His greatest fear was that they were not. No cars were missing. But what if they'd been stolen away by a stranger, in a stranger's car...?

Get a grip, he told himself firmly. How likely was that?

Please God let them be safe.

A hideous memory of Olivia walking into the

500

lake that day he'd waded in after her surfaced in Seth's mind. She'd been having nightmares about her mother's drowning lately, too. What if for some reason — sleepwalking, maybe? — she had gone down to the lake, and Sara had somehow followed? Olivia wouldn't drown herself, not on purpose. He knew she wouldn't. And yet — her mother had. And Olivia might not be aware of what she was doing. That day he had gone in after her, she had almost seemed to be in a trance.

Please God let them be safe.

"I'm going to look down by the lake," Seth told Ira abruptly, and headed for the front door.

"I've already got a man searching the lake area." Ira followed him.

"I don't care. I'm going down there, too."

"I'll come with you."

Seth emerged onto the veranda, and was glad to see that a deputy was stationed by the front door: He recognized him as Mike Simms, a good man.

"Stay inside with my little girl, would you?" he asked Simms abruptly. "I don't want her coming up missing, too."

With a quick glance at Ira for confirmation, Simms nodded and went inside.

Seth, with Ira trailing, headed down toward the lake.

chapter 54

"No! No! No!" Olivia's head slewed around so fast that for an instant it left her dizzy as she strained to see what Charlie was doing. He was moving behind her, out of her line of vision, and when he reappeared he was carrying Sara, her own sweet Sara, clad in the Cinderella nighty that was her particular favorite, like a baby in his arms. She was obviously groggy, her eyes blinking, her head lolling against his chest, her arms dangling.

"Uncle Charlie, no!" Olivia begged, straining uselessly against her bonds. "Please don't hurt her. She's only a baby. Please let her go. Please."

All the terror she'd refused to let herself feel now boiled to the surface for Sara. Despite the stifling heat, she was suddenly cold as ice. Her heart pounded. Her breath sobbed in her chest. Her limbs shook.

Please, God, please. Save Sara.

She got a glimpse of her own reflection in the brass plaque to her left. She was struggling, fighting her bonds, her head and shoulders lifting away from the metal in a futile attempt to reach her child. She was struggling so much that it was almost as though she were seeing double, as if there were two of her reflected in the brass. . . .

"Don't you see, Olivia, I'll be giving her a kind of immortality. She'll be a sweet, innocent little eight-year-old forever."

"Please don't hurt her," Olivia begged. Please God please God please . . .

"Mommy?" Sara lifted her head from Charlie's chest to blink sleepily at Olivia. "Mommy, what's wrong?"

Olivia's desperation seemed to be penetrating Sara's drug-induced stupor. Sara looked around, blinking, then stiffened in Charlie's arms, and began to flail.

"Ah-ah," he said to her, almost tenderly, as he restrained her by wrapping his arms tightly around her. "None of that, now, or Daddy will have to punish you. Here, let's put you right in your nice little cage until Daddy is ready to play."

He walked around the foot of the table, and through another of the brass plaques Olivia saw the reflection of a large dog cage with a padlock on the front. He was going to lock Sara in a dog cage! A finger of ice ran down her spine.

"Uncle Charlie, no! Please, no! Sara! Sara!"

"Mommy . . . !"

Again Olivia saw the double images of herself in the brass plaques, and saw, too, that one of the images now appeared to be standing beside the table while the other image was lying upon it, still restrained, just as she was. She thought the standing image had a wider jaw, a longer nose — and a white nightgown.

"Mommy! Mommy!"

"Mother, help me!" Olivia cried, and smelled the faintest hint of White Shoulders perfume. As Charlie, clasping a now-struggling Sara with only one arm, bent over to jerk the padlock free, Olivia looked wildly around and saw the battery-powered lantern perched on the edge of the table near her feet. She gathered her legs and kicked downward with all her strength — and the lantern flew across the room, although she never felt her bare feet actually make contact. It crashed into the metal door of the crypt, shattering, sending sparks flying everywhere. In the instant before the bulb flickered out and the crypt was plunged into darkness, Olivia saw Charlie whirl toward the sound of the crash, stumble, fall to one knee — and drop Sara sprawling on the floor. The blow from the lantern had knocked the crypt door open just a crack. A burst of cool air whooshed past Olivia's face. The charcoal-gray of the night beckoned just beyond the door.

"Run, Sara! Run, Sara! Run, run, run!" Olivia shrieked.

Sara ran, scrambling to her feet, bursting

through the door, screaming as if all the demons of every nightmare she had ever dreamed were chasing her, as indeed they were. Charlie went after her, shouldering through the door, his big body a ponderous shadow plunging through the night. Olivia lay in her duct-tape prison and screamed, screamed at Sara to run, screamed for help, screamed until her lungs ached and her throat was dry and she was gasping for breath.

She screamed until Charlie stumbled back into the crypt, alone, a large dark presence blocking the charcoal-gray of the night. Sara was safe. Sara had to be safe, or he wouldn't be alone. Olivia sagged with relief, thanked God in a rush of dizziness, sank back against the table and took a deep, shuddering breath. . . .

And watched as Charlie lurched to the metal cabinet, fumbled with the doors, and removed something from it.

A second later he was coming toward her. The gray light filtering through the open door showed her the filled syringe in his hand.

Dread iced her veins anew.

"Uncle Charlie," she croaked. Nothing else would emerge from her scream-parched throat.

He stopped by the table at about her waist level and smiled at her. She could see the gleam of his teeth through the darkness.

"Olivia, dear, what I have here is a syringe filled with potassium chloride," he said, almost pleasantly. "If you remember, this is the one that stops your heart."

chapter 55

When the screaming started, Seth was standing on the bank of Ghost Lake near the spot where Olivia had walked into the water that day. He was playing the beam of his flashlight over the lake's surface and praying with all his might.

At first, the screams were hardly distinguishable from the cries of predators and prey that routinely split the night. Seth stiffened as the first one reached his ears, and then, as it was followed by another and another, wondered if perhaps something was attacking the flock of peacocks. But he was running even as he wondered it, running in the direction of the sounds, stumbling more than once as he pounded along the uneven path that led around the side of the lake, and shouting for Ira as he went.

By the time he knew for certain that they were screams, human screams, Olivia's and Sara's screams, a small, plump figure was hurtling down the trail that climbed the bluff toward the old graveyard. Picking her out with the beam of his flashlight even as he ran toward her, Seth recognized Sara with a rush of both terror and relief. Sara was alive, and screaming her lungs out, and running as if the hounds of hell were on her tail — but where was Olivia?

Oh, God, where was Olivia?

"Seth, Seth, Seth, Seth!" Sara collapsed into his arms as he reached her, wrapping her arms around his waist and clinging like a monkey, shaking, shivering, gasping, crying. "Seth, he's got Mommy! He's got Mommy!"

"Where?" Seth demanded, even as he bellowed for Ira. He could tell the sheriff was not too far behind him from the bobbing yellow beam of light that labored up the trail in his wake.

"Up there! In the graveyard!"

"Go to Ira! See that light? Run there!" Seth detached Sara and thrust her in Ira's direction. Without waiting to see if she obeyed, he took the trail in great bounds, his heart pounding, a cold terror driving him.

The screams had stopped.

The graveyard gate was around to the side, and a glance showed him that it stood open, but Seth didn't even hesitate. He put one hand on top of that fence and leaped it like it was two feet high. Up here, in the shadowy sanctuary where his mother lay in her freshly dug grave, where stone angels stood sentinel and the moon and passing clouds combined to give them eerie life, the silence shrieked at him.

"Olivia!" he bellowed. "Olivia!"

"Seth!"

Her voice was faint, muffled even. Seth ran his flashlight around the graveyard, looking everywhere — and almost missed the fact that the door to the mausoleum stood ajar, just a little bit.

He sprinted toward it, and yanked it wide. It swung open with surprising ease, as if someone had recently oiled the old hinges.

As the inside of the crypt was exposed to his view, what he captured with the beam of his flashlight stopped him dead in his tracks.

Olivia was looking at him, her head lifted away from whatever unholy thing it was that she was lying on. Her face was white as paper, her eyes were huge, and she was trussed up like a Thanksgiving turkey, unable to move. Charlie stood beside her, right beside her head, a hypodermic needle poised to inject just below her ear.

Seth wasn't sure exactly what was happening, but he knew it wasn't good.

"Charlie, don't," he said hoarsely, warningly. And thought, where the hell is Ira with his gun?

"If you come any closer, I'm afraid I'll have to inject this directly into Olivia's carotid artery," Charlie said, sounding so much like his normal self that Seth had a hard time believing what he was hearing and seeing. One glance at Olivia told

508

him that Charlie was in deadly earnest. "It's loaded with potassium chloride, you see. It will stop her heart within minutes."

Seth took a deep breath. "You don't want to do that," he said calmly. "We've always been friends, you and I, haven't we? I love her, Charlie. You don't want to hurt her, because if you do you'll hurt me. That's how much I love her, Charlie. Enough so that anything you do to her, you do to me."

"I don't want to hurt *you*, Seth, but you see . . ." Charlie paused as the approach of Ira and what sounded like a whole posse of deputies reached their ears.

"Charlie, please . . ."

"They're coming for me," Charlie said. He glanced down at Olivia, and, then, as Seth readied himself for the leap of his life, looked at Seth.

"Have somebody check what's in Big John's IV bags, Seth," he said. "I've been keeping him heavily sedated. Once he's not, he should recover."

"The nurses at the hospital already found out. They told David, and that's why he brought in another doctor. Everyone thinks you just made a mistake. It's all right, Charlie."

"Ah, nurses," Charlie said disparagingly. "Mommies! Women! Why can't they just stay little girls?"

He glanced down at Olivia again, hesitated, then turned the hypodermic needle on himself.

"Charlie!" Seth leaped forward, knocking the needle away from Charlie's hand, but it was already too late. The syringe was empty. A little trickle of blood ran down Charlie's neck where the needle had pierced his skin. Charlie sank to his knees, gasped once, then fell forward onto his face. "God*damn* it, Charlie!"

Ira and his henchmen came bursting through the door then, brandishing guns and flashlights.

"We need CPR here," Seth said, staightening away from Charlie, who no longer seemed to be breathing. He turned to Olivia, who had collapsed limply back against the metal surface she was lying on.

"And somebody better call for an ambulance. Charlie just shot himself in the neck with potassium chloride." Then, to Olivia, as he found and unfastened the mesh strap that held her to the table, "Did he hurt you?"

"No." Olivia took a deep, shuddering breath. "Sara?"

"She's safe," Seth said, lifting her into his arms. It was stultifyingly hot in the vault, and smelled like something about the size of a horse had crawled in there and died. To top it off, there was a sickly sweet note to it, like bad perfume. Two deputies were crouched on the floor, giving Charlie CPR, and Seth stepped carefully around them. Another was outside the crypt, talking into a cell phone, presumably summoning an ambulance.

"Call down to the house and let them know

we're all right up here," Seth instructed, and the man nodded.

As Seth put Olivia down on the grass just outside the crypt, he heard Ira exclaim to one of his deputies, "Hell's bells, will you come over here and look at this!"

Whatever it was, Seth didn't, at the moment, particularly want to know.

"What is this, duct tape?" Seth asked, feeling the silvery bonds that made Olivia look half mummy.

"I think so."

She was shivering despite the fact that it was a warm night, and Seth guessed that she was suffering from shock. And no wonder. He felt pretty shocked himself, and he hadn't endured anything near what she had. He had only endured the thought that he might lose her. But that, to him, would be the worst thing of all.

"Hold still." Reaching into his pocket, he found the Swiss Army knife that Big John had given him years ago and pulled it out. After that, it took just a few minutes and some judicious sawing to free her. Gingerly, he pulled the tape away from her skin, taking care not to hurt her. When it was off, he chafed her arms and legs to restore her circulation, then helped her to stand up. She leaned against him for support, resting her head against his chest, and he wrapped both arms around her, holding her tight.

"You saved my life," she said. "Thank you."

"I saved my own life," he corrected, pressing

his mouth to the top of her bent head. "I couldn't have lived if you'd died in there."

"Seth, what we've got in there looks pretty bad." Ira emerged from the crypt, shaking his head and looking pale. "You need to come take a look."

"Charlie — he . . ." Olivia shuddered in his arms. "He murdered four little girls. Their bodies are in there. And he drowned my mother. He told me."

Seth looked at Ira, who nodded grimly.

"Sit down here a minute," Seth said to Olivia, and left her on the single step leading into the crypt, leaning against one of the marble angels.

When he emerged, he felt sick to his stomach.

Olivia cast a fleeting look up at him. "Charlie was going to do that to Sara. He was going to do that to me, when I was a little girl. That's why he killed my mother. She saved me."

"Jesus," Seth said, and sat down beside her on the step as she told him everything that had happened.

In the distance, just faintly, came the wail of a siren. The ambulance itself arrived moments later.

When EMTs came bustling into the graveyard, Seth pulled Olivia to her feet.

"Can you walk back to the house, do you think?" he asked.

She nodded.

"Come on, then," he said. "You don't want to see this."

512

With his arm wrapped around her waist, they moved slowly out of the cemetery and started down the path. Seth was careful to set an easy pace, but Olivia seemed to gain strength as they went. In the places where she had to walk in front of him, Seth looked at her dark, bent head and sweetly curved form in the fluttering nightgown, and thanked God that he had her still.

He had thought there was plenty of time for the two of them. But tonight, time had almost run out.

They were in the woods now, under the sheltering darkness of the trees. The night was alive with sounds. The rustling canopy overhead blocked the moon, but moonlight filtered through, dappling the path. Barefoot when they had started out, Olivia was now wearing his socks to protect her feet. His shoes were so big she couldn't keep them on.

"Livvy?" They were walking arm in arm, with her leaning slightly against him, moving in the direction of the house. Ghost Lake glimmered off to the right. The stone steps that led up to the lawn were ahead of them.

"Hmm?"

Seth cleared his throat. He was clear about what he wanted to say, but sometimes it was hard to get the words out. "I love you."

"I love you, too."

It was as simple as that.

When they reached the top of the steps, Chloe and Sara came running toward them, with

Martha in hot pursuit. Seth wasn't clear on the time, but it had to be about four A.M.

"Mom!"

"Olivia!"

Both girls flung themselves at Olivia. She hugged them, then wrapped an arm around each as they all headed toward the house, the girls chattering incessantly about their thoughts, feelings, and actions during the night's adventures as they went. Seth didn't really listen, and he didn't think Olivia was listening, either, because all she did was nod and smile.

When they reached the house, Chloe stopped suddenly, which halted the whole group, and looked around, waving.

"What are you doing?" Sara asked, looking around, too.

"Waving to my nana," Chloe said. "See? She's that blinky star there."

Sara squinted up into the star-studded sky. "There's two of them, blinking together."

Seth looked, and Sara was right. There was a binary star winking and blinking at them from high in the western sky.

Olivia was looking, too. "Wave, Sara," she instructed with a smile. "I think one of those stars is Chloe's grandmother, and the other one is yours."

Both little girls waved madly.

"Is it okay to wish on Nana-star?" Chloe asked Seth, a slight frown wrinkling her brow.

"Sure," Seth said. He figured if his mother was

now a star, she wouldn't mind being wished on.

"Starlight, star bright, first star I see tonight, I wish I may, I wish I might, have the wish I wish tonight." Then Chloe closed her eyes and scrunched up her face, apparently wishing very hard.

"What did you wish for?" Seth asked curiously when she opened her eyes again.

"I wished that the four of us could be a real family," Chloe said, taking his hand. "Could we, Daddy?"

Seth looked at Olivia over the children's heads. "We could," he said slowly. "If Sara's mom will marry me. Will you, Livvy?"

Olivia met his gaze. Her expression was very solemn for a moment, and Seth wasn't quite sure what to expect. Then her face broke into a wide smile.

"I will absolutely marry you," she said, and walked right into his outstretched arms. As he kissed her, his daughter, and hers, danced around them, cheering. And two bright stars, bound together for eternity, winked and blinked in the night-dark sky.